**Praise for the novels
of Mary Jo Putney**

Uncommon Vows

"*Uncommon Vows* is my favorite among Mary Jo Putney's books. . . . Few authors can pull off a medieval backdrop without stripping the era of its darkness or allowing its dramatic historical politics to overshadow the romance, but Putney makes it seem effortless. . . . The result is some of her strongest and most inspired writing. . . . A romance that definitely qualifies as uncommon." —All About Romance

Dancing on the Wind
Winner of the RITA Award

"Another A+ read from one of the very best. I count on Mary Jo Putney for a compelling story with characters who live and breathe, and most of all, love. . . . [This] love story is intense, emotional, and deeply satisfying." —Under the Covers

"Magnificent Mary Jo Putney has provided her fans with another winner and proves the adage that writers do not age, they just get better." —*Affaire de Coeur*

"Mary Jo Putney has a gift." —*The Oakland Press*

"The characters are appealing, the situations unusual, and the story fascinating. You won't be disappointed!" —The Time Machine

Praise for Mary Jo Putney

"Woven throughout the story are musings on regret and forgiveness, madness and sanity, and on the importance of learning to look beyond the surface of what we see. . . . The plot winds and twists and finally ties up neatly. . . . Putney's strong points are her thoughtfulness and her well-drawn cast of compelling and very human characters." —*Booklist*

"In her superb, inimitable style, Putney . . . takes a pair of magnetic, beautifully matched protagonists, places them in a dark, impossible situation, and makes it work." —*Library Journal*

"Mary Jo Putney never fails to deliver a winning story with heartwarming characters. She is a pleasure to read . . . always." —*The Literary Times*

"Fascinating." —*The Romance Reader* (4 hearts)

"Intelligent, passionate characters flow through this powerful love story. . . . Putney delivers another superior story, beautifully written with her penchant for eloquently portraying her heroines as unique individuals filled with life." —*Rendezvous*

"Passionate. . . . The author has created a realistic, well-crafted story, laced with elements of suspense and mystery and featuring sympathetic protagonists whose biggest mistake was marrying too young." —*Publishers Weekly*

"A winner." —*Midwest Book Review*

"Ms. Putney is one of the very best authors who excels at historical romances." —*Rendezvous*

Uncommon Vows

Mary Jo Putney

A SIGNET BOOK

SIGNET
Published by New American Library, a division of
Penguin Group (USA) Inc., 375 Hudson Street,
New York, New York 10014, U.S.A.
Penguin Books Ltd, 80 Strand,
London WC2R 0RL, England
Penguin Books Australia Ltd, 250 Camberwell Road,
Camberwell, Victoria 3124, Australia
Penguin Books Canada Ltd, 10 Alcorn Avenue,
Toronto, Ontario, Canada M4V 3B2
Penguin Books (N.Z.) Ltd, Cnr Rosedale and Airborne Roads,
Albany, Auckland 1310, New Zealand

Penguin Books Ltd, Registered Offices:
80 Strand, London WC2R 0RL, England

Published by Signet, an imprint of New American Library,
a division of Penguin Group (USA) Inc. Previously published in a Topaz
edition.

First Signet Printing, December 2003
10 9 8 7 6 5 4 3 2 1

 REGISTERED TRADEMARK—MARCA REGISTRADA

Printed in the United States of America

PUBLISHER'S NOTE
This is a work of fiction. Names, characters, places, and incidents either are
the product of the author's imagination or are used fictitiously, and any resemblance to actual persons, living or dead, business establishments, events, or
locales is entirely coincidental.

BOOKS ARE AVAILABLE AT QUANTITY DISCOUNTS WHEN USED TO PROMOTE
PRODUCTS OR SERVICES. FOR INFORMATION PLEASE WRITE TO PREMIUM MAR-
KETING DIVISION, PENGUIN PUTNAM INC., 375 HUDSON STREET, NEW YORK, NEW
YORK 10014.

To my editor, Hilary Ross,
who gets embarrassed when her authors
say how lucky they are to have her

Foreword

THE DEATH OF King Henry I in 1135 precipitated the period sometimes called the Anarchy. Henry was a ruthless and capable king, but while he had over twenty illegitimate children, his only legitimate heir was his daughter Matilda, who had been married to the German emperor at a young age. She was much loved in Germany, but was widowed in her early twenties and returned to England, where she was afterward generally called "the empress."

Henry then married his daughter to Geoffrey, the fourteen-year-old heir to the Count of Anjou, a union distasteful not only to the principal parties but also to the entire Norman baronage, since Normandy and Anjou were ancient enemies. Even so, the king had enough power to bully his barons into swearing that they would accept Matilda as Henry's successor.

However, as soon as Henry died, his nephew Count Stephen of Blois (who had been the first to pledge loyalty to his cousin Matilda, and who may once have been her lover) promptly coopted the crown and the treasury. Stephen was affable and chivalrous and the barons and the Church were happy to accept him as ruler instead of Matilda. However, Stephen's ambition outstripped his abilities and over the next several years he alienated the Church and many of his subjects.

Robert of Gloucester, the oldest bastard son of King Henry, was one of England's greatest landholders and was widely respected for his ability and integrity. In the spring of 1138 he decided to support his half-sister

Matilda's claim to the throne and formally defied King Stephen. The west and south of England supported Robert and the country plunged into civil war.

Most battles occurred on the frontier between Matilda's supporters in the west and the eastern majority of the country, which was loyal to Stephen. Many barons welcomed anarchy as a way of increasing their own power and impartially accepted bribes of land and titles from either side. The carnage was notable even for an age of brutality, though Robert of Gloucester did a decent job of keeping order in the lands he controlled.

Matilda came very close to winning the crown but did not succeed. (She was frequently accused of arrogance and high-handedness, traits that would have been considered fairly normal in a king, but which struck the male chroniclers as intolerable in a female. Things haven't changed much.)

After Robert of Gloucester died in 1148, Matilda went back to Normandy. She never returned to England, but her young son Henry took up the Angevin cause (so named for Anjou, home of Matilda's husband and sons). A true descendant of the Conqueror, Henry first invaded England at the tender age of fourteen. He achieved nothing militarily, but in a piece of unbelievable farce, Henry successfully persuaded his cousin King Stephen to pay off Henry's Angevin mercenaries.

By 1148, when most of *Uncommon Vows* takes place, the country had subsided into an exhausted stalemate. The old division still held: the west for Matilda, the east for Stephen, with friction along the frontier between them.

Prologue

Fontevaile Abbey, Shropshire
December 25, 1137

THE PALE Christmas sun set on a day of disaster, and the two knights set off on their mission with the embers of the ravaged keep still glowing against the night sky. They rode hard and fast, and through the long, bleak miles they spoke not at all.

It was near midnight when they crested the final hill. By unspoken consent, both the young knight and the old pulled their horses to a halt and gazed into the barren valley below, where the cold silver light of a full moon touched the abbey of Fontevaile with unearthly tranquillity.

"I wish to God you were not baseborn." The older man's bitter words were a measure of the grief this evil day had laid on him. Walter of Evesham was captain of the de Lancey guard and had known all of the family, had almost been one of them. In the aftermath of disaster, he wished he had died with them.

The younger man's mouth quirked up with the wry acceptance of one who had early learned his station in life. "You can't wish it more than I, but wishing will not change the fact that my mother was my father's maidservant, not his wife."

The captain's gaze lingered on his companion. Richard FitzHugh had the lanky frame of a lad not yet fully grown, but he was a brave and skillful warrior. Just the previous week he had been knighted, and all who knew him had agreed that he deserved the honor though he was only eighteen. "You are the best of Lord Hugh's sons, Richard," Walter said morosely.

"It would be far better for Warfield if you were the heir."

The young knight shrugged the compliment aside and gestured at the sleeping abbey. "Don't underestimate my brother Adrian."

"Bah, a sickly, undersized, overgodly boy," the old captain growled. "It will be best if he stays at Fontevaile and takes his vows. What can he do to preserve his patrimony in a land gone mad?"

"A good deal. I know Adrian rather well, and I warrant that there is nothing wrong with either his sword arm or his sense." Richard pulled his wool cloak tighter around his hauberk. In the bitter December wind the metal links were cold as carved ice, but with rebellion stalking the countryside they dared not ride unarmed. "Though he is young, I think he will hold Warfield as well as anyone might."

"I'd forgotten that you both were sent to Courtenay for fostering." Sir Walter spurred his horse down the shadowed hill, his brow furrowed as he wondered if Richard's optimism might be well founded.

"Aye, we were, and we shared a pallet and trained together for five years, until Adrian decided to enter the Church." Richard urged his own mount down the rough track, remembering how two boys who would not admit to homesickness had drawn together amongst so many strange faces. They had truly become brothers, and Richard would fare better with Adrian as his liege than he would have under any of Lord Hugh's other legitimate sons.

"Adrian had aptitude for arms?" There was surprise in the captain's question, for the image did not fit his memories.

"Aye, he had aptitude, and an invincible will as well. We tested our skills on each other, as boys will do." Richard smiled wryly. "Had I not had three years more growth and experience, I would never have defeated him. As it was, the honors were about even."

"He could defeat *you?*" Startled, Sir Walter looked

up from the rough track, convinced that the younger man was jesting, but for once there was no levity on his companion's face.

"Adrian came to Fontevaile because he loved God, not because he feared man." Richard knew that his words were less than the whole truth. Though he had known his younger half-brother well, he would not be so bold as to think that he knew all the reasons Adrian had decided to become a monk. "And because as youngest son, there was naught for him to inherit. Now that has changed."

Still unconvinced, Sir Walter was about to reply when he glanced up at the moon above the abbey. "Sweet mother of God," he swore, his hand clenching on the reins and pulling his mount into a nervous halt.

Richard looked up also, then sucked his breath in when he saw what had startled the other man. The full moon had been a perfect circle of silvery white, but now a shadow was devouring the light. The darkened section of moon glowed a dark sullen red, like a lantern from hell.

"It means nothing," Sir Walter said, his voice sharp with anxiety, his eyes fixed on the drama in the night sky. "I have seen this before. It will pass. It means nothing." He did not believe his own words. An eclipse had always been regarded as an omen of great and ominous events, and perhaps it fit this disastrous day. The question was, he thought wearily as he spurred his tired horse toward the abbey gates, did it bode well or ill for the youth who was the new Baron of Warfield?

The porter surveyed the two knights mistrustfully and asked their business before bidding them enter; in these times, even God's servants were wary, and with good cause. They stabled their horses, then crossed the court to the abbot's quarters as fugitive dead leaves skipped before the chill wind with a brittle rasp. The moon was almost half-covered now, the earth tinted with ominous ruddiness.

Then the pure, fragile sound of monks singing matins floated through the frigid night air from the church. The beauty of it was a reminder of a higher, better world, and it brought comfort to Sir Walter's weary soul. His left hand tightened on the scabbard of the scorched sword he carried. God willing, perhaps Richard was right about Adrian.

The abbot's receiving chamber was simple, with the plainest of furniture and a crucifix the only decoration, but mercifully there was fire and wine to warm the visitors' frozen bones while they waited for the service to end. Sinking onto a bench, Sir Walter sipped the wine gratefully, though he was unsurprised to find it thin, poor stuff; Fontevaile was one of the new Cistercian houses, an order grimly determined not to be corrupted by greed for gold and easy living. The captain had been surprised when Adrian had insisted on Fontevaile; apparently the boy had a passion for austerity.

Richard FitzHugh paced about the shadowed chamber, drinking his wine, too restless to sit even after the last exhausting days. Sir Walter watched him fondly. The young knight cut a fine figure, golden-haired and handsome, a courageous fighter. It was Sir Walter who had suggested that he join the Warfield guard when he left Courtenay, and secretly the captain thought of him as the son he had never had. Lord Hugh had enough sons; surely he could spare the least important of them. Then Sir Walter sighed and devoted himself to his wine. Lord Hugh was dead, and Richard could never be Baron of Warfield in his place. Some things could not be changed, and bastardy was one of them.

After matins and lauds were done, Abbot William returned to his quarters. Forewarned of visitors, his features were drawn into a frown. Abbots must be worldly men to guard the interests of their houses, but

William had the ascetic face of a monk who had not forgotten that God must be served first.

After the briefest of greetings, the abbot asked, "You wish to see Adrian de Lancey?"

Tersely Sir Walter explained why, adding, "He has not yet taken final vows, has he?"

"Nay, he lacks a month of his sixteenth birthday." The lines in the abbot's long face had deepened at the grim recital. "Now I suppose he will be lost to us. A pity. I think he has a true vocation." Without further comment he instructed his servant to summon the novice, then sat and waited, his hands folded before him on the table, his eyes hooded.

A few minutes later the object of Sir Walter's mission stepped across the threshold. Only a single lamp burned and the visitors were hidden in the shadows, so Sir Walter took the opportunity of studying Adrian while the youth's attention was on the abbot. The knight had paid little heed to his lord's youngest son in the past, but now he craved knowledge of his new master—knowledge and reassurance.

Adrian de Lancey was no longer the slight, undersize lad of Sir Walter's memory. On the verge of manhood now, he had reached average height, and under the coarse white Cistercian robe his body was healthy and well made. He moved across the chamber with the physical grace of a warrior, not the other-worldly abstraction of a cleric.

Rather than the golden coloring of his father and brothers, Adrian's hair was so fair as to be almost silver. His finely cut features wore the tranquil containment of a monk, showing neither surprise nor alarm at being summoned from his pallet in the dead of night. That air of containment had always been part of him from the time he was an infant; perhaps those grave, reserved eyes were why Sir Walter had never been quite comfortable in the lad's presence.

Adrian bowed to the abbot. "You wished to speak

with me, Father?'' His voice was low and pleasant, as cool and controlled as his appearance.

"You have visitors.'' William gestured toward the shadows.

The young man turned. When he saw his half-brother, for a moment warmth was visible in the gray eyes. "Richard!" With surprise and obvious pleasure he stepped forward to take his brother's outstretched hand.

Richard gravely returned his clasp. Then Adrian's gaze penetrated the dark to recognize Sir Walter, and warmth vanished, to be replaced by wariness at the realization that this could be no ordinary visit. Releasing his brother's hand, he said, "Sir Walter, I bid you welcome. You bring news from Warfield?''

The old knight got heavily to his feet. "Aye, Lord Adrian, and it is evil news indeed." Moving forward into the light, he knelt before the novice and mutely proffered the sheathed sword he had brought with him.

Sir Walter's gesture and salutation conveyed the essence of disaster, if not the detail. For an endless moment the young man stared at the engraved bronze pommel of the Warfield sword. It did not need to be said that the weapon would never have been relinquished while its owner lived.

When it seemed the silence might shatter from tension, Adrian asked softly, his face utterly still, "What happened?''

"Two nights ago, the manor at Kirkstall was attacked and Richard and I took most of the men-at-arms and went in pursuit of the raiders. By chance, all three of your brothers had come to Warfield to celebrate Christmas, so I told Lord Hugh that there was no need for him to come with us, that he should enjoy the time with his sons and new grandson.'' Sir Walter's voice was heavy with self-condemnation. "I think the raid on Kirkstall was a feint to draw us away. While we were gone, Warfield was attacked before dawn on Christmas morning, while everyone was sleeping.

The keep was burned, all within slaughtered. A few of the villagers were drawn by the sounds of fighting and saw what happened from the wood. Your father and brothers fought bravely with what arms were at hand, but they had no chance. It was a deliberate massacre.'' He nodded at the weapon in his hands. ''We found your father's sword by his body. It was one of the few things to survive the fire.''

Adrian's face had changed during the recital. Without a single muscle moving, the planes and angles shifted and firmed in a new pattern, no longer that of a youth. And his fair coloring and pale habit no longer seemed cool; instead, he glowed with the white heat of molten iron. ''Who?'' he asked, his voice still soft but with a lethal edge that penetrated every corner of the room.

''Guy of Burgoigne.'' Sir Walter's bitterness made the name a curse. ''A bandit who seeks to build his own kingdom in the northern Marches.'' Forgetting where he was, the old knight spat on the floor. ''As one of Stephen's strongest supporters, he knows the king will not punish him. But who would have guessed Burgoigne would come so far south to slaughter another baron in his own keep?''

Adrian turned and knelt before Abbot William, who had been silently watching. ''My lord abbot, I must leave Fontevaile, deeply though it grieves me. Will you give me your blessing?''

''Aye, you have it.'' Laying a hand on Adrian's silver-fair head, Abbot William murmured a few sentences in Latin, then sighed. ''Strive for self-mastery, my son. You are your own most grievous enemy.''

''I know that well.'' Adrian stood and turned, his gray eyes blazing as he took his father's sword from Sir Walter's hands and pulled the weapon from its scabbard. For a moment he ran light fingers along the blade, which glinted lethally beneath the marks of soot and blood; then he kissed the charred hilt, which had worn to his father's hand.

Watching, Sir Walter inhaled and took an involuntary step back, shocked to his core as he saw a resemblance he had never noted before. In the deadly purity of rage, Adrian might almost have been his maternal grandfather, the Sire of Courcy, a warrior of legendary strength and viciousness. Courcy's daughter, Lady Eleanor, had been a sweet and gentle mistress of Warfield, and Sir Walter had never thought to see her father's face in her sons. It was a startling, and not wholly welcome, recognition.

Adrian lifted his head, his eyes no less lethal than the steel of his sword. "Sir Walter, make me a knight."

"But . . . but you are only fifteen. You have not prepared, not bathed or fasted." The captain shook his head. "To be made a knight is one of life's most solemn moments. It is not right to do it in haste."

"I have been trained in the basic skills of arms, and for over two years I have been praying and purifying myself," the youth said with noticeable dryness. "Even now Burgoigne might be moving to capture the Warfield demesne, and there is no time to be lost. If I am to command, I must be a knight, and I ask that you confer the accolade."

Sir Walter paused uncertainly, too tired for such a momentous decision. Then Richard's quiet voice sounded from the shadows. "Adrian is right. A hard task lies before him, and he must face it as a man among men." When Sir Walter still hesitated, Richard continued, his voice quieter yet, "If you will not dub him, I will. But it would be more fitting from you."

Sir Walter bowed before inescapable logic. There was precedent for dubbing a youth who was coming into his inheritance, or a squire on the eve of battle, and both those conditions were true now.

It was customary to say a few words on the occasion, and the captain cleared his throat, his gaze meeting that of the young man who stood before him with dangerous stillness. "To be a knight is a great privi-

lege, and an equally great responsibility. A knight must
serve God and the Church, give fealty and obedience
to his lord, and defend the weak.''

He paused, and Richard stepped forward and girded
Lord Hugh's sword around his brother's lean waist.

Sir Walter continued, ''May God grant you courage,
wisdom, and strength, that you might live, and die,
with honor. Be thou a knight, Sir Adrian.'' The captain gave Adrian the *colée,* the ritual blow on the
shoulder, and the ceremony was done.

It should have been an incongruous sight, a youth
wearing a sword over the white robe of a monk, but it
was not. Richard stepped forward and embraced
Adrian, then lifted the abbot's gospel from the desk
and swore the formal oath of fealty to his brother.
Reminded of what was fitting, Sir Walter did the same.

After gravely accepting their oaths, Adrian turned to
face the simple crucifix that hung on the abbot's wall,
and sank to his knees. Drawing his sword, he raised
it before him so that the cross shape of blade and hilt
was aligned with the crucifix. ''I swear before God
and man that I shall rebuild Warfield stronger than
before,'' he said, his voice harsh with intensity. ''And
I further swear that my family and all those others who
died with them shall be avenged, no matter how long
it will take, even if it should cost me my life.''

Of the three men listening, only Richard appreciated the significance of the fact that Adrian's oath was
not to *attempt* rebuilding and vengeance, but was a
solemn promise to achieve those ends. Knowing what
he did of his brother, Richard did not doubt that the
vow would be fulfilled.

Outside in the courtyard, the abbot's servant escorted Sir Walter and Richard to the guest hall so they
could have some much-needed rest. Adrian knew better than to reclaim his own pallet; the contradictory
emotions warring within him would make sleep impossible. Glancing at the sky, he saw that the moon

was almost totally obliterated and gave a faint, humorless smile. An eclipse was said to be a portent of great change, and certainly that was true now: after tonight, his life would never be the same. He turned right and crossed the court to the abbey church.

The vast, echoing interior was lit only by a few scattered candles, and the stone emptiness had a bone-biting chill worse than the winter air outside. An hour earlier Adrian had been here with the other novices and choir monks, chanting hymns to the Lord. There had been warmth in the bodies standing close together in the choir, harmony in their uplifted voices, and peace in the belief that he would spend the rest of his life here. Now peace was gone, perhaps forever.

Lifting a burning taper, he carried it to the rack of votive candles and lit a flame to the memory of his father, Lord Hugh of Warfield. The baron had been a stern and unsubtle man, inspiring more respect than love, but he had believed in honor, and done his duty as he saw it.

Adrian set three more candles ablaze for his eldest brother, also called Hugh, and for the wife and infant son who had died with him on Christmas Day. Hugh the younger had been in the mold of his father, and as heir to Warfield he had been more than a little arrogant. But he had also been unflinchingly brave, and Burgoigne's men must have paid dearly for his death.

Another candle flared for Amaury de Lancey, a year junior to Hugh. Resenting that he was a landless younger son, it had been Amaury's special mission to prove that he was his older brother's equal in all things, and, for better and for worse, he had been.

Baldwin was the youngest of the three brothers who had died. He and Richard had been of an age, and Baldwin had always treated the bastard with disdain. Ironic that his despised half-brother had survived because he was pursuing raiders in bitter December weather while the legitimate de Lanceys had enjoyed the comfort of the Christmas feast.

Adrian took a deep breath, inhaling the faded fragrance of incense and the acrid scent of burning tallow. Was it wicked to be grateful that the one member of his family who survived was Richard, the brother whom Adrian most loved?

His mouth twisted humorlessly. Wicked he might be, but he could not deny how he felt.

Then, as he always did, he lit a candle for his mother, though surely her soul needed no prayers. Instead he made a humble plea for God's forgiveness. When Lady Eleanor had died the year before, too quickly for Adrian to go to her, he had raged at God for taking a woman of such gentle goodness too soon. He should have had more faith; now he could see that it was God's mercy that his mother had passed quickly and peacefully rather than in the flames of Warfield, surrounded by the screams of her dying family and household.

Finally, his face grim, Adrian lit every other candle on the rack until dozens of flames blazed, defying the dark with their heat and light. These were for the cooks and scullions, the grooms and guards who had also died at the hands of Burgoigne and his men. As a child Adrian had known most of them, had played with some, learned from others. May God have mercy on their souls. They had had a right to expect protection of their master, and Lord Hugh had failed them. Pray God that Adrian never did the same.

His sandals slapping softly, he crossed the nave to the Lady Chapel, where a candle illuminated the statue of the Holy Mother. He had always loved this chapel, for Mary's gentle face held a timeless serenity that reminded him of his own mother, and of all that was sweet and pure in life. There was deep truth in the fact that men spoke of Holy Mother Church, for the Church was the force of civilization and compassion among nations, just as women brought mercy and gentleness to men.

He knelt and laid his sword before the altar. Usually

candidates for knighthood prayed over their arms the night before, asking for strength and humility, but Adrian reversed that order. Bowing his head, he covered his face with his hands and drew a shuddering breath, indifferent to the chill of the stone beneath his knees.

As he tried to pray, fragments of thought and feeling swirled within his mind, plans for the future warring with his turbulent emotions. He must protest to the king about Burgoigne's murderous behavior. Stephen would not punish one of his favorites, but perhaps in his guilt the king would waive or reduce the amount of the relief that must be paid for Adrian's right of inheritance. Money saved there would be most useful, for Adrian must rebuild Warfield in stone, not timber, so it could never be burned again. And on another site; Adrian had once suggested that the old keep was too vulnerable and Lord Hugh had scoffed that a mere boy questioned his father's judgment.

But fees and castles were just worldly problems, capable of solution. What could not be solved was the fact that he was now a baron, with life-and-death power over hundreds of men, women, and children. The life of a monk was not easy, but there was a simplicity to it, and here at Fontevaile he could have governed the dark, destructive side of his nature.

His mother had recognized her father's savage temper in her youngest son, and she had done her best to curb him by her example of love and gentleness. It was Lady Eleanor who had suggested that Adrian enter the Church. He had recognized the wisdom of her advice, for even as a boy, tilting at the quintain or practicing swordcraft, he could taste the treacherous joys of bloodlust. As a result, Adrian had early taught himself rigid control. For a time he had believed that he could successfully be both warrior and godly man. Then the stirrings of manhood had intensified his passions, convincing him that his capacity for violence exceeded his ability to control it.

Adrian exhaled, his breath clouding the cold air as he thought of all that he was losing, not just a way of life, but possibly his very soul. He had entered the Church believing that it offered his only hope of living a devout life, and in renouncing the world he had found fulfillment.

More than fulfillment, there had been joy in knowing he would spend the rest of his life working and praying at Fontevaile, amongst the silences and songs of praise, surrounded by learning and beauty. Few were the worldly temptations here, and the great battles were those of the spirit, noted only by one's confessor, though no less challenging for being private. Lust and pride and anger were part of him, and even in a monastary, far from temptation, he had found them to be opponents of overpowering strength and threat.

But now the world had claimed him for its own. The very sins he struggled against were often honored by worldly men, who considered pride fitting in a nobleman, fury a virtue in a warrior, and unbridled lust a proof of manliness. It would be so easy, so exquisitely easy, to become a monster like the Sire of Courcy. Adrian was terrifyingly aware that under his shock, under the grief and regrets for the slaughter of his family, there was fierce exultation that God had not seen fit to leave him at Fontevaile.

Prostrating himself on the floor before the altar, the icy stone rough against his cheek, he prayed for the strength he would need in the struggle ahead. Not the strength to defend his patrimony, or to rebuild Warfield, or to protect the people under his care. Those things he knew he could do.

The true test, the one Adrian feared he might be unequal to, was to master himself.

1

IT WAS a glorious high summer day. Meriel de Vere
stopped at the top of the hill and unhooded the kestrel,
then cast it into the wind, watching in delight as the
little falcon soared upward. With equal delight, she
pulled off her veil and wimple, closing her eyes blissfully for a moment as the wind blew through her
straight black hair. She had hastened through the first
part of her errand to allow time for lingering on her
return, and she intended to enjoy every moment of
freedom. Not that Mother Rohese would scold her for
tarrying; the prioress had always been wonderfully tol-
erant of her wayward novice.

Meriel sighed, reminded once more how quickly
time was passing. She had first come to Lambourn
Priory as a student when she was ten, and in the five
years since she had spent more time with the Benedictine sisters than with her own family at Beaulaine. Sir
William de Vere had sent his daughter to the priory
with the idea that she would eventually take the veil,
and the previous year Meriel had begun her novitiate.

Lambourn was a small house, which was why it was
a priory, not an abbey, but it was a happy place and
Meriel loved the sisters and the way of life. Nonetheless, the closer she drew to final vows, the harder it
was to imagine spending the rest of her life within the
confines of the cloister. The very thought was suffo-
cating.

Which was exactly why Mother Rohese often chose
Meriel for errands to the village and the manor, as a

way of relieving Meriel's restlessness. But would she be so restless if final vows were not so near?

Realizing that her thoughts were starting to chase one another, Meriel set them aside, loath to cloud the perfect day with fretfulness. She hitched up the skirts of her black habit and settled on crossed legs to watch the kestrel. She had named the little falcon Rouge, because of the reddish-brown bars on its upper body, but had not trained the bird for hunting. Quite apart from the fact that she didn't have enough time for the slow work of training, falconry would have been most unfitting for a novice nun. It was enough to have the pleasure of Rouge's company, both in the priory and on these occasional expeditions into the country.

Meriel loved animals: horses, birds, dogs, even cats. Regrettably, she lacked the wisdom to appreciate spiders, but perhaps when she was older and more godly she would learn to love them too.

The first glee of free flight having worn off, Rouge was now hovering about twenty feet above the meadow, her tail fanned, her gaze intent as she searched for unwary mice or other prey. Amongst falcons and hawks, females were the birds of choice because they were larger, stronger, and steadier in temperament than the males. However, kestrels were so small that even the female could not take game much larger than a sparrow.

Meriel smiled dreamily and pulled a sprig of meadow timothy, placing it in her mouth so she could suck the tender end while she let her imagination run free. What would it be like to be a falcon, to have the lightness and freedom to ride the wind, to hover and glide with the swift powerful beat of wings, to cleave the air fiercely as she seized her quarry?

With a grin, Meriel decided not to go as far as imagining what a grasshopper tasted like; that was one part of the kestrel's life she had no desire to share.

Linking her hands around her knees, she watched Rouge fondly. Kestrels were the most lowly of all hunting birds, and were sometimes contemptuously called hoverhawks. Indeed, they were the only breed which could lawfully be flown by those of peasant birth, but what kestrels lacked in dignity, they made up for in charm. Rouge was a playful and affectionate creature, and she had become a pet to everyone in the priory.

The bailiff had found the starving young falcon in the spring, and Meriel, who had spent much time in the Beaulaine mews, had nursed the bird back to health. Now Rouge followed her about, fluttering from perch to perch to be near her mistress, occasionally even invading the church when the sisters were at their devotions.

Once the kestrel went so far as to perch on the statue of the Virgin during prime. After the service Mother Rohese had said rather dryly that, while the Blessed Virgin would doubtless forgive the transgression, it would be well if the bird was persuaded to stay out of the church when the bishop visited. Meriel had agreed meekly, tactfully refraining from mentioning the priest at Beaulaine who brought his sparrowhawk to services and tethered it to the altar rail while he performed the Mass.

After half an hour of drifting, uncomplicated enjoyment, Meriel reluctantly stood and prepared to return to the priory. Rouge had hunted her fill and didn't wait for the lure, but flew down and perched on her mistress's gloved hand, then hopped to her shoulder, making soft mewling noises. The girl winced as claws stabbed through her habit, but she had to smile when Rouge playfully took the lobe of Meriel's ear in her beak. The great gyrfalcons and peregrines were splendid creatures, with the beauty and power of avenging angels, but they were never so tame as the little kestrels and merlins.

Meriel scratched delicately at Rouge's head, then glanced at the sun. Seeing that the afternoon was far advanced, she frowned. If she didn't hurry, she would miss vespers.

Keeping Rouge on her shoulder, Meriel picked up her veil and wimple and set off at a brisk pace. The most direct route to the priory was a steep path over a high wooded hill, and she climbed steadily for a quarter of an hour, warmed by her exertion even though she moved in the shade of the trees.

At the top of the hill she stopped to catch her breath, her gaze scanning the valley far below, where a road to the north followed the river. This part of England had been relatively unscathed during the last years of civil war, but safety could never be taken for granted.

The hard flash of light reflecting from bright metal caught her gaze and she narrowed her eyes to study it further. Her brother Alan said that she had spent so much time with falcons that she had their vision, and perhaps he was right, or she would never have been able to discern the ambush below.

Chilled, Meriel drew in her breath when she realized that armed men lined both sides of the road just north of a curve. It was impossible to guess who the ambushers were, or for whom they waited, but from the sizable cloud of dust being raised on the road, their prey was at hand, riding into the trap.

Even as she watched, a troop of perhaps two dozen knights and men-at-arms rode into view a scant hundred yards from the waiting ambush. There had been rumors of fighting to the south, and she guessed that the groups below were warring adherents of King Stephen and Empress Matilda.

In a way, it did not matter who they were. Any group of armed men was a threat to the innocent, and atrocities had been committed by both sides. Indeed, the whole of England was being torn not just by those who fought for their causes, but by outlaws whose only loyalty was to themselves, whose only goal was plunder. Sober men lamented the passing of King Henry, whose iron hand had kept his barons in check.

Sensing Meriel's tension, the kestrel stirred restlessly on her shoulder, and she quickly hooded the bird so it wouldn't fret. Her instinct was to race back to the priory to warn of possible danger, but she stayed, hoping for more information.

The group riding down the road looked weary and battle worn, and Meriel drew in her breath, wishing she could warn them but knowing her voice would never carry against the wind. Though she knew nothing of the men below and what they stood for, her sympathies lay with the travelers who were about to become victims of treachery.

When the riders were almost within the ambush, the man at their head raised a hand and sharply reined back his horse, alerted by some sign of danger. Immediately the attackers sprung the trap, spurring their mounts into the road.

The two groups clashed and exploded into a wild melee. Three of the ambushed riders went down in the first onslaught and Meriel feared there would be a massacre, for the attackers had greater numbers as well as surprise on their side. Her fingers gripped the bark of the tree that sheltered her as she watched helplessly. She had seen squires and knights in their ceaseless training, but never before had she seen the deadly results. There was an eerie horror in watching the distant figures hacking and stabbing in near-total silence, though occasionally the wind brought the sounds of particularly violent blows, and the anguished screams of men and horses.

But even as the attackers struck, the leader of the riders began to rally his men, pulling them together to protect each other's backs, then taking the offensive with lethal skill. The leader was everywhere, a demon of ferocity, striking down attackers, shoring up a weak spot in his group, and there was an unholy beauty in his wild courage.

As the riders recovered from their first shock, the balance of power shifted. Several of the attackers were unhorsed, and suddenly the whole group withdrew, turning to flee north along the road.

Meriel waited to see no more. The track to Lambourn Priory branched from the road a mile to the north and there was a chance the fleeing soldiers might choose that route for their escape. And if they did, they might decide that the walled priory would be a good place to withdraw and take a stand.

With a silent apology to Rouge, she wrapped the kestrel in her veil and tucked it inside the folds of her habit where it would be safe. Then she lifted her skirts and raced down the hill toward the priory. The mile-long journey seemed to take forever. Twigs tore her habit and once she tripped and fell to the ground, scraping her palms and knees painfully as she protected the kestrel from injury.

As Meriel neared the priory, pain stitched her side and she had to slow, gasping for breath. The bell was tolling for vespers as she entered the gates, and with the last of her energy she darted across the yard to intercept the prioress, who was emerging from her lodging to go to the church. "Mother Rohese!"

The prioress turned, her surprise turning to amusement when she recognized the figure racing across the yard. "Yes, child?"

Meriel skidded to a stop and ducked a quick curtsy as she gasped, "Two bands of knights just fought on the far side of the hill. One group is fleeing north, the others may pursue them."

The prioress's amusement vanished. Raising her voice, she summoned one of the passing sisters, saying tersely, "Tell the porter to ring the bell to summon our people from the fields and the village." Then she commanded of her novice, "Tell me all that you saw."

Meriel described the ambush, the size of the two bands, and the extent of the fighting. When she was done, Mother Rohese asked, "Do you remember any of the knights' emblems?"

Meriel closed her eyes, trying to recall what she had

seen during those chaotic minutes. "I think the leader of the attackers carried the device of a wild boar, in blue," she said slowly. After further thought, she was rewarded by a vivid image, the flashing, upraised shield of the man who had kept his troop from destruction. "The leader of the ambushed group bore a hawk, in silver." Opening her eyes, she asked, "Does that help?"

"The blue boar belongs to Guy of Burgoigne, I think. The silver hawk might be Adrian of Warfield," the prioress said, her brow furrowed. Then, as her attention returned to her novice, a lighter note entered her voice. "I assume that is Rouge under your habit. Perhaps you should set the poor bird free."

Meriel glanced down and saw the upper part of her habit heaving indignantly. Suddenly aware of her dishevelment, she extracted the kestrel, then tried unsuccessfully to put her veil on with her free hand. "I'm sorry, Mother," she said, blushing as she pushed back her wind-tangled black hair. "I should not have lingered on my way back from the grange."

"Perhaps it was God's will, for if you had returned promptly you would not have seen the fighting," the prioress said. "But go now and make yourself presentable. If you hurry, you won't miss the beginning of vespers."

Accurately interpreting the doubtful look on her novice's face, Mother Rohese added with gentle admonition, "Of course services will continue. Can you think of a better time to pray than when danger threatens?"

Adrian was in the high, wild state where fighting was a pure and deadly madness, where he sensed his enemies' blows before they fell, where he blocked and struck back from infallible instinct. He had lost count of how many men he had engaged, though he had killed at least one of the attackers, possibly more. With a powerful blow of his sword, he unhorsed another opponent, who went crashing to the ground to lie stunned on his back. Leaning forward to set the tip of his blade on the man's throat, between hauberk and jaw, the baron was about to finish his opponent when Sir Walter's shouted "Adrian!" pierced his lethal concentration.

The compelling note in the captain's voice caused Adrian to hold back the killing stroke. Withdrawing his weapon, he realized that his quarry was not a knight but a terrified squire, a boy scarcely old enough to carry a blade, certainly not a danger to an experienced knight.

Moreover, the skirmish was ending, most of the ambushers fleeing up the road, those remaining no longer a threat. His breath coming in great gasps from exertion, Adrian told the squire, "Stand and surrender your sword."

Trembling, his face greenish-white, the squire obeyed and offered the hilt of his weapon to his captor. As he accepted it, Adrian felt the wave of reaction that always followed battle, and his stomach churned at the thought of how close he had come to needlessly killing the boy. Though he had killed more than his share of men in battle, he always tried to avoid unnecessary slaughter; thank God Sir Walter had stopped him in time.

Speaking brusquely to conceal his emotions, Adrian ascertained that his captive was a nephew of the Earl of Sussex. As he placed the lad in Sir Walter's charge, Adrian thought wryly that God was rewarding mercy, for the squire alive would be worth a pretty penny in ransom. Such ransoms had rebuilt Warfield.

Turning to more urgent matters, he dismounted and made a quick survey of how much damage they had sustained. Two of his men were seriously injured, four more had taken wounds that needed attention. The attackers had suffered heavier casualties, with three dead, two mortally wounded, and three more injured but likely to survive.

A Warfield man-at-arms who had grown up in this part of Wiltshire supplied the welcome information that they were very near Lambourn Priory. Not only was it a blessing that the casualties could be nursed by the nuns, it also meant that the Warfield troop could resume its journey with little delay.

With the efficiency of long practice, the wounded were crudely bandaged, the dead lashed to horses, and the journey resumed. During the slow trip, Sir Walter dropped back to ride beside his lord. "They were Burgoigne's men, weren't they?"

"Aye. Lord Guy himself was with them. I had a clear sight of him before he ran off. He's vastly skilled at protecting his precious hide." In a voice of supreme detachment, Adrian continued, "After abandoning King Stephen at Wilton, Burgoigne obviously decided this was a perfect opportunity for an ambush. We were lucky. If one of his horses hadn't neighed and given us a moment's warning, he might have finally succeeded in killing me."

"Where you're involved, lad, luck isn't needed." Sir Walter sighed heavily and rubbed his thigh where he had taken a bruising blow during the skirmish. For all his advanced age, he had given a good account of himself. "I've lost count of the times Burgoigne and Warfield have clashed over the years. Since you hold land he covets, it will not end till one of you is dead."

"And that one will be Burgoigne," Adrian said grimly. He had not forgotten his vow to destroy the man who had murdered his family, but there had been other priorities and challenges to meet in the years since he had inherited Warfield. Indeed, within twenty-four hours of leaving Fontevaile, he had fought his first battle, killed his first man, taken his first wound; in the next twenty-four hours he had had his first woman.

After that chaotic reintroduction to the world, Adrian had first concentrated his strength and will on holding the barony together, then on increasing Warfield's strength. In the midst of civil war, there had been neither time nor resources for a lengthy siege of Guy's stronghold. But someday Guy's hour would come, and when it did, he was a dead man.

Mother Rohese forwent vespers to supervise the ingathering of all the priory's tenants, and not a few of their most valuable beasts. After sending out the best poacher in the parish to see what he could learn, there was nothing to do but wait and see if danger materialized, or if the priory would escape unnoticed. There had been false alarms before and the prioress prayed that this would be another. Her serene face showed none of her concern as she sat quietly in the courtyard, her rosary twined around her left hand and a village infant drowsing on her lap.

Vespers were long past when the serf keeping watch on the wall shouted that visitors had arrived, his voice cautious but not fearful. Rohese handed the sleeping infant to its older sister, then made her unhurried way across the court. As she reached the main gate, a single knight was admitted while her bailiff and his men watched him with armed vigilance.

A silver hawk was embroidered on the knight's blue surcoat, and the prioress guessed he was leader of the band that had been ambushed. A dark gold growth of beard dusted his face and he looked as if he had been in the saddle for a week, but fatigue was not allowed to soften his erect carriage.

Seeing Rohese, the knight approached her and bowed, the links of his hauberk jangling faintly. "I am Adrian of Warfield," he said. "We were ambushed nearby, and I beg the assistance of Lambourn Priory in caring for the wounded."

"I have heard of you, Adrian of Warfield. You have the reputation of a man who respects the Church." The prioress inclined her head. "All godly men are welcome here."

She studied her visitor curiously. He was not what she would have expected in a knight of such fierce reknown. Beneath whiskers and exhaustion were the sensitive, fine-drawn features of a scholar; moreover, he was scarcely more than a boy. It was a sign of her own advancing years to be surprised, she realized ruefully; Warfield's cool gray eyes were a reminder that warriors came of age early, or not at all. "How many are injured?"

"Eleven, two of them mortally. Besides the wounded, I would also leave three men-at-arms to guard our prisoners."

Correctly interpreting Mother Rohese's expression, the baron said, "Don't worry, those I leave can be trusted to behave themselves in a nunnery."

"You are sure?" She gave him a peaceable smile. "Forgive my caution, Lord Adrian, but in these times, even the threat of God's wrath is not always enough to protect his servants."

"I promise you there will be no trouble," he said with dry humor. "My men may doubt the sureness of God's wrath, but they know better than to doubt mine."

"Very well, my lord." The prioress's eyes twinkled at his assurance. This was a very forceful young man, and she decided that his followers would behave as they ought. Lifting her hand, she gestured for her bailiff to open the gate.

As the task of settling the injured men in the infirmary began, Mother Rohese said to her visitor, a faint question in her voice, "Rumor says there was a battle to the south."

"Aye," Warfield confirmed, "outside Wilton. Stephen left the town to avoid being trapped in the castle, and Robert of Gloucester put him to rout. Had not the king's steward, William Martel, put up a stout defense, Stephen would have been captured again. Martel himself was taken prisoner."

"The king will pay a high price to get him back," the prioress said thoughtfully, assessing the implications. "You fought with Earl Robert?"

"Yes. My brother and most of my knights are still with him, aiding in the pursuit." Lord Adrian's eye was sardonic. Doubtless he knew that Stephen's Queen Maud was a patron of Lambourn Priory, but by tacit consent the baron and the prioress avoided declaring political loyalties.

Mother Rohese sighed. "So another battle was fought, more men have died, and England is no closer to a resolution."

"Too many men profit by chaos," he observed cynically. "As long as the king and the empress are deadlocked, there are rich pickings for vultures, so men change their loyalties like weathercocks."

Many men did, but the prioress knew that Warfield had held steadfast to the empress through the years of civil war. Though Matilda had a reputation for arrogance, she must also have some finer qualities or she could not have held the loyalty of men like Robert of Gloucester and Adrian of Warfield.

After giving Rohese his news and a generous recompense for the priory's aid, Warfield signaled for his horse, impatient to be off. Surprised, the prioress asked, "You do not spend the night? It is dusk and your men look very tired."

"There is a good moon tonight, reverend mother. We'll not halt for another few hours yet." The baron swung onto his mount.

"Very well. God keep you, Adrian of Warfield." The prioress inclined her head with grave respect, then turned away.

Adrian scanned the milling group of men-at-arms, and under his stern eye they began forming up to leave.

During the baron's discussion with Mother Rohese, the nuns had been moving among the visitors with food and wine, and now one approached the baron. It was not true that all nuns looked the same in their habits, for he had noticed this particular sister earlier. The shadows of the courtyard had eliminated details, and she had been an abstraction of pure grace as she walked from man to man, her step light and her black skirts swaying about her. As he talked with the prioress, his gaze had followed her with absent pleasure, the same pleasure he would have found in a flower or a sunset.

Stopping by his stirrup, the little nun carefully filled a goblet from her wineskin, then lifted it to him. She was very young. "Will you take some wine, my lord?"

"Thank you, madame," Adrian said, using the courtesy title accorded all religious sisters. He emptied the vessel in one long swallow, noting that the Benedictine sisters kept a better cellar than the Cistercians of Fontevaile did, then handed the cup back.

"I was on the hill above the road when you were ambushed, and I saw the whole fight." She reached into her pouch for bread and cheese, then handed them to him. "It was a cowardly attack, but you and your men fought them off with splendid bravery."

In the dusk her upturned face was a small pale oval, the veil covering her forehead almost to the dark brows. It was not a beautiful face, but her expression had a sweet guilelessness that moved Adrian in spite of his fatigue. "There is no splendor in fighting," he said brusquely as he accepted the food. "You were a fool to wander outside the priory."

Startled by his harshness, she gazed at him with wide blue eyes as he continued, "All over England abbeys and churches have been despoiled when it has suited one side or the other. Bands of dispossessed men rove the country like wolves, and your habit will not protect you from danger."

Her light laughter held the same sweetness as her face. "If even Lambourn's walls are no sure protection, why should I stay always within them?" Amusement faded under his hard gaze. "It is good of you to be concerned, my lord," she said contritely. "Pray forgive my levity. In truth, very seldom does an errand take me from the priory, and I never venture far."

"Take more care in the future, madame." Adrian

raised his arm to signal his men, then turned and led his troop out the gate. As they trotted through the woods to the main road, he chewed the bread and cheese absently while he wondered why he had been so rude to the little nun. She had been a sweet little thing, and so graceful. . . . Abruptly he realized that she had aroused not just his protectiveness but his desire.

Realization was accompanied by a surge of self-disgust. He had left Fontevaile knowing that chastity would be impossible in the world. In time he had come to believe that the pleasures of the flesh were one of God's gifts to suffering mankind and that it was no sin for men and women to find comfort and satisfaction together. But lusting after a holy sister was a kind of adultery. Worse than adultery.

Behind him, one of his men said to another, "Did you see the little sister with the great blue eyes? Pity that one is wasted as a bride of Christ."

"Aye," the second said. "She should be warming a mortal man's bed."

Both laughed, then stopped abruptly when their lord's cold gaze swept over them. He was known as a man with more piety than most, one who lived almost as simply as a monk and who brooked no blasphemy within his hearing. Wise men did not anger him without good cause.

As they rode north under a waxing moon, it did not improve Adrian's mood to know that in his heart he was as guilty of profane thoughts as his men were.

Meriel's lips moved as she read the elaborate script, translating the well-loved words from Latin in a soft whisper. *In the beginning was the Word, and the Word was with God, and the Word was God.* She wasn't entirely sure what the phrase meant, but to her it had always symbolized the mystery and joy of faith. And tonight, less than forty-eight hours before the ceremony that would forever separate her from the world, she needed to find that joy again.

She sat cross-legged on her pallet, the heavy volume in her lap, and absently traced the illuminated border with her forefinger. The design was composed of woodland creatures, with a luminous blue kingfisher twined into the initial capital. The artistry of the work awed her, but even such beauty could not lighten her heavy heart.

At Lambourn Priory, a novice about to take the veil spent three nights in a private cell and was excused from all duties except singing the divine offices. The time was to be spent in prayer and purification, much as squires did before the ceremony of knighthood. Meriel had the use of one of the priory's precious gospels and candles to read it by. She even had her kestrel, and Rouge now slept on a perch in the corner.

When Meriel had begun the purification, Mother Rohese had urged her to look deeply within herself for guidance. Doubtless the prioress, who knew everything from the least transgression of the newest student to the great political questions of the day, also knew that her novice was divided in heart.

Meriel closed the book and stood, then paced the narrow confines of the cell. Four steps one way, six the other. If she wished, she could open the door and go out to watch the night sky or pray in the church. If it were daylight, she could have gone to the priory fields and helped with the harvest. That being the case, why did the cell seem so much like a prison? Why was she unable to sleep, feeling as if she could not breathe when her eyes closed?

And blackest of all, why could she not pray? Meriel had always found it easy to pray, conversing with the Blessed Mother, Father, and Son as easily as with her earthly family. Yet tonight, when she should be preparing her soul for the most solemn moment of her life, she felt cut off from the wellspring of faith that had always been at the center of her being, and her spirit was parched by the deprivation.

Stopping by the perch, she unhooded the kestrel and scratched its throat as it blinked its brown eyes in sleepy amiability. Meriel had never been absolutely sure that she wanted to become a nun, and looking back, she could pinpoint the exact time when her doubt had crystallized: two months before, when the knights had come. The day had been the most eventful of all she had spent at Lambourn, and she could recall with precision her pleasure in flying the kestrel, the shock and terror of seeing the battle on the road, then fear as the community waited to see if catastrophe would strike the convent.

Later, when the knights had arrived with courtesy, not blades, the atmosphere had changed from fear to giddy relief. Meriel had volunteered to serve food and drink to the visitors, feeling as if her feet must scarcely be touching the ground. That brief half-hour of talking and walking had reminded her of how much she liked, and missed, the male half of the race. She had enjoyed the good-natured teasing of the men-at-arms, and herself had gently teased a young squire who was so shy his eyes would not meet hers. Meriel had even enjoyed the brusque leader with a face like Lucifer fallen, whose scolding about her incaution reminded her of her older brothers.

She began to pace again, circling the cell, her fingertips grazing the rough stone walls. It was not as if she never saw a male face. Men worked the priory fields. There were visitors, and the occasions when she was sent on errands. Nonetheless, Lambourn Priory was essentially a community of women.

As Meriel paced, she spoke aloud to the kestrel. "You know I must take my vows, Rouge, there is no other choice. My father was not a wealthy man—Beaulaine is scarce large enough to provide for William and his family. Papa was most clever to find marriages for Alice and Isabeau, and their dowries took all of Mama's own marriage portion. As the youngest of five, I must be grateful there was enough to pay my dowry here at Lambourn.''

The kestrel performed the alarming falcon trick of turning its head upside down, as if questioning her conclusion. Meriel continued earnestly, ''As a nun, I will have respect, the companionship of the holy sisters, the joy of doing God's work.'' Her voice rose. ''There is no other choice. Tomorrow evening my family will arrive for the ceremony. William has already ordered the celebration feast. It will be a great occasion. It is too late for me to change my mind. It has been too late since the first day I came here.''

Rouge stirred uneasily and Meriel realized that her agitation was disturbing the kestrel. ''This is where I belong,'' she said more quietly, as if by convincing the bird she could convince herself. ''Mother Rohese, the other sisters, the students—they are my family now. It would be different if Papa was alive. Though he would have scolded me for leaving, in truth he would have been glad to have me back at Beaulaine. But William and his wife . . . he will not refuse to take me in, but Haleva will say I am taking bread from the mouths of her babes, will treat me scarce better than a servant. I cannot turn back!''

Meriel drew a shuddering breath, then said with sudden determination, ''When I have become one of Christ's brides, I will know that I have done the right thing.'' She pulled off her veil. A novice's hair was cut just before taking final vows, as a symbol that the world was renounced. To cut her hair now would prove that she had made her decision, would surely end her tortured doubts.

Meriel lifted her knife, which she kept keen-edged for sharpening quills, eating, and a myriad other daily tasks. Pulling one of her long plaits forward, she tugged it taut so the knife would cut quickly. The ebony strands gleamed in the candlelight. Meriel knew that to be beautiful one must be tall and blond like her sisters, but secretly she had always thought her hair was rather nice in spite of its color. When she brushed it out, it fell almost to her knees in a glossy rippling mantle.

Vanity! The sooner her hair was cut, the better. She laid the edge of her blade against the plait, as close to her head as possible. Her fingers tensed on the knife to begin the downward stroke, then froze, incapable of completing the action.

Meriel was halted by a paralysis that had nothing to do with vanity. She felt as if great weights constricted her chest, dragged at her wrist, halted her breath. As her heart beat frantically, she closed her eyes for a moment, seeking to calm herself. Instead, she had a terrifying sense that the stone walls were closing in to crush the breath and life from her.

The illusion was so powerful that when her eyes flew open, for a moment it seemed as if the walls actually moved, pressing inward with the lethal inexorability of fate.

Meriel felt terror such as she had never known in her life. The knife dropped from her nerveless fingers and she fell to her knees and buried her face in her hands as she began to shake convulsively, her slim body as cold as death. Desperately she cried out, "Blessed Mother, help me. *Help me!*"

At first it seemed that her anguished prayer would go unanswered and that she would drown in her rising panic. Then, twining through the maelstrom, came a thread of peace.

At first it was the frailest of strands, but it grew, weaving a cloak of protection around the novice, as if the Blessed Virgin had come to embrace her anguished daughter.

Quite clearly Meriel saw a vision of herself standing at a crossroads. The road on the right ran through a cloister. It was a clear path, as safe and predictable as it was confining.

The left fork was as dark as the right was bright.

The road lay swathed in dark mists, and she knew that the shadows held both danger and joy, freedom and peril.

Yet, in truth, there was no choice. For an instant a vision of terrible beauty appeared before her inner eye: an archangel with flaming sword and a face of pitiless purity barred the right-hand path that led to the religious life.

Before she had time to draw a second breath, the vision was gone, leaving profound certainty in its wake. Meriel had asked for guidance and received it. Now she must follow the unknown path into the mists, no matter what trials and dangers lay there.

Tears still glittering on her face, she took her candle and wove her way through the narrow corridors to face her first trial. The bell was tolling for matins as Meriel knocked on the door of the prioress's quarters.

Mother Rohese bade her enter. The older woman was preparing to go to the church, and even at this dark hour of night she was a figure of otherworldly serenity. Looking at her novice without surprise, she said softly, "Yes, child?"

Meriel sought for words to explain why she had come, but in the end all she could do was say brokenly, "I can't do it, Mother, I just can't."

Understanding immediately, the prioress opened her arms. "It's all right, child, truly it's all right."

Meriel set down her candle and flew into the older woman's embrace, gasping through her tears, "I love God, and the Blessed Virgin, and the priory, but I can't be a nun."

"There is more than one way to serve the Lord," Mother Rohese said, her voice rich with comfort. "Mary herself was a wife and mother, and the world was a better place for that." She stroked the girl's bare head. "There are many reasons why women take the veil, but for you, child, it would be wrong to become a nun without a true vocation."

"I know in my heart that I am doing the right

thing," Meriel whispered, "but I have no idea what will become of me. My brother William will be most displeased."

"I do not doubt that God has plans for you, and in his time, you will discover what they are." Mother Rohese was unsurprised by Meriel's agonized decision. With her knowledge of the human heart, she had guessed the girl was not meant for the cloister, but Meriel might have taken vows from lack of other alternatives. Though she would have made a devout and honorable nun, it was better that she had the courage to turn away.

Selfishly Mother Rohese knew she would miss the girl's special kind of sweetness, the joy she brought to everyone and everything she touched, but the outside world had more need of sweetness and joy than Lambourn Priory did. "I will send a message to Beaulaine in the morning, to tell your family of your decision so they will not come for the ceremony."

Meriel nodded, then reluctantly stepped from the prioress's sheltering arms. While she knew beyond doubt that her choice was the right one, she did not look forward to the consequences.

The day when Meriel was to have taken her vows came and went. Her change of mind had created a stir at Lambourn. While a few members of the community had offered shy approval and best wishes, most avoided her, as if her failure of vocation might be contagious. As she continued with her usual tasks, Meriel herself was impatient, feeling that it was time to take her first uncertain steps into the mists of the unknown.

Three days after her decision, one of the lay servants came to the scriptorium to tell Meriel that her brother had come for her. She glanced around the large room, where half a dozen sisters engaged in the painstaking work of copying manuscripts. Meriel would never set foot in here again, and already she missed it. Carefully she blotted her quill and laid the pen down, suddenly sorrowful. Someone else would finish copying this page, and Meriel would never see the result.

Automatically she straightened her veil modestly across her forehead. Meriel still wore her black habit since she had no other gown. It could be reworked into a regular garment when she returned to Beaulaine; the heavy wool was still sound and would last for years.

She hesitated outside the guest parlor, hoping that William had accepted her decision and would not try to change her mind. Doubtless he and his wife, Haleva, had spent the last three days arguing what to do with his undutiful sister. Surely William would be at least a little glad to see her? He took his responsibilities very seriously, but usually she could coax a smile from him.

Opening the door, Meriel stepped inside, then stopped, astonished at the sight of the handsome young knight who waited for her with teasing eyes. "Alan!" she cried, and hurled herself across the room into his arms.

Laughing, her brother swept her from her feet with his hug. "No wonder they wouldn't have you as a nun, Madame Mischief!"

Alan was her favorite brother, five years older than Meriel. They were the two youngest de Veres and she had adoringly trailed him around Beaulaine, in the process learning to ride, hawk, and swim. Like Meriel, Alan had inherited their Welsh mother's raven-black hair and vivid blue eyes, but while Meriel had also inherited her mother's slight build and lack of inches, her brother had the height and strength of their Norman father.

"Why are you here? I thought Lord Theobald was keeping you in the north?" Meriel frowned, suddenly concerned. "You are still one of his household knights, aren't you?"

"So many questions!" Her brother set her down on her feet and both of them took seats. "Never fear, his lordship is far too wise to dismiss such a fine fellow as Alan de Vere." More seriously, he continued, "He needed a message delivered to Winchester and gave me leave to see my little sister made a nun on my way back, so I was at Beaulaine when the prioress's message arrived. In truth, I was glad of the news, for I did not think you should be a nun. You have too much life in you to spend it all within these walls."

Meriel gave him a look of affectionate exasperation. "If you and Mother Rohese were so sure of my lack of vocation, why did neither of you tell me? It would have made my life much easier these last months."

"I know little of vocations, but it seemed to me, and surely to the reverend mother, that such a decision must be one's own, no matter how great the difficulty. Besides"—Alan sighed—"it seemed the best choice, if you were content."

Meriel's face sobered as she remembered her circumstances. "Are William and Haleva dreadfully angry with me?"

"Well, Haleva is breeding again and you know what that does to her temper."

Meriel nodded; her sister-in-law, not particularly amiable even at her best, became positively shrewish toward the end of her pregnancies.

Alan continued, "She refuses to have you back."

Stricken, Meriel stared at her brother, her eyes huge and round. "But I will work hard and cause no trouble. Even Haleva has said that I am good with the children." She swallowed hard. While she had known her family would be unhappy, she had never considered that she might not be allowed to return to Beaulaine. "Did . . . did Haleva say why she does not want me?"

Her brother raised his hand quickly. "Don't worry, everything will be all right. Better than all right, in fact. As to why Haleva doesn't want you"—he grinned—"she is jealous, afraid you will put her in the shade."

"Jealous!" Meriel gave a peal of laughter. "Alan,

you're teasing me again. Haleva is beautiful. I would draw no attention from her.''

"Haleva is a handsome wench, for all her sharp tongue,'' Alan admitted, ''but you . . . you are Meriel.'' Before his sister's puzzled expression could become a question, he continued, ''But don't worry, you can come back with me to Lord Theobald's castle and attend his wife, Lady Amicia. I think you will be happier at Moreton than at Beaulaine. And later, a few years perhaps''—he paused portentously, drawing out the moment—''you will be able to live with me at my manor.''

Meriel caught her breath, scarcely daring to believe that her brother's announcement could be true. Landless younger sons took service with the great lords in the hope of eventually earning land of their own, but few were successful, fewer yet at so young an age as Alan. ''You mean Lord Theobald is going to enfeoff you?''

Alan nodded, a proud smile spreading across his face.

"How wonderful!'' Unable to contain her delight, Meriel jumped up and gave him a strangling hug. ''Tell me all about it! Did you do some great deed to earn Lord Theobald's gratitude?''

"We were attacked, I came to my lord's aid as any knight would,'' he said succinctly.

"Then you saved his life.''

"Perhaps. Certainly I saved his freedom and the ransom he would have had to pay to buy it back.'' Alan gave a deprecating shrug. ''At any rate, Lord Theobald decided I should be rewarded. One of the manors he holds is called Avonleigh, in eastern Shropshire. The knight who holds it now is old, with failing health and no heirs, so Lord Theobald has promised I shall have the manor when the present tenant dies.''

"I am so happy for you,'' Meriel said, her face glowing. ''You will be a man of property. You will be able to marry, perhaps an heiress who will increase your holdings.'' Her eyes danced. ''You will become a greater lord than William.''

''You go too quickly, little sister,'' Alan cautioned. ''It is not a great estate, just a single knight's fee, and it is not mine yet. Even if all goes as planned and Lord Theobald enfeoffs me, there will be much to be done, for the old knight is lax in his management.'' He leaned forward, his blue eyes earnest. ''I need you, Meriel. When—and if—Avonleigh becomes mine, I want you live with me, to run the household and oversee the manor when I am away serving my lord. I will need someone I trust, and I can think of no one who would be better than you. Even when you were a tiny maid, people were always glad to obey you.''

He gave her a conspiratorial smile. ''If I do take a wife, I shall be sure she is one you will be happy to call sister. And who knows? Perhaps I will take a rich captive and earn a ransom that will let me dower you.''

''I'm not sure I want a husband, Alan, for I'd not make an obedient wife.'' Meriel laughed, thinking how good it was of her brother to say that he needed her, when in truth, she needed him far more. ''But it will be my great pleasure to assist you in any way I can.''

Blissfully she leaned back against the whitewashed wall. Further along there were still mists, but for now, the first stretch of her path lay clear and bright before her.

2

Montford Castle, Shropshire
March 1148

"THERE'S A SIZABLE party coming from the south, my lord."

Alerted by the lookout, Richard FitzHugh raised a hand to shade his eyes and tried to discern the device on the banner barely visible in the distance. The mild spring weather had brought him up to the battlements to survey the castle defenses and decide what improvements to make over the summer. As he peered into the distance his gaze was wary, for the long civil war was about to enter an uncertain phase and spring might bring danger after the cold safety of winter.

The lookout said, "It's Warfield, my lord," at the same time that Richard made out the silver hawk on the banner. A minute later he fancied that he saw his brother's silver-gilt head shining in the sunshine at the head of the band of riders.

"Adrian made good time," Richard said with pleasure. "I had not thought to see him back in England before April." He turned and went down the stone steps to tell his seneschal to prepare a welcoming feast for Montford's liege lord. A pity it was Lent and they were restricted to fish, but the end of winter was not the time for fatted calves anyhow. No matter; it would be good to see Adrian, and to discover what conclusions he had reached during his sojourn in Normandy.

The feast was very presentable, even though it featured herring and cod in a number of guises. After eating, Adrian and his brother withdrew for a private conversation, leaving the Montford household and the Warfield knights to drink themselves cheerfully under the trestle tables.

Though the days were growing milder, the nights still had the bite of winter and Richard knelt at the hearth to build up the fire as Adrian prowled around the solar, glad to be back on his own land again. As he had done many times before, Adrian gave thanks that he had a brother whose loyalty, judgment, and battle skill were beyond question.

The last years had been busy ones. After the construction of Warfield Castle was well under way, Adrian had decided that a second castle was needed at Montford to defend the southern part of his holdings. He had designated his brother as castellan, and most of the work had been done under Richard's supervision. As a result, Montford bore the mark of Richard's mind and taste, just as Warfield showed Adrian's.

Finished with the fire, Richard stood and brushed his hands. "How is the empress?"

Adrian's journey across the channel had been as escort to the Empress Matilda, who was returning home after nine tumultuous years in England. Taking a chair, Adrian replied, "She has not given way to despair, though she mourns her brother's death greatly."

"It was a grievous loss for all who knew him," Richard said somberly. The Earl of Gloucester's sudden death the previous October had been a crushing blow to the empress's hopes. Once he had decided to support his half-sister's claim to the throne, Earl Robert had devoted his considerable wealth, loyalty, and military skill to her cause. For Adrian and the other barons who had also been loyal to Matilda, loss of her chief supporter could mean political disaster if King Stephen now achieved ascendancy.

"Matilda may win the ultimate victory by sitting quietly in Rouen." Adrian smiled with unaccustomed mischief. "I swear the king is his own worst enemy— no sooner does he gain an advantage than he throws it away. Stephen must be mad to clash with the Church now.''

Richard nodded agreement as he poured them both French wine from his own private stock. ''Having antagonized the Archbishop of Canterbury, the Pope, and Bernard of Clairvaux, Stephen can hardly expect the Church to be enthusiastic about confirming his son as heir to England.''

''Certainly Eustace is Matilda's best ally. Stephen must be the only man in England who doesn't see that his son would be a disastrous king, with most of Stephen's faults and none of his virtues.''

Adrian took an absent sip of his wine and stretched out in his chair, thinking of the red-haired youth he had visited in Anjou. The desire to know Matilda's son well enough to make a judgment for the future was one of the reasons he had escorted the empress to Normandy. ''I like what I saw of Henry FitzEmpress. Though he is only fifteen now, in a few years he will make a king to equal his grandfather. If—and when—it comes to a choice between Eustace and Henry, I think England will prefer Henry. Even the greediest of barons are tiring of civil war and anarchy.''

''Let us hope so,'' Richard said pessimistically.

''When Henry inherits his father's lands, he will have the strength to take England if it is not freely offered. Matilda's allies here in the west country need only stand together and wait to be on the winning side.'' A note of amusement sounded in Adrian's voice. ''To encourage continuing loyalty, the empress is being most generous with grants and charters. After all, such gifts cost her no more than the parchment they are written on.''

''What did she grant you?'' Richard asked with interest.

''Written license for Warfield and Montford castles, plus permission to build another should I deem it necessary.''

His brother whistled softly. "A valuable charter indeed."

"Especially since Henry told me that when he becomes king, he means to destroy all unlicensed castles." Adrian chuckled. "The lad lacks neither confidence nor common sense."

"Did Matilda have any other rewards for you?"

"A few minor privileges, such as the right to hunt in the royal forest, plus one major one." Adrian paused to sip his wine, then said offhandedly, "She made me Earl of Shropshire."

"Jesu!" Thoroughly startled, it took Richard a moment to assimilate the news, then make an accurate deduction. "Was this prompted by the fact that shortly after you left England, the king created Guy of Burgoigne Earl of Shropshire?"

"Exactly. When word reached Rouen, I was not pleased." Adrian's voice was very dry. "Knowing how I felt, Matilda offered me the same rank, thinking that it would increase my incentive to fight Burgoigne for control of the shire." He stared into the fire, his face impassive again. "I did not tell her that no such incentive was required."

It was not the first time that king and empress had created rival earls for the same county. In practical terms, control of the shire and its revenues went to whichever of the two claimants was stronger. Richard nodded, approving the empress's strategy. "Since Guy forced the demoiselle of Chastain into marriage and now controls half of Shropshire, you are the best choice to hold him in check."

"Very true." Adrian sighed. "One can pity poor Cecily of Chastain. Marriage by kidnap and rape is harsh even for an heiress. I would not wish Burgoigne on the worst termagant in Christendom."

His brother shrugged philosophically. All heiresses were wards of the king, to be handed out as prizes for royal supporters with no regard for the maids' own wishes. The demoiselle of Chastain had merely been unluckier than most. "When we kill him, she'll be free." Dismissing the subject, Richard poured himself more wine. "Speaking of heiresses, are you now officially betrothed to Isabel of Rouen?"

"I talked with her father again, but no final decision has been made."

Surprised, Richard raised his brows. "I thought you were set on the marriage. She has a fine dowry, and is said to be a handsome wench."

"It is a good match, but I can't say the girl appealed to me when I met her. Handsome, yes, but in a large and boisterous fashion." Adrian thought of the lady in question and the uncomfortable meeting they had had, then gave a self-mocking smile. "Nor was I to her taste."

Richard knew him well enough not to point out that one's wife did not have to be appealing—that's what mistresses were for. Instead he asked, "Are there any other girls of suitable rank that you prefer to Isabel?"

"Alas, no." Adrian shrugged. "I daresay Isabel and I can learn to be comfortable together. The idea of marriage has not been dropped, merely set aside for the moment." He made a dismissive gesture with his hand. "For the moment marriage is of minor importance. What matters is that soon there will be open war between Burgoigne and Warfield. We will have to patrol the area along the boundaries to ensure that Guy doesn't destroy our villages and fields. I'm thinking of quartering small bands of men-at-arms in several of the villages, so they can respond more quickly when Burgoigne attacks. What do you think?"

"It would make better sense to take the fighting to Burgoigne and burn *his* crops and fields."

"Which would hurt a lot of innocent villeins more than it would hurt him. There is no need to go after Guy, for he will surely come to us," Adrian said patiently. Laying waste an enemy's territory was a standard tactic, but he was unable to forget that in the eyes of God, peasant lives and souls were as valuable as any other. More than once it had occurred to Adrian that a conscience was no asset to a baron. "Which villages do you think would be best for placing bands of men?"

The conversation turned to practical preparations for the coming conflict, which kept them occupied until the fire had collapsed into embers. Finally Adrian yawned and got to his feet. "We've made a good beginning. I'll return home tomorrow, but I'd like you to come to Warfield in a fortnight or so—there is still much to discuss." Then he bade his brother good night.

Despite his fatigue, sleep eluded Adrian. Though tonight he had brushed aside talk of marriage, the subject could not be ignored forever. Dutifully he had contracted a suitable marriage five years before, but the girl had died before reaching marriageable age and he had avoided choosing another.

He twisted restlessly in the feather mattress, knowing why he hesitated. It was foolish of him to want more of marriage than a good dowry and a healthy woman who would give him strong sons. For men of his rank marriage was a practical and political decision, and pleasure could be had easily enough outside the marriage bed. Unfortunately such a solution would not suit a man who meant to obey the Church's commandment of monogamy, so Adrian must show more than usual care in selecting a mate. He wanted a wife who was a friend and lover as well as a "good match"; ridiculous though the idea was, he wanted a wife he could love.

Idly Adrian wondered what an ideal wife would be like. While the girl must be of gentle birth, she needn't be a great heiress. A man must find his wife reasonably attractive, but unusual beauty was not essential. More important was intelligence and the rarer quality of wisdom; the sweet piety and gentle nature that had characterized his mother; the grace and bright charm of a young nun he had once seen and never forgotten;

the good humor and easy sensuality of his first mistress, Olwen.

Five years older than Adrian and of common birth, Olwen had been a widowed serving woman when she had initiated her young master into the pleasures of the flesh. It was she who had taught him what pleased a woman, and had convinced him that guilt and shame had no place in honest loving.

Olwen had been his mistress for years, until the day she told him that she wished to marry a miller who had recently lost his wife and been left with four young children. With her calm good sense she had explained that she was fond of the miller and liked the idea of having four sweet children to raise, since she seemed to be barren herself. Though she did not say so, perhaps she also craved the respectability of marriage.

Adrian had given his mistress a generous dowry as a parting gift, though he greatly regretted her loss. Indeed, he missed her still; the mere thought of Olwen made him burn with desire, for it had been months since he had had a woman. While he had come to terms with his need for physical passion, a difficult legacy of his religious schooling was that he had never learned to take a woman casually, forgetting her in the morning. It would have been far easier if he had never left the cloister—or had never entered in the first place.

After reviewing the qualities he wanted in a wife, Adrian smiled wryly into the darkness. No wonder he had never found a woman he wished to marry—it was doubtful that such a paragon existed. And if she did, she would want a husband of equal perfection, which would eliminate Adrian from consideration.

He rolled over and buried his head under the pillow. There was nothing really wrong with Isabel of Rouen, and the match was a splendid one which would give him great holdings in Normandy. Doubtless when several months had passed without seeing the girl, Adrian would find the prospect of marrying her more congenial.

3

MERIEL HAD WORKED late the night before, then gotten up early to finish her most important tasks quickly so that she could slip away for a few hours. While she would take her falcon and hope to find game for the pot, her real goal was simply to take advantage of the beautiful spring weather to commit the sweet sin of slothfulness.

After starting the household servants on tasks that would occupy them all day, Meriel scanned the courtyard with a practiced eye as she walked to the mews. The court teemed with life as villagers baked their bread in the new oven, carpenters raised the frame for another storage building, a thatcher balanced on the smithy roof, and the smith himself hammered on a set of iron hinges for the rising barn. It was a scene of happy productivity, far different from the decay and lethargy the de Veres had found when they had first arrived at Avonleigh. It had been almost two years since Alan had been enfeoffed, and they had been years of unremitting work for him and his sister.

Alan was in Normandy performing his military service with Lord Theobald and would be gone at least two months, so Meriel was lord as well as lady of the manor until his return. Even on the short walk to the mews she was stopped to issue judgment on whether a serf's hen was robust enough to be accepted as rent for his cottage. The bailiff claimed the fowl was sickly while the serf insisted that the hen was perfectly stout, though something of a runtling, but all his hens were small this spring.

By custom, the hen was deemed healthy if it could jump over a fence or onto a stool when frightened, so Meriel duly witnessed the serf's attempts to make his hen perform. The problem was not the hen's health but its stupidity; three attempts were necessary to get the bird to jump in the right direction. Voice grave but eyes dancing, Meriel accepted the hen as a suitable payment, then slipped into the mews before she could be intercepted again.

Meriel closed the door behind her and turned to speak, then held her tongue when she saw that Edmund the falconer was sewing shut the eyelids of a newly caught goshawk, a process called seeling. While the bird was temporarily blinded, it would be tamed through taste, touch, and sound. In a few days, when the hawk was accustomed to being handled, its eyes would be unseeled.

They had been fortunate to find a falconer as skilled as Edmund. He was an elderly man who had spent most of his life in the mews of a baron, then been turned off when his lord had unjustly blamed him for the death of a valuable Norwegian gyrfalcon. Now Avonleigh benefited from Edmund's magnificently trained hawks.

When the falconer had finished his task, Meriel said softly, "I've come to take Chanson out."

Edmund gave her a dour glance. "Be careful with her, she's nervous today."

"When am I not careful?" Meriel asked with amusement as she made her way through the dimly lit mews without disturbing any of the roosting inhabitants.

"You haven't ruined a hawk yet," he allowed, unable to suppress an affectionate smile. At first Edmund had had doubts about Meriel's assisting him, but eventually he had come to accept that her passion for falcons, and her gift for working with them, were the equal of his own. Her actual knowledge had not been as great, but his teaching was remedying that lack.

Crooning softly, Meriel took the great hooded falcon onto her gauntleted left wrist. Chanson mantled with pleasure, fluffing her dark feathers while her bells jingled, then stretched her neck to be scratched. She was a peregrine falcon, the largest and noblest of the hunting birds that nested in Britain, sometimes called the falcon-gentle because only people of gentle birth were allowed to possess them.

Chanson was one of two shrieking eyases that Meriel had taken from a nest the previous spring when she was visiting her mother's cousins in South Wales. The other falcon had been trained and presented to Alan's Lord Theobald as a special thanks for enfoeffment, but Chanson was Meriel's own, and she loved the falcon as much as she had loved her kestrel Rouge, who had died two years before.

Leaving the mews, Meriel crossed to the stables, where Ayloffe, the groom, held her mare. Since she was going hawking, she would ride cross-saddle, which gave a firmer seat than a sidesaddle.

After helping her mount, Ayloffe said, "I'll be ready in a moment, mistress."

"No need to interrupt your work," she replied. "I want to ride alone today."

Ayloffe looked doubtful. "Sir Alan won't like it if I let you go off by yourself."

"Since he's in Normandy, he won't know, will he?" Meriel pointed out with irrefutable logic, then added reassuringly, "I'll not leave Avonleigh, so there's no need for you to worry."

Unconvinced, Ayloffe said, "With two earls quarreling over Shropshire like mongrels over a bone, it's not wise for a maid to ride alone."

"I'll be safe enough—the whole of the royal forest lies between us and the rival lords." Her mouth quirked up wryly. "If one of the earls decided to ravage Avonleigh, everyone on the manor fighting together couldn't stop him.''

"It's not the manor I'm worried about, but you,'' the groom said sternly. "What if you meet with robbers?''

"Enough!'' Meriel chuckled and stroked the mare's glossy chestnut neck with her free hand. "If I encounter robbers, Rosalia will outrun them.''

Before Ayloffe could object further, Meriel released the mare and rode out of the yard, Chanson balanced on her wrist with the skill of long practice. What was there about her, she wondered with amusement, that made men act like worried uncles? Indeed, all of the servants, both male and female, treated their mistress with a combination of respect and protectiveness that was endearing but sometimes a nuisance.

As she trotted down the lane, serfs who were weeding and planting straightened from their labors and waved, none of them resenting her frivolity since it was known that the mistress worked harder than anyone save Sir Alan himself.

When Meriel was past the fields, she gave Rosalia her head so that the mare could gallop her high spirits off. As the flower-scented wind whipped her long braids out behind her, Meriel laughed aloud from sheer pleasure. Impossible to believe that a day so lovely could harbor menace.

Every hour of this freedom was a gift she would never have known if she had become a nun. On the rare occasions when Meriel felt nostalgic for the peaceful life and companionship of Lambourn, she closed her eyes and recalled the archangel with the flaming sword, and knew that she had made the right decision.

Moments of doubt had been very few. She had enjoyed her years in Lord Theobald's bustling household, serving his amiable and absentminded lady, and even more she enjoyed life at Avonleigh, where every day was different and satisfying.

Beyond the communal pasture was open wasteland that had been cultivated in the years before the Conquest, and which Alan hoped to bring under the plow again. When she was well into the open countryside, Meriel halted her mount and unhooded Chanson. "Will you catch some game for the pot, sweetling?"

She scratched the falcon's neck once, then cast it into the wind. With thunderous wings the bird swept heavenward, reveling in flight, tumbling across the sky from pure joy. Meriel watched with a pleasure and envy so intense that they were nearly pain. No wonder men imagined angels as having wings, for what could be more glorious than having the power and freedom of flight?

When her playful paroxysms had worn off, Chanson wafted on so high above Meriel's head that she was scarcely more than a speck in the sky. Then, when she spotted prey, the falcon stooped, diving from the heavens with the power and beauty of God's own angels, the wind screaming through her bells like no other sound on earth.

Chanson was in good form today, and two hares, a partridge, and a grouse went into Meriel's game bag as she followed the falcon across the grasslands. While the short-winged hawks were birds of the woods, the long-winged falcons were creatures of the open sky and it was easy to ride great distances when hunting with them.

In midafternoon Meriel crested a hill and looked down to see a broad expanse of woodland. Though she had never ridden this far before, she knew it must be the royal forest. Regretfully she said, "We must turn back now, Rosalia."

Immense tracts of English countryside were designated as royal forests, and only the king and those bearing his warrant had the right to hunt or take the timber. The harsh Norman forest law that enforced royal prerogative was heartily disliked by every rank of society. The greatest of barons and bishops could be fined heavily for killing the king's royal deer, and commoners could be imprisoned for taking even so humble a creature as a hare.

Meriel took out her wooden whistle and the lure, which was a dummy bird on a cord which was used to attract a falcon back to its owner. First she used the whistle to play a series of notes the falcon had been trained to; then she swung the lure around her head. Looking up, she saw the falcon sweeping down as prettily as any owner could wish for.

Chanson was almost back to her mistress when the bird's attention was caught by a startled magpie darting upward from a nearby shrub. Unable to resist the challenge, the falcon stooped toward the magpie but missed. Frantically twisting and zigzagging in a series of short flights and glides, the magpie raced toward the trees in a black and white flurry of wings and tail.

Peregrine falcons are better at stooping than tail chases, but Chanson did her best to catch the rudely squawking upstart. It would have been amusing, except that, as Meriel watched, the magpie disappeared into the forest, Chanson in hot pursuit.

"Sweet Mary," Meriel said with dismay. "Why must Chanson go raking off *here?*" Falcons were very easily lost in the woods, where they couldn't see the lure, and this was the royal forest, the last place Meriel would have chosen to pursue a wayward falcon. Riding across Avonleigh and the wasteland, she felt perfectly safe, but on the far side of the royal forest were the two rival earls, and both of them the sort that humbler folk should avoid.

Telling herself that it was foolish to worry—Jesu, she'd not seen another soul all afternoon!—Meriel rode down the hill and into the cool shadowed woods. She followed Chanson westward, traveling along a dimly visible game trail and led by the elusive sound of bells. Periodically she stopped and played the wooden whistle, hoping the sound would bring the falcon back to her. It was a maddening business, for the trees distorted the bells and made it difficult to know if Chanson was near or far. Even Meriel's keen eyes never caught a glimpse of the falcon, and she wondered with exasperation if the bird was playing some kind of avian game—Chanson had always had a playful disposition.

The further she traveled into the forest, the more uneasy Meriel became. Scant sunlight penetrated through the branches to the damp forest floor, and in the dimness the very trees seemed threatening. It was easy to believe that unknown dangers sheltered here—masterless men, perhaps, living in the forest as outlaws. In open country Rosalia could outrun any robber, but this was not open country. . . .

Firmly telling herself that her fears were foolish, Meriel continued ever deeper into the forest. It was hard to judge how much time passed, but eventually she was forced to admit that she must turn back. She was alone and far from home, and her anxiety was increasing with every step the mare took. It would be better to return tomorrow with Edmund and Ayloffe and hope that Chanson would not have gone too far. Bells could be heard for half a mile, so with several people searching they should be able to locate the falcon and lure her back.

She had just reached her decision when disaster exploded out of the shrubbery. It was a giant squealing boar, the most vicious and dangerous beast in the forest, capable of killing a man or horse with a single swipe of its tusks. As the boar slashed at Rosalia's belly, the terrified mare trumpeted and reared onto her hind legs.

Meriel was an excellent rider, but most of her attention had been on the treetops and she was hurled from her mount before she had time to react to the attack. For a startled instant she tumbled through the air. Then she crashed into the ground with stunning force.

The impact knocked all of Meriel's breath away, leaving her helpless as the bellowing boar wheeled and charged toward her. With horrible precision Meriel

saw light slide along the curving yellow tusks and
looked into the beast's small, mad eyes. There was no
time for terror, and only an instant for the despairing
prayer: *May God have mercy upon my soul.*

At the last possible moment, the beast swerved
around her, so close that moist earth spattered her face
and she smelled its hot, fetid breath. Preferring Rosalia as quarry, the boar pursued the terrified horse
down the forest path. The pounding of hooves and
screams of equine fear were audible long after both
animals were out of sight.

When Meriel had regained her breath, she shakily
pushed herself to a sitting position. "Sweet Mary,"
she murmured, trying for levity, "if Alan finds out
how careless I've been with horse and falcon, he will
never let me forget it."

There would be bruises aplenty tomorrow, her ears
were ringing, and her plain brown gown was muddy,
but at least she was alive and unhurt. Then she tried
to stand and pain shafted through her right ankle. Meriel subsided to the ground again, her vision temporarily darkening, then prodded the aching joint. At length
deciding that the ankle was only twisted, she tore a
strip from the bottom of her shift and bound the ankle
so that it would bear her weight.

The bag containing her game and hawking gear had
also been thrown, so she slung it over her shoulder
and started limping back along the path. The game bag
was heavy enough that she could wish the day's hunting had been less successful, but she'd not throw good
food away just to lighten her load.

It would be a very slow journey back to Avonleigh
and she would not be home until long after dark. Everyone would be in a panic when the mare returned
with an empty saddle. Meriel's lips curved into a rueful smile; she would never be able to escape without
escort again and it would serve her right. Sweet Mary,
but she'd been careless! She should have stayed home
and helped with the bread baking.

After a quarter mile or so she saw that the boar's hoofprints veered away from the path while the horse's continued straight along. There was no sign of a scuffle, so Rosalia must have escaped unscathed, saints be praised. If Meriel were lucky, she would find her mount grazing somewhere ahead on the path, but more likely the horse would run all the way back to her stable.

Perhaps a mile farther, Meriel heard a familiar *ek-ek-ek* as she entered a sizable clearing. Looking up, she saw Chanson perched in a tree on the far side of the clearing, the picture of innocence. Wrathfully she exclaimed, "You wretched crow-feathered bug-catcher!"

The falcon twisted her head upside down as if hurt by her mistress's words. Wasting no more time on insults, Meriel donned the heavy leather gauntlet, then swung the lure. Chanson flew across the clearing to seize the lure and a few moments later was safely hooded on her mistress's wrist. Carrying the falcon would make Meriel even more tired, but the bird's recovery meant that the day was not a complete disaster. Now, if only Rosalia was grazing somewhere ahead . . .

When she thought back later, Meriel realized that her concentration on the falcon made her miss the sound of approaching horses, but at the time it seemed as if a band of fairyfolk had materialized. One moment she was tightening Chanson's hood; the next she looked up into a chaos of hooves and horses and blazing colors. She gasped, too startled to be frightened, too slowed by her twisted ankle to dodge out of the way.

"Halt!" a man's voice called out, and the group jangled to a noisy stop when the closest horse was scarcely six feet away.

It took a moment for Meriel to sort out the confusing images and realize that she had been discovered by a hunting party. Judging by the quality of horses and clothing, the hunters came from the highest level of the nobility, and all six of them were staring at her and Chanson with frank curiosity. Meriel tensed, all too aware that she was a woman alone with a group of strangers. While in theory a knight would never offer insult to a lady, in practice the ideals of chivalry were not always upheld.

Surely the band before her must include one of the rival earls of Shropshire. The question was, which one? Meriel tried to remember what she had heard about the two earls, but could recall little beyond the fact that both were renowned for ruthless military skill. As a member of a household loyal to Stephen, she would probably be allowed to continue undisturbed if this was the king's earl, Guy of Burgoigne. But if this was the empress's man, she might be in trouble.

The horsemen were ranged in a loose semicircle before her, and from the richness of his dress, she guessed that the man in the center was the leader. He was possibly the handsomest man she had ever seen, as tall and golden-haired as if he had just ridden out of a jongleur's romantic ballad. Effortlessly holding his restless horse in check, he exclaimed, "Jesu, the wench has a falcon-gentle!"

Meriel understood his surprise, for usually only noblemen had peregrine falcons. Thank heaven his expression was amused rather than furiously disapproving. Her relief lasted only until an older man with grizzled hair said gruffly, "Aye, a falcon, and she's been hunting with it." The man dismounted, handed his reins to one of the servants, and walked over to her. "Well, girl, who are you, and what have you to say for yourself?"

Before Meriel could answer, a different man said quietly, "She might not understand Norman."

Ruefully Meriel glanced down at her plain muddied gown and couldn't blame them for thinking her a peasant girl rather than a Norman gentlewoman. Before she could correct the misapprehension, the grizzled man said in Norman-accented English, "Make your bow to the Earl of Shropshire, girl."

Still wondering which earl was before her, Meriel prepared to curtsy to the golden man, then paused at sight of his amused expression. He looked like a man anticipating diversion, and under these circumstances it would likely be at her expense.

What if he was not the earl? That would certainly be a rich jest on her. Warily Meriel scanned the entire group, and her gaze came to rest on a smaller man with silver-gilt hair, the one who had suggested that she didn't understand Norman. His mount stood next to that of the golden knight, and Meriel had assumed the man to be of lesser importance, but as she looked squarely at him, she hesitated. He was not half so magnificent as the golden man, his clothing was far plainer, his expression as inscrutable as drifting smoke. Yet though he did not draw the eye quickly as his companion did, once Meriel looked at him, it was hard to look away. There was something about him, a quality like thrumming steel, an air of authority . . .

Praying that she was choosing correctly, Meriel dropped into a deep curtsy before the young man with the silver-gilt hair. The group broke into appreciative laughter and the golden man said, "The wench has an eye for an earl, Adrian."

"Perhaps," the earl said, unimpressed. "More likely she saw me somewhere in the past." Though his voice was dispassionate, he was watching Meriel with disconcerting intensity.

There was a strong resemblance between the two blond men. Brothers, perhaps? As Meriel studied the finely chiseled features, she decided that the silver earl was very nearly as handsome as his golden companion, though they were as different as crystal-cold ice and warm sunshine.

The grizzled man approached her, his hand out and his expression grim. "Give me your game bag."

Knowing that he would take it from her if she didn't

cooperate, Meriel slipped the bag from her shoulder and reluctantly handed it to him.

The man looked inside, then pulled out the grouse and one of the hares. ''A poacher,'' he said, scowling at the limp bodies. ''What's your name, girl, and where are you from?''

A poacher! Stunned, Meriel stood mute, her mind racing frantically at the unexpected charge. She had caught the game fairly on her brother's land. Yet how could one prove where a particular hare came from? If they chose not to believe her . . .

She felt a bone-deep chill of fear. Poaching was a serious crime—so serious that in these uneasy times it was not impossible that the empress's earl might use Meriel's trangression as an excuse to attack Avonleigh. For a greedy lord, almost any pretext would serve to take land from men of the opposing side, and hunting the royal forest was a grave offense.

The grizzled man said impatiently, ''Are you dumb, girl? What is your name?''

The earl said, ''From the look of her, she's probably Welsh, and may be as ignorant of English as Norman.'' Then, to Meriel's surprise, he addressed her in slow but accurate Welsh. ''What is your name and where do you live?''

Meriel made an instant decision. Alan was not home to defend his property and the manor had only a half-dozen men trained to arms. But the earl would have no excuse to threaten Avonleigh if he did not know that she came from there. Very well, since they thought her lowborn, she would act the part. Bobbing a meek curtsy, she said in English, ''Indeed I am Welsh, my lord, though I speak English too. My name is Meriel.''

Too late it occurred to her that she should have given a false name, but Meriel was not uncommon in Wales and the Marches. Earnestly she continued, ''I swear I was not poaching, my lord—the hares and fowl were caught in the wasteland east of the forest, where anyone may hunt the beasts of the warren.''

The grizzled man snorted. "A likely story for someone afoot in the western half of the forest." He stepped toward her. "And in England, it's against the law for a serf to possess a falcon-gentle. Give me the bird.''

"No! I am no English serf, and the falcon is mine.'' Meriel raised a protective hand to Chanson, horrified to realize that she had trapped herself in her own lie. As the daughter of a Norman knight she had the right to have a falcon-gentle, though it was an unusual choice for a female of any rank. But for someone of humble birth, possession of any falcon greater than a kestrel was unlawful.

She opened her mouth to confess the truth, then stopped. If she admitted her identity, she might bring danger to Avonleigh. Perhaps her fears were ridiculous and she was starting at shadows, yet dare she take a chance? Knowing that she had only a moment to decide whether to tell the truth or maintain her deception, Meriel raised her gaze to Earl Adrian, who watched her with implacable stillness.

Abruptly she remembered something Alan had said to his seneschal just before he left for Normandy. Meriel had been busy with her spinning, not really listening, but now in her head she heard Alan say: *The new Earl of Shropshire is one of the wickedest men in England, capable of anything.*

Could that be true of this quiet, contained man? Meriel looked searchingly at the earl, then caught her breath as she realized that the measureless depths of those gray eyes were not quiet, but blazed with dangerous emotion.

Sweet Mary, this man *was* capable of anything, ice on the outside and fire within. His dangerous, unarguable power reminded her of the angel of her long-ago vision, that bright, sword-brandishing being who had barred her path to the nunnery. But if the earl were an angel, he must rank among Lucifer's fallen, for she saw no compassion or gentleness in him. His masked intensity was more frightening than obvious brutality, and her throat went dry with fear.

The faces of her people at Avonleigh flashed through Meriel's mind, all of them trusting her to do her duty by them. From the chaos of her agonized thoughts emerged a solemn vow: she would say no word, do no deed, that might bring harm to Avonleigh. Nay, not even if the earl had her whipped or cast her into a dungeon.

Her frantic calculations had taken only a few moments, just long enough for the grizzled man to reach for Chanson. "I took the game lawfully," Meriel said, backing away from him, "and in Wales there are no foolish laws about who can possess a falcon."

"You're in England now, girl," he said impatiently.

"No! She is mine!" Meriel repeated as she continued to back away. There would be no escape into the forest; if she turned to run, they would have her in an instant. "I found her myself in a nest high on a cliff, and trained her too. You have not the right to take her from me."

The golden knight said reassuringly, "If what you say is true, you'll have her back, but let Sir Walter hold the bird until the matter is settled."

As if a nobleman would return a falcon-gentle to a woman he thought a peasant! Meriel might be at the earl's dubious mercy, but grimly she resolved that he would not have Chanson as well. Swiftly she loosed Chanson's jesses and bells, the fingers of her right hand hidden by her gauntleted left arm.

"You heard what Sir Richard said," the grizzled man said as he extended his gloved hand. "We'll not keep the bird if you can prove you've a right to possess it."

As he spoke, she slipped the hood from Chanson's head, then hurled the falcon skyward with all her strength, not casting into the wind like a hunter, but down the wind, the traditional way of returning a hawk to the wild. "You'll not have her!" Meriel cried. "If she is not mine, she will belong to none but herself."

For an instant Chanson seemed startled by the suddenness of her mistress's action. Then, freed of the jesses she had worn for a year, the falcon soared heavenward with all the speed and strength of her kind, her four-foot wingspan casting a broad shadow across the clearing, her bold flight drawing the mesmerized gazes of the watching men.

"God's blood!" Sir Richard gasped. "The wench has whistled a falcon down the wind."

Meriel blinked tears from her eyes as she watched Chanson spiral upward, but she had no regrets, save that she could not fly away as well. Swallowing against the tightness in her throat, she lowered her gaze to the earl.

Of all the men in the clearing, he alone watched her rather than the diminishing form of the falcon. "You should not have done that," he said, his voice low and intimate, as if they were alone in the clearing.

"She was mine to do with as I chose, my lord."

Though her voice was soft, there was nothing humble in the tilt of the girl's chin or in the eyes that met Adrian's without flinching. Yet she was not defiant— defiance implied anger, but he saw no anger in her. The night-blue depths of her eyes were free and pure, and he knew intuitively that she was as untamed as the falcon she had released to the wind.

As he regarded the girl's slim figure and tangled raven-wing hair, Adrian felt something dark and dangerous shift deep within him. He wanted her, with the same savage intensity that he felt when fighting for his life. In a distant part of his mind he knew that this madness would wane, for a man could not live at such a peak without being consumed. But for the moment, he had only the most fragile of control over his actions.

Adrian knew that he should send the girl on her way

with a simple warning to be more careful where she hunted, but he would not—*could* not—let her go. His voice strange in his own ears, he said brusquely, "And as a poacher, mistress, you are now mine to do with as *I* choose." He gathered his reins in one fist. "We have wasted enough time here. Bring her back to the castle." To touch her himself would be disastrous, so Adrian wheeled his mount, leaving his men to obey his orders.

As he rode off without looking back, he tried to define what he had seen in the girl. Once he understood her allure, he would be able to treat her impartially, as he would treat any other peasant girl. But no matter how hard he tried to argue away his sudden, fierce attraction, Adrian was unsuccessful. The girl called Meriel was special. And the word that haunted him as he rode away was "invincible."

4

MERIEL STARED at the earl's retreating back, not quite believing that her freedom could be taken from her so casually. She had always lived within the security of a household or community, subject to rules but also having rights, and to be utterly powerless was profoundly disturbing. Even worse was knowing that not just her freedom was at stake—her honor and her very life were equally vulnerable.

Both Sir Walter and Sir Richard looked surprised at the earl's command. Then the latter shrugged and rode after his lord. Before remounting his horse, Sir Walter gestured to one of the retainers. "Ralph, you take her."

A young man spurred his mount over to Meriel and extended his hand. "Come, mistress," he said, not unkindly.

Of course a servant would be given the distasteful task of conveying a muddy, common-born poacher, Meriel thought acidly; God forbid a knight should so demean himself. Once more she considered flight, but there would be no hope and less dignity in trying to escape, so she gripped the servant's proffered hand and let him lift her onto his horse.

With Meriel settled uncomfortably in front of the saddle, they began the journey to the earl's castle. The horse's steady gait was soothing and soon Meriel recovered her composure, though her ankle throbbed, she ached all over, and her fatigue was so great that it was difficult to stay upright.

The group rode single file along the narrow track, with Meriel and her guard at the end of the line. She was surprised at how soon they left the forest; she had followed Chanson much farther west than she realized. No wonder Sir Walter had been skeptical of her statement that she had been hunting to the east.

As they entered an area of broad, well-cultivated fields, Meriel decided to learn what lay ahead of her. Ralph seemed a decent young man—at least he had the decency to keep his hands on the reins, where they belonged—so perhaps he would answer some questions. "What do you think the earl will do to me?"

"Since there is no proof you took the game in the forest and they were all humble beasts, you've naught to worry of, mistress. Earl Adrian is a stern lord, but a just one," Ralph said reassuringly. "Most likely he will scold you and let you go. At most, he'll levy a fine." He chuckled. "Mind, it would be a different story if you had been caught skinning a roe deer."

Meriel twined her fingers in the coarse black hair of the horse's mane. "I've no money for a fine, not so much as a quarter penny," she said in a low voice.

"Then he can't make you pay one, can he?" Ralph said, unperturbed. "Don't worry, the earl thinks it a waste of good labor to keep men in prison for any but the most serious crimes."

Meriel was not entirely convinced by Ralph's belief that she would not be severely punished; since she was not one of the earl's serfs, he would lose none of her labor by imprisoning her until the forest court next met, and that could be weeks, even months, away. Still, it was not uncommon to release minor offenders who had no worldly goods, and she was certainly of that number. And, of course, she was innocent of wrongdoing.

Her spirits rising, Meriel tried to calculate how long it would take her to walk home after she was released; probably two or three days unless she chanced on a cart going in the right direction. She hated to think how upset everyone would be at Avonleigh, but there was naught she could do to relieve their anxiety, so she returned to her questions. "Are the earl and Sir Richard brothers? They look like close kin."

"Half-brothers. Sir Richard is the elder but base-born," Ralph replied. "He is castellan of Earl Adrian's other castle, Montford, to the south of here, but he's visiting at Warfield."

Warfield! Sweet Mary, the empress's earl was Adrian of Warfield, who five years earlier had brought his wounded men to Lambourn Priory, and who had scolded Meriel for going out alone. She cast her mind back to that brief meeting, which she had almost forgotten. No wonder she had not recognized the earl as the same man; not only had it been dusk on the earlier occasion, but Lord Adrian's distinctive silvery hair had been hidden by his mail coif, and the growth of beard that had obscured his features was of a darker, more golden hue than his head.

Mother Rohese had mentioned that the group of soldiers had been led by Adrian de Lancey, Baron of Warfield, but the incident had been a minor discord in the gentle life of the priory, soon forgotten after the wounded men left through death or recovery. While the visit had helped Meriel decide that she should not take the veil, Lord Adrian himself had made no particular impression on her. How strange to find him now an earl.

She had not thought of the skirmish in years, yet Meriel had only to close her eyes to see Lord Adrian rallying his men to beat off the ambush, fighting as if possessed by the devil. The new Earl of Shropshire certainly deserved his reputation for military skill—and, she though acerbically, he still did not believe in women traveling alone across the countryside.

Perhaps the earl was right. Several hours earlier she had been enjoying a quiet day of hawking and now she was a prisoner, just the sort of situation Lord Adrian had once warned her of. There was a certain bizarre humor to the thought, though Meriel did not feel like smiling. "Is Sir Walter one of the earl's household knights?"

"He is captain of the castle guard and has been for many years. They say the earl offered to enfeoff him, but Sir Walter wants neither land nor family of his own. I've often heard him say that women are the work of the devil." The young man chuckled and gave Meriel's nicely rounded flank an appreciative pat. "The old fellow doesn't know what he's missing."

She ignored the pat, which was the sort of casual gesture that a girl of common birth would be accustomed to. Then Ralph's horse crested the large hill they had been laboring up, and what Meriel saw in the middle distance drove all other thoughts from her head. "Sweet Mary!" she breathed. "That is Warfield Castle?"

"Aye," her guard said proudly, halting his mount so she could absorb the full glory. "Lord Adrian found a master mason who had traveled to the Holy Land and studied Saracen fortifications. I doubt there is another castle in England so strong."

Ralph was surely biased, but Meriel suspected that his opinion was correct. Warfield Castle stood on an upthrust of rock that was almost an island, surrounded on three sides by a river. A moat cut across the neck of land on the fourth side so the only access was over a drawbridge. Two separate rings of curtain wall protected the keep and the inner bailey, and the village below the castle had a wall of its own. Wonderingly she said, "So many towers. And why are they round, not square?"

"The mason said round towers are stronger." Ralph set the horse moving again. "There is enough food stored inside to withstand a siege of a year, and we'll never run out of water."

"Has Warfield ever been besieged?"

"Nay, who would dare?" Ralph scoffed as they rode down the long hill. "There isn't a lord in England who

could hold an army together long enough to force Warfield to surrender.''

As they rode through the prosperous village, Meriel's awe increased. This close to the castle, it was
impossible to imagine any force successfully storming
the walls which stood so tall and sheer above the river
and moat. The horse's hooves rang hollow and ominous as they trotted over the drawbridge, and she could
not repress a shiver of fear as they passed through the
massive gate. These walls would not only keep enemies without but also prevent any within from leaving
against the lord's will.

Close up, the castle looked raw and new and several
outbuildings were under construction. All the buildings were stone and even the humblest sheds were
roofed in slate rather than flammable thatch. Warfield
would no more be burned than stormed or starved into
submission.

Meriel had thought the courtyard at Avonleigh was
busy, but the Warfield outer bailey was a veritable city
of craftsmen, laborers, and beasts. Even Lord Theobald's sizable keep would go inside three or four times
over. A still more formidable wall protected the inner
ward, its towers commanding the whole of the outer
bailey.

They rode through the chill shadows of the gate to
the inner ward. In front of the massive keep, the earl
stood in conversation with his brother and his captain
of the guard. Ralph reined his horse to a halt and dismounted, but before he could help Meriel down, the
earl came over and assisted her himself, his hands firm
and strong on her waist.

Meriel hoped her weakness would not betray her,
but her ankle had stiffened during the ride and it buckled when she touched the ground. The earl's grasp
tightened, holding her steady while she regained her
balance. Warily she looked up into his face and was
relieved to see not the hidden fire which had so

alarmed her in the forest, but a cool impersonal detachment.

Might Lord Adrian recognize her from that brief meeting five years ago? If so, he would know that she was probably Norman, for nuns were almost exclusively from the ruling class. But it had been dusk then, and she had been swathed in veil and wimple. Surely he had forgotten her existence even before he had left Lambourn, for she was not a memorable person.

The earl asked, "Are you injured?"

"Not seriously, my lord," she explained. "Merely a twisted ankle."

"Can you walk up a number of stairs?"

Pride made Meriel say, "Of course, my lord." But her ankle refused to obey, and when she turned to climb the stone steps, she almost fell again.

With a smothered oath the earl caught her before she could crumple to the ground and scooped her into his arms. Without further comment he carried her up the stairs and into the keep's great hall. He was very strong and supported her weight effortlessly, his right arm encircling her rib cage and his left under her knees.

Even through her exhausted dizziness, Meriel was astonished. What on earth was an earl doing assisting a muddy suspected poacher? She had not been cradled in a man's arms since she was a very small child being borne off to bed by her father, and the earl's welcome warmth dispelled the chill of her tired body.

But she was no longer a child and she could not be unaware of the intimacy of their closeness. Meriel had a lover's-eye view of the smooth texture of the earl's lightly tanned skin, and of the silver and pale-gold strands that comprised his bright straight hair. With a slight shift of his grip he could have stroked her breast or knee, or touched his lips to hers.

The direction of Meriel's thoughts embarrassed her, for there was nothing lecherous in the earl's touch. She might have been a sack of grain for all the emotion he showed, and for that she was profoundly grateful. It was only her fatigue that gave her such strange, improper fancies.

As Meriel studied Lord Adrian's still profile, it occurred to her that he was too cool, too unemotional, for such abnormal circumstances. She had seen his hidden fire, and uneasily she wondered if the fact that he concealed it now was ominous.

The thought increased her dizziness and she closed her eyes and rested her aching head against the earl's shoulder, her right hand masking her face. Dimly she was aware that she was being carried up another long flight of steps. At the top was a passage with several doors opening from it. The earl stopped at one of the doors and dexterously opened it with one hand, then carried her inside.

The room contained a bed with a small chest at the foot, and for a moment Meriel was roused from her drowsiness by the alarming thought that she had been brought to the earl's own chamber. But the room did not have an air of occupancy; Warfield Castle must be large enough to have the luxury of a guest chamber.

The earl laid her on the yielding surface of the feather mattress. Then, without asking permission, he lifted her injured ankle and expertly examined it, his fingers probing the crude bandage. Though his touch was gentle, Meriel winced, biting her lip to keep from exclaiming.

"Nothing is broken, but you had best stay off your feet for the rest of the day," he said at length.

When he released her, Meriel immediately tugged her skirt over her legs and feet. "Thank you for your concern, my lord."

His intense regard was making her uneasy again. As she could feel the moods of a horse or a hawk, she sensed that his present cool indifference was a facade, that behind that beautiful, pitiless face there was still dangerous wildness. But for the moment, at least, the earl offered no threat.

"Rest," he said quietly. "I will speak with you to-morrow."

Before he had reached the door, Meriel had slid into exhausted slumber.

For the rest of the day Adrian carried on his normal routine, but all the while he was aware of the girl sleeping upstairs, and the thought of her pulled him like a lodestone. After supper he excused himself, leaving Richard and the other knights to an earnest discussion of the best method to tunnel into a castle. His departure caused no comment, for he was known to have an unnatural appetite for privacy.

He unlocked the door to the girl's chamber and quietly entered. The sky was darkening outside, but enough light came through the two window slits for him to see her clearly. She lay on her side, her long lashes dark against the subtle curve of her cheek, one thick ebony braid trapped under her slim body while the other spilled over her shoulder to her waist.

Indeed, she was so still that for a moment he was afraid, until he saw the steady rise and fall of her breasts. Using every shred of his hard-won discipline, he had suppressed the perilous madness she had initially inspired in him, and by the time they reached Warfield he had been able to touch her without risk of losing control. Now he rewarded himself with the pleasure of studying the girl as she slept.

Meriel. He repeated the name silently in his mind, thinking that the gentle musical sound suited her. Though she was slightly built, her softly curving body was that of a woman, and he guessed that she was at least eighteen, possibly older. Certainly old enough to be a wife, though she wore no ring. Considering her age and station in life, likely she was not a maid even if she was unwed, and he was glad of that.

What was it about her that drew him so? Certainly she was pretty, but not a striking beauty. Was it the graceful freedom of her movements that reminded him of the young nun he had glimpsed years earlier, forbidden but never forgotten? Or was it her quality of innocence?

Adrian studied the girl's calm sweet face, then shook his head. What she had was far rarer, for what men called innocence was usually no more than inexperience. The clear, unconquerable simplicity he had seen in Meriel's gaze and manner was not an accident of youth, but a wise honesty that came from the soul.

Or perhaps he deluded himself that a young peasant woman possessed qualities he had never found in a woman of his own class; perhaps it was just her Welshness that made her seem so rare. The Welsh were a wild strange folk, whose women had far more freedom than the womenfolk of the English and Normans.

Adrian ached to touch her but restrained himself. Instead, as he gazed hungrily, his fingertips burned with the memory of the petal-soft texture of her skin. With equal exactness he recalled how she had felt in his arms when he had brought her here, and the precise shade of her eyes, that brilliant Celtic blue that made the summer sky seem pale. Meriel's small bones, glistening shadow-black hair, and flawless white complexion had the distinctive look of the Welsh, a beauty very different from the Norman ideal, but nonetheless comely.

The night would be cold, and she lay on top of the embroidered coverlet, protected only by her shabby gown. Moving quietly so as not to wake her, Adrian took a woolen blanket from the chest at the foot of the bed and laid it over her, folded in half for maximum warmth.

This close he could no longer resist the desire to touch her, and he gently cupped her cheek with his hand. She stirred, her eyelids fluttering as if she was on the verge of waking. Then she turned toward his palm, her movement making his gesture a caress. As she settled again, he felt the delicate structure of bones beneath her silken skin and drew his hand away carefully, his fingers trembling with the strain of suppressing desire.

Even more than desire, he felt tenderness, the wish to shield her from all harm. He surrendered to one last temptation and leaned forward to brush his lips against her forehead in a gossamer kiss. Her hair had the faint, sweet tang of mint.

Adrian straightened, cursing himself for having yielded to the mad impulse to bring her here. He had released greater offenders with no more than a warning. Indeed, Meriel claimed to have committed no crime and there was no reason to disbelieve her. Tomorrow he would discover where she lived and return her to her home with an escort for protection.

He walked to the door, then turned and looked back at Meriel, who was a barely discernible shape beneath the woolen blanket. His mouth tightened. For the benefit of his soul and hers, he should send her home— but in his heart he already knew that he would not.

When she woke, Meriel blinked in confusion, wondering why she was alone in the bed instead of sharing it with her maid, and why the hangings were rich blue, not faded gray. She sat up, and so many sore muscles complained that memories of the previous day flooded back: her hawking, the accident in the forest, releasing Chanson, and the stern earl who brought her to Warfield Castle.

The sun was just coming up and the household would be stirring soon. She pushed aside the wool blanket, wondering who had covered her during her exhausted slumber. Gingerly she set her feet to the floor, and was grateful to find that her injured ankle gave no more than a twinge or two. Besides the massive bed and the chest at its foot, the room contained a small table and two stools, clothing pegs, a plain screen concealing a wooden bathtub, and a finely carved crucifix hanging on the wall. The rushes on the floor were clean and sweetly scented.

Most surprising was a fireplace built into the wall. Meriel examined it with interest. She had heard that the French had such luxuries, but had never seen such a thing in England. Lord Adrian clearly believed that his castle should have all modern comforts as well as impregnable fortifications.

The two narrow slit windows overlooked water. Apparently this wall of the castle was built on a sheer cliff rising directly above the wide river. It must be the Severn, but she could not be sure. This country was as foreign to her as the wilds of Ireland, though it lay only half a day's ride from her home.

As she absently watched a brilliant blue kingfisher hover above the water, a key turned in the door and she looked up to see a maid enter with a tankard of ale and hunk of fresh bread. "Good morning," the girl said as she set the tankard and bread on the table. "My name is Margery. Are you feeling better? I saw you arrive yesterday and you looked poorly."

"I'm very well, thank you. All I needed was rest. But tell me, are suspected lawbreakers always treated so hospitably?" Meriel gestured around the chamber.

"Nay," Margery said cheerfully, "usually you would have been put in the dungeon, but just now it holds a couple of drunken louts and likely Lord Adrian thought a female would not be safe with them."

"Thoughtful of him," Meriel said rather dryly, thinking it would have been more thoughtful yet if he had let her go.

Deaf to nuance, the maid agreed, "Aye, he's a good lord."

"Who is the lady of the castle?"

"There is none," Margery said regretfully. "They say Lord Adrian is on the verge of contracting himself to a great heiress, Isabel of Rouen. I'll be glad when they are wed. 'Twill be good to have a lady here."

As she had asked Ralph the day before, Meriel now asked the maid, "I was brought here as a suspected poacher, though I am innocent. How do you think the earl will judge me?''

"Since it was naught but hares, he'll just scold you and send you home. Lord Adrian went out this morning, but doubtless this afternoon he will see you. He's not one to keep folk idle.'' Margery cocked her head to one side curiously. "Mistress Adela, the housekeeper, said I'm to ask if you need anything.''

That was definitely not the sort of question most prisoners were asked! Uneasy, Meriel started to refuse, then stopped, deciding to take advantage of Margery's offer. "Would it be possible to have a bath?''

"A bath?'' Margery was startled, but after a moment she shrugged. "I don't see why not. I'll bring up hot water and towels.'' She eyed the visitor. "And a comb.''

Margery was as good as her word, and half an hour later Meriel was happily immersed in steaming water scented with tangy herbs. The warmth soothed her bruised muscles and she leaned blissfully against the wooden staves until the water cooled.

She washed her hair, but reluctantly decided not to do the same to her clothing since the woolen garments would take hours to dry. Still, shaking and brushing her overtunic with her hands removed the worst of the caked mud and the garment's dun color concealed most of the rest. By the time she was clean and dressed, her hair combed straight and drying around her shoulders, she felt quite respectable.

After eating the midday meal that Margery brought, Meriel knelt before the crucifix to pray. Usually her prayers were praise and thanks for her many blessings, but today she also prayed that the people of Avonleigh would not be too distressed by her absence. For herself, Meriel asked for strength and wisdom to face what might come.

She always imagined the Father, Son, Holy Spirit, and Blessed Mother as points of light in the center of her heart, and as she prayed, the light expanded, flowing through her body and soul, smoothing away knots of guilt and sorrow and fear until her whole being glowed with harmony. When Meriel was done, she felt such peace that it was impossible to believe that any dreadful punishment would be inflicted on her. She drew a stool beneath one of the windows and sat with the breeze gently stirring her long damp hair as she considered what was likely to happen.

Meriel herself gave justice at Avonleigh when Alan was away, and from her experience she guessed that the earl would question her informally. She would say that she was Welsh, on her way to visit relatives in Lincoln, and that she had caught her game in the open wasteland, not the royal forest. Apart from concealing that she was Norman and lived at Avonleigh, she would speak the truth rather than risk becoming trapped in lies. Both Ralph and Margery had assured her that Lord Adrian was a just man, so when he saw that no crime had been committed he would release her.

Looking at the events of the previous day, Meriel reached the rueful conclusion that if she had not loosed Chanson in such a provocative manner she would not have been taken into custody. It was hard now to recall exactly why she had been so fearful the day before. Doubtless her accident had scrambled her wits.

In spite of the civility with which she had been treated, Meriel still thought it wise not to draw the earl's attention to Avonleigh, for while he might be just, he was the empress's man. The most important thing was to avoid speaking Norman. She was amazed that the earl spoke English flawlessly and Welsh very well; most of the great lords spoke only Norman, and perhaps a few simple English commands. It was different for Meriel, who had learned Welsh from her mother and who had grown up on a manor so small that most of her playmates had been English. For the same reason Alan was adept at languages, and his ability was one of the reasons Lord Theobald valued him.

Peaceful in mind, she sat quietly with her hands

folded in her lap, her mind drifting in much the same way as the clouds outside the window. She was half-dozing when a serving man entered and said, "The earl will see you now."

Aroused to full alertness, Meriel stood, instinctively raising a hand to her head. "It will take me but a moment to braid my hair."

"Nay, come along now," the man said briskly. "The earl does not like to be kept waiting."

It served her right for daydreaming, Meriel thought with amusement. Now she would receive justice with her hair loose about her like a child. Doubtless at the sight the earl would not be able to get rid of her soon enough.

The servant led her to the door at the far end of the hall, ushered her inside, and left. Meriel stood just inside the door and examined the large room with interest. Rather than a solar for the whole household, this appeared to be the earl's private chamber and it was a place such as she had never seen before. The bed and hangings were not unusually lavish, no more so than Lord Theobald's, but beneath her feet was a brightly colored carpet such as Alan had once seen in Normandy and described to her. A carved wooden case full of books stood against one wall, its shelves holding as many volumes as Lambourn Priory had possessed. And in the far wall . . . !

Meriel was so astonished that she forgot etiquette, forgot that she was here to be questioned, forgot everything but the huge window opposite the door. It was not open to the air, but filled with glass like the brightly colored windows of a great church. Here, however, only a band across the top was colored. The rest of the pieces were clear and let in so much light that the chamber was as bright as the world outside.

Mesmerized by the sight, she crossed the room and knelt on the wide cushioned seat set in the wall beneath the window. Rectangles of glass were held together by thin lead strips, and she touched a joint curiously. Most of the glass was somewhat wavery, distorting the outside world, but the piece directly in front of Meriel was almost as clear as air. Like the guest chamber, this room also overlooked the gray-green river, and in the distance she saw the rugged profile of the Welsh mountains.

"The view is very striking, is it not?"

The soft voice was that of Lord Adrian and the sound brought Meriel back to her circumstances with a jolt. Whirling, she saw that he was seated behind a wide carved desk, a faint smile lightening his stern features. The earl had the inward-looking face of a scholar or cleric, yet even in relaxation he had the indefinable air of readiness that marked a knight, plus a quality of cool control that was very much his own.

Coloring from embarrassment, she dropped into a deep curtsy. "Forgive me for my distraction, my lord. I have never seen such a window, nor even heard of one."

"There may be no other like it anywhere." The earl set down the piece of parchment he had been perusing. "It occurred to me that what could be done in a church could be done in a castle, but with clear glass, so that more light might come through."

All that glass must have been incredibly expensive. Most noblemen preferred the more obvious extravagance of gold and jewels, but Meriel was learning that Earl Adrian was not obvious. She glanced at the window again, fascinated by the flood of sunshine and the stunning view. "During a siege, might not arrows and stones be hurled through?"

"Shutters can be hung across the glass. The width of the river is also a defense."

Meriel turned her gaze from the window to the earl and was again struck by how simply Lord Adrian dressed for a man of his rank. His dark blue tunic was of fine fabric but very plain, with only a narrow border of silver embroidery. Perhaps he did not believe in ostentation, or perhaps he knew that he did not need gold or jewels to compel attention.

She crossed the room and stood before the desk, casting her eyes down modestly. "You wished to speak to me?"

The amiability he had shown when discussing the window fell away and he became the judge seeking information. "Do you have any name other than Meriel?"

She almost answered "de Vere" before remembering that the answer would brand her as Norman. Instead she said, "In Wales we do not use family names, my lord."

"Where is your home?"

Meriel hesitated. Her mother's family lived near Kidwelly in the Norman-controlled south of Wales and she knew that area well, but it would be no kindness to direct unwelcome attention toward her kin. As her silence stretched, the earl said, "You do not know where you live?"

" 'Tis a small place, my lord, you would not know the name. It lies in the north of Wales, in the country of Gwynedd," she said hastily, plucking names at random. "Perhaps you have heard of Dolwyddelan, which is not far from my father's farm."

"How did you come to fall and injure yourself yesterday?"

"My horse was frightened by a boar and threw me."

"You were riding?" Lord Adrian said, surprised.

What a fool she was, for not thinking that a peasant girl was most unlikely to be mounted. "It was a sorry beast, my lord, too old to till the soil," Meriel improvised. "My father let me have it for my journey."

"Yet it was healthy enough to bring you from Wales to England," he murmured. "Where were you going?"

"To Lincoln." That didn't seem like enough answer. Why would she be going to Lincoln? After a moment's quick thought, Meriel added, "My sister will be lying in soon and wanted me to be with her."

"You were carrying a falcon all the way from Gwynedd to Lincoln?" he asked incredulously.

"I . . . I brought her to hunt game on the way." When the earl's golden brows rose in patent disbelief, she continued, "And because I thought this journey a good opportunity to further her training." Of course he wasn't convinced; even to Meriel, her explanation sounded nonsensical.

"You were traveling alone?"

"Yes, my lord."

"What kind of father would let a pretty young girl travel across the width of Britain alone?"

"In truth, my father recently died and my brother's wife did not want me to stay on the farm," she said, drawing on her own history. "I took the horse, knowing that my sister would let me stay with her in Lincoln."

"No doubt she will need help with the new baby," he remarked. "What is your sister's name?"

Spinning a believable tale was far harder than Meriel had thought it would be. She had never been interrogated like this, and she found that under the earl's skeptical gaze her wits worked slowly. There was a dangerous, too-long pause before she thought of a suitably Welsh name. "Bronwen, my lord."

"You have no other kin in Wales? You were so desperate that you risked your life on a journey through country torn by civil war and robbers?" The satirical glint in the earl's eyes did not augur well for his belief in her story.

"I did not realize how great the distance was, my lord," Meriel admitted, then could not resist adding, "However, I met with no danger until I encountered you."

His mouth quirked up with fleeting amusement, conceding her the point before he turned his queries in another direction. "Did your sister marry a Norman knight?"

"Of course not, my lord, he is but an English cobbler," she said, widening her eyes as if astonished by the question. "Though in a good way of business."

"Granted that in Wales you have the right to possess a falcon-gentle, what did you mean to do with the bird in England?" he asked. "Possession of a falcon is forbidden in the households of cobblers, even those 'in a good way of business.' "

"I did not know ownership was illegal in England until I was told yesterday." Meriel did her best to look apologetic. "You guessed correctly, my lord, I did not have my falcon for hunting, but because I did not wish to give her up. If I had left her with my brother Daffyd, I would never have seen her again."

The earl leaned back in his chair, elbows on the wooden arms and fingers laced together across his flat midriff. "Where did you catch the hares and fowl?"

"In the wasteland east of the royal forest, my lord." She spoke more confidently, sure of her ground. "A serf told me that no man owns it and that anyone might take humble game there."

"You say that you were traveling from western Wales to eastern England. Yet you claim to have caught the game east of the forest, then doubled back miles to the west?"

Once more using the truth, Meriel explained, "My falcon raked off into the forest after a magpie, so I went in pursuit. That is when the boar frightened my horse and I was thrown. You and your men found me not long after. I was hoping to find my horse along the path as I walked east."

"Being a sorry beast, it would not have run far," he agreed. His expression hardened. "There may be some truth in what you are telling me. Then again, your story may be lies from beginning to end. Can you give me any good reason why I should not lock you in the dungeon for poaching and theft?"

"Theft!" Meriel gasped, beginning to feel fear. "But I have stolen nothing, nor have I hunted illegally."

The golden brows rose again. "By your own admission you stole your brother's horse. It must have been a decent beast to bring you safely from Gwynedd to Shropshire, if indeed you came from there, which I doubt. Yesterday I noticed that under the dishevelment of your fall, you seemed remarkably clean and neat for a woman who claims to have been traveling for days."

Curse the man for his keen eyes, which saw too much. Grasping at straws, Meriel explained, "I was not sleeping on the ground but staying in monastery guesthouses. And I did not steal the horse!"

"No, you 'took' it, which of course is a very different matter," he said, lightly sarcastic. "What are the names of the religious houses at which you stayed?"

Meriel's mind went blank. There were few monasteries in wild northern Wales, and she could name none on the road from Gwynedd except the one that was so close that the earl could easily check her story. Still, even a forlorn answer was better than none. "Two nights ago I stayed at the Benedictine abbey in Shrewsbury. The other houses were in Wales and very small. You would not know them."

"I think I would know them better than you appear to," he said dryly. "I wonder, will anyone in Shrewsbury remember you?"

Meriel shrugged. "The abbey is a very busy place and accepts many travelers. It is quite possible that a humble person such as I made no lasting impression."

"I shall be astonished if anyone does recollect you," the earl murmured. Returning to the attack, he said, "While you can't be charged with stealing a horse which no one else saw, there is still the matter of the falcon. The most likely explanation is that you either stole it or caught one that was lost, then released it so you could not be convicted of the crime. Did you know that the penalty for finding a lost falcon and failing to return it is that the bird be allowed to eat six ounces of flesh from the culprit's breast?''

Meriel had never truly believed that the matter would go this far, and she felt the blood drain from her face, leaving her pale and so weak she could barely stand. What she felt was less fear of punishment than revulsion that the earl should be treating a minor misunderstanding as a major crime. What manner of man was he? *A man capable of anything.*

Seeing Meriel's expression, the earl said, ''Don't worry, I would never impose such a penalty, even if I had the falcon in hand.'' His gaze flickered over her. ''It would be a great waste.'' He switched to speaking Welsh, his words slow but accurate. ''I will give you another chance to tell me who you are and where you come from. Will you give me the truth?''

Speaking in the same language, she said with dignity, ''Most of what I have said is true, and that which I wish to conceal does not bear on your charges. I swear by the Blessed Virgin that I am innocent of poaching and theft, and if you are an honest man, you will believe me. You have no evidence that any crime has been committed.''

''Had I found you outside the forest and without the falcon, that would be true,'' he said, watching her with disturbing intensity. ''As it is, I have quite enough evidence to imprison you indefinitely.''

''Then bring me before a jury of freeman, as is my right under English law,'' she demanded. ''No honest court will convict me of wrongdoing. As God is my witness, I am guilty of nothing!''

''If you know anything of law,'' he said coolly, reverting to English, ''you must also know that the lords of the Welsh Marches have authority far beyond that of other barons. As Earl of Shropshire I have the power of high and low justice. If I wish, I can take your ear or hand as punishment for poaching. I could even take your life and none would gainsay me.''

''The laws of men may give you the right, but this is not justice in the eyes of God!'' Meriel cried, anger overcoming fear.

Ignoring her words, he said thoughtfully, ''Though I am not an expert on Welsh speech, it sounds to me as if your accent is of southern Wales, not the north, and your English is flawless. Are you an English-woman born of Welsh parents? Perhaps a serf who ran away from her master after stealing a horse and falcon?''

Meriel took a deep breath to calm herself, then looked directly into his unreadable gray eyes. ''No, my lord, you are entirely wrong. I am a freeborn woman, not an English serf, and never in my life have I stolen anything from anyone.''

''Then summon witnesses who can attest to your identity and character,'' he challenged her. ''That is another provision of English law. I won't require ten—if you can produce five people who will swear for you, I will release you immediately.''

Less than a day's ride away were dozens of people who would swear for her, but this strange interrogation had reinforced Meriel's belief that revealing her identity might endanger Avonleigh. ''I cannot summon witnesses, my lord, and well you know it. All my friends and neighbors are too far away, and I know no one in this district,'' she replied, lifting her chin and speaking with the calm pride of a Norman lady. ''Why do you treat me so harshly? Surely all minor offenders are not so ill-used. Why have you singled me out for this persecution?''

Lord Adrian stood and walked across the room to gaze out his window for a moment, then turned to face her. ''I am not persecuting you, simply demonstrating the gravity of your situation. You were found with evidence of a serious crime and you refuse to give an honest account of yourself,'' he said quietly. Against the bright sunlight she could not see his expression, but the tension in his lean body was clearly visible. "While I have sufficient evidence and authority to punish you with great severity, it is not my desire to do so."

"Then what *is* your desire, my lord?" Meriel asked, utterly bewildered by this strange nobleman who had the semblance of a reasonable man, but who said such unreasonable things.

There was a lengthy pause. Then he crossed the room to her, a lithe silhouette against the bright light. He stopped an arm's length away and drew a deep breath before saying, "I want you to become my mistress."

5

MERIEL STARED AT HIM, her vivid blue eyes stark with astonishment. "You are mad," she said with conviction.

"Not at all," Adrian replied, uneasily aware that speaking so directly might not be wise, but unable to think of a better way. "For men and women to come together is the most natural thing in the world."

"But why me?" she asked in honest bewilderment. "I am no beauty, I have never inspired men to intemperate lust. If you desire a mistress, there must be a hundred women on your lands prettier and more suitable than I."

Adrian studied her slim graceful figure and the shining raven hair that cascaded sensuously about her, amazed that the girl had no notion of how attractive she was. "I don't want another woman, I want you."

"But I do not want you, Lord Adrian," she said as her gaze met his searchingly. "I want only my freedom."

What was between them changed. Before, they had been nobleman and commoner. Now they were man and woman. "Have you a husband?" he asked.

Meriel shook her head.

"A sweetheart?"

She shook her head again.

Though her answer was a relief, at the same time Adrian felt an odd kind of sorrow for the honesty that made her vulnerable. Meriel had already demonstrated that she was a dreadful liar, and she didn't even think to attempt the one falsehood that might have freed her. "You would have been wiser to have lied," he said. "Though it would have been difficult, I could have accepted your refusal if your heart or hand belonged to another man. Since they do not, I intend to . . . to win you for myself."

"I am not a prize to be 'won,' " she said tartly. "If threats are your notion of wooing, no wonder you are in need of a mistress. You would do better to ask your steward to find a willing girl. I'm sure he can easily find many who will be not only willing but also eager to lie with their lord." Her eyes narrowed. "Unless the thought of rape excites you? For that is the only way you will have me."

"I am not interested in rape. I hope to persuade you to willingness." Adrian surrendered to desire and stepped forward, lightly placing his hands on Meriel's shoulders. She tensed and lifted her head to look at him. Her face was mere inches away, her long sooty lashes emphasizing the clarity of her blue eyes, her grave regard a question and a reproach.

Whether or not she was beautiful could be debated, but Adrian was not interested in the opinion of others. What mattered was that to him this slim young woman was irresistible. He bent his head and kissed her, not with the passion that she had roused in him from the moment he saw her, but gently, with all the restraint he could muster.

For one sweet moment Meriel accepted the kiss, her soft mouth welcoming his with innocent pleasure and exploration. With a rush of hope Adrian thought that his wooing would be easy, that she desired him as he desired her. His arms went around her and he drew her close so that her warm contours molded against him.

She stiffened immediately and pulled away, moving so quickly that her glossy black hair swirled about her like smoke. When she had put a safe distance between them, she said in a shaking voice, "Surely there is nothing in English or Norman law that gives you the right to ravish a suspected offender, Lord Adrian.''

He forced himself to stand still rather than follow her. ''As I said, I do not want to ravish you. What I am offering is a position of honor and respect, with all the comfort that money and power can provide.''

''Honor? To be your whore?'' she asked incredulously. ''And when you have wed your heiress, to be your companion in adultery? You may have no thought for your immortal soul, Lord Adrian, but I feel otherwise.''

She had found the flaw that lay at the heart of his desire, for he had always sworn that he would never commit adultery. Nor did he intend to do so in the future. Uneasily Adrian decided to face that problem later, suppressing the inner voice that taunted him with the knowledge of his own hypocrisy. ''There is no adultery if both man and woman are free as we are. Fornication is no great sin. Some think it no sin at all.''

''Men are more inclined to approve of fornication, my lord, for the consequences bear lightly on them. A woman who is not more careful is a fool,'' she said dryly. ''Men have ever used arguments like yours to casually seduce and abandon young girls.''

''I have never been interested in casual seduction, nor am I now. If you trust me, I will not betray and abandon you.''

''Fine lies, my lord, but why should I believe them?''

''I am not lying,'' he said steadily, knowing how important it was to convince her of his sincerity.

She raised her dark brows. ''Why should I believe you any more than you believed me?''

''Unlike you, I happen to be telling the truth.''

Meriel's gaze shifted away and the movement confirmed that she was too honest to uphold her own falsehoods. It was easy to know that she was lying; a pity that Adrian could not as easily guess what she was so determined to conceal. But in truth it did not matter what her past was, for she could have committed any number of crimes and it would make no difference to him.

"I told the truth when I said I was innocent of wrongdoing," she said, a catch in her voice, "and I tell the truth now: even if I had no care for my honor, I will never go willingly to the bed of a man who holds me prisoner."

He stepped closer and she edged away, retreating until her back was against the carved wooden bookcase. She stood rigid, her hands curled around the edge of a shelf behind her.

"If I took you outside and freed you now," he asked quietly, "then asked again that you become my mistress, would you accept?"

Meriel's eyes flashed. "Release me and find out."

"Do you think you would survive traveling alone to Lincoln, if that is indeed your destination?" He had to admire her courage even while he deplored her lack of sense. "You think me harsh, but I will not use you half so cruelly as a band of robbers or drunken soldiers will."

"Then you mean to keep me prisoner?" she asked, her fair skin becoming still more pale.

"You can be my prisoner or my cherished mistress," he said, his voice implacable. "The choice is yours."

Meriel caught her breath, realizing that he was deadly serious. "That is not a choice, Lord Adrian, for either way I am a prisoner."

"Life is a prison," he said, an edge in his mild voice. "We are all bound by our responsibilities, by our places in society, by the choices we make, and by the ones that are thrust on us. Only those who care for nothing and nobody are truly free this side of the grave, and they will spend eternity in chains."

At another place and time Meriel might have admitted that there was some truth in his words, but not now, not here. "Your argument is too subtle for me," she retorted. "Being a simple creature, all I know is that yesterday I was free to choose my own road, to give or withhold my body, to risk my life on my journey if I wished to. Now my only choices are a dungeon or your bed, and of the two, I prefer the dungeon. At least then my honor will be unstained."

"I have heard that the women of Wales take pride in being descended from the ancient kings of Britain. That they believe there is no sin in giving themselves where they love, and that they are known for the courage with which they follow their hearts." His brows rose in mock surprise. "Is that not so?"

Meriel hesitated, impressed at his knowledge of a people so different from his own. Her mother had been a Welshwoman such as he described, and Meriel had much of her mother in her. "Even more than love, Welshwomen revere freedom, and I can never give my love to a man who has taken my freedom away."

"Never is a very long time."

Meriel closed her eyes and kneaded her temples, temporarily defeated by the stubbornness with which the earl held to his absurd passion for her. Perhaps such passions were a habit of his, and a week from now his regard would fall on another woman and he would forget her. She would pray for that, and hope that it was true that he did not believe in rape.

Uncannily reading her mind, Lord Adrian said, "You think I am acting on whim and my fancy will soon pass to another, but that will not happen, for I am not a whimsical man. I hope that when you have had time to consider what I am offering, the idea will become more appealing."

"Time will not change my mind," she said, opening her eyes and matching his determination with her own.

He asked softly, "Do you find me repugnant?"

Meriel examined the chiseled masculine elegance of his features, his angel-bright hair, the controlled

strength and power of his lean body. He had the untamed beauty of a hawk, and like a hawk, his dangerous grace touched something deep inside her. "You
are a comely man," she said with reluctant honesty,
"but how can I welcome the advances of my jailer?"

"Perhaps a few days of confinement will answer that
question," he said, his voice dry again. "Come."

Silently she accompanied him back to her room. The
earl stepped aside to let her in, then stood in the door,
watching her. She turned to face him, her expression
wary. He did not try to kiss her again, simply touched
her aching temple, gently brushing back her hair.

Meriel flinched away and he dropped his hand immediately. She was startled by the yearning in his face,
and might almost have been sorry for him, had she not
been the target of his unwelcome desire.

"Rest well," he said, his voice without inflection.
"We will speak of this again."

Then he closed and locked the door, the heavy rasp
of the turning key like the trumpet of doom.

Drained by the interview, Meriel lay down on the
bed but sleep eluded her. It would be comforting to
think that she was experiencing a nightmare caused by
green apples, but Warfield Castle and its uncommon
master were too vivid to deny. Lord Adrian was different from any man she had ever met, and she spent
some time groping to define the difference, because
understanding him might be vital to her future.

While she had been fascinated by that great glass
window, the most unusual feature in his chamber was
the case full of books. It was remarkable that the earl
could read, more remarkable yet that he had a library
that would do credit to a monastery. Apparently the
pious scholarly expression his face wore in repose was
genuine. And oddly enough, she believed that he
would indeed have released her if she had had the wit
to claim that she was bound to another man.

Yet side by side with the scholar lived a ruthless

warrior, accustomed to imposing his will on everyone and everything around him. Meriel shivered, remembering the terrifying intensity she had seen in the earl's eyes when they had met in the forest. Though today he had behaved with restraint, she sensed that beneath his surface calm, a devil lay waiting for the opportunity to break free.

The Church warned that there was a bit of the devil in everyone, which must be true of her because for a moment she had enjoyed the earl's touch, had wondered what it would be like to let him continue. Between her years in the priory and her large, protective male relatives, she had reached the advanced age of twenty-one with a singular lack of experience, and it had been quite educational to learn how pleasant a kiss could be. Passion was not a subject Meriel had ever much considered, but it was suddenly easier to understand why many peasant girls went to their marriage beds with a babe already on the way.

Her lips thinned in disgust at her weakness. Everything that Lord Adrian had done today had emphasized that he was a dangerous, unpredictable man. Meriel might be only a weak woman, but with the Blessed Mother's help she would be strong enough to do what was right for Avonleigh, no matter what that beautiful fallen-angel earl might do to her.

Adrian had seen enough of his little Welshwoman to be sure that her will was great, and that she was determined not to yield to him. Therefore, suspecting that boredom might prove to be a better ally than threats of violence, he decided to leave his captive alone for a full week before he spoke to her again. She would be allowed all comforts save those of companionship.

Suppressing his conscience, he ordered that the maid who took her meals should not linger, and that no one else be permitted to visit her. To ensure that his resolve to leave her alone did not falter, he personally

led a patrol along the border between his lands and
those of Guy of Burgoigne. His rival had launched a
series of raids, and the grim work of fighting, commanding, and rebuilding took much of Adrian's attention. Nonetheless, the thought of Meriel was always in
the back of his mind, and at night, as he lay restless
and longing for sleep, the image of her sent fire
through his veins, an unholy mixture of desire and
guilt.

Uneasily he recognized that he had mishandled her
badly, a mistake he had never made with horse or falcon; yet he could not undo what had been done. To
release the girl now would be to lose her, quite possibly to send her to her death. A masterless man or
woman was prey to all manner of dangers even at the
best of times, which was why every village needed a
lord to protect its people. Now, with war brewing between the rival earls of Shropshire and Guy of Burgoigne controlling the roads that led northeast, Meriel
would be running straight into disaster if she really
meant to go to Lincoln.

No, he must continue as he had begun. If Meriel
could be persuaded to accept his advances, surely in
time she would come to feel the affection that usually
grew between bedmates. She had thought him comely,
and God knew that he did not wish to harm her; most
women entered marriage praying that they would be
so fortunate.

In return for accepting him she would have rank and
wealth such as few women of her birth ever attained.
Once she had had time to consider, that prospect
should be enough to win her willingness. If not . . .
He refused to think of what he would do if that was
not enough.

There was some concern when the mistress's horse
returned alone to the Avonleigh stables, but real fear
did not set in until darkness fell and Meriel was still
missing. Though nothing could be done that night, at

dawn the next morning searchers went out, led by Henry, the manor steward.

The searchers were hampered by the rain that had fallen overnight, and the manor's keenest-nosed hounds were unable to trace the missing woman much beyond the fields of Avonleigh. The search continued for days with increasing desperation, through the wasteland, to all the neighboring manors, even to the edge of the royal forest, but without success: no one had seen any sign of Lady Meriel de Vere, either dead or alive.

When all hope of finding her had been exhausted, the steward sent word to Lord Theobald's castle. The next messenger that his lady sent to her husband in France carried a note to Sir Alan de Vere, informing him that his sister had disappeared and was presumed dead.

Amidst the constant demands of a busy household, Meriel had sometimes thought wistfully that it would be pleasant to have nothing to do, and often in the clamor of the great hall she longed for unlimited privacy. After a day of inactivity, she knew how foolish those wishes had been.

The first day after Lord Adrian had issued his ultimatum had not gone badly. She slept for hours and woke refreshed, feeling no more effects of her accident than a few twinges in her ankle. Then she had prayed, asking the Blessed Virgin to protect her and her chastity. By the next day, restlessness was gnawing at her. Sweet Mary, how did anyone survive years in a dungeon? Meriel preferred not to think further along those lines, since there was an unpleasant chance that she would find out.

She measured the confines of her chamber, five paces long, six wide. She counted the stones in the wall. She prayed for patience, with minimal success. She requested a bath every day and stayed in the water so long that her skin wrinkled. She identified the number and variety of dried flowers mingled with the rushes on the floor. She thought wistfully of Lord Adrian's treasure trove of books in the next room, but of course asking for one was out of the question since Meriel the lowborn Welshwoman could not possibly know how to read.

On the fourth day, inspiration struck and she persuaded Margery to bring her wool, distaff, and spindle. The maid had been doubtful first, but Meriel prevailed with the argument that the earl liked people to make themselves useful. Thereafter she spent most of her days spinning by one of the narrow windows where she could see the sky.

Occasionally she saw a bird fly by and her hands would fall still as her heart ached with longing to be free. Being unable to face a lifetime confined within walls was a great part of the reason that she had left Lambourn, and now Meriel was held in a far narrower confinement. Then she would resume her spinning, for it helped to have her hands busy.

The days were bearable, but anxiety haunted her nights and she often woke from restless slumber gasping with fear. How long could she maintain her composure, even with the Blessed Mother's help? How long until her mind and spirit shattered? There was no answer except prayer, and the hope that Lord Adrian would tire of his captive before she reaching her breaking point.

Cecily of Chastain tensed at the sound of heavy, familiar footsteps in the hall, then glanced up, her expression neutral. She had hoped her husband would be away from the castle for several days longer and did not welcome his early return.

The furious expression on Guy of Burgoigne's face when he entered confirmed her misgivings. He was a large man, so dark and broadly built that Cecily, with the secret dry humor that enabled her to keep her sanity, sometimes wondered if his mother had lain with a bear.

At Burgoigne's heels was his chief lieutenant, Sir Vincent de Laon, a Frenchman whom Cecily loathed almost as much as her husband. Scowling, Guy made an impatient movement of his hand and Cecily's three women instantly picked up their handwork and took flight to a more comfortable spot.

Scarcely looking at his wife, Burgoigne tossed her his helmet. "Unarm me."

Guy continued his conversation with Vincent as he bent over so that she could pull first his surcoat, then his hauberk over his head. He must have been living in his armor for days, because he stank like a goat.

Even for a large, strong woman, the chain mail was heavy. As Cecily turned, the hauberk slipped from her arms and crashed noisily to the floor. Annoyed by her clumsiness, Guy swung a surly fist at his wife. Cecily could have avoided it, but had long since learned that it was better to accept a glancing blow, for if he missed entirely, he would strike again, harder.

In a corner of the room stood a wooden frame for holding the hauberk. As Cecily arranged the mail over it, she listened to the men carefully, wondering what had put her husband in a mood that was foul even by his low standards.

"Damnation!" Guy swore as he peeled off his quilted gambeson and dropped it on the floor for his wife to pick up. "We should have been able to loot and raze three of Warfield's villages. Instead, the bastard was there even before we could burn the first one. How does he always know where to be?"

"A pact with the devil?" Sir Vincent suggested as he removed his own helmet. He was from Paris and never troubled to conceal his disdain for the crude northerners among whom he lived.

"Bah, that puling Christ-kisser would faint at the thought," Burgoigne snarled. "He's a monk in all but name."

"For a monk, he fights rather well," Vincent murmured. The French knight was the only man who actually conversed with his choleric lord rather than merely obeying orders. Sometimes he even dared disagree.

Guy gave the harsh bark that was his version of laughter. "Aye, I'll give him that, Warfield does fight well, though not so well as I. Someday I'll meet him in single combat and carve his heart out and feed it to the dogs. But just now, sending him to his savior is less important than capturing his lands so there will be no question who is the true Earl of Shropshire. He is the one collecting most of the shire's third penny in taxes, and it gives him a great advantage over me." He flicked his dark hair impatiently. "The only way I'll defeat him is by hiring mercenaries."

"You're thinking of bringing in outside troops?" Vincent asked, surprised. " 'Twill be costly."

"Which is why I've not done it yet. But with fifty good mercenaries, I could raze Warfield's lands and have him mewed up in his castle before the summer was done," Burgoigne said. "No chance of taking Warfield Castle, more's the pity, but no matter—if I can stop him from interfering for a month or two, I'll have all Shropshire under my hand."

"There is still the matter of Richard FitzHugh and Montford Castle," Vincent said. "He may be his brother's lapdog, but he is not to be dismissed lightly."

"All I need do is lay siege to Warfield Castle when FitzHugh is visiting and they'll both be out of the way. Or mayhap the bastard can be bribed to turn his coat in return for being enfeoffed with some of his brother's lands." Burgoigne brooded. "The question is, where can I find the gold to hire the mercenaries? The worst of them are a greater danger to their master than his enemies, and the best will not settle for mere promises of future plunder."

"Does the lady of Chastain," Vincent nodded to

Cecily with mocking respect, "have any jewels worth selling?"

"Most of them went last year, for rebuilding the wall. Unless she held some back, like the sly cow she is." Burgoigne raised his voice. "Wife, attend me!"

Cecily dared not disobey; rebellion had been beaten out of her before her wedding night was over. When she was within her husband's reach, he grabbed her arm and twisted it harshly behind her. "A good and faithful wife like you would not withhold any of her treasure from her lawful lord, would she?"

She tried to keep her expression impassive, knowing how much her husband enjoyed the sight of another's suffering. "No, my lord," she said, then gasped as he twisted harder and pain lanced through her shoulder. "You have had most of the gold plate and all of my mother's jewels, save for a few valueless trinkets."

"Bring me your jewel box," he commanded, shoving her away so hard that she almost fell.

Clumsily she caught her balance, then crossed to the wardrobe and removed the small chest that had once contained her mother's jewelry. Removing the key from around her neck, she unlocked the casket before presenting it to her husband. With no real hope he poked around in the interior, sneering at the simple enameled brooches and glass beads. "Bah, I've seen village whores with better."

"Very likely," she agreed with a trace of dryness, then cast her eyes down when he glared at her.

"They're good enough for a fat cow like you," he said as he removed a pretty circle brooch. "I'll take this one."

"Yes, my lord," Cecily murmured as she returned the casket to her wardrobe. She knew that Guy would give the ornament to one of the whores currently enjoying his favors. The brooch had been a gift from her father when she was a child and she had cherished it, but if it helped keep her husband from her bed for a night or two, she'd not regret the loss.

"Who has money, apart from Adrian of Warfield himself?" Vincent mused, then answered his own question. "The Church and the Jews, that's who."

"What good does that do me?" Burgoigne snapped as he sat in his tall chair of state. "Once the Church gets its greedy hands on gold, it never lets go, and the Jews are all in London."

"I agree, it would be folly to risk excommunication by plundering any of the Church's treasures," Vincent admitted as he sat in the chair that was usually Cecily's, "but the Jews, now, that's a different story."

"You've a plan?" Burgoigne said with interest.

Cecily did not doubt that the Frenchman had a plan; it was his evil, fertile mind that made him so valuable to his master. Silently she poured silver goblets of wine for both men, served them, then took her embroidery and retreated to a stool at the far end of the chamber. She would have preferred to withdraw, but her husband required her to be available to wait on him.

"It's true that all the Jews used to live in London, since that was where the old king had invited them. But I heard something interesting at Stephen's Easter court. Over the last few years Jews have moved to smaller cities. Now there are Jewish communities in Norwich, Lincoln, Oxford, several other towns as well." The French knight paused to sip his wine. "Perhaps some of them can be persuaded to bring themselves and their gold to Shrewsbury."

"What good will that do me? Shrewsbury is Warfield's city, not mine," Burgoigne growled. It was a sore point with him that his rival controlled the shire's largest community and its revenues.

"But the road from London to Shrewsbury crosses your territory," Vincent pointed out. "When they pass through, you can relieve them of the gold they've leeched from honest Christians."

A slow, unpleasant smile crossed Burgoigne's face. "Do you think you can persuade a rich Jew or two to make the move?"

"I think it quite possible, if they are assured of the personal protection of the Earl of Shropshire." Vincent held out his empty cup. Across the room, Cecily saw his signal and quickly refilled both men's goblets with wine.

"If you like the idea, I will go to London and see if I can find a lamb for our fleecing," the Frenchman continued. His smile broadened. " 'Twill be a particularly nice touch if I say that I represent Adrian of Warfield. Then he will be blamed for the robbery, which will do his lily-pure reputation no good."

Burgoigne roared with laughter, his earlier ill-humor gone. "I like it well. The king would be displeased if he knew I had robbed some of his Jews, but he'll not find out." And to ensure that there would be no hint of Guy's involvement, he would take their lives as well as their gold. "Go you to London and use that silver tongue of yours to persuade a moneylender to bring his business to Shrewsbury."

Cecily's lips thinned and she jabbed her needle into the fabric with unnecessary violence. Even if they were Jews, she could not help but feel sorry for anyone fool enough to fall into her husband's web.

6

MERIEL GLANCED UP, surprised when the key turned in the lock, for Margery had already brought dinner and should not be back until suppertime. But it was Lord Adrian who entered, and when she saw him Meriel felt an odd twist of emotion, not quite fear, certainly not pleasure. Perhaps it was . . . anticipation, for now there would be a break in the tedium.

As the earl entered and closed the door behind him, she saw that though he wore his sword, he looked scholarly and contained today, with no dangerous wildness in his eyes. The thought also occurred, and was hastily suppressed, that he was dangerously handsome. "Good day, Meriel," he said, his voice mild and reasonable. "Have you been served well in my absence?"

She gave a wry chuckle. "Since when does the jailer ask his prisoner about the accommodations?"

He looked uncomfortable. "I am not your jailer."

Her dark brows rose. "What then?"

"Perhaps I am your fate."

"You flatter yourself, my lord." As they spoke she remained seated, her deft fingers twisting thread onto the spindle.

"Who set you to work?" he asked, eyeing the distaff and spindle with disapproval.

"No one. I thought to make myself useful. Since it is well known that you don't believe in slothfulness, it was easy to persuade your servants to let me spin."

As his mouth tightened, she said quickly, "The fault is mine, my lord. Do not punish any of your people."

"I won't, but it is obvious that I should have given more detailed orders." As the earl spoke, he stared at her with such intensity that Meriel began feeling uncomfortable. He had been calm enough when he entered; what was it about her that made the man become unbalanced? She braced herself, expecting him to ask her if she had reconsidered his proposal, but he surprised her. "Would you like to go for a ride?"

Scarcely daring to hope, she asked, "You mean go outside?"

"Of course." He smiled. "I have heard of knights who ride their horses inside their keeps, but I like to think that we are above such behavior here."

Meriel laughed, so happy at the thought of leaving her prison that anything would have amused her. Laying down her spinning, she accompanied him downstairs, through the great hall, and outside to the stables, delighting in the fresh scenes and faces. She was interested to note that everyone from knight to stable lad treated his lord with deference, but there was no fear, and not a few friendly smiles from his people. It was very much the way people at Avonleigh behaved with Alan, and implied that the earl was better liked than she would have expected.

Meriel herself was studied with open curiosity, and, in the case of one or two young females, with hostility. Knowing what everyone was thinking embarrassed her, but Meriel kept her head high. She was not here of her own free will, nor was she responsible if the lord of the manor was neglecting his usual bedmates.

Two saddled horses were waiting in the stables. It was not surprising that he thought she would accept his offer. Or had he intended to force her to come, no matter what her own wishes? She would do well to remember that his courtesy did not change the fact that she was entirely in his power.

The mount Lord Adrian had chosen for her was a

sorrel mare, as pretty and sweet-tempered as her own Rosalia. Meriel almost asked why the mare did not carry a sidesaddle, but just in time recalled that as a female of humble birth she would be expected to ride cross-saddle. No matter; she was experienced with both styles and would have ridden bareback to get out of Warfield Castle.

Since Meriel preferred that the earl not have opportunities to touch her, she swung into the saddle without waiting for his help. "What is the mare's name?"

"Call her whatever you wish," he said as he mounted his own black stallion.

"Rose," she said, deciding on a humble version of her own mare's name.

It was a sunny day, with a stiff breeze whipping fluffy clouds across the sky, and as they trotted out of the village gate Meriel threw her head back and laughed from sheer delight. Never in her life had she so much appreciated God's sweet green world. The sky was bluer, the flowers brighter, the very air tasted better than she had ever noticed before.

As they came onto the broad meadow that stretched beside the river, Lord Adrian remarked, "I don't suppose I need to warn you that it would be futile to try to escape."

"No, my lord," she replied, casting a sapient eye over his stallion. "Even the swiftest of mares could not outrun that great black devil of yours." Her eyes gleamed mischievously. "That doesn't mean that I will forgo the pleasure of feeling the wind in my hair."

Meriel loosened her reins and urged the horse forward, leaning over the mare's mane as they went tearing down the meadow. Rose had a pretty turn of speed and Meriel gloried in it, feeling very nearly free as the wind whipped her braids out behind her and fluttered her skirts above her knees. Vaguely she was aware that the earl was keeping pace with her, staying a stride or two behind, and she was grateful that he made no attempt to stop her wild flight.

As they approached a small flock of grazing sheep, Meriel slowed down so as not to disturb them. Her eyes glowing, she turned to her companion. "That was wonderful. Rose is a superb mount."

Reining back his own horse, Lord Adrian said, "This is just a taste of what you might have if you agree to my proposal."

Meriel's pleasure died and she turned away, ignoring him as if he had not spoken. Rather to her surprise, the earl was content to ride in silence rather than pursue the point. The trail swung away from the river's edge, and soon they were traveling through light woodland. Good country for hawks, though not suitable for falcons.

Even as Meriel enjoyed the ride, part of her mind was calculating the chances for escaping. Granted that her horse could not outrun the earl's in an even contest. But what if he dismounted for some reason and she had a good lead before he came after her? Better yet, what if she could lead or drive his stallion off and leave her captor on foot? He would never catch her then.

She glanced askance at her companion, then gave an inward sigh. In spite of his casual air, it was unlikely that Lord Adrian would be easily caught off-guard. Still, if by some chance an opportunity arose, she'd be off with a speed that would do credit to Chanson.

After two or three miles, the trail entered a wide area of wasteland. Meriel frowned as she considered it. Wasteland was land that had once been farmed, then abandoned, usually in the troubled years after the Normans conquered England. But these fields had been cultivated more recently; judging by the size of the scrub trees scattered across the old fields, perhaps ten or twelve years earlier.

Then she saw the unmistakable flattened cone shape of a motte rising before them. The top of the mound was crowned by the blackened ruins of a tower. To the right lay the bailey, a mass of vines and tall grasses obscuring the sad remnants of stables, workshops, and living quarters. An unnatural silence lay over what once had been a Norman keep, as if even the birds and insects preferred to keep their distance.

The overgrown trail led to the ditch that surrounded the motte and bailey, and Meriel reined her horse in at the edge, her gaze scanning the ruins.

As the earl drew up beside her, he said, "This was the original Warfield keep."

Puzzled, she asked, "Did you destroy the keep after the castle was built so that robbers could not take it over?"

"It was burned by Guy of Burgoigne." His voice was flat, but there was an underlying note that caused Meriel to glance at him. Catching her gaze, he smiled humorlessly. "The other Earl of Shropshire. Were you aware that there are two claimants to the shire?"

"I had heard that," she replied cautiously. "It is said that you were appointed by the empress, Burgoigne by the king."

He nodded. "The same thing has happened in several other counties—Cornwall, Wiltshire, Hereford. It is an inexpensive way for Stephen and Matilda to persuade barons to do their fighting for them," he said cynically. "An English county is a rich prize, for the earl is entitled to a third of all royal tax revenues in return for keeping order."

"So you and Burgoigne will butt heads like spring rams while the people of Shropshire endure endless *dis*order." She did not trouble to keep the contempt from her voice; sweet Mary, it would be a better world if women ruled. "No doubt the two of you will fight until one of you is dead. A pity that the common folk have no voice in who will rule them."

He did not flare up in anger, just sighed and looked at the blackened ruins of the keep. "I'm told that most of the shire hopes that I will win, and do it quickly. Until the civil war began, Guy was no more than captain of a band of robbers, but he was shrewd enough to see the advantage of being one of the few knights in the west to declare for the king. Sure enough, Stephen rewarded him richly for his support. Next Guy forced an heiress to the altar, which made him master of a large part of Shropshire and extensive estates in Normandy as well. He is now one of the most powerful barons in England—but he still has the black lawless heart of a bandit.''

''Are you so much better a man than Guy of Burgoigne?'' she asked caustically.

He shrugged. ''I keep order in my lands, and I do not burn dwellings, then slaughter all who escape the fires.''

It took Meriel a moment to understand what he wasn't saying. Then she inhaled sharply, glancing from the ruins back to the earl's still profile. ''That is what Burgoigne did here?''

There was a long silence before Lord Adrian replied. ''He struck before dawn on Christmas Day. My entire family was inside, save only my half-brother Richard.'' The steadiness of his voice did not disguise the sorrow. ''Guy took great care that no one—not man, woman, or child, Norman lord or English servant—escaped.''

She found herself aching for an old tragedy whose pain still echoed down the years. ''How did you survive?''

''I was at Fontevaile Abbey, preparing to take vows.''

''You, a monk?'' she exclaimed.

''I daresay that seems strange to you,'' he said, smiling faintly as he set his horse in motion away from the keep.

As Meriel followed, she thought that on the contrary, Lord Adrian's words explained a great deal: his reading skill and library, the austerity of his dress, perhaps even the strange duality of his character. It also gave Meriel a surprising sense of kinship with the earl to know that he too had experienced the religious life. Had he had felt the same suffocation she had? "A monk's life is a limited one," she commented as the ruins disappeared behind them. "Were you glad to leave the abbey?"

"Limited only on the surface. Within the boundaries of prayers and books lies a wider world than the one visible around us. As to whether I was glad to leave—part of me was, part of me was not." He turned his palm up apologetically. "I can give you no better answer than that."

It sounded as if Lord Adrian had been more suited to the cloister than Meriel, who had never regretted leaving. "Which part of you was sorry and which part was not?"

"The better part of me was sorry." He smiled wryly. "Doubtless I've already earned a few extra decades in purgatory, for the world offers many more temptations than an abbey does and I have not the saintly strength to resist them all." His glance slanted over to her. "Your presence is proof that I am not good at resisting temptation."

"Then for the good of your soul, you had best set me free," she said, her voice light but edged.

His self-mocking humor vanished, leaving his gray eyes utterly serious. "Never."

Sweet Mary, why her? Chilled, Meriel pulled her gaze away and there was no more conversation as they picked their way through the waters of a shallow stream.

A few minutes later, ignoring their last exchange, the earl asked, "Are you hungry?"

"A little," she admitted. "I had scant appetite for my dinner."

He rummaged in a small pouch hanging from his saddle, then pulled something out and tossed it to her. "Catch."

Meriel was so startled that she bobbled the object and almost dropped it. "An apple!" she said with delight just before biting into it. After chewing a mouthful, she gave him a quizzical glance. "It tastes fresh, not like one of last autumn's crop, but isn't it rather early for apples?"

"It came from France." He bit into his own fruit.

Impressed, Meriel stopped eating and examined the apple with awe. "Goodness, I don't know if I should eat it. This apple is better-traveled than I am."

The earl laughed. Meriel had never seen him laugh before, and humor transformed his face from austerely handsome to quite irresistibly appealing. She laughed with him, until she realized what he was doing and her amusement abruptly ceased. Since a straightforward invitation to his bed had failed, Lord Adrian was now trying to charm her into submission. He probably thought that after a few hours of conversation, and perhaps a gift or two, she would be eager to spread her legs for him.

Meriel sank her teeth viciously into the apple and tore out a large piece. What did he think she was, a randy goosegirl with neither morals nor sense? It took a moment for her to realize that she could hardly blame him for thinking that when she was doing her best to act like a simple peasant wench.

Ruefully she nibbled away the last of the apple flesh, then tossed the core into the high grass. For the first time she wondered if her brother could have meant Guy of Burgoigne when he had referred to the vicious Earl of Shropshire. After a moment's thought, she mentally shrugged. There was no way to know which of the two earls was more villainous, since she would be a fool to trust one man's words about the character of the other. Besides, it didn't really matter, for even if Adrian of Warfield was less vicious than his rival, he was still a ruthless man and a danger to Meriel.

Licking apple juice from her fingers, she resolved that the earl would be no more successful with his charm than he had been with his threats. If he was the honorable Christian knight that he sometimes appeared to be, in time he might be shamed into releasing her, particularly if another female caught his fancy. She would pray for that to happen soon.

They were taking a different path from the one they had ridden out on, and it wound through higher, more heavily wooded ground. Perhaps a mile from the burned keep, they entered a clearing where about two dozen standing stones were set in a circle. Fascinated, Meriel rode to the nearest and slid off her horse to investigate further. The stone stood easily twice her height. "I have heard of these stone rings where our ancestors worshiped, but have never seen one before."

"Your British ancestors might have worshiped here, but mine were Northmen who sailed around in long-boats and raided honest folk." The earl dismounted also, tethered his mount, then gestured toward the center of the circle, where the ashes of a fire could be seen. "This may have been built in ancient times, but it is still used, apparently within the last few weeks."

"Do you really think some of your people worship the old gods?"

"I'm sure of it, but there isn't much that can be done to stop them." He drifted across the circle, his step light, his brow furrowed. "Executing everyone suspected of following pagan superstitions would not necessarily save their souls, and would certainly deprive the fields of much-needed labor."

"That is a wise and practical way to deal with them." Meriel chuckled and flattened her hand against the coarse surface of the standing stone, feeling the sun's warmth in it. "Life is hard for serfs. Doubtless the folk who come here are good Christians—they just don't want to risk angering any older gods who might still linger."

Abruptly she noticed something much more important than ancient forms of worship. The stallion was tethered only a few feet from Meriel, but the earl himself had moved away. Now he was on the far side of the circle, examining the stones, his back turned to his captive.

Trying not to betray her excitement, Meriel mentally rehearsed her actions. She held the reins of her own horse in her hand. All she need do was untie the stallion, mount Rose, and she'd be off with both horses. Lord Adrian would never catch her on foot.

Swiftly she untied the stallion's reins and swung onto Rose's back. Then she turned the mare back the way they had come and kicked her in the flanks.

So far, so good. But then events went wrong with shattering suddenness. Alerted by the sounds of harness and hooves, the earl turned, instantly saw what Meriel was about, and exploded into action. A shrill whistle split the air and the stallion reared up, jerking the reins from Meriel's hands and coming down directly in front of the mare. Lord Adrian himself was closing the distance between them with terrifying speed.

Meriel abandoned hope that she could take the stallion, and concentrated on regaining control of Rose, who was panicking under the nips and harassment of the other horse. Since the stallion blocked their path, Meriel wheeled Rose about so she could escape in the other direction. But before the mare could stretch into full gallop, the earl was there, diving through the air to grab the bridle with one hand.

Desperately Meriel pulled her foot from the stirrup and kicked the earl's right wrist, hard. He gasped with pain and released the bridle, and for a moment she thought there was still a chance of escape.

Instead, he twisted like a cat and lunged for Meriel herself. The clawing fingers of his left hand missed her shoulder but caught in the neck of her gown, his falling weight tearing the fabric before he managed to get his arm solidly around her waist. Meriel was jerked from the saddle to tumble helplessly through the air. She landed on her back with jarring force.

Lord Adrian had fallen next to her, and with one quick movement he pinned Meriel to the soft turf with his hard, furious body. His head and wide shoulders loomed above her and his heaving chest pressed against hers as he fought for breath. Meriel herself could scarcely breathe, and not just because of his crushing weight. She had seen dangerous intensity in him before, but his present annihilating rage terrified her. She was so close that she could see the darker gray that rimmed his clear light pupils, and the grim lines carved around his mouth.

Violence sizzled in the air like heat lightning. Meriel's shift and bliaut had been ripped almost to the waist, exposing her right breast, and as the earl lifted the upper part of his body away, his fierce gaze raked over her nakedness. "You should not have tried to escape."

Meriel knew that he was perilously close to raping her. With what breath she could muster, she replied, "You are right, it was foolish of me to try. To be honest, I never dreamed that you could move so quickly."

His expression eased, still furious but no longer wild. "A knight does not survive long if he is either slow or stupid."

"My experience of escaping from knights is limited," she said lightly, as if his loins were not pressed against hers like a lover's.

A spark of humor showed in his eyes. "Not limited. Nonexistent."

He lowered his head and she tensed, fearful that he would force a kiss on her. Feeling her stiffen, he hesitated. Then, instead of capturing her mouth, he kissed her ear, using lips and tongue in a sensual and wholly unexpected way. Meriel gasped, shocked by the intensity of the sensation, and by how distant, previously undiscovered parts of her body were reacting.

Gentle and implacable, his mouth traversed the length of her throat as one of his hands moved into a caress. Her exposed flesh was chilled by the air except where he touched her. There she felt fire. First his questing hand molded the shape of her breast; then he found her nipple and rolled it delicately between thumb and forefinger. As dark, compelling warmth unfolded deep inside her, Meriel cried out, confused and frightened by how her body was responding.

"Please . . . please stop," she begged, terrified that he might be able to persuade her body to permit an act that was utterly against her will. The thought was somehow more frightening than that he might take her by force; to be ravished was physical violation, but turning her own body into an enemy would violate her spirit. "Don't punish me like this. It would be better if you beat me."

To her amazement, after a taut moment he did stop. "I had not thought of this as punishment," he said, and from the dry note in his voice she knew that the danger had passed.

The earl rolled away and sat up. She stiffened when he reached out again, but he merely pulled the torn shift across her bared flesh, his hand lingering for only an instant. When he stood, his movements were slow and precise, as if he were brittle and would shatter if he moved too quickly. Then he extended his hand to help Meriel. As she regained her feet, his sleeve fell back and she saw that his right wrist was bandaged, and that blood was seeping through the fabric.

Meriel gasped, covering her mouth with her hand. "Did I do that when I kicked you?"

He glanced at his wrist. "My wrist was slashed in a skirmish last week. Your aim is excellent—you managed to catch the wound dead center and open it up again."

She bit her lip. "I'm sorry. I just wanted to escape—I didn't meant to hurt you."

"No?" His golden brows raised skeptically as he tugged at the bandage in an attempt to reduce the bleeding.

"No," she repeated firmly as she intervened. "I would never have aimed deliberately at a wound." While the earl watched with ironic amusement, she unwound the bandage to examine the damage. The gash was ugly and would scar but it was not deep and there were no signs of infection. While his wrist must hurt like the very devil, she decided that her kick had done him no real harm.

Since her shift was already in dire straits, she had no compunction about tearing off another strip of fabric. She folded the original bandage into a pad, closed the edges of the wound and placed the pad over it, then wrapped his wrist with the fabric stripped from her gown. "This should hold the bleeding until you get back to Warfield, but it must be dressed again."

"Are you quite finished?" he asked mildly.

"Yes, my lord," she said, unable to repress a note of mischief. "Should the situation arise again, I shall do my best to avoid kicking sensitive parts of your anatomy."

"I sincerely hope so. There are things more sensitive than an injured wrist." He put two fingers to his mouth and gave a piercing whistle. The stallion, which had been grazing nearby, raised its head. The earl gave a different whistle and his horse trotted to where the mare grazed on the far side of the clearing and herded the smaller animal back.

Meriel watched the stallion with admiration. "Remarkable. Do you use him as a destrier?"

"No, Gideon's gift is swiftness, he isn't large enough to carry full armor for long distances. But he has a destrier's training, and some other tricks as well. One can never tell when a casual ride might turn into a skirmish. Or an escape attempt."

Refusing to rise to the bait, she walked to Rose and spent a moment stroking the mare's muzzle and murmuring soothing words in Welsh. While she did that, Lord Adrian removed his mantle and tossed it to Meriel. "Wrap this around yourself or I will not guarantee my behavior."

Glancing down at her torn gown, she blushed and did as he ordered, almost disappearing under the folds of fabric. When Meriel started to mount the mare, the earl said, "Don't bother. You will ride in front of me."

Dismayed, she turned to face him. "Is that necessary?"

"I have no faith that you have learned the futility of trying to escape," he said as he swung onto his own horse.

"If you were held prisoner, would you not take any chance to try to win free?"

"Of course," he agreed with perfect good humor. "That is why I don't trust you an inch."

Meriel bit her lip in frustration, hating the idea of being brought in on his saddle bow like a naughty child. "If I promise not to try again, will you let me ride Rose?"

"Not to attempt to escape ever again?"

"I'll not try between here and Warfield," she replied, unwilling to swear away future chances.

She could see him considering her request, weighing whether she would keep her word. Finally, to her relief, he said, "Very well." He smiled faintly. "If nothing else, I don't intend that you will find another opportunity today."

There was a curious amiability between them, and they talked easily for the rest of the ride back, but when they reached the castle, Meriel found it almost impossible to reenter. As the walls loomed oppressively above her, icy tendrils of panic began curling around her heart and it took a major act of will not to wheel her horse and dash off in futile flight. When, if ever, would she leave the castle again? After her failed escape attempt today, she doubted that the earl would take her riding another time.

She should have been prepared for his next move, but she was not, and it was an unpleasant surprise when he picked up her distaff and spindle when they reached her chamber. "What kind of host would I be if I allowed a guest to work?" he murmured. "Sleep well, my little Welsh falcon.'' Then he collected his cloak and turned to go.

Her lips thinned but she refrained from comment, guessing that the earl knew just how much the spinning had done to alleviate her boredom. If she pleaded to keep her tools he might be amused or he might be regretful, but she was sure that he would not change his mind.

As Meriel watched the door close behind his lithe, broad-shouldered figure, she knew that there was war between them, a war of wills as clearly drawn as a chess game. His latest action was simply one more move in a game where he held all the strongest weapons, except one: the fact that she would never allow herself to be defeated.

7

BACK IN HIS own chamber, Adrian set down Meriel's spinning, then drifted across the room to stare sightlessly from the great window as he recalled how achingly lovely she had looked when flying down the meadow on the sorrel mare. What a rare creature she was. Though he held her captive, her spirit was as free as a falcon's, as impossible to hold as a shower of sunshine.

His smile faded. A wild falcon could be tamed, but could Meriel be? Perhaps a creature could not be gentled unless it was wild. Therefore, since she was already gentle, perhaps she could not be further tamed, perhaps she would always be the way she was now, rejecting him with soft implacability.

Fiercely he dismissed the bizarre thought. She was merely shy of him because he had behaved so clumsily at the beginning. Falconers began training a wild hawk by "manning" it, which meant accustoming it to the presence of men. Like a falconer, he was now doing exactly that with his little Welshwoman. Today's ride had not gone badly, except for her ill-judged attempt to escape. She had relaxed in his company, had laughed, and even bantered with him. Her mind was quick and lively; once she realized that he meant her no harm, she would come to him willingly.

Absently Adrian rubbed his aching wrist and tried not to think of how arousing her soft curves had been when she had lain beneath him, and how lovely was the body revealed when her shabby gown had been

torn away. She deserved finer than rags, and he made
a mental note to have more suitable garments made.

Even wholly at his mercy, Meriel had shown no fear,
but had teased him out of his fury when he was perilously near dishonoring them both. Though the memory was a torment of both guilt and desire, he forced
himself to think objectively about what had happened.
There had been genuine pleasure in her reaction to his
caresses, he was sure of it, but pleasure had been coupled with equally genuine distress.

The combination made it likely that she was virgin
in spite of her years, which meant he must be even
more careful in his dealings with her. But Jesu! it was
difficult to maintain his control. It had been almost
impossible when she was in his arms, and was little
easier now, when he was all too aware that she was
only a few steps away.

There was a large chapel in the outer bailey and a
parish church in the village, but except for Mass,
Adrian preferred the privacy of his own chapel. Hoping to cool his fevered mind and body, he walked to
the far end of the room and through the narrow door
into his personal sanctuary. The chapel faced south-
west, and late-afternoon sunshine poured through the
small stained-glass window to cast brilliant swaths of
color across the floor and altar.

In the years since Adrian had inherited Warfield, he
had never faltered in his Christian faith or practice. He
obeyed the laws of the Church, gave alms to the poor,
generously endowed Fontevaile Abbey and several
other religious houses. Once or twice a year he left the
world and withdrew to Fontevaile for several days to
remind himself of what was truly important.

Nonetheless, in spite of his best efforts, he knew
that he was falling away from God. Though he prayed
and meditated regularly, and with increasing desperation, it had been long—too long—since he had felt
the profound sense of peace that had once been the
center of his existence. He missed that ultimate one-

ness with a sorrow so acute that sometimes it nearly
disabled him.

Ever since he was a child, Adrian had had a mental
image of his soul as a silver chalice. In the days when
his cup had been filled with the Holy Spirit, it had
been as bright as newly polished silver, with only a
few flecks of darkness to mar its shining surface. But
as the years passed, tarnish and grime had accumu-
lated until the silver was dull and lifeless. Was his soul
blackening because of the worldly life he had been
forced to live, a life of cunning, compromise, and violence? Or was the fault more basic, a flaw in his own
spirit that was becoming more visible with time?

He knelt at the rail and tried to pray, asking for the
strength and wisdom to woo Meriel with patience and
wisdom, but he was too torn by desire to achieve calm.
After a weary interval he opened his eyes so that he
could contemplate the small statue of the Blessed
Mother. Her serene image had never failed to soothe
him.

He began to whisper the Hail Mary, but today the
words were empty, without meaning. The harder he
tried to concentrate on the statue, the more Meriel's
face came between them. Meriel, first with her sweetness and transparent honesty, then with desperate un-
happiness when he had begun to make love to her.

Her reproachful face was before him even when he
closed his eyes again. His breathing harsh, he tried to
eliminate her image but failed. He had known stern
old monks who claimed that all women were of the
devil, and such men would have said that Meriel had
been sent by Satan to try to steal his soul. But Adrian
knew better; the fault was not in her, but in him.

Though his prayers had lost much of their clarity
with the years, this was the first time that he had been
unable to pray at all. Despairing, he raised his eyes,
past the statue of Mary, past the golden crucifix which
hung on the wall. Higher than both was a jewel-bright

stained-glass window which had been formed into the image of the dove of the Holy Spirit.

As Adrian gazed at the dove, a pitiless inner voice commanded: *Set her free.*

A piercing chill accompanied the words, and it spread through his body and lodged in his soul. His icy hands clenched spasmodically as Adrian confronted the devastating truth that he had tried to conceal from himself: no matter what his legal authority, no matter how much he cared for Meriel or claimed to be holding her for her own protection, what he was doing was utterly wrong. It was a sin of the most selfish and despicable kind, committed against an innocent for the basest of reasons.

No wonder he had lately been "too busy" to find time for confession; how could he confess to such wickedness? God help him, not only had he been incapable of admitting his sin, even now he could not feel the true remorse and wish to atone that were necessary for confession.

As clearly as if the words had been spoken aloud, he knew that if he sent Meriel away he would be able to pray again. Releasing her would not cleanse his soul to the bright luster of his youth, but at least he would be able to contemplate the Blessed Virgin without an anguished face interfering. He could be shriven and receive Holy Communion again.

His breath came in anguished gasps and his hands curled so tightly that the nails drew blood. *Set her free.* Such a simple act, the right and proper thing to do. But he could not do it; may God forgive him, not even to save his soul could he let Meriel go.

Sir Vincent de Laon had never been in the home of a Jew before, and he trod warily, unsure of what to expect. But in the event, he found that the house of Benjamin l'Eveske differed little from the home of any other rich merchant, save that it was built of stone, not wood. For protection, perhaps?

Benjamin l'Eveske proved to be a man of advancing years, with a great hooked nose and a flowing dark beard liberally streaked with gray. Though he sometimes lent money, his principal occupation was trade, and he had the shrewd black eyes of a man who knew how to drive a hard bargain.

Even though he wished to curry favor with the Jew, Sir Vincent could not bring himself to bow to the man—after all, he himself was a Christian and a knight. But he would do his considerable best to be affable and persuasive, for the unbeliever might aid Guy of Burgoigne to greater wealth and power, which would increase both for Vincent.

After the preliminary greetings had been observed and wine poured for both men, Benjamin said, "I understand that you have been making inquiries about me in the Jewry."

Sir Vincent nodded. "Aye. I had heard that you are considering relocating your business and family to a provincial city, and I wished to learn more about you."

Benjamin's expression was noncommittal. "I have thought of moving," he murmured. "But it has been no more than a thought."

"My Lord Adrian, the Earl of Shropshire, looks to benefit his city of Shrewsbury," Sir Vincent said. "Men like yourself, successful merchants and bankers, would be made welcome."

"And what would my advantage be if I should move to Shrewsbury rather than Lincoln or York?"

"Shrewsbury is a growing town, placed to profit from the Welsh wool trade." The Frenchman paused to sip more of his excellent wine. "There is no Jewish community at present, so there would be more opportunities for you. Also, you and your household would be placed under the earl's personal protection. Lord Adrian will even give you escort between London and Shrewsbury should you choose to come."

The black eyes were ironic. "My people are under

the king's protection now. How would we be safer with the earl's?''

Sir Vincent shrugged. ''London has the most dangerous mobs in England. When the idlers, drunkards, and apprentices run wild, even the king's soldiers cannot always contain them. And the king has greater worries than protecting his Jews.''

Benjamin's eyes grew even more unreadable, and Sir Vincent knew that he had aroused the other man's interest. Best not push now, but leave the merchant to discuss the matter with his family. The knight finished his wine and rose. ''I shall be in London for some days longer. May I call on you again? In case you have any questions about Shrewsbury and the Marches?''

The old man stood also. ''Perhaps there is merit in your lord's suggestion. It is true that the west of England is not so well served by merchants as the east and the Midlands. But such decisions must not be made in haste.''

Sir Vincent left feeling well pleased with himself. From the information he had gleaned earlier, Benjamin l'Eveske was more than mildly interested in relocating, but had not yet made up his mind. The prospect of becoming the chief merchant in the Marches would surely be enough to bring him to Shrewsbury.

For several more days—it was getting hard to keep track of how many—Meriel was left alone in her prison, save for the all-too-brief visits of Margery. Meriel did not make the mistake of believing that the earl had forgotten her; no, this was a ploy to make her so lonely that she would crave his companionship, might even be willing to pay the ultimate price for it.

She refused to think what would happen if his patience expired before his interest did. Instead, Meriel spent long hours meditating and saying cycles of rosaries. She luxuriated in her daily bath. When she could not sit still a moment longer, she paced around her chamber, moving and turning swiftly in the limited space. She visualized different scenes from the places she had lived, Beaulaine, Lambourn, Moreton, Avonleigh, then pretended that she walked among their familiar hills and trees.

To occupy her restless fingers, she unraveled threads from her torn garments and made painstaking repairs so that she was decent, even if disreputable. Then she took the longest floor rushes and wove them into crude mats and baskets. When she ran out of suitable rushes, she disassembled her handiwork and began again, experimenting with new patterns and forms.

She was reweaving a mat when Margery entered carrying a tray and a covered basket. "There is a nice bit of chicken with your dinner," the maid said, a sparkle of amusement in her eyes.

Meriel stood and stretched. "Why don't you eat it? I find these quiet days give me little appetite." Then her attention was caught by strange sounds coming from the maid's basket. A moment later an indignant young cat scrambled out and jumped to the floor. The cat immediately began to explore and soon arrived under the table where Margery had placed the food. As the small creature looked up hopefully, Meriel asked, "Is that your cat?"

The maid turned a bland face. "What cat?"

Perhaps solitude was blunting Meriel's wits; it took a moment for her to understand. Then she gave her first genuine smile in days. "It must have been my imagination. For a moment I thought I saw something hiding in the rushes." Taking the chicken leg from the platter, Meriel pulled off a strip of meat and offered it to the little cat, who accepted eagerly.

"There's a double handful of cats in the kitchen and pantries, but I've never seen one up here," Margery commented as she picked up the empty tankard left from breakfast.

"There must be few mice for them to catch on the

upper level,'' Meriel said gravely. ''A pity. I've always liked cats.''

''Time I was off,'' the maid said cheerfully.

Even before Margery had closed the door, Meriel was furthering her acquaintance with the cat. It was a comical-looking beast, a female not quite fully grown, with scrubby whiskers and gray fur irregularly splotched with tan. Meriel christened her new companion Kestrel, in memory of Rouge.

Even a mouse in the rushes would have been welcome company, but Kestrel proved to be a rare delight, the friendliest feline Meriel had ever encountered. She slept on Meriel's lap during prayers and meditations, and Meriel had only to lie down on the bed to have Kestrel jump onto her chest, settle down with her paws under her mistress's chin, and begin to vibrate with purrs.

Kestrel adored playing with the end of a rush when Meriel dangled it in front of her, and in the absence of other games the cat would sometimes chase her tail. Regrettably she woke far too early and thrust her inquisitive nose into Meriel's face, but that was a small price to pay for such wonderful company.

Revitalized by her new friend, Meriel thought of another diversion and wove a long, narrow reed mat, then wedged it into the bottom of one of the slit windows so that part of the mat projected outside. Then she tore up her unwanted bread and placed the crumbs on the little platform. Within a day small birds were coming to gobble the bread. At first it was necessary to hold Kestrel back from attacking, but soon the cat learned that hunting birds was not permitted and she did no more than cast an occasional longing eye.

Sometimes a bird accidentally flew in through the window, then hurled itself about the chamber as it sought an exit. Meriel found the shrill cries and battering, self-destructive attempts to escape unbearable, for they were an exact mirror of her own barely suppressed emotions. As soon as possible she would catch the bird, then release it outside.

During her activity-filled days, Meriel told herself that surely she could keep her mind and body strong enough to defy the earl until he had lost interest in her. Yet in the dark, endless nights, she was haunted by the knowledge that the barrier that kept her fears at bay was very frail. And in the shadow of that knowledge lurked desperation.

Several more days passed before Margery made an unexpected visit, her arms piled high with garments. "Lord Adrian had clothing made for you," she said, laying her load on the foot of the bed. "He wants you to change into one of the new gowns and discard your old one. He will send for you shortly."

"My own garments are perfectly satisfactory." Meriel eyed the clothing with the same enthusiasm she would have shown a nest of angry wasps. "You may take these back to his lordship."

Margery looked shocked. "Oh, I couldn't possibly. He's quite reasonable, for a Norman, but he doesn't like to be crossed." She stroked the garment on top longingly. "Besides, these are such lovely things."

"Nonetheless, I do not want them." Seeing the maid's dismay, Meriel continued, "Don't worry, you needn't tell him that. I will myself when he sends for me."

Margery opened her mouth as if to remonstrate, then thought better of it and left, shaking her head.

Meriel stared at the pile of clothing with pursed lips. She had guessed that the earl would woo her with conversation and gifts; did he really think she could be bought by a new gown? She was so irritated that she seriously considered tossing everything out the window, and she went so far as to lift the garments in her arms and carry them across the room. But after a lifetime of frugality, she found it quite impossible to throw good clothing away. Such waste would be a sin.

And as Margery had said, the garments were very lovely. There were two white shifts of the finest, softest linen, one with collar and sleeves embroidered in gold thread. There were also three bliauts, two of wool for daily wear, and one of velvet for great occasions. And the colors! Rich blue, lush green, bright scarlet. There was a heavy crimson mantle trimmed with miniver, two gauzy sendal veils and a jeweled circlet to hold them in place, a girdle threaded with gold, even silk ribbons to weave into her hair in colors matching the gowns. The simplest garment here was finer than the best Meriel had ever had.

It was a wardrobe fit for a princess. Or a whore.

At the thought, she very nearly did pitch everything out the window, but once more her thrifty nature defeated her anger. Instead, she carried the clothing back across the room, then folded the garments one by one and stacked them in a neat pile by the door. Meriel's mood was lightened by Kestrel, who interfered at every opportunity, diving in and out of the clothing and very nearly tearing a delicate veil.

When Meriel was finished with her task, she scratched Kestrel's chin until the cat was purring, then encouraged her friend to sleep under the bed. If the silly beast had the sense to stay there, she would not be noticed by whoever came to collect the prisoner. Then Meriel sat down, eyes closed and hands folded, and attempted to meditate. Calm seemed the best way to prepare for a summons by the disturbing earl.

Only he did not summon her. Instead, a short time later Lord Adrian himself entered. Meriel glanced up, and immediately thought that he was different in some way. Not physically, his silver-fair beauty was unchanged. Yet something about him seemed darker, more strained. Was his struggle with the rival earl going badly, or was something more personal tormenting him?

At sight of his prisoner in her shabby gown, the

earl's face hardened. "Why aren't you wearing what I gave you?"

Meriel stood without haste. "I prefer not to accept your generous gifts, my lord. My own garments are quite suitable to my needs and station."

"Your own garments were shabby to begin with, and now they are in rags. Since I was responsible for the damage, it is only fair that I replace them."

A clever argument, though she did not waste time admiring it. "Had I not attempted to escape, no damage would have been done. You are under no obligation to clothe me, my lord." Meriel paused for emphasis, then added, "Nor do I wish to be under obligation to you."

Her words stirred his unpredictable temper, and he stalked across the room to her. Before Meriel even had time to become alarmed, he grasped the neckline of her faded gown and ripped downward. The fabric tore along the line of the earlier repair and beyond, almost to her knees.

The force of the earl's action jerked Meriel forward and he swiftly caught her shoulders so that she would not fall. She stared up at him, holding her breath as she waited for his next move. She was acutely conscious of the fact that she was covered only by her shift, a garment so worn and patched that it was almost transparent.

The hot, dangerous flare in Lord Adrian's eyes showed that he was equally aware. For a moment his grip on her shoulders tightened, his fingers digging deep. Abruptly he released her. "If you don't change into one of the gowns I gave you, I will tear your shift off also, and I will make no promises about what would happen next." He turned away and headed for the door. "I will return soon, and I expect that you will be decently clothed."

Meriel was left to wonder if she should stand her ground defiantly and refuse to obey, or quietly submit. At length she decided to obey, partly because her own clothing was no longer fit to be worn, but more because his gifts were only symbols, unimportant in themselves. In his present black mood, she would be a fool to anger him needlessly over something trivial.

Once she had decided, she changed quickly, fearful that he would return at any moment. She slipped into the plain shift, unable to repress a shiver of pleasure at how deliciously smooth it was against her skin. Then she pulled on the simplest of the bliauts, the blue one, which had only a narrow band of embroidery edging the neckline and sleeves. The seamstress had guessed well, for the upper part of the garment hugged her figure as closely as if it had been fitted to her.

The girdle must have been intended for a larger woman, for she had to wrap it around her slim waist an extra turn or the fringed ends would have trailed on the floor. She refused to weave the ribbons into her hair, but on impulse she donned the veil and the circlet. Perhaps if she looked more like a lady, he would be less likely to treat her like a round-heeled serf.

Meriel had just finished putting all the clothing, old and new, into the chest when the earl returned. Once more he stopped in the doorway, but this time his expression was so admiring that she blushed and looked down, self-conscious about the close fit of her gown.

"This is how you deserve to look," Lord Adrian said. He crossed to Meriel and put a finger under her chin, lifting it so that she was looking at him. "Why do you fight me, *ma petite?*" he asked softly. "I want to do well by you, but time and again, your actions bring out the devil in me."

Meriel stared at him, unable to believe his words. "How dare you!" she exploded, batting his hand away from her chin. "You have abducted, imprisoned, bullied, and threatened me, yet you have the audacity to blame *me* for your behavior?"

So much for her resolution not to anger him unnecessarily! As Lord Adrian rocked back on his heels, Meriel braced herself, expecting that his temper would dissolve in flames. Instead, he gave an utterly enchanting smile that took the shadows from his eyes. "Of course I am blaming you. That is far more comfortable than admitting that I have been behaving like a perfect ass, which is the only other alternative."

His reaction was so unexpected that Meriel laughed, as much from tension as amusement. "Oh, no one is perfect."

"Very true," he said, his expression serious again, but with humor lingering in his eyes. He was about to say more when Kestrel shot out from under the bed, pounced on an invisible enemy in the rushes, somersaulted over her tail, then skidded to a stop by the earl.

Startled, he looked down, then leaned over and scooped up the cat. Suddenly fearful for the cat's safety, Meriel exclaimed, "Please, don't hurt Kestrel."

Lord Adrian examined his captive, and was rewarded by a raspy pink tongue licking his wrist. Meriel watched with exasperation; Kestrel had no judgment at all. Not only was the cat too foolish to stay safely under the bed, she had to hurl herself at the earl and try to befriend him.

After a moment, Meriel decided that perhaps she had maligned the cat's wisdom, for the earl's dry humor was still in evidence when he said, "I have the lowering feeling that you value this foolish beast more than you do me or anything I might offer you.

"Don't answer that," he added as he set the cat on the floor. "I would rather not know your true opinion just now. It's a beautiful day. Let us go for a walk on the walls."

"Will you force me to go if I do not wish to?" Meriel asked, reckless in her relief.

He regarded her thoughtfully. "No, if you would rather not, I shall not insist."

"Very well. In that case I accept." She walked past him to the door.

He grinned. "You are not entirely a reasonable person yourself, little falcon."

"I never claimed to be. In fact, our parish priest once said that no woman is capable of true reasoning."

"That is the problem with a celibate clergy," Lord Adrian murmured as he opened the door for her. "They forget what the world is really like."

Meriel laughed again as they went down the hall. "Monks who never see women might forget, but priests do not. All those sermons admonishing women to be obedient are examples of priestly wishful thinking."

"Not just priestly, but masculine wishful thinking." He gave her a rueful glance. "I think that most men sometimes wish that women did not have minds of their own."

"Woman was created from man's rib, to stand next to him, not from his feet, to lie under them," she retorted, calling a saying of Mother Rohese's.

He chuckled again and they proceeded amiably to a stairwell that led to the roof. At moments like this, the earl was such pleasant company that it was easy to forget his dark, dangerous side. As she went first up the narrow spiraling steps, she slanted a quick glance back at him and was struck by a startling new thought.

As the daughter of a poor knight, early destined for the nunnery, Meriel had never looked at men as potential mates because she knew she would never marry. Even after leaving Lambourn, marriage was still a distant, unlikely prospect, for it would be years, if ever, before Alan could afford to dower her, and she was by no means sure that she wanted a husband.

But now she found herself wondering how she would feel about her captor under different circumstances. What if Adrian de Lancey was a knight with a single manor rather than an earl, and he had asked for her hand rather than demanded her body? If she had never seen his dark side, might she have desired to have him as a husband?

The answer was a surprising "yes," for Lord Adrian was the most fascinating man she had ever met. Apart from his strange and threatening obsession with her, he was intelligent and reasonable, with unexpected humor and undeniable charm. He had even been amused by Kestrel. And though she feared his ardor and loathed what he was doing to her, there was something secretly satisfying about his interest. Men had always treated Meriel like a little sister in need of protection or a lady too virtuous to insult with passion. The earl made her feel, for the first time in her life, that she was a desirable woman.

She sighed and concentrated on climbing the steps, knowing that such speculation was singularly profitless. She was the earl's prisoner, not his guest, and his intentions were strictly—and dangerously—dishonorable. Even if he knew her as Lady Meriel de Vere, they would have been hopelessly divided by circumstances as well as politics. Her family was at the bottom of the Normal social scale; in worldly terms, the de Veres were much closer to their own English villeins than to the great Norman barons. Lord Adrian's bride was already chosen, and she came from a family whose wealth and power equaled his.

As they stepped out onto the parapet that circled the edge of the keep, she set aside her bleak thoughts, wanting to appreciate every moment in the open air. A brisk wind was blowing and her veil billowed up, the swirling silk temporarily blinding her. Lord Adrian came to her rescue and neatly caught the veil, twisted it loosely, then tucked the rolled fabric under the back of her girdle.

Meriel thanked him, amused that his hand hadn't even lingered on her backside. He was certainly on his good behavior today. Then she looked at her surroundings with pleasure. The roof of the keep was the highest point of the castle, and the castle itself was set on

a high thrust of rock. They had come onto the roof
facing east, overlooking the castle wards, the village,
and the Shropshire hills. How many miles was it to
Avonleigh? She suppressed a sigh. "What a wonderful
view you have from here. I have never been so high
above the earth."

"It is beautiful," he agreed, "and also practical. A
lookout here can see a very long way."

Meriel glanced about and saw that there was indeed
a guard. The young man nodded respectfully to his
lord, then withdrew beyond earshot to the other end
of the roof.

They strolled around the perimeter of the keep until
they came to the side facing the river. Meriel leaned
between the crenellations to peer over the edge of the
wall, then gasped at how sheer the descent was. "If I
dropped a pebble, I think it would go straight down
into the river."

The earl nodded. "Very likely. The cliff below here
is almost as steep as the castle wall."

She knit her brows, calculating. "We must be just
above your chamber. Why did you build the keep on
the very edge of the cliff rather than in the center of
the peninsula? Is there some good defensive reason?"

"No." He leaned on top of one of the upthrust merlons, his arms crossed as he watched the river. "I just
liked the idea that I could look this way and not see
walls and men-at-arms."

"I see what you mean," Meriel said, feasting her
eyes on the peaceful flowing water. At the far right a
water gate led from the river to the castle postern, and
in the distance she saw two fishermen in a small boat,
but there was no other sign of man or his works. It
was very different from the bustling view in the other
direction.

She glanced at the earl's still profile. He wore his
quiet, ascetic face again, his thoughts turned inward,
his danger leashed, his hair bright as pale polished
gold in the sunshine. Except for his height, which was

only moderate, he exactly fulfilled the fair, gray-eyed Norman ideal of beauty. Perhaps someday he would have daughters lucky enough to inherit his good looks.

After a lazy, comfortable interval, Meriel remarked. "No one could ever attack Warfield from this side."

"Not true." Lord Adrian gestured toward the cliff. "To prove to my men that no castle is impregnable, I once climbed up from the river, and if I could, others can as well."

Startled, she looked at the water far below, then back at her companion. "You're joking."

"God's own truth," he assured her. "I did it at night, without alerting anyone to expect attack. I didn't try to come all the way up here, though. I chose a spot under the curtain wall, which was much easier to breach."

"Sweet Mary!" she exclaimed, appalled. "You could have been killed. Why did you do such a thing?"

"I probably would have survived a fall to the river. As to why"—he smiled faintly—"when the guard who had been careless in his watching found my dagger at his throat, it impressed him—and all his fellows—much more than words ever could have."

"You didn't kill the man, did you?"

"Of course not. That would have wasted the lesson."

Meriel studied the earl uncertainly, unsure whether his words were proof of ice-cold blood or desert-dry humor. Perhaps he had both. "In spite of your assurances, I still have trouble believing that anyone could climb up here."

He shrugged. "Even the sheerest of cliffs has cracks and projections. If you have climbed to take eyases from their nests, you should know that."

She shook her head. "I've never climbed such a cliff—when we were taking eyases, my brother would lower me from the top with a rope." Thinking of the distance to the river, she shivered. "Much easier that way."

The golden brows arched. "Your brother permitted you to risk your life like that?"

"I was quite safe. And it was necessary, since I was hardly strong enough to lower *him* down the cliff."

His expression was bemused. "Apparently the stories about the wild Welsh are true."

"Indeed they are, my lord, as wild as they are free." She looked beyond the river, toward the distant Welsh mountains. "Wales will never bow to the Normans."

"You are wrong. No matter how brave your people are—and they are brave, insanely so—in the long run they will lose, because they are a nation divided, too independent to accept one king as their overlord." He shook his head. "Too much of Wales's courage, too many precious lives, are spent by petty princelings fighting their brothers for greater shares of their inheritance."

"It is more just for all of a man's sons to inherit equally," Meriel said sharply, thinking of her own two brothers. "Where is the justice in the Norman way, where the eldest inherits everything and his younger brothers are scarcely more than beggars?"

"Dividing the patrimony equally may be more just," he conceded, "but less wise. There is no war more bitter than that among brothers. The Norman custom creates strength for everyone. Look how England has suffered under a weak ruler. And who suffers most? The common people, who have no stone walls to hide behind. Yet they are the wealth of the land. Without men to till the soil, the whole society is beggared." Lord Adrian's expression was grim, perhaps in memory of what he had seen in the years of civil war. "When England has a strong king again, northern Wales will be conquered as the south already has been. It is only the wildness of the mountains that has enabled the north to remain unvanquished for this long. And though you will not agree with me, Wales will be better for Norman rule."

"Never, my lord. Freedom is in our blood." Meriel

was infuriated by his words. She had always admired the spirit of her mother's kinfolk, and as the earl spoke she forgot that she herself was half-Norman—for the moment, she was pure Celt. "A true child of Wales would rather die than live in chains."

He studied her gravely. "I have the feeling that the conversation had just moved from the political to the personal."

"Very discerning of you." His assertion that her mother's people would be better for being ruled by the Normans was as arrogant as his belief that she would be better for being ruled by him, and the anger that had been building since her capture erupted. "How long do you intend to hold me prisoner, Lord Adrian?" Meriel challenged. "I have been charged with no crime, tried in no court. I swear that I will not change my mind about being your mistress, any more than my Welsh brethren will concede that the Normans are destined to conquer them and hand over their swords without a fight."

His gray eyes were as inexorable as cold steel. "I will hold you for as long as necessary to persuade you to stay of your own free will."

"Outrageous!" she exclaimed, then reined her temper in a little, hoping that logic might work where fury would not. "You seem to be an intelligent man, Lord Adrian, and a learned one. You very nearly became a monk, and by your own testimony left the cloister only from necessity." Her eyes narrowed. "Where is your morality? More than that, where is your pride? How can you bear to let yourself be ruled by lust? I am an insignificant female, without wealth or birth or beauty. Ravishing me will not add to your reputation as a lover, nor have I a courtesan's skills to drown your senses in passion."

The air between them pulsed with tension. "What I feel for you is nothing so simple as lust," he said softly. "To me you are unique and irreplaceable, and I will not let you go. I have said as much before, but apparently you did not believe me.'' His voice hardened. "The sooner you accept that I mean what I say, the sooner you can come to terms with your future.''

Meriel stared, aghast. "If I truly believed that you intend to imprison me forever, I would throw myself over that wall.''

He stepped forward swiftly and grasped her upper arm. "I trust that you do not mean that, but I will take no chances. It is time you returned to your room.''

"My dungeon,'' she snapped, flinging the words over her shoulder as the earl shepherded her down the twisting stone stairs. "If I were to submit because of your threats, would it be any less rape than submitting because of your sword?''

He did not reply and there was no more speech until they arrived back in her chamber. When they were inside and he had shut the door behind them, he released her and she whirled to face him again.

"Even if I were fool enough to want to be your mistress, what kind of future would I have? Will your wife be so compliant that she will let you keep your leman under the same roof? Or would you imprison me elsewhere in the castle, to spare her pride? What would you do about your bastard children?'' Meriel threw her hands up in exasperation. "You are a practical man, my lord earl. What are the answers to these practical questions?''

She saw shame and guilt in his eyes and guessed that beneath his arrogance there was still some honesty, perhaps even a trace of conscience. At length he said, "You would always be honored and protected, as would any children.''

"A whore's wages,'' she said with contempt. "I will never come to you willingly, my lord, and the sooner *you* accept *that,* the sooner you will be able to think about *your* future, about the suitable Norman heiress you will take to wive.''

His mouth twisted with wry admiration. "You have

the mad courage of a goshawk. Most women would be quaking in fear.''

"What good would fear do?" Meriel said bitterly. "You are a lord in your own castle and can do anything you wish, but rape will not make me any more willing than I am now. Quite the contrary."

"As I said before, I have no interest in forcing you." He stared at her with the intensity he might have used on an opponent in battle. "You are stubborn, but so am I, and I will wait as long as necessary. In time, you will change your mind."

Meriel met his stare with equal intensity. "Mark my words, my lord earl. You can rape me, you can murder me, you can break my body in a thousand ways, but I will be of no value to you broken." Her voice dropped to a chilling whisper. "And I vow on my mother's grave that you will never make me bend."

8

FROM THE MOMENT Adrian had met Meriel, unruly desire had frayed his hard-won control. Now, as she cried her defiance, standing straight and proud and infinitely desirable, the last frail threads of restraint snapped and the dark demons of violence raced through his veins. "Damn you," he swore, "if you will not bend, then I have no choice but to break you."

Meriel was no longer a woman to be won, but an enemy to be vanquished. Beyond thought, beyond conscience, beyond everything but the overwhelming need to conquer, Adrian closed the distance between them with one long step and lifted her in his arms, then hurled her into the middle of the feather mattress. He followed her down, pinning her slim body beneath him. With rough, impatient hands, he tore open a seam of her bliaut, then ripped the shift beneath.

Meriel fought him in grim silence, not bothering to cry for help in her attacker's own castle. She twisted and clawed with surprising strength, and when he raised himself to unfasten his chausses she brought her knee up savagely, almost managing to smash him in the groin.

Adrian's battle-sharpened instinct saved him and he twisted away so that her knee hit his thigh. Before she could strike again, he threw his body over her so that she could not move, then struggled until with one hand he pinned both her wrists to the bed. "It will be easier for you if you don't fight me," he said, panting for breath.

''Never!'' Meriel's voice was scarcely a whisper, but she was undefeated. Their faces were inches apart, and he saw that her blue eyes held an unholy blend of defiance and despair.

He reached down and caught the hem of her bliaut and raised it, along with her shift, then stroked her thigh, his hand gentling when he touched her silken skin.

As his hand moved upward, Meriel shuddered, but did not plead or beg or cry. Instead, her voice breaking, she gasped, *''Holy Mary, Mother of God, pray for us sinners now and at the hour of our death.''*

To Adrian, her despairing words were like a knife in his belly. He wanted to force his mouth over hers, to silence her so that she could not waken his honor, but it was too late. Now when he looked in her face he saw not just the features of Meriel, but those of the sorrowing Virgin, the all-loving, all-forgiving mother who interceded with God on behalf of wicked mankind.

Though his body and soul burned with need and no one but Meriel could quench the fire that threatened to consume him, Adrian could not continue. With sickening clarity, he knew that rape would be more than an unpardonable sin against Meriel; it would also destroy forever the part of him that was capable of tenderness, and would condemn him to a hell beyond any hope of love or forgiveness.

Trembling, he released Meriel and stood. ''Jesus Christ,'' he gasped, his voice a desperate prayer. ''Sweet Jesus, help me.''

Words could not begin to relieve his madness. Convulsively he turned and grabbed the chest at the foot of Meriel's bed and hurled it into the stone wall with all his strength, his muscles straining to the limit, his voice a howl of wordless anguish. The chest broke with a thunderous boom as the iron bands split. Then it crashed to the floor, bright fabrics spilling onto the rushes.

The destruction relieved a little of the tumult within

him, but not enough, not nearly enough. Adrian turned and his gaze met that of Meriel, whose blue eyes were wide with shock and horror. "Forgive me," he whispered. "Forgive me, little falcon."

Then he swept from the room, automatically locking the door behind him. Earlier he had planned to spend the afternoon on the training ground, testing the skills of the older squires, but to do that now was out of the question. In his present crazed mood he would kill one of them.

To pray for peace was impossible. Only action might relieve his fury, so blindly he headed to the stables. Those members of his household who saw him took one look at the molten rage on his face, then stepped quickly from his path.

After saddling Gideon, Adrian rode out, barely managing to hold the horse's pace in until they were clear of the crowded bailey. Once they were free of the castle and village, he turned Gideon loose and they raced north, the horse responding to his master's madness with a wild, heedless gallop.

Adrian had no idea how long he rode, relying on the horse's instinct to save them both from breaking their necks, but when he finally slowed, Gideon was badly blown, his black coat lathered with foam, and Adrian himself was little better. His mind churned with horror and disgust at what he had done, yet even now, he was not free of desire. He still wanted Meriel with an intensity that was pain. But everything he had done since they had met had pushed her further and further away, and after today he doubted that he could ever induce her to trust him. God knew that he did not trust himself.

When the first wild fury had faded to weary self-disgust, Adrian pulled his horse in and looked for landmarks to determine how far he had come. It took him only a moment to realize that there had been a method to his madness, for he was within a mile of the home of Olwen, his former mistress.

Several times a year he would call on her when he was in the area. Though they had not been lovers since she had wed her miller, Brun, they had remained friends. Olwen was a woman with a gift for contentment. Happy in her marriage, she was always a pleasure to visit, a soothing contrast to his usual life. Because she was a woman and Adrian trusted her, he could speak to her of things he would never mention to another man. And today of all days, he craved her wisdom and kindness.

The miller was an important man in the community, and Brun's cottage was larger than most and set at a distance from the village, near the mill itself but with no other buildings within sight. When Adrian rode up to the cottage, he was grateful to see Olwen working alone outside, with none of her stepchildren in attendance. She was brewing, her brown braids falling forward as she leaned over the great kettle, but at the sound of his horse she looked up, then gave a broad smile of recognition. "Greetings, my lord," she said cheerfully.

Adrian had meant to behave properly, but that resolution went by the wayside at the sight of her affectionate welcome. Without speaking he dismounted, tethered Gideon, and took Olwen in his arms. At first she stiffened in surprise, but almost immediately she sensed that he sought not sex but comfort. Her arms went around him. "Ah, lad, something's wrong, isn't it?" she said softly, then leaned her head against his.

For a long time it was impossible to answer. He simply held her close, needing her warmth and acceptance.

Olwen was almost as tall as he and had always been as plump and pretty as a young partridge, but as his chaotic emotions calmed, Adrian realized that she was rounder than usual. Loosening his embrace, he asked, "You are with child?"

"Aye," she said happily, patting her growing belly.

"Who would have thought an old woman like me would finally learn the knack of it?"

The news was a shock. Olwen had thought herself barren, not having conceived in her first marriage or in her years as Adrian's mistress, but apparently Brun had succeeded where the other men had failed. For the first time Adrian wondered if he himself was incapable of fathering a child. It was a painful thought in a day that was already disastrous.

But for Olwen, who was over thirty and had long despaired of having a babe of her own, the event was one of great joy. He smiled and kissed her lightly on the forehead. "Congratulations. I am very happy for you."

"You mustn't think 'twas your fault I never conceived," she said, direct as a blade. " 'Tis obvious I'm a mare that is not easily bred."

He had to laugh. "Olwen, I hope you never change." In spite of the time that had passed, she knew him better than anyone. "If you wish, I will stand godfather to the child."

Her first reaction was pleasure, but then she frowned. " 'Twould be a great honor, but people may get the wrong idea if you do."

"Perhaps you should discuss it with Brun," Adrian agreed. "Even if you prefer that I not be godfather, you know I will be pleased to look after the child's interests as it grows."

"Aye, I know." She gave a fond smile. "Brun's eldest, the one you helped into the abbey at Shrewsbury, has become such a scholar. You'd not know he was just a village boy."

"He's an intelligent lad and deserved the opportunity to study. Perhaps in time he will come back to the village as priest."

"Ah, that would be something, wouldn't it? But it's early days yet, he is but a student." She turned her head at a bubbling sound. "Will you excuse me for a moment, my lord? The water is boiling and I must pour it in with the malt.''

"Let me do it,'' he offered.

'' 'Twould not be fitting, my lord,'' she said, scandalized. "I'm no delicate lady who cannot lift a pot.''

Adrian chuckled and helped anyhow, carrying the hot water to the kettle and pouring it slowly under her direction. Olwen stirred the mixture with her besom, explaining that this particular clump of broom was responsible for the fact that she made the best ale in the whole village of Shepreth, for she'd been using it for years. To prove her claim, she poured two tankards from her last batch, and they settled companionably on a crude wooden bench that Brun had built under a chestnut tree. Olwen kept an eye on her brewing while they talked easily of things that didn't matter.

His former mistress was the reason that Adrian spoke English so well, for a bed made a fine schoolroom. More than language, from her he had also learned much about how the common folk thought and felt, and the knowledge had made him a better lord than if he had stayed only within the circle of Norman nobility. Perhaps now she could give him some insight into Meriel.

Though his mood eased, Adrian was unable to broach the subject of his distress until Olwen said, "You looked sore troubled when you arrived. Might it have something to do with the maid you have at the castle?''

He shot her a startled look. "How do you know about Meriel?''

"The lord's doings are of interest to everyone.'' Olwen chuckled. "One of the Shepreth girls serves at the castle and she told everyone about your new mistress when she visited her family a few days hence. She has long hoped you would take her to your bed, and it's jealous she is. A pretty wench, but vain.''

Adrian sipped his ale thoughtfully. He tended to forget how visible his doings were. Or perhaps he preferred not to think of it. "Meriel is not my mistress."

"And that is the problem?"

He looked up, his rueful gaze meeting her hazel eyes. "You know too much."

"I know very little, my lord, just a bit of gossip, and likely most of that wrong."

"Do you think you can forgo calling me 'my lord' for a little while?" he asked, thinking it would be easier if they recaptured some of their old closeness.

"Very well, Adrian," she said quietly. "Will you tell me about your Meriel?"

"She's not my Meriel, though it's not for want of trying." He gazed into the tankard, as if divining the future in its amber depths. "I know almost nothing of her. She has the look of the Welsh and speaks their tongue, but she speaks English equally well. I doubt that she's a serf—perhaps she is daughter to a Welsh smallholder or a merchant. She is not from this part of Shropshire, for I made inquiries throughout the area and no one knew of her. Yet no one remembers seeing her at the abbey where she claimed to have stayed while journeying from Wales. She has told me very little, and even that seems to be lies."

"What is she like?"

He shrugged. "Small. Black hair as straight as rain, blue eyes to drown in. Not beautiful, but very . . ." He searched for the right word. "Winsome."

Olwen shifted on the bench and rubbed her back, which tended to ache these days. "I didn't mean what she looks like, but what she herself is like."

Adrian sighed and leaned back against the chestnut tree. "That is harder. Intelligent. Lively. Sweet and good-natured, except when I am abusing her."

"You have abused her?" Olwen, who had known only kindness from Adrian, had trouble believing that.

He swallowed hard, the tendons in his throat tautly visible. "Olwen, earlier this afternoon I almost raped her. It was so close, so very, very close. And though

I stopped in time, I did terrify her, which is almost as bad.'' He closed his eyes, shuddering, then went back to the beginning. ''I found her in the forest with a falcon and a game bag and used that as an excuse to hold her in the castle. When I told her I wanted her as a mistress, she was appalled. I thought that she would reconsider in time—she claimed to have no sweetheart or close family, nothing that would call her elsewhere.''

He sighed and kneaded his temples with one hand. ''I tried to move slowly, to let her come to know me better, but the more I saw of her, the less I could bear the thought of losing her. As a result, the more I bullied her. She is like a . . . a madness in my blood. Yet the fault is not in Meriel, she is innocent. The madness is in me.''

Olwen watched him with pity. She was a simple woman and had never really understood the complicated depths of Adrian's nature, but she knew that he was a man who asked much of himself, always forcing his body and mind to the limit to achieve what must be done, more forgiving of others than of his own human weakness. Years of such demands had taken their toll on him. Now it seemed that a little Welsh girl had pierced the walls he had built around himself and found her way into his heart. ''Is it just that you want to lie with her?'' she asked, testing her theory. ''Might another wench do as well?''

''If only that were true.'' He ran his fingers through his bright hair distractedly. ''That kind of desire I can control well enough. No, I want more than that from her.''

''In other words, you are in love with her.''

''In love? I don't want to write songs about how I languish for her glances.'' He spoke slowly, trying to define something new and alien. ''From the first moment I saw her, I felt that . . . that she was a missing part of me. That I would never know peace again unless she was near.'' He laughed bitterly. ''Instead, I haven't known a moment's peace since I met her.''

"That sounds like love to me, Adrian. You have never found time for much love in your life, which is why it hurts so much now." She sighed, a little envious of this young woman who affected him in such a way. He had never pined for Olwen like this. "There is an easy solution, my dear. Marry her."

"Marry her?" His head swiveled around in astonishment.

"Aye. There is no law against marrying a common-born woman, you know." Olwen's gaze was challenging. "You already have great wealth and power. Do you really need a wife who will bring you more?"

There was a long silence while Adrian weighed her words, his light eyes blank and unreadable. "You must think me a fool not to have seen such an obvious answer."

"No more a fool than most men," she replied, then tilted her head back to empty her ale pot. "Marriage is a practical business—even the poorest serf weighs what the other will bring to the match. Having been raised to consider your obligation to your name and family, it's not surprising that you forgot to consider your obligation to yourself. But if the lass brings you peace of mind, that is a dowry beyond price."

His expression darkened. "I'm not sure that offering marriage will persuade her to accept me. Meriel may no more want me for a husband than for a lover."

Olwen's gaze drifted down Adrian's lean frame, from gilt hair to well-muscled legs, recalling what it had been like when all of that beautiful masculine strength had been focused on and in her. At the thought, she felt a little shiver of remembered delight. It was quite impossible to believe that any poor girl would turn down a man who was handsome, wealthy, powerful, and mad for her as well. "Ask her and find out. I guarantee that offering marriage will make a difference in her opinion. A modest godly girl with sense will hesitate to become a mistress, but to be a wife is very different. An offer to wed is a much greater compliment than a simple invitation to lie with you."

"Meriel is not a woman like any other." His smile was crooked. "She hates me, I think, and with good reason."

"Has she always acted as if she hated you?"

Adrian thought back over the times he and Meriel had been together. "No, there were moments of ease and amusement between us, when she seemed not ill-pleased to be in my company."

"There you are, then, a basis to be lovers and friends." Olwen nodded approvingly. "And didn't St. Paul himself say that it is better to marry than to burn?"

Adrian laughed, feeling lighter and freer than he had in years. "He did indeed. Lord knows I've been burning, and the prospect of wedding Meriel seems like heaven itself in contrast."

Olwen grinned, but added more seriously, "You know that your own kind, the Norman lords, will think you have run mad if you marry a common English girl."

"I know. But none save the empress have any right to censor my actions, and she needs my support more than I need hers." He leaned forward and impulsively kissed his companion. "You're a marvel, Olwen. Thank you."

He glanced up and saw that the miller was just returning home from his work. Brun halted at the sight of the earl, his expression wary and sullen. Adrian stood without haste, understanding the miller's resentment. A poor man had no recourse if the lord came after the man's wife. While Adrian had no reputation for seducing his tenants, Olwen was different, for everyone knew what they had been to each other. "Good day, Brun. I was congratulating Olwen on her condition. It seems that you're a better man than I."

The miller was too cautious to comment directly, but his expression eased at the earl's self-deprecating remark. "Aye, we're all pleased, especially my youngest, who looks forward to having someone smaller than her.'' He glanced fondly at his wife. ''Did you wish to speak to me, my lord?''

''No, I just called to say hello to Olwen. Take good care of her, Brun.'' Adrian swung up onto the stallion. ''Good day to you both.'' Then he rode off, wondering what was the best way to offer marriage to a woman whom one has gravely wronged.

After Lord Adrian stormed out of her room, Meriel curled up on her bed, her chilled body shaking and her breath coming in rough gasps. She had secretly thought that the virgin martyrs who had chosen death before dishonor were a little unreasonable, particularly Saint Catherine, said to have turned down the emperor Maxentius' offer of honorable marriage. If all women chose virginity, what would happen to mankind?

But now Meriel understood that the true horror was not loss of virginity in itself, but the violation of spirit that accompanied the rape of the body. And there was a special horror in the fact that the earl was not a wholly evil man. There was a bright, endearing part of him that fascinated her, but the dark side of his nature was stronger.

Lord Adrian was mad, possessed of the devil, and the madness was growing stronger every day. A small part of Meriel could still find compassion for him. It must be a foretaste of hell to feel one's will and honor shredding away, overcome by one's own wickedest impulses; she had seen that from the frantic pain in the earl's face before he had left.

But much stronger than her compassion was her fear, for the mental wall that she had used to keep panic at bay had shattered. Today the earl had come within a hair's breadth of losing control. It was just a matter of time until his will broke, and then he would break her. Perhaps, if she was fortunate, she would die of the assault, but more likely she would survive to be assaulted again and again.

The earl had said he would never let her go, and

finally she believed him. For whatever mad reason, he would keep her captive, like a songbird in a cage, and soon she would be too defeated to care what he did to her. She would be a prisoner until she died of her imprisonment, and the prospect was a horror that made death pale by comparison.

Kestrel jumped on the bed and meowed curiously, then came over and nudged her mistress's nose. Meriel wrapped her arm around the cat and pulled the little animal's warm body close. Almost immediately Kestrel fell asleep, snoring softly, but Meriel could not rest. Her mind still churned, replaying the terror of what had happened, and fearing what was to come.

She wondered what would be the worst aspect of her fate. Would it be the loss of dignity? The physical pain? Perhaps being forced to bear the child of a madman? No, the worst part would be her captivity itself. Never again would she know the freedom of the open sky, the liberty to walk and talk as she chose, the simple exercise of her will.

Meriel opened her eyes and stared at the stone walls with hatred. Then she shuddered, experiencing the same illusion she had known at Lambourn: that the walls were moving in to crush the life and breath from her. But this time, no decision of hers would free her— she was at the mercy of another's will, and that was the worst horror of all.

Her heart pounded and her breath came in ragged gasps as Meriel fought the spiraling descent into madness. *It would be better to be dead.* If she had still had her knife, she would have turned the blade on herself, but it had been taken away when she was captured.

She recoiled, appalled by her thoughts. To kill oneself was a mortal sin. Suicide would condemn her to endless damnation, an eternity of flame and anguish. It was unthinkable.

Yet the blessed Ursula had stabbed herself in the heart to escape from being ravished, and she had been made a saint. Perhaps suicide was permitted in the defense of one's virginity? Wearily Meriel tried to puzzle it out, but she could remember no priest addressing the question.

Hours passed as she wavered between fearing what suicide would cost her soul, and possible means to achieve that end. Perhaps she could hang herself with the girdle he had given her? But there was nothing to tie it around.

Periodically she tried to convince herself that her situation must improve, that Lord Adrian would tire of his uninteresting captive and release her to freedom. But she did not believe that; to the very marrow of her bones, she knew that in some mysterious way they were bound together.

Freedom . . . it was as close as the sky outside her window, as distant as the length of her life. As dry sobs shook her body, Meriel wondered despairingly if she would ever be free again.

When Margery arrived with Meriel's supper, she looked at the prisoner with shock and asked some question, but Meriel ignored her and soon the maid went away. Eventually Meriel rose and placed the food on the floor for Kestrel to eat. With numb fingers she removed her torn finery and donned her old shift and bliaut. Then she lay down again, dully wishing she could sleep.

It was still light when the key turned in the door again, and the sound roused Meriel from her stupor enough to fear that it was the earl returning. Instead, it was a man-at-arms that she did not recognize. "Please come with me, mistress."

Slowly she stood. There was no sensation in her hands as she reflexively smoothed her gown, then followed him down the hall to Lord Adrian's chamber. The sun was low in the sky and a flood of golden light poured in the great window, but it did not warm her.

The earl himself awaited, standing behind his desk a safe distance away. He spoke and she made an effort to follow his words. He was stiffly apologizing for his behavior. Of course. He was always sorry for what he had done.

Lord Adrian came around his desk and she forced herself to stand still, not retreat. Strange how a man so comely could be so dangerous. He was still talking, but his words streamed by like the wind.

Then Meriel noticed the sheathed dagger on his belt and she felt a spark of interest. If he came close enough, might she be able to snatch it from him? She would have to move swiftly.

According to legend, Saint Ursula had pierced herself in the breast, but Meriel was dubious—too many ribs in the way. And if she didn't strike true, she might not have time for a second attempt. Better to cut her throat. Perhaps she would feel pain, but no matter. Soon she would feel nothing at all. Except, God willing, free.

Adrian raised his voice a little. "Meriel, have you heard anything I have said?"

He had thought that her blank stare was a way of ignoring him, but as he drew closer he saw that her deep blue eyes were as empty as the sky and guessed that she had withdrawn to some corner of her mind where nothing could harm her.

His guilt twisted deep inside him. He wanted to touch her but dared not for fear of distressing her further. *Set her free.* If she refused his offer of marriage, he would have no choice but to obey that internal command and let her go, even if she took his soul with her.

He stopped an arm's length away. Meriel did not move or flinch, simply looked straight ahead, her eyes at the level of his chest. She was dressed like a beggar in her old clothing, but to Adrian she was still the essence of womanly grace.

It was hard to speak in the complete absence of response, but doggedly he began again. "Meriel, I've wronged you from the moment I met you. I did not have good cause to take you prisoner at the beginning, and there was even less cause to keep you here, except that I was . . . greatly attracted to you.'' Impossible to say the word "love" when she stood as still as stone. "I tried to convince myself that . . ."

Before he could finish the sentence, Meriel moved with a speed he would not have believed possible, her hand darting out to seize his dagger and wrest it from the sheath. She stepped back and raised the weapon. For a critical moment Adrian fell into a defensive posture, sure that she intended to stab him and determined to reclaim the dagger without harming her.

Instead, under his appalled gaze, she plunged the dagger toward her own throat. Adrian leapt forward and grabbed her wrist before she could complete the slash. She had the strength of desperation but he was able to divert her arm so that the tip of the blade only snagged her gown.

"If you will not let me go, then for pity's sake, let me die!" Meriel begged. Her eyes were alive now, wild with despair as she struggled to escape his grip.

"Meriel, you must not hurt yourself," Adrian said desperately. "I swear I will not keep you captive any longer." Hating the necessity, he twisted her slender wrist until her fingers loosened and the dagger dropped behind her and skidded away.

As earnest of his good intentions, he released her, then promptly blurted out what he had intended to work toward gradually. "I want you for my wife."

Her great expressive eyes widened, stunned. "You want to marry me?"

"Yes, both because I care for you, and to make amends for what I have done." He felt a moment of relief as he saw her expression change. Olwen had been right; offering marriage made a difference. "You would be the Countess of Shropshire, with all the honor and respect due my wife."

She took a step back, then another, and he abruptly realized that her expression was not pleasure but rising hysteria. "Sweet Mother of God, you want to *marry* me!" she burst out. "Then I would never be free of

you, would I? Jesu, I should have let you rape me!
Then I would have had the hope that you would tire of
me. If you turned me over to your guardroom to amuse
your men, someday I might have been able to escape.

"*Don't come near me!*" she screamed as Adrian
made an involuntary movement toward her.

Adrian froze, not wanting to alarm her any further.
"Meriel, please, calm yourself," he said softly. "I
swear before God that I will never hurt you or coerce
you again."

"You have been sorry for your actions before, then
come back and done worse the next time," she scoffed,
retreating farther.

The fallen dagger was now within her reach. Afraid
to risk her seizing it again, Adrian threw himself forward in a shallow dive and swept the weapon from her
reach.

Thinking that he was attacking, Meriel darted away.
As Adrian hit the floor rolling, he looked up and saw
her frantic eyes as she glanced about the room, desperate to find escape.

"I will never be caged again. Never!" Meriel's flight
had taken her into the glare of light that poured through
the window. Like a flower she turned to look into the
setting sun, her face illuminated with unbearable
poignancy. Then she smiled, her expression transcendent, as if she had just been offered the keys of heaven.

Opening her arms as if to a lover, Meriel raced
across the room toward the giant leaded-glass window.
Time seemed to slow, every moment stretching lan-
guidly as Adrian watched her spring onto the window
seat. She was graceful as a doe, her movements so
lovely to behold that she seemed to be performing
some exotic dance.

Without slowing for an instant, Meriel raised her
right arm before her face and hurled herself headfirst
into the window.

9

THE SCENE in front of Adrian was an image from hell. Outside the sky blazed with the orange and gold fire of sunset. Silhouetted in the center of the window was Meriel, her slim figure suspended in time and space. It seemed as if he could reach out his hand and pluck her from the sky with one leisurely gesture.

"Meriel, don't!" he shouted, scrambling to his feet and racing forward to stop her, but he was too slow, a lifetime too slow.

Her body arced and tilted forward at the same time that the sound of shattering glass struck his ears. Then she was gone. Shards of splintered glass and twisted lead strips edged the gaping hole, and a gentle breeze blew through the broken window.

For an endless instant Adrian felt paralyzed, unable to accept what had happened before his very eyes. Then, with a wordless cry of anguish, he reached the window and looked down, thrusting his head through the gaping hole Meriel had made.

The water below the castle was very deep, and from its churning he saw that she had struck several feet out from the cliff face. Meriel had not yet resurfaced, and in her heavy woolen garments, perhaps she would not. If she was still alive, she was surely unconscious from her plunge through the glass and the impact with the water. If she was not dead yet, she would be within minutes.

It would take a long time, too long, to go down through the castle to the river and find a boat. By the time he did that, she would be beyond help or hope.

But Adrian was a powerful swimmer, and if he went after her there might be a chance. Without making a conscious decision, he stripped his clothing off, his fingers fumbling with haste, then wrapped his tunic around his arm and enlarged the open area of window so he would not be shredded by broken glass.

He paused before he jumped, marking where Meriel had gone down. The height was great, but if he dived cleanly he should be able to retain consciousness when he hit the water. And if he did not and drowned also, it would be better than living with the knowledge of what he had done.

Adrian spent one instant on prayer, a short, violently intense invocation to the Blessed Mother, that she might spare Meriel. Then he launched himself headfirst into the air. The evening wind chilled his naked body as he arrowed down in an endless fall. He heard a shocked shout from the castle walls as a guard saw him.

Then Adrian struck, cleaving the water with an impact that knocked the air from his lungs and took him far below the surface, almost to the bottom of the river. As he turned and swam upward, he opened his eyes, searching for Meriel. When he reached the surface he dived again as soon as his lungs filled with air, exploring the area between where he had dived and the cliff, allowing for the current, which would be taking her downriver. Thank God that at this season the water was fairly clear.

Lungs burning, he dived twice more before he found her. The weight of her heavy clothing kept Meriel from rising, and she floated half a dozen feet below the surface like an enchanted doll. Her eyes were open and sightless and her twining hair and garments drifted around her. There was an expression of dreamy peace on her face.

Adrian looped his arm around her chest and kicked for the surface. When they broke into the air, he held Meriel's head above the water while scanning the shore to see how far the current had carried them. They were well below the castle, but he saw men shouting from the shore, and farther up the river someone was launching a boat.

Wearily he began swimming toward the river's edge. The water was shallower here, and as he neared the shore two men plunged into the river and waded out to assist him. Adrian recognized them as Warfield fishermen. "Don't mind me, do what you can for her," he gasped.

One of the fishermen laid Meriel facedown on the grass and pressed rhythmically on her back until water gushed from her mouth. He continued pressing until no more water came, then held his palm in front of her mouth. "Don't think she's breathing, my lord," he said grimly.

Concerned with the earl's dignity, the other fisherman took off his own tunic and pulled it over Adrian's head. The man was burly and the garment hung in copious folds, but the warmth was welcome in the chilly dusk. Adrian knelt beside Meriel, feeling helpless, then thought to put his hand on her throat. Her pulse still beat, though it was weak and thready.

What happened next was pure instinct. Since Meriel needed breath, he should share his with her. Adrian took a deep breath, then leaned over and forced air into her mouth. Her lips were cold as death. When he raised his head, he pressed on her chest and another thin trickle of water came from her mouth. Once more he forced air into her mouth, and this time she coughed convulsively, then began to breathe on her own.

Weak with relief, Adrian closed his eyes and bent his head, uttering his prayerful thanks that Meriel still lived. Blood stained her hair and saturated clothing, so there were injuries, perhaps serious ones.

But for the moment, God be thanked, she lived.

After a long hard ride, Richard FitzHugh arrived at Warfield in early evening and found the castle lying under hushed, expectant silence. He sent his men off to find themselves food and sleeping space, but he immediately sought out Sir Walter of Evesham, whose urgent message had brought Richard to Warfield.

As Richard entered the solar, Sir Walter's tired face lightened. "Thank God you've come."

"What has happened?" Richard said sharply as he peeled off his gloves. "You said Adrian was in dire straits. Is he ill?"

"Not exactly." Sir Walter signaled to a serving man to pour wine, then sent the man off for food. "Do you remember that girl we found in the royal forest? The one with the falcon?"

Richard nodded. "Of course. Pretty little thing. Named Meriel, wasn't she?" He drank deeply of his wine. "At the time I was surprised that Adrian took her into custody for so little cause, but I presumed he had his reasons."

"Aye, his loins were on fire for her," the old knight said with disgust. "He's held her captive ever since, trying to persuade her to become his mistress. God knows why, but she turned him down. Then four days ago, he asked her to marry him—Jesu, he wanted to *marry* the wench!—and she responded by jumping through that damnable window of his." He regarded his wine sourly. "I always knew it was unnatural. Glassed windows are meant only for churches."

"Saints preserve us," Richard said blankly, having trouble imagining his cool contained brother in the throes of uncontrollable passion. "So the girl is dead?"

"No, but so near it's just a matter of time. Adrian risked his own life by diving into the water after her, the bloody fool. Managed to pull her ashore before she drowned, but she hurt her head and has never recovered consciousness."

The serving man returned with a tray of food, and Richard paused to carve off a substantial piece of beef.

He chewed a bite, then asked, "A strange tale, but why did you send for me?"

"Because Adrian seems to have gone mad," Sir Walter said bluntly. "He spends all of his time either by her bed or praying in his chapel. I don't think he's slept since the accident. He threw one physician out for trying to bleed her—claimed that the girl had no ill humors and had lost enough blood. Then he sent to Fontevaile for Abbot William's infirmarer. He's fit for nothing, Richard, and all because of a lowborn female. Holy Mother, he could find a dozen prettier wenches down in the village!"

The old knight brooded over his wine. "What if Burgoigne attacks? I wish to God the girl would die and be done with it."

"If Burgoigne attacks, you and I will defeat him without Adrian if we must," Richard said tersely. On the whole, he was more concerned with his brother's state of mind than with the military situation, which he could manage capably. But Adrian, complicated, high-strung Adrian, who burned with inner fires and never relaxed—what would happen to him if the girl died? Richard would rather not find out. "Where can I find him?"

"Try his chapel first. If he's not there, he'll be in the guest chamber next door, the one you usually use. That's where the girl is." His tone made it clear that he did not approve of that either.

Richard drained the last of his wine, then set the goblet down and went in search of his brother. Adrian's chamber was lit with a branch of candles, and he saw that parchment had been stretched over a gaping hole in the window. He winced at the sight, trying to imagine what state of mind could send someone through it to plunge into the river so far below.

He crossed the room to the door of the chapel and looked in to see Adrian kneeling before the rail, his head bowed. His brother's back was toward the door, and there were traces of blood on his tunic. Richard's mouth tightened with the knowledge that Adrian must have flagellated himself.

Richard had never had a tithe of his brother's piety. Occasionally he regretted the lack, thinking that a strong belief in God must be a great comfort, but at the moment he was very glad that he lacked his brother's faith and the tormenting guilt that went with it. "Good evening, Adrian," he said quietly.

His brother stirred, then turned to face the door. His face was drawn into stark bone-tight planes, more like a skull than a living man. "I suppose Walter sent for you?"

Richard nodded, rigidly controlling his shock at his brother's state. No wonder Walter had summoned him.

Adrian got slowly to his feet, his movements brittle. "Don't worry, in spite of what Walter might have said, I'm not mad. At least, not yet."

"How is Meriel?"

Adrian's face eased slightly. "I'm glad you remembered her name. Walter always calls her 'the girl.' He accords more dignity to his horses."

Richard put his arm around his brother's taut shoulders. "Come into the other room and tell me about her."

So Adrian did, talking in short choppy sentences, showing little emotion, except in his haunted eyes.

Richard sat drinking wine and listening, astonished at what Meriel had come to mean to his brother. How strange that a humble peasant girl had called forth so many buried aspects of Adrian's nature. Was it simple lust on Adrian's part? But Richard, who in this arena was far more experienced than his brother, knew that lust was not always simple. And when he remembered how Meriel looked when she whistled her falcon down the wind, his brother's feelings were easy to understand.

At the end of his recital, Adrian was slouched wearily in his chair, his face hidden behind his hand. "And the worst of it is . . . ." His voice broke. "Suicide is a mortal sin, Richard, condemning a soul to eternal damnation. I have been praying that I might take Meriel's sin upon my own sôul, for if she dies, it will not be suicide but murder. I am as responsible for her death as if I had stabbed her through the heart. Surely God will understand and not punish her for my crime?''

''I can't believe that the Blessed Mother will not understand and intercede for her.'' Though Richard had his doubts about heaven and hell, if there was a just God, innocents would not be punished in the afterlife. Nor would his brother's agonized remorse go for naught. Softly he added, ''And she will intercede for you too, Adrian. To be a fool is not the same as to be evil.''

''The results can be evil in either case,'' Adrian said bitterly.

''I am no theologian, but as I recall, what is in one's heart is supposed to be more important than one's actions.''

Adrian sighed and lowered his hand. ''I hope you are right, for I can do no more than hope.'' He stood. ''I'm going to sit with Meriel. Do you want to see her?''

Richard didn't, not really, but clearly Adrian wanted him to. He nodded and followed his brother to the sickroom. By the bed sat a Cistercian monk, the Fontevaile infirmarer presumably. The girl looked very small and frail, her face as pale as the white bandage threaded through her black hair, only her labored breathing proving that she still lived.

By the flickering light of the single candle, it took Richard a moment to identify the furry ball curled up on the foot of the bed. ''Is that a cat?'' he asked in surprise, keeping his voice low even though this was one case where waking the patient would be a blessing.

''It's Meriel's cat. She named it Kestrel. She was . . .''

Adrian caught and corrected himself, "she is very fond of it."

As if knowing it was under discussion, the little animal lifted its head and regarded the newcomers with golden eyes for a moment before tucking its nose under its tail again. Richard supposed that it was no more foolish to have a cat than it was to have the reliquary that also sat on the foot of the bed. Probably it was a relic that the infirmarer had brought from the abbey in the hopes that it would help the patient.

Richard thought rather cynically that Fontevaile was doing its best to please the patron who had contributed so generously over the years, but it was also true that Abbot William and Adrian were good friends, and that the abbot was a compassionate man. Richard's gaze went to the girl's still face again. The relic was as good a treatment as any, for it would take a miracle to preserve this life.

The monk rose and approached Adrian, his face grave. "She will not last the night, Lord Adrian. You must call your priest so that the last rites can be administered."

Richard could feel his brother's vivid pain without even looking at him, but Adrian's voice was steady when he said, "Very well, Brother Peter."

Within a few minutes the Warfield priest had arrived and in a murmur of Latin he performed extreme unction, anointing Meriel's eyes, ears, nostrils, lips, hands, and feet. If he had doubts about ministering to a woman the whole household knew had attempted self-destruction, he wisely did not speak them.

Then there was nothing to do but wait. Adrian realized that Richard was still present, sitting tiredly against the wall. He went over and said quietly, "There is no need for you to stay. You must be exhausted after riding from Montford. Take my bed—I won't be using it."

Richard looked up, groggy with fatigue but still game. "You are sure?"

"Yes." When Richard stood, Adrian clasped his hand. "Thank you for coming."

Richard squeezed back, offering what silent comfort he could, then left. The priest had also gone, leaving only the monk dozing in the corner and Adrian. He pulled a stool up to the bed and sat down. Because Meriel was far beyond caring what he did, he allowed himself to stroke her face once. Her bones were delicate beneath the white rose-petal skin. To think that soon she would be gone, her bright sweetness buried beneath the earth, was quite unbearable.

Adrian believed that there had been moments of real sympathy between them, but his unforgivable actions had destroyed any possible future. As he studied her face, trying to memorize every line and curve, a bleak thought occurred to him. Often he had yearned for the lost life of the monastery, but never had he wondered about being a freeman of modest fortune. If he had been born to the same rank as Meriel, had met and won her as his wife, he would have found more happiness than he would ever know as an earl.

Hours passed, the castle slept, and each breath came with more difficulty than the last, yet still Meriel breathed. Helplessness was a torture as terrible as being stretched on a rack, and Adrian could feel tension building steadily inside him. When Meriel died, the rack would be tightened the final turn and he would be torn into shrieking fragments. Or perhaps he would go mad, as Walter feared.

He scanned the chamber's handsome furniture and solid stone walls. Many of his guests thought this the most luxurious place they had ever stayed, but how had Meriel felt about it? What thoughts had filled her mind during the lonely hours?

His lips thinned with guilt as he remembered how he had deliberately deprived her of all companionship and activity, trying to drive her into his arms through boredom. Instead, she had cultivated a cat, fed birds, found small tasks to keep her mind and hands busy.

She was a resilient woman; in her quiet way, formidable. He remembered how she had sat beneath the window and watched the sky.

Watched the sky . . . a thought sliced through Adrian's musings with a shaft of absolute certainty. Knowing what he must do, he stood and pulled the covers from Meriel. Her slim, shift-clad body was wraithlike, as still as the grave. Taking a blanket, he wrapped her carefully.

Aroused by the sounds, the Cistercian woke. "My lord?" he questioned, blinking with sleepy confusion.

"No wonder she can't die, trapped here within these walls," Adrian said harshly as he lifted her in his arms. "The last—the only—thing I can do for Meriel now is to let her die under an open sky. She would have wished it."

"But the night air can be deadly," Brother Peter cautioned.

Adrian smiled humorlessly. "How can that worsen her condition?"

After a moment's thought, the monk nodded. "Very well." He lifted the candle from the bedside, then lighted the earl's way downstairs, through the sleeping bodies in the great hall and out the heavy iron-bound door.

There was a waxing half-moon, enough to guide them through the castle wards to the postern gate. The monk's quiet explanations saved Adrian from having to speak himself, and for that he was grateful. The guard at the postern wanted to send an escort to protect his lord, but in a few savage words Adrian refused. Then he sent the monk back to his rest.

Finally it was just the two of them. Adrian supposed that if he had the full strength of his conviction, he would find a quiet place to set Meriel down, then leave her, but he could not bear to let her die alone or to deprive himself of what moments of her life remained.

Following a footpath, he carried her upriver until even her slight weight bore heavily, then found a spot on a bluff overlooking the water. There was a tree and he settled down against it, then arranged Meriel across his lap, her head supported by his shoulder.

It was a peaceful place. Moonlight burnished the flowing water. Below the bluff, reeds rustled gently in the wind, and now and then a water creature splashed. Across the river he saw the soft white shapes of sleeping sheep. Sometimes one more restless than the others gave a plaintive bleat.

Doubtless it was Adrian's imagination, but Meriel's breathing seemed a little stronger now. He touched her cheek and it seemed warmer, but perhaps that was just because his fingers were cool. In the moonlight, her face showed the innocent peace of a sleeping child. The explosive tension he had felt in the castle had drained away, leaving the calm of resignation.

The sun rose very early at this season, and as the first faint light defined the horizon, Adrian began to talk. Since Meriel was beyond hearing, he spoke in Norman, his mother tongue, the language of his heart. "Abbot William says that the purest, highest love is for the divine, because when mortal men love mortal things, they often kill what they most love. And that is what I did," he said with deep sadness, his gaze fixed on the pale oval of her face.

"I loved you from the moment I saw you, but was too blind a fool to know my own heart." He sighed and tilted his head back against the tree trunk. "So being mortal man and a sinner, I set out to possess you, to clip your wings and cage you so that your songs would only be for me. But in the end you found another way to fly, and so defeated me."

He drew a shuddering breath. "May angels carry you to your rest, *ma petite.*"

He had the fancy that angels did hover near, waiting for Meriel to slip from her body. Then they would take her by the hand and fly away, leaving Adrian alone forever. "Ah, God! If only one could turn back time!" he cried out, anguish overwhelming him. "If only I could start again, I would do everything differently. I would try to win your love through kindness rather than compel it by force, and if I failed, I would accept your will and wish you joy on your own path.''

Meriel had been quiescent in his arms, but for the first time she moved, a subtle shift of weight, as if nestling more closely. Adrian stared down, knowing her movement had not been his imagination. Her breath really was stronger now, and quieter, not so labored as before. Was it possible that she really was improving? He laid two fingers at the base of her throat and found her pulse easily.

The intoxication of hope surged through Adrian's veins, and he closed his eyes and prayed aloud, his voice choked and breaking. ''Holy Mother, I know that you must want Meriel's sweetness and joy in heaven, but if it is not against God's will, then spare her. *Spare her.* Grant me a chance to atone for what I have done, and I swear and vow that I will do anything in my power to make amends. Whatever her wish, I will grant it, even if she would ask that I cut out my own heart. Because I love her, Blessed Mother, I love her, and of all the saints in heaven, you know most of human love.''

Then the miracle occurred. After aching years of inner emptiness, once more Adrian knew the exultation of spiritual grace. He had fallen away from God, but now he could pray again, once more he was enfolded in the mantle of divine love. And part of his joy was his knowledge, beyond question and doubt, that Meriel's soul was safe. After her spirit departed, he would find comfort in the fact that she would be in realms of light.

He felt a gossamer touch on his head, like an angel wing, or a mother's kiss for a sleeping child, and with it came an insight into why Meriel had instantly meant so much to him. Over the years Adrian had lost touch with the gentle, loving side of himself, the side that had found fulfillment at Fontevaile, and Meriel was not just her own beloved self, but an emblem of his own lost soul. No wonder he had loved her with desperation. Even if she died in his arms, he would still have the healing he had found through her. And he would be able to hope that someday, in heaven, he might find her again. "Thank you, Holy Mother," he whispered brokenly, "thank you."

For a long time he neither moved nor thought, simply sat content in the deepest peace he had ever known. Then Meriel stirred and he opened his eyes. The edge of the sun was over the horizon now and there was light enough to see her face, delicate and pretty as a fairy child's. She shifted again, then opened her eyes and looked up at him.

Adrian caught his breath with delight, not quite believing that there might be a second miracle. He whispered, "Meriel?"

She said nothing, just stared at him, like a grave blue-eyed baby owl. There was no recognition in her eyes, but there was intelligence, like the wisdom sometimes seen in the eyes of newborns, when all the world is new and strange to them. Her cheeks had color and she looked as healthy and pretty as the first time he had seen her. "Meriel, do you know who I am?"

Her brows drew together and she blinked thoughtfully. Remembering that he had spoken in Norman, Adrian repeated his question in English, but she still did not answer. Chilled, he wondered if her mind had been damaged. She had taken a great blow on the side of the head and Brother Peter was sure there was damage to her brain, but there had been no way to know how much.

Then Adrian relaxed. "I prayed for your life, and if your injuries keep you forever in a state of innocent simplicity, I will love you still. There might even be a special grace in that, if you cannot remember how ill I treated you." He smiled, then kissed her lightly on the brow. "I swear that I will care for you always, *ma petite*, and that none shall harm you while I draw breath.''

And as the final miracle of the night, Meriel smiled back at him.

Alan de Vere stopped to buy a hot apple pastry at a street stall in Evreux and received a saucy smile as well. He smiled back, for the baker's girl was a pretty wench. Perhaps he would come by here again when he had more time to dally. But now it was time to attend Lord Theobald at the castle.

Alan walked briskly, munching the pastry and feeling well pleased with the world. Lord Theobald had come to Normandy to reach terms with Geoffrey of Anjou and had been successful in his mission. Geoffrey was the empress's husband, and while there was no love lost between the two, he had been happy to use his wife's claim to her father's lands as an excuse to make himself master of Normandy. With Geoffrey's encouragement, Theobald had taken the castle of a baron who had been a thorn in Geoffrey's side.

During the siege, Alan had been fortunate enough to capture a prosperous knight, and the ransom had been very handsome. Most of the money must go to Avonleigh, but he had come into the town today especially to find a gift to take back to Meriel. She worked so hard, always gay, never complaining, and he wanted to buy her some special luxury.

It had been hard to decide, for the local merchants had a dazzling array of wares, but at length Alan's choice had fallen on a brightly polished silver mirror. Unlike silk or velvet, it would never wear out, and it would show Meriel her own pretty face. He chuckled, thinking how she believed that her tall blond sisters had all the family's beauty. Neither of them, nor William's wife, were half so appealing as Meriel.

Within another year or two Alan should be able to dower his sister to a knight like himself, though he would surely miss her when she married. He wouldn't pick just any man; Meriel's husband must be a man of honor and kindness, one who would treat her well. Aye, and Alan would let her meet and approve the man for herself before any contracts were drawn.

Then he could think of finding a wife for himself. He licked honey-sweetened sauce from his fingers. Lord Theobald had hinted that he might put in a good word for Alan with the king. Not all heiresses were daughters to barons and out of his reach. Some were heir to modest manors like his, and such a one would be a perfect match.

A half-hour later, washed and combed, he went to Theobald's solar to see if his lord needed him, and found the baron seated at a table, brooding. The older man looked up at his entrance, then waved to a chair. "A message arrived from Lady Amicia this morning. There's bad news, I fear."

Alan took the indicated seat. "Is there illness? Surely the castle is not threatened."

"Nay, the bad news is not mine." Theobald was a short, powerfully built man, fearless in battle, but now he toyed with his dagger, cleaning his nails, not meeting Alan's eyes. Finally he looked up. "My wife received a message from Avonleigh to send on to you. Apparently Lady Meriel went riding one day and never came back. Her horse did, but your men could find no trace of her when they searched. She is presumed dead." His voice broke for a moment. "Amicia sends her condolences. You know how fond she was of your sister—she often told me that she had never had a waiting woman she loved more. Indeed, we were all very fond of her. She was like a spring day. I'm sorry, lad."

It wasn't possible. Numbed, Alan tried to make sense of the baron's words. She couldn't be gone, not Meriel, with her gifts of life and laughter. Who could want to harm her? "She isn't dead," he said hoarsely. "You said they did not . . . did not find her body. They just did not look hard enough. Perhaps she had an accident and a villager is taking care of her. Mayhap she is home already, apologizing for the worry she caused.''

"The fact that they did not find her means nothing, Alan, you know that," the baron said, compassionate but unwilling to encourage self-delusion. "Robbers could have killed and buried her. She could have been thrown from her horse and broken her neck and the wolves would leave no trace.''.

"No!" Alan said, unable to face the image conjured up. "I will not believe she is dead until I have searched for her myself." The thought was a bracing one. There was no one who would seek Meriel as hard as he would. He knew how her mind worked, he would see something that the others had missed. He looked at the baron, his voice pleading. "You have achieved your goals for the season and do not plan any further campaigning. Please, my lord, give me leave to return to England.''

"If you must, I suppose I can manage without you." Theobald sighed, his eyes sad. "But do not deceive yourself, Alan. How could Meriel be alive and your men not have heard of it?''

"I don't know," Alan said, his voice grim. "But I intend to find out.''

After leaving Lord Theobald, Alan swiftly packed so that he would be ready to leave at first light. The sight of the silver mirror almost shattered his fragile control. Had it been just this afternoon that he had so blithely chosen it for Meriel? His long fingers stroked the chased pattern on the back. Until he had learned what happened to his sister, he would carry the mirror as a token of his determination.

And if she was truly dead, and had perished from human treachery, Alan would not rest until he had avenged her.

10

FIRST THERE had been light, a pure joyous flood of light that illuminated her within and without. The light had been full of beauteous beings, exquisite and diaphanous as they caressed and healed her. She had almost gone with them, but the voice drew her back. While the exact meaning of the words had escaped her, their pulsing emotion had caught her heart.

Curious and moved, she had turned away from the light and followed the voice until she discovered the most beautiful creature she had ever seen. Indeed, he was the first being she could remember seeing clearly. The rising sun had touched his hair to silver-gold, and he had looked at her with such tenderness that she had thought he must be an angel. Then she had gotten confused, trying to remember exactly what an angel was, and who had told her of them. But it hadn't mattered. He had kissed her on the forehead and she had known that she was safe, so she had drifted back to sleep.

He was there again when she woke, but too far away, not holding her as he had the first time. She had looked at him reproachfully and he had come closer. He spoke again, and this time the meaning of the words was nearer, just out of reach, and she knew that soon she would comprehend.

Intently she watched the people who came and went from her chamber. There was a man in a pale robe, with gentle hands and no hair on the top of his head. He was called Brotherpeter. There was a young female who brought food, and combed her hair, and spoke

friendly words. She was called Margery. There was
another kind of creature, small and furred, with a
comical face. It slept on her chest and woke her in the
morning, and she was very pleased with herself when
she remembered that it was called Cat. One or two
other people came into the room from time to time,
looking at her curiously, as if there was something odd
about her. Perhaps there was.

But the most important one, her angel, was called
Lordadrian. Always there was tenderness in his eyes,
along with sadness. He didn't touch her. She didn't
like that. She had been happy and safe when he held
her, and this was not as good.

When next she woke, he was sitting by the bed.
When her eyes opened he said softly, "Good morning,
Meriel."

This time she understood what the words meant,
and she was vastly pleased. She was equally pleased
that his hand lay on the edge of the bed. She reached
out and took firm possession of it. "I am called Meriel?" she asked. Her voice sounded strange, unused.
She must use it now.

Lordadrian's face lit up as if he had swallowed the
sun. He had beautiful eyes, transparent gray, and she
could ready every shift of emotion in the depths. Indeed, she could close her eyes and still know what he
felt. What he felt now was happiness.

"Yes, you are Meriel. Do . . . do you remember
what happened?"

She pondered. Meriel. She liked that. "We were
under a tree. You . . ." She fumbled for a word, found
it. "Kissed me. I slept. Then I was here."

"That is all you remember?"

She knew that he was feeling an odd mixture of
disappointment and relief, and she wondered at that.
Later she would ask what it meant, but just now she
wasn't sure that she would understand the answer. It
was hard enough to remember the words to answer
Lordadrian. "Should I remember more?"

"There was . . . an accident. I . . . we feared that you would die. You don't remember the accident, or any of your life before it?"

She thought again. "Angels."

"If one can only remember one thing, angels are a fine choice." He smiled with great sweetness, and she wished he would kiss her again. A brilliant idea struck her. Perhaps it was her turn. Perhaps he would not kiss her until she kissed him.

She—she must try to think of herself as Meriel— pushed herself to a sitting position. She frowned when she realized that she could not reach his forehead, but surely allowances would be made. She leaned forward and kissed him.

As her lips pressed against his cheek, she felt a wave of startled tension ripple through his entire body. She pulled back and asked anxiously, "Did I do that wrong?"

She felt the effort he made to relax and say reassuringly, "No, I was just surprised. I see you are feeling very much better. Do you hurt anywhere?"

Meriel thought about it, touched the back of her head. A small area had been shaved and a neat bandage applied. It ached, but only a little. She sat up in the bed and pulled down the neck of her shift, baring her left shoulder. Another bandage, and when she poked it her shoulder throbbed. She realized that her left leg had a similar throbbing, so she pushed the blankets away and lifted her shift to investigate. Another bandage, this one running from mid-thigh to calf, but no serious pain. "I don't hurt much," she decided, flexing her leg in the air.

Then she looked at Lordadrian and saw that his eyes were fixed on her legs with fascination, as if he had never seen such a sight before. Meriel looked down, then ran a questioning hand along the curves from heel to hip, but they were simply legs. She looked at Lordadrian uncertainly. "Is something the matter?"

He raised his eyes to meet hers, and smiled again,

though she sensed again that it was difficult for him. "It is just that you are recovering so quickly. Yesterday you lay still all day and didn't speak at all. Indeed, we thought that perhaps you could not. But now you seem almost ready to get out of bed."

What a splendid idea. She swung her legs over the side of the high bed and slid off, but her legs did not want to work. Perhaps that was why Lordadrian had stared at them.

As she crumpled toward the floor he swiftly caught her. His clasp brought her close to his body. Meriel smiled. This was exactly what she had wanted. She wrapped her arms around his waist and cuddled against him, savoring the warmth and strength of his encircling arms. He had a nice scent. She would know it anywhere. Pressing her body against his, she asked, "Isn't it your turn to kiss me?"

"What?" His tone was baffled, and she felt tension in him again. She pressed closer, fascinated by the way part of him was hardening and changing shape.

"You kissed me the first time, so I kissed you," she explained, a slight questioning lift to her voice. She turned her face up, trying to understand. "I thought it was your turn to kiss me. That is not how it is done?"

His lips were inches from Meriel's. Might a kiss be even better if both people pressed their lips together? She liked the shape of his mouth. What would it taste like?

To her dismay, she did not have a chance to find out, for Lordadrian scooped her up in his arms and laid her back on the bed. Before he could move too far away, she captured his hand again, so he sat on the edge of the bed. His eyes grave, he explained, "Kisses are very special. They are sometimes exchanged by people who are very fond of each other, but it is not done all the time, or by all people."

She frowned, not liking the implication. "You are not fond of me, so you don't want to kiss me again?"

He looked a little helpless, and she wondered if he was having as much trouble understanding her as she was understanding him. Then he gave her the tender smile that was the very first thing she remembered clearly, and reached out to stroke her cheek. "I am very, very fond of you. But you have been ill, and it is not the best time for kisses. You must get your strength back, and then . . . and then we can talk about it again."

Perhaps he was right, for she was very tired. Lordadrian must have known, because he got off the bed, removed his hand from her clasp, then pulled the covers over her. "Rest now, Meriel. I will come back tomorrow."

She reached up and touched his bright hair. The texture was as lovely as its appearance, soft and live, like threads of spun silk. "Perhaps . . . perhaps just one kiss? For luck?"

"One for luck," he agreed, bending to kiss her forehead again. The touch of his warm lips made her want to purr like the cat. They felt lovely, soothing, yet also . . . exciting. He had said that when she was stronger they would discuss kissing again. She thought that an excellent reason to get well as soon as possible.

Meriel fell asleep almost instantly, a smile on her lips. Adrian could only stare at her, shaken. He had never before wondered what came after a miracle, but it appeared that he was going to find out. Yesterday they had feared that her mind was hopelessly damaged and she would be unable to do more than watch the world through solemn eyes.

Today she was a whole different person. No, not really different, she was still Meriel, merely shorn of the memories that define a life. Would she soon remember more of her past? He must find Brother Peter and tell him how Meriel had improved. Perhaps the monk would have some idea of what would happen to her next.

He smiled ruefully as he left her room. Any child old enough to walk and talk had some idea of what was proper, but Meriel seemed to have lost her propriety along with her other memories. Her casual display of large expanses of her exquisite body had seriously undermined his self-control. It had been even worse when she fell, then made herself at home in his arms. Jesu, but she had felt so right there!

He should have known that repentance for his behavior was not enough, that there must still be punishment as well. It appeared that God had an unexpected sense of humor, for Adrian had wanted Meriel to come to him willingly, and now she had. Yet he could not honorably accept, for she had no more idea of what she was doing than an infant. It was the subtlest, most frustrating punishment imaginable, a special kind of hell. The fact that he had not accepted her invitation proved that he was much closer to a saint than he had ever imagined.

Meriel had recovered greatly in the space of a day. In the space of another, she might recover entirely and have both her memory and her hatred of Adrian. He would be a villain and a fool to take advantage of her present innocence; all of his concern must be for her and her welfare. But in time, when she was fully healed, if she still wanted kisses and closeness . . . He had sworn to grant her every wish, and he had no intention of breaking his vow.

Adrian sought out Brother Peter in the castle herb garden, where the monk was taking cuttings, and described Meriel's miraculous improvement.

Brother Peter listened with interest. "There is often some memory loss after a blow to the head, but usually it is just for the events around the accident. Though I have heard of complete memory loss, I have never seen such a case myself. I think it possible that eventually she will remember her past, but it is in God's hands." He crossed himself. "The young lady's survival was a miracle, so only he can say what will happen. I will examine her when she wakes. After that I will return to Fontevaile, for I can do no more here.''

Adrian nodded agreement, then returned to his chamber and summoned his steward. After dealing with the normal business, the earl ordered that no one in the household was to tell Meriel how she had come to Warfield, or what had happened after.

Then, because Meriel would need a woman's guidance, Adrian called the maidservant Margery. Given the tendency of young females to chatter to each other, they had probably become friends. Adrian could have ordered that the maid be kept away from Meriel, but he knew from experience that such prohibitions could be easily circumvented if the wench thought it her duty to tell her friend what had happened. Far better to win her willing cooperation.

Sure enough, Margery bowed her head submissively when he ordered her not to enlighten Meriel about her past, but there was a rebellious gleam in her eye. Adrian leaned back in his chair. ''I think you do not agree with the order. Do you wish to say something? Speak freely, you will not be punished.''

She looked at him suspiciously, then decided to take him at his word. ''You treated her very badly, my lord. She really ought to know.''

''You are quite correct on both counts,'' the earl agreed. ''She deserves to know the truth, and I intend to answer all of her questions. However, I prefer to do it in my own time, after she is more fully recovered.''

Margery thought about that. ''Are you still keeping her captive?''

Adrian shook his head. ''Her door is not locked, nor will it be again. Though I hope Meriel will stay, she is free to leave at any time.''

Margery's gaze fixed the earl squarely. ''Why are you talking to me like this, my lord? I am just a maid.''

''You have seen how Meriel is today?'' When Margery nodded, Adrian said, ''Then you must see that she needs a woman to help her, not just as a maid, but to teach her what most grown women have already learned. You are the best choice for that, and I would rather have you working with me than against me.''

''Very well, my lord, I shall tell her nothing of her past, since you say that you will do so.'' Margery curtsied, preparatory to leaving, but could not resist another question. ''Is it true that you asked her to marry you?''

''Yes, and when she is well, I will ask her again.''

Margery left with a broad smile on her face, doubtless pleased by the romantic thought that the lord wanted to marry a girl of humble birth. On the whole, Adrian preferred the maid's response to that of Sir Walter, who was more than half-convinced that the earl had lost his wits.

Adrian spent the rest of the day working with the newest men-at-arms, which was good training for them and equally good practice for him. Richard joined in, since he was still at Warfield, and the two brothers climaxed the afternoon by fighting each other with swords. They were very equally matched and their demonstration left the recruits slack-mouthed with awe.

Besides having an exhilarating bout, it was always a good thing if the men-at-arms had a proper respect for their leaders. Even Sir Walter had to admit that while the earl's wits might be in question, there was nothing wrong with his sword arm.

After a pleasant and profitable sojourn in London, Sir Vincent de Laon had returned to Chastain Castle. Guy of Burgoigne greeted him impatiently. ''You took long enough. Did you find a rich Jew interested in moving to Shropshire?''

Sir Vincent took his time, drinking deeply of his wine before answering. ''I did indeed, one Benjamin l'Eveske.''

The earl nodded with satisfaction. ''What trade is he in?''

"A variety of things—wool, spices, wine, timber. And moneylending, of course. A very rich goose for the plucking."

"When will he be coming?"

Sir Vincent held up his hand. "Patience! The man did not earn his fortune by being a fool. He wishes to visit Shrewsbury, talk to the other merchants, find a house." After a pause, he added with a trace of malice, "And of course he wishes to meet his sponsor and protector, Earl Adrian."

"God's bones, Vincent, what game are you playing?" Guy exclaimed. "He can't be permitted to meet Warfield, and I'll be damned if I'll pretend to be that whey-faced bastard myself."

"No need." Sir Vincent smiled lazily, pleased with himself. "Benjamin has made inquiries and been assured that Warfield is an honorable man and Shrewsbury a well-defended city, so he is already inclined to accept the invitation. I will meet the Jew in Shrewsbury and explain that the earl is busy defending his tenants from dastardly neighbors. Perhaps this is a good time to attack that small keep of Warfield's, I forget the name, but it would draw Warfield well away from Shrewsbury.

"At any rate, after extending your deepest regrets that you cannot meet him, I'll show Benjamin that empty house you own near the castle. It is fine enough to please even a rich merchant. I will say that he may live in the house rent-free if he moves himself and his business to Shrewsbury. That should be enough to persuade him. Jews are greedy devils."

Guy considered. Occasionally his lieutenant's oversubtle mind irritated him, but this seemed a good plan. All that was necessary was to lure the Jew into coming to Shropshire. As soon as the man and his gold entered Guy's territory, he could be plucked like a ripe fruit. "Are you sure he will come?"

"Aye, I made a number of inquiries and was told that Benjamin is anxious to leave the city as soon as he finds a suitable spot. He fears that the fickle London mob may decide to turn on the Jewry as happened in Norwich a few years back.'' Sir Vincent shrugged. ''The Jews may be under the king's personal protection, but Stephen has never been fully master of his kingdom, and after so many years of civil war he is grown tired. Benjamin believes that in a smaller city, where people are known to one another, there is less likelihood of violence, for it is easier to burn a stranger than a neighbor who is known to you.''

The earl snorted, unimpressed. If Benjamin l'Eveske's life was that precious to him, he would pay handsomely for the privilege of keeping it. If he paid enough, Guy might even let him live, though likely he would not. The lives of Jews were a matter of supreme indifference to Guy of Burgoigne.

Before Richard left for Montford the next morning, he joined Adrian for a last meeting. They spent some time discussing coordination of their regular patrols. Then Richard turned to something else that had been concerning him. ''I know you have had other things on your mind, but have you noticed how strange Burgoigne's behavior has been?''

Adrian gave his brother a quizzical look. ''What do you mean? He has been very quiet, surprisingly so.'' He stopped and thought about what he had just said, then nodded. ''I see what you mean. Guy has been too quiet, hasn't he?''

''Exactly.'' Richard got up and wandered over to the large window. Fresh, pale lead strips showed where the broken glass panels had been replaced. Adrian's gaze avoided the window, which was hardly surprising. Richard returned to his chair. ''Guy has been raiding steadily and has caused us some damage, but there has been no major attack. Whenever we retaliate, he pulls back quickly. I wonder what he is planning.''

Adrian leaned back in his chair and frowned. Since his attention had been on Meriel, he had been absentmindedly grateful for how quiet things had been this season, but the situation wasn't natural, especially since control of Shropshire was in the balance. "I don't suppose he has learned wisdom and knows that he can't defeat us."

"Guy? Wise? He has no more sense than a mad boar." Richard snorted. "More likely he is trying to lull us into complacence. Since he would need twice as many men to seriously threaten Warfield or Montford, more likely he is planning some treachery instead."

"Maybe that is the answer," Adrian said slowly. "When I was in Normandy earlier in the year, I heard that an English lord was inquiring about mercenary troops, but that is not unusual, so I thought nothing more of it. But what if Burgoigne is thinking of strengthening his forces, perhaps to the point where he could take Shrewsbury?"

"If that is a possibility, we would be better off striking first. A waiting game is well enough when two foes are equally balanced, but if Guy is going to change the odds, we should take the battle to him."

"Perhaps you are right," Adrian said reluctantly. He had avoided such tactics because of the high toll of destruction they caused, but perhaps he could no longer afford his scruples. "I'm not ready to strike out of hand, but I'll send word to Normandy and see if any of our friends have news that might indicate that Burgoigne is hiring mercenaries."

Before Richard could say more, the door swung open and Meriel peeked in cautiously. When she saw Adrian, she gave a heart-stopping smile and entered. She was dressed in the blue bliaut he had given her, which someone had repaired so well that it was impossible to tell that it had been torn. Apart from a slight stiffness in Meriel's gait, there was nothing to indicate how near death she had been. "May I sit with you awhile?" she asked. "I will cause no trouble."

"Of course," Adrian said, quite unable to resist her

elfin charm. He gestured to his companion. "This is my brother, Sir Richard FitzHugh. He will be leaving in a few minutes. After he has gone, we can go for a walk if you like."

"Oh, yes, please." Meriel dropped into a curtsy before Richard. "I am honored to meet you, my lord."

Richard bowed with the same courtesy he would have accorded the empress while Adrian watched the exchange with amusement. Had Meriel remembered how to curtsy, or had Margery already begun training her in manners? He would ask later. As the two men returned to their discussion, Meriel drifted about the room, touching and lifting objects curiously, studying textures with her fingertips. Adrian devoutly hoped that she would never remember the last disastrous occasion when she had been in this chamber.

When Richard rose to take his leave, Meriel approached the men shyly. "I'm sorry, I could not help but hear. You are fighting a war?"

"Not really a war, more like quarreling with a bad-tempered neighbor," Adrian explained. "However, Warfield will be safe. It is one of the strongest castles in Britain."

He would have said more, but a sudden realization struck him dumb. The two men had been speaking Norman. Meriel had not only understood their discussion, but she now spoke Norman herself, as fluently as Adrian and Richard.

Meriel was looking at him with puzzlement, sensing something wrong. Forcing himself to appear calm, Adrian said, "I didn't know you spoke the Norman tongue."

"Norman?" Meriel asked curiously. Then her face brightened. "Oh, I see, it is a different language. And the one we spoke before is English, is it not?"

"It is." Adrian switched languages. "You also knew Welsh. Do you still remember that?"

"Yes!" she answered in the same tongue. "And the other one is called Latin." She skipped over to Adrian's bookcase and pulled out a volume, thumbed to a particular page, and read a few lines in Latin, then looked up like a puppy who has just performed a new trick.

Since Adrian seemed temporarily deprived of the power of speech, it was Richard who asked, "Do you know what they mean—the lines you just read?"

"Of course, it is from the Gospels." Meriel glanced down at the volume and translated, *"In the beginning was the Word, and the Word was with God, and the Word was God."* She looked up apologetically. "I am not sure that I know that it *really* means, but those are the words. It is very lovely, is it not?"

"Very. And you read it well." Adrian swallowed hard. "Meriel, may I ask you to wait for me in your room? I will come in a few minutes."

"Of course," she said sunnily. She made a grave curtsy to Richard and a saucy one to Adrian, then left the chamber as both men stared after her in stunned disbelief.

"Her appearance is Welsh," Adrian said rather feebly.

"But she speaks like a Norman lady. You said that her accent was of southern Wales, so perhaps she learned Norman there, serving a Norman noblewoman." Richard gave a wicked chuckle as he went to the door. "When you went hunting that day, you certainly caught a most unusual prey. Perhaps you should find out if she reads Greek as well."

"You have a deplorable sense of humor," Adrian said, unamused.

"Of course," his brother agreed cordially. "Farewell—I wish you joy in solving the puzzle of your mysterious maiden."

Dourly Adrian watched the other man leave. Who the devil was Meriel and how much else had she successfully concealed from him? As he thought about it, he realized that she had never denied speaking Norman, but she had certainly encouraged his belief that she was ignorant of the language.

Her ability to speak Norman was nowhere near as much a shock as the fact that she could read as well as he could. Whatever her background, it had included an excellent education. It was still possible that she was the Welsh girl of modest birth that she had claimed to be—the Welsh revered education—but she could be almost anything else. Despite her distinctively Welsh appearance, Meriel could even be Norman, or partially so, but the possibility was remote. A Norman lady would not have been alone in the forest, and she had certainly not been dressed as a lady.

He sighed and went to Meriel's chamber. At this point, he and she were equally ignorant of her history, but by careful observation of what she remembered, he might be able to deduce her background. At least now Meriel wasn't deliberately trying to conceal anything from him.

She gave her shining smile when he entered her room, as if the sun rose and set on him. Her regard was very humbling. No man could possibly live up to such veneration, and perhaps enduring it when Adrian knew himself unworthy was another subtle punishment. "Do you feel strong enough for a walk in the garden?"

"Oh, yes, I feel very strong today."

Meriel's expression was hopeful, and he remembered that he had said that they would discuss kissing again when she felt stronger. It would be interesting to see which would win, his honor or her innocent sensuality. As he escorted her down the stairs, her slim hand clasped trustingly in his, he would not have gambled much on his honor.

Lordadrian said apologetically, "I fear that it is rather plain. The castle is still quite new and there has been little time to give the garden proper attention."

In spite of her claims of complete recovery, Meriel

had tired quickly. They had found a shady spot on a stone bench beneath the trees that had been left in the corner of the large walled garden. A thorn fence divided the area in half, and on the other side was the kitchen garden, well planted with herbs, vines, and young fruit trees. On this side of the thorn there were some formal plantings of shrubs and flowers, but most of the area was plain grassy turf. "Much could be done here," Meriel answered. "Perhaps a fountain there . . ." She pointed to a spot. "Do you think water could be brought here for a fountain?"

"If you wished it, it could be done."

"And around it, raised beds with flowers in them. Roses, of course, like these lovely white ones." She lifted the perfect blossom in her hand and inhaled with pleasure. It smelled all the sweeter because he had picked and presented it to her. "But there should be other varieties like violets, lilies, pansies—enough kinds that there will be flowers from early spring until frost. Some could be in tubs, then brought into the solar for the winter." Seeing his amused expression, Meriel stopped, abashed. "I am sorry, Lordadrian, I did not mean to chatter on, as if you were not capable of planning your own garden."

"Don't apologize, *ma petite*. Most of my time has been divided between fighting and overseeing my lands. I have thought very little of what should be done here." He gestured toward the open expanse. "A castle garden is usually the special charge of the lady of the household. Since you seem to know a great deal about gardens, you may plan this one if the task pleases you. And don't call me Lordadrian. I would prefer Adrian."

"Adrian is the usual nickname, not Lord?"

" 'Lord' is a title of honor, not a nickname," he explained, his voice grave but with a twinkle in his eye. "My actual name is Adrian de Lancey."

"Ahh," she said, able to place the information in a larger context. "As with Brotherpeter. 'Brother' is an-

UNCOMMON VOWS • 189

other title of honor, is it not, with Peter his true name?"

"Exactly, but to be a brother is a different kind of honor from being a lord." Adrian regarded her thoughtfully. "You remember things almost instantly when you are reminded of them. Perhaps if I ask you questions about your past, you will remember them as well."

"What a good idea." Meriel cocked her head and waited for him to begin.

"Do you recall where your home is?"

She thought and thought, but could not remember. As she frowned, he tried again. "Do you remember your father's name?"

Still nothing came to her, no matter how hard she tried. Distressed, Meriel worried at her lower lip with her teeth.

"You speak three languages well, but which is your mother tongue? Are you Norman?" When she did not answer, Adrian tried again, offering, "Welsh?"

"I'm sorry," she said miserably, her brows knit with anxiety. "I can't do it. I remember Latin and gardens, but nothing of myself."

"Don't worry, *ma petite*," Adrian said quickly, putting a comforting arm around her. "Perhaps your memories will come back to you in time. And if they don't, that is all right too."

Meriel leaned against him, as always feeling warm and safe in his closeness. At the same time, she had the strange impression that Adrian felt some relief that she could not remember more. How could that be? As she pondered, for the first time it occurred to her that her situation at Warfield was an odd one. The more she thought, the odder it seemed. "May I ask you some questions, Adrian?"

Removing his arm, he replied, "Of course. Anything you wish. If I can answer, I will."

"How is it that nothing is known of me or my family? Surely I have a family?"

Choosing his words carefully, he replied, "You were

discovered alone in the royal forest near here. You had been slightly injured in a fall from a horse. You refused to say much about yourself, but claimed to have come from the country of Gwynedd in Wales. You said that your brother had a small farm there, and that you had a sister in Lincoln.''

"But you did not believe me?" she asked, accurately interpreting his tone.

He shook his head. "You contradicted yourself, said things that made no sense. There may have been some truth in your story, but I don't know how much."

"Why ever would I have lied?" she asked, perplexed. "I cannot believe that I would have done so for no reason."

"I'm sure you had a reason, Meriel, but I have no idea what it was." Adrian gave a wry half-smile. "If I did, the question would likely answer itself."

Meriel frowned, inhaling the fragrance of her white rose again. The more Adrian told her, the more confused she became, and the biggest question was yet to come. Hesitantly she said, "I do not understand my position here." She gestured toward the great keep which loomed above them. "This is your castle. You are the most important person in Warfield, while I am just someone whom you found in the forest, of no importance and a liar to boot. You have given me much of your time and consideration, but why? What am I to you?"

There was a long silence before he said, "You are the woman I hoped to make my wife."

Shocked, she glanced up to see if he was joking, but his quartz-clear eyes were completely serious. Seeing her reaction, he asked, "Is marriage one of those things you remember, or should I explain it?"

Meriel swallowed hard, and looked down, nervously twisting the stem of the rose between her fingers. Even the idea of marrying this kind, beautiful, powerful man made her shiver with delight. "I . . . I remember what it means to wed. But why would you wish to marry me? From what I recall, it is customary for people to marry others of the same rank. Surely a lord would marry a lady of family and wealth, and I am not that. Apparently I am not even a lady.''

Adrian laid his hand over hers, stilling her restless fingers. ''It didn't matter what your background was, Meriel, because I loved you from the moment I saw you,'' he said quietly. ''You were so lovely and bright and free—I knew that my life would be incomplete without you.''

Scarcely daring to believe, Meriel looked up and saw such longing on Adrian's face that it humbled her. Remembering how such things were done, she asked, ''Then we were betrothed?''

''No, there had been no betrothal.''

She understood immediately, and her joy faded. ''You said that you *had* hoped that we would wed. That means you no longer wish it, no? You have changed your mind.'' Meriel looked away from him, trying to be strong. ''I understand. I am not the same as I was. You need a woman wise enough and strong enough to be lady of a castle.'' Her eyes dropped. ''Perhaps I would not have known how to do it properly even if I had not had the accident.''

''I have not changed my mind,'' he said swiftly. ''The reason we were not betrothed was because you did not wish to marry me.''

Staggered, Meriel looked up again. ''You are jesting,'' she whispered. ''I could not possibly have refused you.''

''I am not jesting.'' Adrian's beautiful mouth twisted. ''You refused my offer in . . . the strongest possible terms.'' He started to say more, then stopped, shaking his head. Meriel could feel pain radiating from him.

''If I said that I disliked you, I was lying again,'' she said with absolute conviction. ''I may not remember anything, but I know I could not have changed so much.''

''I would like to believe that,'' he said softly, his yearning gaze holding hers.

Wanting to do something, anything, to eliminate his pain, Meriel raised her hands and placed them on both sides of his head, then pulled his face down to hers. Adrian gasped, then responded with raw, aching hunger, his embrace so powerful that she could scarcely breathe.

Meriel discovered that her surmise had been correct: pressing two sets of lips together was even better than a kiss on cheek or forehead. Incredibly better, in fact; this kind of kissing was a whole world of delicious new experience.

Knowing herself ignorant, she followed Adrian's lead, opening her mouth as he did, using her tongue as he did, stroking his back as he did hers. The result was pure enchantment, a blend of passion, fulfillment, and longing for more, though Meriel knew not what she longed for. She wondered if they had ever kissed like this before, but immediately knew they had not. Even if she had died, she would have remembered this.

Then he stopped, lifting his head away, leaving Meriel confused and bereft. "What . . . ?" she questioned, dazed and wondering if she had again done the wrong thing.

Adrian pulled her close again, but holding her against his chest, not kissing her. She felt the pounding of his heart against her cheek, and knew that he was as shaken as she was.

"I'm sorry, Meriel, you have a most unsettling effect on me."

"Why are you sorry?" she asked crossly, not understanding. "I thought that was very nice."

He gave a rather ragged chuckle. "So it was. Very nice indeed. In another few minutes, I would not have been able to stop."

Meriel sighed. "You will think me very stupid again, but I can't remember why we should stop."

"Because . . . because what we would have done is something that is best reserved to husband and wife."

Intrigued, she asked, "Do you mean that only wedded folk do that? People must have great powers of self-restraint.''

"In truth, it is not uncommon for men and women to lie together out of wedlock," he admitted. "But in the view of the Church, marriage and the physical union of man and wife is sacred, and no lesser union can compare.''

Her eyes widened. "You mean it would be even better if we were married?''

Adrian's laughter vibrated throughout his whole body. "I think you are making sport of me, *ma petite.*" He held her back from him, his hands on her shoulders. "I have never been wed so I cannot swear to the difference it would make, but marriage is a solemn vow; a pledge of love and trust. I think it would give a depth to loving that goes far beyond mere physical desire.''

She *had* been teasing him, a little, but now she said shyly, "If you still want to marry me, Adrian, this time I would be happy to accept. More than happy." She thought again. "Much, much more than happy.''

He smiled rather sadly and released her shoulders. "It is too soon, Meriel. What if you suddenly remember all your past, including how much you disliked me?''

"I did not dislike you," she said firmly.

Ignoring her interruption, he said, "I . . . did not always behave honorably to you, and I am determined to do so this time.'' After another silence, he lifted her hand and kissed it very tenderly, then pressed it against his cheek. "But when some time has passed and you are recovered, if you are still willing, I hope you will do me the honor of becoming my wife.''

"I will always be willing, Adrian," she said softly. "I swear it." As she studied his face, even more dear than it was beautiful, it was quite impossible to believe that her feelings would ever change.

11

IT WAS WELL past midnight when the wounded messenger arrived to inform Adrian that Guy of Burgoigne had taken the small keep of Cheston. Woken unceremoniously from sleep, Adrian accepted the news with the grim thought that perhaps it had been unlucky to say that his rival had been quiet lately.

The earl gave crisp orders about which of his men must rise and arm themselves. Cheston was a small place, no more than an old motte and bailey, and they should be able to retake it easily if they struck back soon, before Guy could rebuild the defenses. Adrian and Sir Walter discussed the best way to approach Cheston while the earl's squires armed him.

With the whole castle abuzz, it was not surprising that Meriel also woke and came to Adrian's chamber, her feet bare and her black hair in a single braid that fell over her thin shift. Adrian did not know how long she stood in the corner of the room silently watching before he noticed her, but when he did, he saw that her blue eyes were quietly miserable.

It took only a few minutes more to finish his business with his men and dismiss them to take care of their own needs. When they were gone, he went to Meriel. In the week since her miraculous recovery, they had spent much time together, talking and exploring the castle and its near environs. Adrian had been rigorously proper, no easy task when Meriel was so utterly open to him. It was not just honor that restrained him, for he could not escape the fear that she would wake one morning remembering everything, and forgiving nothing.

As he approached her, she asked, "Will you come back?"

"Of course," he said, surprised. "And I would have woken you to take my leave, not just vanished in the night."

She relaxed a little at his words. Adrian put his arm around her shoulders and guided her back to her own chamber, where a candle by the bed burned through the night.

"It is dangerous, this quarrel with your bad neighbor?"

Adrian started to deny it, then stopped. Meriel's air of simplicity was a part of her nature; it did not mean that she was a child, and he must not treat her as one. "There is always some danger when one goes to war, but a fully armed knight is not easily killed." After another moment of hesitation, he continued, "In most fighting, knights are relatively safe because they are valuable alive but worthless dead. But this case is different—there is a blood feud between Guy of Burgoigne and me. One day I will kill him."

Her eyes stark, Meriel threw her arms around him, hiding her face against his shoulder. "Or he will kill you?"

"That is possible," he admitted, welcoming the feel of her soft body, "but not likely, for justice is on my side. I should not be gone long now, only a few days. I do not think it will be difficult to retake Cheston if we move quickly."

Her voice muffled against his surcoat, she said, "Your hauberk is not comfortable to hug."

"Very true." Adrian laughed as he detached himself from her embrace and tucked her back into the bed. After pulling up the covers, he bent over, bracing his arms on both sides of her head. "I will come back to you, Meriel, and soon. Don't worry about anything.

Sir Walter is in charge of Warfield until I return, and he will guard you well.''

She pulled his head down for a kiss of aching sweetness, a draft so potent that it would have been easy to forget the call of duty and join her in the bed. Conscience intervened in the form of Kestrel, who nudged Adrian's cheek with prickly whiskers. He laughed and straightened up. ''Here is someone who will not miss me. Your cat is jealous, I think.''

''She is female. Soon she will be in love with you too,'' Meriel said, her grave eyes following him as he left the room.

As an oblique declaration of love, it was a very satisfactory way to be sent off to war, Adrian decided. And since this was a local war, he should be home soon to reap the benefits of being loved.

It took only two days to recapture Cheston, two more to assess the damages and bury the dead.

To Adrian's disappointment, Guy had led the attack on the keep but left after vanquishing it, so once more their confrontation was denied. Several times they had crossed blades briefly in skirmishes, but always the tides of battle had swept them apart before there could be a final resolution of their mutual hatred. Once they had even met face-to-face under the roof of Ranulf of Chester and had had to be civil to one another, a situation that had vastly amused Ranulf. For years Adrian had bided his time, content to wait for the inevitable end, but he found that now his patience was gone. He wanted to fulfill his vow of vengeance, then put revenge behind him so that he would be free to build a new life—a new life with Meriel.

It was raining and very late when he arrived back at Warfield, traveling with only a half-dozen men, since the rest had been left at Cheston until the small keep was reasonably secure again. After his squires had disarmed him, Adrian looked into Meriel's chamber, feasting his eyes on the sweetness of her sleeping face, but refrained from waking her. There would be time enough for greetings in the morning. When he reached his own bed, he fell into exhausted sleep almost immediately.

Meriel awoke gasping with terror, the talons of nightmare stabbing deep in her mind. Every night since Adrian had left, the nightmares had grown worse, until she feared going to sleep. Tonight a breeze had quenched her candle and the darkness was damp and heavy.

As Meriel tried to calm herself, she suddenly caught her breath with relief. He had returned.

She slid from her bed, not waking Kestrel, who slept at the foot. Silently she made her way through the drafty corridor to his chamber.

Her instinct had not misled her: Adrian was there. The bedcurtains had not been pulled and she saw that he lay sprawled facedown across his bed, arms outflung, his profile chiseled by moonlight. In the shadowed night he seemed too beautiful to be human. Even shivering with cold and lingering fear, Meriel could not help but stop for a moment in admiration. Once more she thought of an angel come to earth, masking his power so that those mortals around him would not be consumed by his flame.

She padded over to the bed, moving cautiously so that she would not wake or touch him. Simply being in Adrian's presence would banish her nightmares.

Meriel should have realized that a warrior would sleep lightly. No sooner had she lifted herself onto the mattress than he awoke. In a swirl of vivid motion Adrian seized her by the shoulders, twisted her down, and pinned her to the mattress. His grip was bruisingly powerful, and the flexed muscles of his bare arms and shoulders were pale as sculpted snow in the moonlight.

Meriel gasped, startled but not frightened. Adrian's face was clearly visible above her, and she saw recognition flare as soon as his eyes were fully open. He instantly released her. "Did I hurt you?" he asked, running a concerned hand over her shoulder and upper arm.

She shook her head. "No," she said after catching her breath. "I'm sorry. I did not mean to alarm you."

"Nor I you," he said with a wry smile. He rolled onto his side and lightly caressed her face, welcome warmth in the fingertips that crossed her brow and traced the curve of her cheek. "You are very cold, *ma petite*. Is something wrong?"

"I was just . . . just having a bad dream." To her horror, Meriel started to cry.

Adrian enveloped her in his arms, surrounding her with his warm words and body. "Don't worry, sweeting," he whispered softly, "nothing can harm you here."

When her tears had ceased, he said, "Do you remember the nightmare? Sometimes when bad dreams are spoken aloud, the devils of the night lose their power."

"I . . . I was a prisoner in a stone cell much like my room here, but the walls moved inward, crushing me. I could feel my bones snapping. I could not even draw breath to scream, no matter how hard I tried."

Meriel shuddered at the memory but managed to suppress further tears. "Just outside the cell a demon mocked me, saying that I should trust him, that if I did he would set me free, but I knew that he was lying. And the worst, the very worst part"—she began to shake, her hands clenching convulsively—"was that the demon wore your face."

Adrian's stillness was palpable. Then he lay back on the pillows, pulling her down on top of him so he could caress her back with long, gentle strokes. "It was just a bad dream, love. You know that I would never hurt you."

"Of course not," Meriel said, surprised that he could think she might have believed otherwise. She laid her head on his shoulder and began to relax. "That is why the dream was so horrible—it masked evil with something good and true."

He brushed his lips against her forehead in a light sweet kiss. "It was only a dream. You must forget it now."

The nightmare was already half-forgotten; impossible to remember the demon when Adrian was here, so kind and so tender. As the tension flowed from her body, Meriel molded herself against him, hoping that he would not tell her to leave.

At peace with the world, she ran an idle hand across his chest, enjoying the contrasting textures of smooth flesh and the faint roughness of hair, then winced at the discovery of a gnarled ridge of scars along his ribs. She hated the reminder of what a warrior faced when he fought. What if the blade that made this scar had cut more deeply? She would not think of it.

Her light exploring fingers brushed across his nipple. Intrigued, she toyed gently with the soft point and felt it harden beneath her touch. With her head in the hollow below his shoulder, Meriel was intimately aware of all the subtle changes of Adrian's body, his unsteady breath and quickening heartbeat. Still more interesting were the changes in her own body, for they mirrored his, her own breath and heartbeat changing. Intrigued, she rubbed against him and felt her nipples tauten.

"Perhaps," he said, rather breathlessly, "it would be better if you did not do that. It . . . is not restful."

Obediently she closed her eyes, but without volition her hand continued moving. Beneath the bedclothes Adrian was entirely naked, and she was fascinated by the pattern of his hair, a wide silky span across his chest that narrowed to a whorled line leading down his flat midriff.

When she reached his navel, Meriel circled it playfully with the tip of her middle finger, then continued to quest lower. She was warm now, and he was warmer still. The back of her hand brushed his heated flesh and all of Adrian's muscles went rigid. He groaned and caught her hand, linking his fingers in hers and raising their joined hands to rest on his chest.

"I'm sorry," she said remorsefully. "You would rather be sleeping and I am disturbing you."

He gave a husky chuckle. "On the contrary, because you are disturbing me, I would rather not be sleeping. I would rather be"—he raised her hand and kissed her palm, his lips and tongue searing—"doing this."

Meriel gasped, her fingers curling with pleasure.

Wrapping his arms around her, Adrian rolled them both over until he was above her. "Or perhaps this," he murmured, finding her mouth with his.

His lips were gentle at first, exploring, until she opened her mouth, wanting more. As the kiss deepened, their breath mingled, and as she inhaled his essence something stirred deep inside her. His hand moved up to cup Meriel's right breast, molding and shaping the soft contours through the thin fabric of her shift. When he found her nipple and rolled it with delicately judged pressure, pure pleasure shafted through her, becoming a melting sensation in her loins.

Meriel made a purring noise in her throat. His thigh was between hers and she arched against it in a primal demand for closeness. His body drove once against hers, then stilled, and she felt a shudder run through him. With an effort so intense that the air seemed to vibrate, Adrian lifted himself away. Hoarsely he said, "For my sins you will drive me mad, *ma petite*."

"I didn't mean to anger you," she whispered, shaken. "I still don't always know what is right and what is wrong."

"You didn't anger me," he said, a trace of humor in his voice. "Merely breached my good intentions with amazing ease. What we did was not wrong, merely . . . untimely."

She sat up and swung her legs over the side of the

bed. "I'll go back to my room so that you may sleep."

"No!" Adrian caught Meriel and pulled her back into bed. Lying on his side, he tucked her back against his front and secured her with an arm around her waist. "We can lie here and contemplate our sins together."

She giggled and relaxed, loving his closeness and the feel of his hard body. Impossible to worry with Adrian so near.

As the room began to lighten, Adrian woke, finding that in the night his hand had shifted, coming to rest on the gentle curve of Meriel's breast. She still slept, a smile on her lips. He thought of her nightmare and winced, fearing that her hatred of him must lie just below the surface of her mind. She had such trust in him now, such misplaced trust. When—if—she remembered, seeing the trust on her face turn to loathing would be like a dagger in the belly.

But perhaps that would never happen. Except for that one nightmare, Meriel showed no signs of returning memory, and since she was otherwise fully recovered, perhaps that meant that her hatred was gone as well. "I will atone, *ma petite,*" he whispered, "for everything I did to you."

Early morning was a time when passion reached floodtide, and Adrian was no longer exhausted as he had been when she joined him in the night. Therefore he chose the wiser course and carried Meriel back to her own bed rather than waking her himself, since he had a lively suspicion of how that would end.

The early part of the day was taken with learning what had happened in his absence, but since he had been gone only a few days, duty was easily disposed of, leaving Adrian free to spend the afternoon with Meriel. He decided to take her to the mews. He knew from their first meeting that she was a mistress of falconry, and he was curious to see how she responded. He had an obscure belief that if she did not recover her memory after being introduced to skills and events from her past, he would be safe.

Meriel was happy to do anything Adrian suggested. He was not surprised to see that she donned the leather hawking gauntlet with the ease of total familiarity. Inside the mews, Meriel looked around with a sigh of pleased recognition, then crossed to the nearest perch. Not touching the great hooded bird, she asked softly, "She is a gyrfalcon, is she not? I have heard many tales of them, but never seen one."

Which meant that his lady of mystery had probably never been in the mews of a king or a chief baron, information that Adrian received with relief. Likely she was not Norman after all. "The gyr was a gift from the Empress Matilda," he replied. "She is temperamental, but the fastest bird I have ever flown."

As if to illustrate his point, the gyrfalcon suddenly bated, bolting screaming from the perch until jerked to a halt by the jesses, then swinging upside down, beating her wings while she continued to shriek. Meriel hastily stepped away while the falconer moved in to calm his nervous charge.

At the other end of the mews, Meriel stopped in front of a goshawk. Without even thinking, she untethered the bird and took it onto her gloved wrist. "There is something about the goshawk that is magnificent," she mused as its claws bit deep into the leather. "They are often ill-tempered, they care little for their masters, yet they have such wild courage. I once saw a gos ride on a stag's back, purely for amusement, I think. Another time I saw one on the ground fighting a hare face-to-face, though the hare was twice its size."

"Do you remember where that happened?" Adrian asked quietly.

Meriel froze. Her tenseness caused the gos to stir restively, and she returned the hawk to its perch, her movements overcareful. "No. I remember seeing those scenes, yet when I try to see more, there is nothing."

Adrian touched her shoulder comfortingly and they continued their tour of the mews. The chief falconer had been following at a respectful distance, and at the end he approached the earl. "There are reports of a falcon over toward the edge of the royal forest, my lord." His eyes flickered to Meriel. " 'Twas said that she might be a trained bird that had escaped, so I went to see if I could recapture her. I found her and she stooped to the lure, but raked away before I could take her."

"Really?" Adrian exchanged a glance with the falconer, knowing what was on the man's mind. Falcons had been known to return to a lure years after they had escaped. If this particular bird was the one that Meriel had whistled down the wind, it might return to her even if not to a stranger. Turning to his companion, he asked, "Would you like to see if you can capture a falcon?"

Surprised but game, Meriel replied, "Of course."

After getting precise directions to the area where the falcon was most often seen, Adrian took a bag of the needed equipment and escorted Meriel to the stables.

They had visited here, but Meriel had not attempted riding and she eyed the saddled mare with some doubt. "You are sure that I know how to ride?"

"You are an excellent rider," Adrian assured her as he helped her onto the horse's back.

For a moment, Meriel swayed uncertainly in the saddle. Then a look of pure bliss crossed her face. "Ahhh," she breathed happily, leaning forward to caress the mare's gleaming sorrel hide. "I have missed this."

Chuckling, Adrian mounted his own horse and they rode out of the castle.

Beyond the village, Meriel asked, "What is the mare's name?"

"You may name her whatever you wish."

Meriel cocked her head to one side as she thought. "I shall call her Rosalia."

Adrian felt a prickle on the back of his neck at how similar the name was to the one she had chosen before, Rose. Somewhere in her past, there must be another horse named Rose—or Rosalia—but where? Somehow he doubted that it was the aged horse she had claimed to have taken from her brother's farm.

As they rode east toward the royal forest, Adrian could not help wondering about her background, though he suspected that he would be better off never finding out. A woman who knew Latin and hawking and horses was not likely to be without protectors. But where had they been the day that he had found her?

Meriel herself was blithely unconcerned, content to enjoy the time in Adrian's company and her newfound riding ability. He envied her pristine conscience.

After about an hour's ride they reached a wide expanse of meadowland near the forest and began watching for the falcon, trotting parallel to the woodlands at a leisurely pace. It was a pleasant ride, but the afternoon passed with no success in their mission. Adrian was about to suggest that they return to Warfield when Meriel suddenly said, "There!" pointing high in the sky. "That is the one we seek."

Adrian was willing to admit that the tiny speck was a bird, but it was soaring so high as to be almost invisible.

Meriel, however, had no doubts. She dismounted. "Give me the hood, the lure, and the jesses, then move away," she said briskly, her eyes fixed on the sky.

Very rarely did anyone command the Earl of Shropshire, but Adrian obeyed, amused at her air of unconscious command. He gave Meriel what she needed from his pouch, then moved well back from her. When he was clear, she began swinging the lure with the skill of long practice.

At first it seemed that the bird was a wild one that would not respond. As Meriel patiently continued to swing the lure around her head, Adrian narrowed his eyes against the sun, doubting that she would be successful.

The bird changed the angle of its flight, as if considering. Then it began to stoop, diving at Meriel with the speed and precision that identified it beyond doubt as a falcon. Even the mighty gyr could not match a peregrine's stoop, and it was impossible to watch without feeling awe for what God had wrought.

Seconds later the falcon smashed into the lure with killing force, riding it to the ground. Even at his distance Adrian could hear Meriel's peal of delighted laughter. As the bird greedily gobbled the meat bound to the lure, Meriel moved in and deftly fastened the jesses to its legs. The falcon made no protest and in a few moments she was secured.

When the earl arrived and dismounted, Meriel looked up at him, her face glowing. "She came back to me, Adrian, she came back! There is no thrill greater than when a wild creature returns of its own will."

With feigned casualness he asked, "What is her name?"

"Chanson, of course," Then Meriel faltered, looking from the falcon to Adrian, then back. "How . . . how did I know that?"

"Did I mention that when I found you in the forest you had a falcon, but you whistled her down the wind?" He smiled, trying to conceal both guilt and apprehension. "Even at first meeting you did not trust me, so you set her free. I can't swear that this is the same bird, but I doubt that another would have come to you like that."

Meriel frowned, a gesture that constricted Adrian's heart, then shook her head. "I have no recollection of such a thing." The falcon had finished eating, so Meriel took it onto her wrist and scratched the feathered throat. Chanson made a sound of pleasure and happily fluffed her feathers.

''She has no doubts that she has come home, Meriel.''

She hooded the falcon, then looked up, her bright expression untroubled. ''Isn't it time we did the same?''

At her words, Adrian felt the tightness in his chest begin to ease. If Meriel did not recover her memory even after finding her falcon and being reminded of their meeting in the forest, surely she never would. For the first time he felt really safe. It was almost time to begin planning for the future. ''Yes, *ma petite*, it is time to go home.''

They headed back to the castle, Meriel carrying the falcon on her wrist and singing softly under her breath.

And as they rode, Adrian's sense of well-being shredded away when he realized that the song she sang so joyfully was one of the Latin hymns from the Benedictine service of Lauds, the song of a monk or a nun.

12

HAVING REDISCOVERED RIDING, Meriel was anxious to do more, so the next afternoon Adrian took her out again, following the river north until they came to a tributary and turned east. The day was a very warm one, and it was pleasant to follow the shady path that ran along the stream. Adrian had brought food and wine and they shared it by a hidden pool, laughing and talking of trivial things that were rendered amusing by the company.

Sprawled beneath a tree with Meriel an arm's length away, Adrian could not remember when he had been so content. More than content, happy. Though he was loath to end the day, eventually he sighed and said, "It is time we went back."

It was midafternoon and the hottest day that the young summer had yet produced. Adrian glanced at the stream with regret, thinking that if he had been alone or with Richard, he would have gone swimming.

Meriel had no such inhibitions. "Let us delay for a few minutes longer." Then she stood, untied her girdle, and let it drop to the ground.

Startled, Adrian sat up. "What are you doing?"

She peeled her bliaut off over her head, then removed her shoes and stockings. "Going into the water, of course. It is such a warm day." She stopped at the expression on his face. "Is that one of those things that is not done?" she asked uncertainly.

"It is done sometimes," he admitted, distracted by

how the thin fabric of her shift clung to her perspiration-damped curves.

Before he could collect himself enough to enumerate the conditions under which one was likely to enter a stream, she said, ''Good!''

Lifting her shift by the hem, Meriel pulled it off in one sinuous movement. She was neither brazen nor timid, but instead serenely comfortable with her body, like Eve before the Fall.

Mesmerized by the sight of her slim, perfectly proportioned figure, Adrian was rendered temporarily speechless, but as she blithely headed toward the water he managed to exclaim, ''Jesu, Meriel, can you swim?''

She glanced over her shoulder mischievously. ''I don't remember, but I'm about to find out.'' She wrapped her braids around her head in a coronet, then scampered across the grass and into the water.

Torn between amusement and concern, Adrian stripped off his own tunic, thinking that protecting Meriel from possible danger was a good excuse to do what he had wanted to do anyhow. In a few moments he was as bare as she was. He crossed to the stream and was about to enter when he stopped, his gaze caught by Meriel's.

She stood shoulder-deep in the water, her wide blue eyes fixed on him as if she had never seen a naked man before. Perhaps she had not.

Embarrassed by her grave regard, Adrian was unsure whether to advance or retreat. Before he could do either, she said softly, ''I never knew how beautiful a man can be.''

There was no mistaking the sincerity in her voice. While Adrian could not help but be gratified, her admiration embarrassed him even more and his face burned with rising color. The best cure was at hand, so he stepped into the stream, then dived below the surface and swam underwater toward Meriel. He managed to get a hand on her ankle, but she twisted out of his grip and escaped, squealing with delight.

Concern for her safety vanished quickly, for Meriel swam like an otter. There were people who considered open-air bathing to be unwholesome and a source of contagion, but children often ignored their elders on days such as this, and it was like children that they played, diving and darting and splashing each other. Laughter helped wash away Adrian's painful memories of Meriel's plunge into the Severn and his desperate search for her.

When Meriel made an attempt to duck Adrian and failed, he caught her shoulders and immobilized her. "Now I have you, water sprite," he said, chuckling. "I claim a forfeit."

"I have naught with which to pay a fine, Sir Knight," she said, fluttering her long black lashes piteously. "What is a poor maid to do?"

Laughter dropped away as Adrian looked down at his captive. The outlines of Meriel's lovely body were dimly visible below the surface. Her figure was delicate, not voluptuous but perfectly and exquisitely female.

And because of who she was, she was the most desirable woman he had ever known. "Ah, Meriel," he whispered, "I love you so. You need no forfeit, for you yourself are the richest prize any man could hope for."

Responding to his seriousness with her own, Meriel replied, "And I love you, for now and always." Raising her hands, she pulled his head down for a kiss.

Even as he knew that he should not give in to temptation, Adrian reveled in the taste of her mouth, exploring, greeting, welcoming. Having begun, he could not stop, and he trailed kisses across the fine bones of her cheek to her ear, where he traced the complex whorls with his tongue. She made a soft, rich sound deep in her throat and he sought the source, feeling the vibration of her pleasure against his lips.

Her flawless fair skin was beaded with moisture, and it was a short but infinitely enjoyable journey to her breast. He teased the nipple with his tongue and Meriel's whole body softened in response, until she was supported entirely by Adrian's arm. He kissed first one breast, then the other, while his free hand rejoiced in the subtle curves of her back and hips. Underwater her skin was slick and soft as silk.

When he stopped to draw breath, intoxicated with desire, Meriel leaned back across his arm, her gaze meeting his with absolute trust. Silently she mouthed the words "I love you."

He could not stop himself. His left arm circling beneath her shoulders as support, Adrian bent for another kiss as her body floated free beside him. With his right hand he caressed downward, enjoying every change in texture and consistency between her breast and her knee—here soft, there firm, here curving outward, there tapering in.

Even when he slowly drew his hand up her inner thigh, she did not flinch or draw back. She had no coyness or doubt or maidenly modesty, and her unconditional acceptance was more erotic than practiced wiles could ever be. With infinite tenderness he slid his fingers through her silken triangle of hair to the delicate folds below.

At Adrian's first intimate touch she gasped, not with fear but with delight. He ended the kiss so that they could both breathe, and clasped her against his chest as he penetrated more deeply, discovering her secret depths. He watched her face like a hawk, tuned to every one of her physical and emotional reactions, anticipating when to quicken, when to slow.

Meriel began to tremble, then cried out, her body convulsing uncontrollably against him in an ultimate act of trust. Her arms clenched around him, then relaxed. She did not open her eyes even when he drew her through the water to the edge of the stream, then lay down so both of them reclined on the grassy bank, the upper parts of their bodies out of the water, their lower bodies twined lazily beneath the surface.

Meriel lay across his chest like a pagan water nymph until her breathing had returned to normal. Then she opened her eyes and gazed up into his. "I did not dream that such pleasure existed," she whispered. "But what of you?"

"I have never known greater pleasure than in giving it to you," he said truthfully.

"That is a truth of the heart, but there is also truth of the body. Please, Adrian, make love to me." She reached up and linked her arms around his neck. "Do not deny me the chance to pleasure you."

Adrian ached with desire and she was granting him the right which he so desperately craved. But he would not—could not—accept. He drew a deep breath and marshaled his will, no easy task when Meriel watched with such warmth and when her willing body was wrapped around his. "To make love with you would be the greatest of pleasures, *ma petite,*" he said unsteadily. "But even more than pleasure, I want to do what is right in the eyes of God and man. For the ultimate joining, I will wait for our marriage bed."

Her eyes lit with joy. "Then you no longer think it is too soon to speak of marriage?"

"Perhaps it is, love," he said wryly, "but I can bear to wait no longer." By his actions today, Adrian had taken a kind of virginity from Meriel, and the longer he delayed, the greater the risk that he would take the rest without the blessing of the Church. He had sworn to treat Meriel with all honor, and tumbling her in a stream was hardly the best way of fulfilling his vow. *But he had also promised to do whatever she wanted, and now she wanted him to make love to her.*

Firmly he quashed the thought, knowing it to be self-serving. Marriage was the honorable course and he deserved the torments of waiting. "Shall we set a wedding date?"

Her face glowing like the dawn, Meriel whispered, "Yes, beloved, let us be wed as soon as possible."

She leaned forward to kiss him, and he shivered at her caress. They lay interwoven so closely that he knew he must break the kiss before his body took over from his mind. It would be easy, so easy, to consummate their troth right here. Only conscience barred the way.

Before Adrian could fulfill his good intentions, Meriel's hand slid down between them, moving lightly through the water until she found what she sought.

He was already fully aroused, and his whole body went rigid when she touched him. He gasped, "Meriel . . ." wanting to say that this was not necessary, that he did not want her to do anything that disquieted her. But there was no disquiet on her intent face, just satisfaction that she could kindle him so. And he could not have said more to save his life.

Her clasp was tentative at first, then surer as she studied and learned from his passionate, uncontrollable response. It took very little for her to bring him to the explosion point. Later Adrian wondered that she had been able to breathe as he crushed her to him, but at the time he was aware only of rapture.

This time it was her turn to feel satisfaction at what she had wrought. They lay in each other's arms, half-floating in the water, until finally Adrian said, "The sooner we get married, the better, *ma petite*. If this happens again, we might both drown."

She laughed in delight, then stood and wrung the water from one of her long braids. "I cannot imagine a better way to die."

"Speak for yourself," he said with mock severity as he climbed onto the embankment. "I am not at all sure that I want to enter Saint Peter's presence with that particular smile on my face. It would be too embarrassing to explain."

Meriel laughed again and wrapped her arms around his waist in a gesture of pure affection.

Adrian held her close, not ever wanting to let her

go, but under his pleasure was dark questioning. He had thought her a virgin, but perhaps she was not. Perhaps when they embraced she had drawn on unremembered experience, much as she had with riding and hawking. Though he hated the idea, he could accept that she might not be a virgin—after all, neither was he—but what if Meriel had a living husband? The fact that she was ringless was not proof that she was free.

Suppressing the thought, Adrian kissed her fiercely. Meriel was his, and they both knew it. No matter what her past, nothing would stop him from making her his wife.

It was sheerest chance that Sir Vincent de Laon happened to be in Shrewsbury when Adrian of Warfield and his betrothed visited. Warfield was popular in his city, and the citizens were abuzz with comment and approval as the earl rode through the streets with his future bride at his side, both of them smiling and waving.

Sir Vincent kept his distance even though he was dressed in a fashion that made it unlikely that he would be recognized. Even if he had been, Warfield would probably have done nothing; unlike Guy of Burgoigne, the empress's earl was a soft man, not quick enough to protect his interests. Still, the great lords were an unpredictable lot, and the Frenchman thought it wiser to stay at the back of the crowd.

As usual, the citizens were well informed. By the end of the afternoon, Sir Vincent had learned that the earl's marriage was to be celebrated with unseemly speed, and that he had brought his future wife to Shrewsbury so she could choose fabrics and jewels from the city's finest merchants while the earl transacted business with his sheriff.

Sir Vincent shook his head when he caught a glimpse of the woman Warfield had chosen as his wife: low in stature, hair black as pitch, and, it was said, Welsh.

214 • MARY JO PUTNEY

Since even the greatest Welsh heiress was unlikely to have a large dowry by Norman standards, it was obvious that Warfield could have done much better for himself. Incredible that he should have passed up Isabelle of Rouen for such a creature.

However, anything that weakened Warfield was good for Guy of Burgoigne, and for Guy's faithful supporters. As Sir Vincent rode back to Chastain Castle, it occurred to him that this might be the perfect time to discover if Richard FitzHugh could be persuaded to change his allegiance. Guy agreed and ordered his lieutenant to Montford to see what could be done.

Sir Richard FitzHugh received the Frenchman promptly, his handsome face open and amiable. They had once crossed swords in a skirmish but had never before met socially. After an exchange of pleasantries, Sir Vincent reached the derisory conclusion that the other man's swordarm was superior to his wit. FitzHugh was a typical hulking Norman, good in battle but no match for a man of superior subtlety. The Frenchman loved the process of seduction, whether it was coaxing an uncertain female to his bed or convincing a man to do something against his honor. 'Twould be a pleasure to persuade this simple Norman to sell his brother.

After enjoying an excellent dinner, Sir Vincent asked for a private audience with his host. Not surprisingly, it was granted right away. FitzHugh might have no great intellect, but he obviously had guessed that this was no social call.

The two men withdrew to the solar and began a leisurely discussion of politics over an excellent wine. Sir Vincent discerned little passion for the empress's cause in the other man; likely he served her only because his liege lord did.

When enough wine had been drunk to soften the atmosphere, Sir Vincent said casually, "I understand that your brother is about to take a wife."

FitzHugh rumpled the ears of a greyhound that had

just laid its head on his knee. "Hardly surprising. He has been seeking a wife for some time. The only question was whom he would choose."

"I saw Warfield with the wench in Shrewsbury, and I can't say that I understand the attraction." Sir Vincent hoped that the statement might provoke some juicy item of gossip, for his intuition told him that there must be an interesting tale behind the marriage, but FitzHugh's face remained blank. Perhaps he did not know the true story.

Mildly disappointed, Sir Vincent continued, "I should think it a bitter time for you. For years you have faithfully served Warfield. If something had happened to him, you would have had a very good claim to his honors since there was no legitimate heir." He shrugged delicately. "Within a year or so, that might no longer be the case."

An amused gleam showed in FitzHugh's blue eyes. "Legitimacy is not enough to hold an inheritance—it also takes strength. It will be years before a son of Adrian's will be strong enough to hold the land, or a daughter old enough to wed a man who can do it for her. Many years—and life is most uncertain."

Startled, Sir Vincent realized that FitzHugh might not be quite the stupid oaf he appeared. Testing the waters, he said, "You need not wait years to improve your lot."

The atmosphere changed as the real subject of this meeting came out in the open. FitzHugh's eyes narrowed. "Have you some suggestion of what I might do to better my circumstances?"

Sir Vincent frowned slightly, disapproving of such bluntness. 'Twould be more elegant to circle around the subject longer. But of course Normans were not know for subtlety. "Guy of Burgoigne is a generous lord, and he would suitably reward a man willing to . . . rethink his allegiance to Adrian of Warfield."

After a charged silence, FitzHugh said, "You interest me, but it would take more than vague promises before I would do something so drastic. What would Guy expect of me, and what would he offer in turn?''

''Lord Guy would expect you to bring him Montford Castle and all of the lands you now control. In return, you would continue to hold them for him.''

''How would my situation be better than it is now?'' FitzHugh asked, his left hand absently fondling the fortunate greyhound.

''First, he will enfeoff you so that you will hold the castle in your own right rather than as your brother's warden. Second, joining Lord Guy will place you in the king's camp.'' Sir Vincent waved his hand dismissively. ''Granted, the empress's husband has made himself master of Normandy, but she has lost England and her son Henry will have to content himself with being Duke of Normandy. It is Stephen's son Eustace who will be King of England. Since you have no Norman holdings, which ruler's favor will serve you better?''

Sir Vincent paused to let the force of his words sink in, then advanced to the last major point. ''Also, Lord Guy would be happy to use his influence with Stephen to promote a match between you and a suitable heiress. I have never heard that your brother has done as much, in spite of your loyal service.'' He sipped his wine lazily, drawing out the moment like the serpent making its offer in Eden. ''If Warfield will not reward your courage and loyalty, then take them to a man who will.''

FitzHugh leaned back in his chair and steepled his fingers in front of him. ''What makes you think I wish to take a wife?''

''Because real power is in the hands of married men—you know that as well as I do. For as long as you remain unwed, you are 'a young knight,' no matter what your age, a man of little consequence or influence.'' Sir Vincent leaned forward persuasively. ''If you join Lord Guy, you can begin to build power of your own, not spend the rest of your life waiting on Warfield's caprice.''

FitzHugh's face showed no sign of what he thought. ''Fine words, but the fact remains that of the two earls, Adrian is in the stronger position, controlling more of Shropshire and its revenues. He is also master of an impregnable castle. I am still not convinced that going over to Guy will improve my lot.''

Sir Vincent felt a small stir of pleasure that his persuasive skills were needed. He thought a moment. FitzHugh surely held some resentment for his brother, and the seeds of that could be nourished into a healthy growth. Making his voice low and confidential, he said, ''You and I are in much the same position, landless knights forced to use our wits to survive, not fortunate like Adrian, who had the luck to be born to wealth.

''Because I sympathize with you, I will tell you a secret. Before the summer is over, the balance of power will change. Lord Guy has engaged one of the finest mercenary troops in Europe. After it arrives in Shropshire, Warfield will be broken. It may be impossible to take his castle, but everything else will fall to Guy.''

Sir Vincent leaned back in his chair again, sure that his arguments would prevail. ''If you change allegiance now, Guy will have reason to be grateful to you. But if you wait to see which way the wind blows, it will be too late, for you will have nothing left to bargain with.'' He made a graceful gesture at the walls around them. ''Montford is strong, but it is not so strong as Warfield, and it will be one of Lord Guy's first targets.''

FitzHugh's gaze was unfocused as he considered. Finally he said, ''You have a persuasive tongue, Sir Vincent. But what surety would there be of Guy's good faith?'' A trace of irony entered his voice. ''Forgive me for mentioning this, but there have been occasions when his good faith has been questioned.''

Very true, though Sir Vincent managed to sound indignant when he replied, ''The earl pledges his word, of course. And as a token of his faith, he sent this small gift.''

The Frenchman reached into his pouch and produced a tall golden goblet. It was a masterpiece of smithery, the stem a swirl of repoussé vines, the foot and bowl lavish with filigree. Rainbow-hued jewels were set wherever lines of webbed gold intersected. The cup was one of the best pieces of plate from Cecily of Chastain's inheritance, fit to serve an emperor, and Guy had saved it for some special use.

When FitzHugh took the heavy goblet, the Frenchman noticed that there was a faint tremor in his fingers. Very good; greed was gaining the upper hand.

The Norman rose from his chair and carried the cup to the window and turned it thoughtfully, admiring its artistry. Sapphire and ruby fires flared from the gemstones and the rich gold shimmered and coruscated in the sunlight. ''A pretty bauble,'' he said at last. ''Much more valuable than thirty pieces of silver.''

Before the Frenchman could evaluate that rather disquieting remark, FitzHugh glanced up at his guest. ''Tell me, Sir Vincent, how long have you been with Guy? Five or six years?''

The Frenchman nodded.

''Then perhaps you do not know the origins of the bad blood between Burgoigne and Warfield. You do know that they are more than simply rivals for an earldom?''

Puzzled, Sir Vincent admitted, ''I have heard that the enmity goes back for some years.'' He frowned, trying to remember what he had been told. ''Didn't Lord Guy burn the old Warfield keep back in his robber days? I recall hearing that Lord Adrian was a novice at Fontevaile Abbey when he inherited.'' The Frenchman laughed maliciously. ''Perhaps he should have stayed a monk. He seems not to have the stomach for fighting, and it took him long to find the stomach for marriage. Perhaps, like many monks, he has not the taste for wenches. It would have been better if he had left Warfield to you.''

His voice still calm, FitzHugh said, ''Perhaps no one ever told you that when Guy burned Warfield, he slaughtered all of the inhabitants, including the old baron and all his descendants save Adrian. And me, of course.'' He set the goblet on an oak table near his guest.

Then, moving with explosive suddenness, FitzHugh pulled his sword from his sheath. The sun glittered wickedly on the whirling blade. Aware that somehow he had misjudged matters disastrously, Sir Vincent gaped, terrified that he was about to be spitted like a suckling pig on his host's blade.

Before he could scramble to his feet and grab for his own weapon, the other man smashed the hilt of his sword into the gold cup, crushing the delicate workmanship with a shriek of rending metal. As FitzHugh struck the cup again and again, gems broke from their settings and rattled to the floor.

After sheathing the sword with a savage gesture, FitzHugh seized the crumpled remnants of the goblet. With his bare hands he twisted it until its original shape was unrecognizable. ''Does Guy forget that the family he murdered was not just Adrian's, but mine?'' he raged. ''*My* father, *my* brothers, *my* friends and kin died that day, and I was there to pull their bodies from the smoldering ruins.''

Viciously he hurled the goblet into Sir Vincent's belly. ''*That* is my answer to your master. I would see him in hell before I would lift a finger to aid him. If Adrian had not already marked Guy for his own, I would kill him myself. Perhaps, if I am lucky, I may still be the one to do the deed.''

Sir Vincent struggled for breath, wondering if the thrown goblet had cracked a rib. But since it appeared that FitzHugh was not going to kill him, the Frenchman was emboldened to strike back, furious that he had so badly misjudged his man.

"If you wait for Warfield to avenge your dead, then you wait in vain," he snarled. "Your brother is a coward, and you are either a coward or a fool to wait upon his vengeance." He stood and grabbed his cloak, then shoved the ruined cup into his pouch, preferring not to stay for any further pleasantries.

To Sir Vincent's surprise, his taunt did not anger his host further. Instead, FitzHugh laughed. "If you or Guy think that of Adrian, you are worse than fools— you are dead men. Now, get out, before I forget the laws of hospitality and send you prematurely to the devil."

Sir Vincent was more than willing to obey. Richard watched him scuttle out with disgust. The only thing that had saved the Frenchman's slimy neck was the fact that he had not been with Burgoigne at the time of the Warfield massacre.

It might have been wiser to pretend to take Burgoigne's bribe, then withdraw support at the most critical moment, but Richard knew that he did not have the temperament to play a double game. Adrian probably could, but Richard had been hard-pressed to hold his tongue long enough to learn about the mercenaries. Still, that was valuable information, and forewarned was forearmed.

Two months after his sister had disappeared, a grim-faced Alan de Vere arrived back at Avonleigh to resume the hunt. He began his task by ascertaining exactly what areas had been searched when Meriel had disappeared, finding that his men had gone as far west as the royal forest, and rather farther in the other three directions.

No one had seen a trace of his sister after she had gone out of view of the Avonleigh fields. That fact made Alan wonder if for some reason she might have entered the forest, because if she had ridden in one of the other directions she would almost certainly have been seen by serfs on the adjoining manors.

The forest's dark width divided eastern and western Shropshire like a broad river. Ordinarily Meriel would never have gone that far west, or entered the forest, or crossed into the territory controlled by the empress's men. But something extraordinary could have happened; she might have been pursued by robbers, or have met someone needing help—any number of things could have sent her into the forest and out the other side. If that had happened, word might never reach Avonleigh, for twenty miles could be almost as great a barrier as the English Channel.

Alan decided that the best place to begin his search was at the market in Shrewsbury, and he rode over and spent the night before the next market day.

The next morning he found what he was seeking within the first hour.

The morose apothecary had denied any knowledge of lost Norman lasses, but his chatty wife said, " 'Tis an odd coincidence. You say your sister is named Meriel?"

When Alan nodded, she said, "The Earl of Shropshire, *our* earl, Adrian of Warfield, not that wicked other one, is marrying a girl named Meriel. But she's Welsh, not Norman. I saw her when they came into the town last week."

His interest caught, Alan asked, "What did the earl's betrothed look like?"

The apothecary's wife shrugged. "Welsh, you know. Black hair, blue eyes." She scanned him with critical approval. "Rather like yours, but a little bit of a thing. A sweet-natured lass, she is. Looked right at me and smiled."

Clamping down his excitement, Alan asked, "What is known of her family?"

" 'Tis said she is an heiress from Gwynedd. Well, of course she would be an heiress, noblemen like the earl don't marry just anyone. Still . . ." The woman leaned forward confidentially. "They say Earl Adrian found her in the forest, like a fairy princess, and was so struck by love that he took her back to his castle and locked her in a tower until she agreed to marry him, but I for one don't believe a word of it. The earl has never been one for ravishing wenches." She giggled. "He don't need to, handsome devil that he is. More likely he has to take care that wenches don't abduct *him*."

Alan felt chilled, convinced that the Meriel in question must be his sister, for the story fitted what might have happened. Shorn of the romantic trappings, it was a story of abduction and rape, for Meriel would never have abandoned her friends and responsibilities unless she were being held by force. It was easy to believe that a nobleman would ravish a chance-met girl. Harder to understand was that such a man would marry his victim. Would a hardened villain have felt guilt over ruining a gently born maiden?

"You say that they are going to be wed," Alan said, his mouth dry. "Do you know if the marriage has taken place yet?"

"No idea, lad, I wasn't invited." She chuckled at her wit. "But they say it was going to be a hasty ceremony, so maybe a babe is on the way. Even lords are human, though 'tis not everyone as would agree with me."

Blindly Alan left a handful of silver pennies and walked away, fury raging within him. The earl had the reputation of an honest man, but perhaps the reputation was a false one, because honest men did not ruin innocent young women.

Alan's step quickened as he headed to the inn where he had left his horse. He was going to go to Warfield Castle as quickly as possible to find his sister. He might be only a knight and Lord Adrian an earl, but if the other man could not provide satisfactory answers, Alan de Vere would tear his castle down with his bare hands.

13

"HOLD YOUR ARMS above your head, Lady Meriel," Margery commanded.

Meriel docilely did as she was bidden and the blue silk gown was dropped over her fine linen shift. Knowing that today she would wed Adrian had her in such a state of dreamy anticipation that it was hard to be concerned about clothing. Fortunately Margery and the other women were more than willing to be concerned for her.

Since deciding that it was time to marry, Adrian had spent much time introducing his future bride to the Warfield household. Some were wary of her at first, but all had soon warmed. Adrian said it was because Meriel learned quickly, yet did not try to bully any of the folk who would serve her.

"Is that too tight, my lady?" one of the maids asked as she laced up the gown to fit as neatly as an apple's skin.

"Remember that I must breathe all day, and perhaps eat something later," Meriel pointed out.

The maid giggled and loosened the laces a bit while Meriel drifted back into her thoughts. Learning to be a countess was all well and good, but while Adrian had always been there for company and guidance, he had kept a decorous distance from her, giving not so much as a good-night kiss. Fortunate that the wedding was here, or she might have found herself creeping into his chamber at night to see if she could change his mind.

Meriel sighed. She knew that it was important to Adrian that he act according to his notion of honor. Perhaps if she remembered more, her own morality would be stronger; she could not quite understand his desire to wait until they were wed. Still, she did know that persuading Adrian to do something he would regret later would be a poor way of showing how much she loved him.

Her lips curved into a smile as she thought of the night she had shared his bed. Tonight there would be that and more, for there would be no barriers of honor between them.

The world once more interrupted her reverie as Kestrel galloped over and batted at one of the gold-embroidered sleeves, which trailed almost to the floor. Meriel would have liked to pick up the cat for a quick cuddle, but knew that Margery would not approve of what claws could do to fragile silk. Kestrel's fate was sealed when she pounced on one end of Meriel's new girdle, a gold-threaded cord with good-luck gemstones woven into it. The youngest maid hastily scooped up the cat. "I'll put her somewhere where she can't cause mischief and won't be stepped on, my lady."

Meriel smiled wryly as the cat was borne off; she and Kestrel would be equally glad when the wedding was over! As bride, Meriel's task was much like Kestrel's: to hold still and behave herself.

Margery lifted Meriel's hair out of the way, laid her mistress's crimson mantle over her shoulders, and fastened it across her breast with a golden chain. Then, because Meriel was wearing her hair loose, the maid began combing the heavy black tresses that rippled past her mistress's slim hips.

Stalwart under the tugging comb, Meriel absently stroked the mantle's luxurious velvet folds and miniver trim, thinking thoughts that would have shocked her attendants. Or perhaps not. They were an earthy lot, and there had been a number of frank, enthusiastic comments about what the new countess would have to look forward to in Lord Adrian's embrace.

Finished with combing, Margery lifted the delicate sendal veil, so gauzy as to be nearly transparent. The maid set it over Meriel's cascading hair, adjusting it to frame the bride's face, then fixed the veil in place with a chaplet of tiny interwoven blue and white blossoms. The chaplet was the only item that Meriel had insisted on, since she preferred real flowers to a cold metal circlet.

Margery circled her mistress for a final inspection, tweaking a fold here, smoothing fabric there. Finally she smiled. "There, my lady. You look as pretty as a summer dawn."

Meriel could not resist saying, "As soon as I step outside in the breeze, all this perfection will disappear."

Margery laughed while wiping an incipient tear from her eye. "But I'll have done my job right, my lady."

"You all have." Meriel stepped forward and gave Margery a light kiss on the cheek, then did the same for the other three maids. "Thank you for being my family today."

Her words broke the composure of all four attendants and Meriel left the room accompanied by a storm of weeping. She knew it was traditional for women to cry at weddings, but could not imagine why—she herself was floating on happiness.

There were other people below in the great hall, but Meriel saw only Adrian, who waited for her at the foot of the stairs. Today he had set aside his preference for simplicity and wore the silk-and-velvet grandeur of his rank. His tunic and mantle were in shades of deep blue, banded lavishly with silver embroidery that dimmed beside his silver-gilt fairness. He glowed like an archangel, so beautiful that he took her breath away.

Meriel stopped on the next-to-last step, suddenly shy, not quite believing that this superior being truly wished to marry her. Perhaps Adrian read her thoughts, because he came and caught her hands in his, speaking so softly that no one else could hear. "They say that all brides are beautiful, but there has never been a bride so beautiful as you, *ma petite,* and there never will be again." Then he kissed her hands, first one, then the other.

A shiver ran through Meriel and her fingers tightened around his. "And there has never been a woman more blessed than I," she whispered, "for you have chosen me for your wife."

Together they walked from the hall to their horses. Adrian's brother Richard waited, as splendidly garbed as the earl. Since Meriel had no family, Richard helped her mount, taking the role the bride's father usually had.

Preceded by a band of musicians, followed by the chief wedding guests, with Richard leading her mare and Adrian by her side, Meriel rode from the castle to the village church. The streets were lined with Adrian's tenants. Normally a lord's wedding would have taken place at the bride's home, so the people of Warfield felt particularly fortunate that they could witness this one.

Richard helped Meriel from her horse with a warm smile and a soft "Courage, little sister, soon it will be over."

If Meriel had a brother, she would like one like Richard. For a moment she remembered that she might have a brother, perhaps more than one. She pushed the thought away. Better to think of what she was gaining than what she might never know.

Then she was standing under the church porch, Adrian's right hand clasped in hers. Because Adrian hoped that in time there would be no more distinction between Norman and Englishman, they had chosen to exchange vows in English, using the same words that any villager might.

Meriel felt as if she moved in a dream, her gaze locked to Adrian's as he spoke the vows. *I take thee*

*to be my wedded wife . . . to have and to hold . . .
for fairer, for fouler . . . for better, for worse . . . for
richer, for poorer . . . in sickness and in health . . .
from this time forward . . . till death us do part . . .
if Holy Church will it ordain . . . and thereto I plight
thee my troth.* But words meant less than the expression of his clear gray eyes, where he pledged her his
very soul.

Then it was her turn. Raising her voice, so that no
one could doubt her willingness, Meriel repeated her
own vows. They were similar to Adrian's, but included
the promise to be "blithe and obedient in bed and at
board." When she reached that phrase, Meriel found
herself blushing. Adrian's face was solemn, but his
fingers tightened on hers and a spark of teasing promise showed deep in his eyes.

The priest gave a short homily on the virtues of conjugal harmony, then blessed the ring. Adrian took
Meriel's left hand in his and slipped the gold circlet
over three of her fingertips in turn, saying at the same
time, "In the name of the Father . . . and of the Son
. . . and of the Holy Ghost." Then he slid the band
fully onto her third finger with the quiet words, "With
this ring I thee wed."

Adrian's gaze held Meriel's. Though they were outwardly quiet, both were blazingly aware of the bonds
of spirit, heart, and body that connected them. Now
Meriel understood why Adrian had wanted to wait until they were wed to make her fully his own, and the
understanding brought tears of profound joy to her
eyes.

They might have stood handfast indefinitely if Richard had not begun to distribute the traditional alms.
Brought back to a sense of the occasion, the earl and
his new countess went into the church for the nuptial
mass. Every corner of the church filled with people,
with Meriel and Adrian in seats of honor in the choir.
She ignored the sonorous Latin words; what mattered
was that below the level of the carved railing Adrian

held her hand, his fingers locked around hers as if he would never let go.

After the service the priest gave the kiss of peace to Adrian, who then transmitted it to Meriel. Her new husband's kiss was not overtly carnal, but his lips held hers with aching sweetness. When Adrian finally released her, he whispered, "For now and for always, little wife."

Meriel could not help herself; she departed from dignified custom by throwing her arms around her new husband. As Adrian caught her up against him so forcefully that her elegant leather slippers lifted from the floor, the onlookers broke into cheers and laughter in spite of the priest's quelling expression.

There was one more deviation from custom. As they left the church, they passed under the tower where the bell-ropes hung. Adrian stopped, a mischievous gleam in his eye. Grabbing one of the ropes, he said exuberantly, "I want the whole of Shropshire to know that we have wed."

Above their heads Great Tom, the deep bass bell, boomed out with a resonance that made the tower vibrate. Meriel could not resist joining in. Loving the sunny day, the happy crowd, the whole wonderful world, and most of all loving Adrian, she seized another rope, pulling with all her weight until the soprano bell, Little Nell, pealed out a rapturous chime.

For a few clamorous, laughing minutes Meriel and Adrian rang the bells and the whole parish resounded with their joy. Then the regular parish bell-ringers arrived, apologizing breathlessly for having neglected their duty by being caught in the crowd.

As the ringers took over the bells and the chiming settled into a more normal rhythm, Adrian and Meriel emerged hand-in-hand into the village square to be pelted with seeds. The ride back was slow, as everyone in Warfield seemed to want to wish the new couple happiness. When he helped Meriel dismount in front of the castle, Adrian said softly, for her ears only,

"Only a few hours of feasting and dancing, *ma petite*—then we can be alone."

"And you can teach me how to be blithe and obedient in bed, my dearest lord," Meriel replied, her heart overflowing with love. She hoped that the next hours would fly.

The outer gate of Warfield was guarded by only two men, and the streets visible inside the walls looked deserted as Alan rode up in the late afternoon. When a guard good-humoredly asked his business, he replied, "I am the brother of Lady Meriel."

The guard inspected him. Alan's clothing might be travel-stained, but he was unmistakably a Norman knight and his face confirmed his story. "Aye, you've the look of the new little countess," he said cheerfully. "You were delayed?" Without waiting for an answer, he continued, "You missed the wedding, but the feast is going on up at the keep. Go along now, and give the bride a kiss for those of us who are missing the festivities."

Alan rode through the quiet streets with his teeth gritted. So he was too late. Or perhaps not, since the feast was still going on. A great tent had been set up in the outer bailey, and there the common folk were celebrating. Whole calves and sheep were roasting, with cooks carving off slices as the meat was done. Barrels of ale were everywhere evident and the air was filled with the gay clamor of harps, pipes, and viols.

Alan left his horse at the stables and walked right into the keep. The great hall was somewhat more decorous than the bailey, and the music was better. Jongleurs, acrobats, and singers entertained; guests feasted, drank, and danced; servants scurried about with platters of food and pitchers of drink; dogs and cats foraged for savory tidbits in the rose-strewn rushes. It was everything one would expect at the wedding of a nobleman.

Alan stood in the door, attracting no notice, while

his vision adjusted to the dim light. At the far end of the hall was a table set above the others, and his heart constricted as he saw the small, dark-haired figure of the bride. He could not be sure, but she looked painfully like his sister.

With rapid strides he made his way along the wall completely unchallenged, even though his hard face was not what one usually saw at a wedding. From the edge of the platform he could see the bride and groom from an angle. Maddeningly, he could still not be sure the girl was his sister, for her head was turned away and a cloud of veiled hair obscured her profile.

All the bride's attention was on the man at her side, and Alan shifted his gaze to the groom. So this was the Earl of Shropshire. Turned toward his bride, his face was clearly visible. He was surprisingly young, and surprisingly contained for such a riotous setting. Alan studied the cool, handsome features, wondering if this was a man capable of forcing a girl into marriage, and concluded that it was.

Then the bride laughed and made a quick gesture of her hand, a movement Alan had seen his sister make a thousand times. He came up behind the bridal pair and said sharply, so that his voice would cut through the din, "Meriel!"

The bride turned at the sound of her name and looked up at Alan. His heart leapt at the sight of his sister, alive and well, her great blue eyes shining with happiness. He had never seen her look lovelier, but how the devil had she gotten here?

Meriel smiled up at him with the polite expression of a bride receiving the best wishes of a stranger. Her face was utterly devoid of recognition. "Welcome," she said warmly. "You are a late-come friend of my husband's?"

Not understanding, Alan asked, "Meriel, what is wrong?"

"Why, nothing," she replied, puzzled that a

stranger would ask such a thing. "I have never been happier."

With the devastating suddenness of an ax blow, Alan realized that she didn't know him. It was unbelievable, yet the truth was written on her uncomprehending face. "Jesu, Meriel," he cried in anguish. "Don't you recognize me?"

Her smile faded. "I'm sorry . . ." She faltered, distress clouding her eyes. "I do not."

By this time, the scene had attracted the attention of the nearest people, including the earl. His voice edged, Warfield asked, "You know my wife?"

Alan swung around and looked down into the earl's ice-gray eyes. Later he realized that Warfield showed an odd blend of emotions—surprise, anger, and a kind of fear, though not a physical one—but at the time, Alan was too furious to care. "You bastard," he snarled. "What have you done to Meriel?"

His fingers balled into a fist and he was beginning to swing when a hard hand caught him above the elbow. Alan turned and saw he had been stopped by a tall golden-haired man whose steady eyes were level with Alan's.

His voice pleasant but his grip firm, the man said, "We should be happy to hear whatever you know of Meriel's past, but let us find a better place to speak."

The earl had also risen. Now he assisted his bride to her feet. "An excellent notion, Richard."

The four of them left, scarcely noticed by the revelers. Upstairs, the solar was blessedly quiet. As soon as the door closed, Alan swung around, breaking the grip on his arm. Ignoring the other men, he spoke directly to his sister. "In the name of God, Meriel, what has happened? If you are here willingly, why did you tell no one at Avonleigh?" His voice broke. "They told me you were dead."

Her face pale, Meriel sank into a chair, shaking her head miserably. "I'm sorry, but . . . I had an accident. I remember nothing before the last few weeks."

Adrian went to stand by Meriel, one hand protectively on her shoulder. "Are you sure that she is the woman you think she is? Could you not be mistaken?"

The handsome stranger gave him a look of furious disgust. With one finger he brushed back Meriel's hair, showing a small scar on her right temple. "This was made by a stone, when she tripped and fell. And this . . ." He pulled back a trailing silk sleeve to show a thin, almost invisible scar on her left forearm. "Meriel was bled here when she had the fever."

As if she was used to the man's touch, Meriel did not draw back, simply stared up at him with her brow furrowed, trying to remember what intimacy had been between them.

Adrian's fingers tightened on Meriel's shoulder. He felt as if he had received a mortal blow and his life's blood was gushing forth onto the floor. Harshly he asked, "What are you to Meriel? Friend? Lover? Husband?"

"Of course not," the stranger snapped. "I'm her brother. Have you no eyes?"

The relief was so intense that Adrian's knees weakened. He studied his visitor, the height and powerful build that were so different from Meriel's, then the finely cut features. "You are right, I might have guessed. It is strange, you look as Norman as Meriel looks Welsh, yet the likeness is unmistakable."

Meriel spoke, her voice thin. "Will you stop talking as if I am not here?" She turned to the black-haired stranger. "You say you are my brother. What is your name? What is *my* name?"

The stranger knelt before her, his voice gentling in the face of her distress. "You are Lady Meriel de Vere and I am your brother Alan. Our father William held a manor called Beaulaine in Wiltshire. Our mother was Welsh and you are the very image of her. She died some years ago. You and I are the youngest of five children. For the last two years you have lived with me at my manor of Avonleigh. When I was away serving my lord, you ruled in my absence. You remember nothing of this?''

She shook her head, her great blue eyes stark. "I'm sorry," she whispered, "but I do not."

Alan had thought that learning Meriel was alive would mean unbounded happiness, but he had never imagined a scene such as this, nor dreamed how much it would hurt that she did not know him. Remembering the silver mirror he had bought, he pulled it from the pouch on his belt, where he had carried it as a talisman since learning of Meriel's disappearance.

The earl silently stepped back as Alan put his arm around Meriel's shoulders, then held the mirror up so their faces were reflected side by side in the polished silver. His sister studied the reflection—the deep blue eyes, the black hair, the planes of cheek and jaw told the story.

"I see," Meriel said softly. She raised her gaze to Alan, an expression of wonder and rising joy on her face. Then, with utter simplicity, she leaned forward and put her arms around him.

Alan hugged her back with profound relief. While Meriel might not remember, she did accept him and he was grateful for that.

She loosened her arms and gave him the sweet smile that was the essence of Meriel. "Earlier today I was wishing that I had a brother to see me wed. I am grateful that you found me on this of all days." Her expression became troubled. "I am very sorry that you thought I was dead. It must have been dreadfully difficult for you. If it was through a failing of mine that you heard such evil tidings, I ask your pardon with all my heart."

Alan shook his head. "I am sure the fault was not yours. You were ever the kindest and most considerate of sisters. That is why everyone at Avonleigh was sure you must have died. It was unthinkable that you would have gone off without a word."

Then Alan swung around, his voice low and dangerous. "But you, my lord earl, have a great deal to answer for. It is said in Shrewsbury that you found Meriel in the forest and kept her prisoner until she promised to marry you. How dare you do such a thing to a girl of gentle birth!" His voice roughened. "And what the devil did you do to her, that she remembers nothing of her life and family?"

Adrian watched his new brother-in-law with wry respect. Though he was alone in a castle surrounded by Adrian's men, Alan de Vere flung his challenge without fear. Even if there was not the family resemblance, that heedless goshawk courage confirmed that this was Meriel's brother.

He drew a deep breath, wondering if the day of reckoning for his crimes against Meriel had arrived. "The story you heard in Shrewsbury is essentially true, though more complicated than the bare facts. I did discover your sister in the forest when I was hunting. Meriel had been slightly injured in an accident. She was on foot and carried a falcon, and a game bag that implied she had been poaching. She claimed to be a Welshwoman on her way to Lincoln. I doubted her story." A faint smile touched his lips. "Your sister is a terrible liar. Not knowing who she was, and concerned for her safety, I was reluctant to turn her loose."

Puzzled, Alan de Vere glanced at his sister. "Why did you say such a thing?"

Her voice barely audible, Meriel said, "I don't remember." She rubbed her temple, looking so forlorn that Adrian took her hand again. Her cold fingers gripped his convulsively.

Richard had been leaning on the edge of a table, his arms folded across his chest. Now he said, "You mentioned Avonleigh. That is part of Theobald of Moreton's honor, is it not?" When de Vere nodded, Richard continued, "Lord Theobald is a follower of the king, while Adrian supports the empress. Could Meriel have been concerned about possible repercussions to Avonleigh if she identified herself? Particularly since you were away?''

Sir Alan frowned. "It seems like something Meriel might do," he said slowly, "if she had reason to be concerned.''

Honestly bewildered, Adrian said, "Where could she have gotten the idea that I might attack a manor without cause?''

"With all due respect, Adrian, your demeanor is not always such as to inspire trust," Richard said with a hint of dry amusement. "Besides, that may not be the correct answer. It is merely one possibility.''

"A plausible one." De Vere's eyes narrowed. "I want to hear more about the 'accident' Meriel had. How was she injured so badly that she remembers nothing?''

"She had a fall," Adrian said tersely. Then, before de Vere could inquire further, he continued, "I am sorry for the distress your sister's disappearance caused you and your household. I swear that if I had known Meriel's true name and residence, I would have returned her safely to her home, then asked to marry her in the proper manner.''

His fingers tightened on Meriel's. "The circumstances were unfortunate, but that is in the past. Your sister freely consented to marry me. The match is a good one in a worldly sense and you will have no cause to complain of how I treat her." He paused to let that sink in, then said with cool emphasis, "Since the marriage is an accomplished fact, I hope you will accept it with good grace.''

Alan de Vere's deep blue eyes, so like Meriel's, gleamed with fury. "You expect me to accept with complaisance the fact that you have seduced or ravished my sister? Never! And the law is on my side, for the Church says a marriage that results from an abduction is invalid, even if the man later frees the woman.''

The atmosphere was explosive. Adrian felt his stom-

ach tighten, knowing that the legal and moral ground
was very soft beneath him. But that was merely the
law; if Adrian had to defy the pope, the king, and the
empress to keep Meriel, he would do so. "I neither
ravished nor seduced your sister," he said, deciding
that it was time to use his strongest weapon. "Meriel,
do you wish to go with your brother?"

Her dismayed gaze shot up to his. What she saw in
Adrian's face reassured her, for she stood and walked
to her brother, taking his hands in hers. "Please, if
you have a care for me, do not try to alter what is
done. Adrian is my husband—he has been all that
is kind and I love him dearly. Can you not accept that
for my sake?"

It would have taken a heart of stone not to be moved
by her plea. De Vere's anger faded, leaving his face
sad and empty. "Very well, Meriel, if it is truly your
wish. But remember that you have a home at Avonleigh. If you ever change your mind, if anything at all
happens, you will always be welcome there." His voice
shook a little. "And perhaps . . . you might visit us."

"Of course." She smiled up at him warmly. "It is
strange. Though I do not remember any of the past, I
know that we have been close and I pray that we will
be again. Perhaps, in time, I will remember more."

"You are welcome to visit Meriel here whenever
you wish, Sir Alan," Adrian added. No matter how
uncomfortable such a visit might be, he owed the other
man all possible consideration.

De Vere's venomous expression did not augur well
for future visits, but he said nothing that might distress
Meriel. "Treat her well," he said tightly, then turned
to his sister. "Good-bye, Meriel. May God keep you."

"You will not stay for the feast?" she asked shyly.

With some effort, her brother smiled at her. "I am
in no fit mood for a wedding celebration." Remembering the silver mirror, he handed it to her. "Here,
a bride gift. I bought it for you in France before I
heard that you had disappeared."

Meriel stood on her toes and kissed him. "Thank you for caring enough to find me, and for understanding."

Wanting some questions answered before Meriel's brother left, Adrian said, "I assume that if your sister was already betrothed or married, you would have said so?"

De Vere nodded. "I had been considering possible marriages for her, but nothing had been settled."

Probably that meant her brother had not been able to afford to dower her, which must have hurt his pride. Adrian understood pride. Not showing his thoughts, he said, "I've also wondered if Meriel was educated at a convent."

Her brother paused, one hand on the doorknob. "More than just educated. She spent several years at Lambourn Priory and came within two days of taking the veil." Then he left the solar, closing the door behind him rather harder than necessary.

No wonder Meriel could read and sing Benedictine hymns. And Jesu, Lambourn Priory of all places! Adrian stared at his bride. Meriel had been looking after her departing brother, but now she turned to face Adrian, her face strained and vulnerable.

After a perceptive glance, Richard pushed himself off the table where he had been perching. "I suspect that neither of you is in the mood for further feasting or a formal bedding. Fortunately, no one downstairs would dare try to persuade an earl to do either against his will. Shall I take it on myself to ensure that the wine continues to flow, the dancers to dance, and that no young hothead starts a brawl?"

"I would be eternally grateful," Adrian said with a weary smile. "I feel an intense need to be alone with my wife."

He took Meriel's hand and together they walked down the corridor to his chamber.

14

WHEN THEY had reached the safety of Adrian's room and he had locked the door behind them, Meriel silently turned into her husband's arms. He held her tightly, seeming almost as shaken by Alan de Vere's angry visit as she was.

Meriel was genuinely glad to have met her brother. He seemed a fine man; she did not doubt his identity, nor that he loved her. Yet the meeting had been a disturbing interlude in a day that had started out as pure, uncomplicated pleasure. For Meriel, her world had begun with blazing light, and with Adrian. The life Alan de Vere described had been that of a stranger.

Abruptly Adrian released her, then paced across the room to stare out the large window, every line of his body taut. "Is there anything you want to ask me? Any questions your brother raised that you want answered?"

So that was why he had been upset by Alan de Vere's visit. Meriel thought about it, then shook her head. "I know that you are afraid of what I might ask, and afraid of what you might have to answer," she replied gravely. "But there is nothing I need to know, except that you love me."

He turned swiftly to face her, his soul in his eyes. "You are a miracle," he said, his voice unsteady, "and I don't know what I have done to deserve you."

She smiled as he walked over to her. "Is love something that must be earned?"

"Not in heaven perhaps, but on earth few things are

given freely.'' Adrian removed her flower chaplet, now somewhat the worse for wear, and set it on a table.

Dropping her gaze and rubbing her temple, Meriel asked, "There is one thing I do want to know. Am I very different from the way I was before I was injured?"

Adrian stood quite still for a moment. Then he placed warm hands on her shoulders. "No. The essence of you—gentle, loving, and free—is the same. Perhaps losing your memory has made that essence more visible, stripping away some of life's wariness, but it did not change you."

"Then . . . if I ever recover my memories and become as I was before, you will not cease to love me?" she asked hesitantly.

"Jesu, Meriel, of course not." His fingers tightened on her shoulders. "When your brother said that you had been at Lambourn Priory, I realized that I met you there once about five years ago. Though we exchanged only the briefest of words, you have flitted through my dreams ever since. You must have been a novice, but I thought you were a nun and was thoroughly ashamed of myself for desiring a holy sister."

"Truly?" she asked, surprised and pleased.

He nodded. "It was not chance that brought us together, *ma petite*, but fate. If I had known that you had not taken your vows, I think I would have offered for you then. Since I did not, fate gave us another chance." His mouth twisted. "Or perhaps two more chances."

She liked the idea of that, because from the time she woke up after her mysterious accident, she had felt that they were bound together. Perhaps she should take this opportunity to ask just what kind of accident she had suffered, but she shied away from the question, sensing that it might be better not to know.

Adrian removed her veil and tossed it toward a chair. The gauzy silk opened in the air and floated silently to the floor. In the distance Meriel heard the music and voices of the wedding feast, which would continue through the night. But even though she had longed to be alone with her husband, between shyness and fatigue she found herself not quite ready to discover the mysteries of the marriage bed.

After a perceptive scan of her face, Adrian suggested, "Let us lie down and just relax in each other's arms. I've often thought that having the wedding and the bedding on the same day is a mistake. Beginning a marriage when husband and wife are both tired and anxious is difficult at best, and today has been more distressing than either of us expected."

Meriel nodded with relief and started toward the bed, so tired that she was ready to lie down in all her finery.

Adrian caught her by the waist and deftly untied her girdle, then turned her around and began unlacing the tight silk gown. "You will relax more without this."

He was right; she felt immediately better after Adrian peeled off her gown and draped it over a chair. Bemused, Meriel wondered if he would suggest that she would feel better yet without her shift.

Instead he swept her up in his arms. Before she had uttered more than a small squeak of surprise, he deposited her in the middle of the bed. Then he removed her elegant slippers and hose and spent a few minutes rubbing each of her bare feet between his hands. "That feels wonderful," she said, wiggling her toes in surprise. "I didn't know feet could feel that way."

Adrian chuckled. "It isn't easy to be feet. There they are, carrying all our weight, supporting us day in and day out. They deserve a little kindness now and then."

Lying back on the feather mattress with a sigh of pure pleasure, Meriel smiled at his whimsy. Then, as Adrian took off his own shoes and outer tunic, she glanced toward the window. The setting sun flooded the chamber with glowing orange light. She found something oddly disturbing about the sight, and in spite of the room's warmth, she shivered.

Before she could define her unease, Adrian lay down and drew Meriel into his arms so that her head was pillowed on his shoulder. She sighed and relaxed against him, her arm across his chest, the steady beat of his heart beneath her ear. Adrian's hand gently massaged her head, easing the ache. She had not known how exhausted she was until she lay down, and within moments she was asleep.

It was full dark when Meriel opened her eyes again. In the distance sounds of celebration could still be heard, but they were unimportant. The true reality was her husband's nearness. In the velvet darkness she was acutely aware of the length of his body against hers, his warmth and subtle masculine scent, the faint sound of his breathing.

When she stirred, Adrian lifted his hand and brushed her heavy hair back from her face. "Feeling better, *ma petite?*"

Though the air had cooled, she felt warm and safe under his arm, and she sat up with some reluctance. "Much better, but you must be very stiff from holding me."

"A thousand years of holding you would not be too long." Adrian leaned over to strike a light for the tall candle by the bed. Then he punched up a pillow against the headboard and leaned back lazily, candlelight etching the planes of his face and gilding his bright hair. "Are you hungry, or would you like some wine? I gave orders earlier that food and drink be left here so that we would not have to venture out."

"Such wisdom." She smiled, amused and touched by his thoughtfulness. But it was not his consideration that was in the forefront of her mind. Even relaxing, even shadowed, Adrian compelled attention, and she could not take her eyes from him.

Abruptly Meriel remembered the day they had gone swimming, and the image of his lithe body was so vivid that it was as if he were naked now. She knew precisely how broad were the shoulders beneath his tunic, how supple and tight his muscles, how lean his waist and hips.

As she looked at Adrian, something warm and powerful began to move deep inside her, and the anticipation she had felt earlier in the day returned. With a slow smile she said, "It isn't food or drink I need."

A phrase from the Song of Solomon floated up from the mysterious well of Meriel's memory. Leaning forward, she took his face in her hands and touched his lips with hers, murmuring, *"Kiss me with the kisses of thy mouth, for thy love is better than wine."*

Adrian's relaxed demeanor disintegrated instantly at the touch of her lips and he reached up and pulled her down so that she lay full-length on top of him. *"I slept, but my heart wakens,"* he said softly, quoting also from the Song of Songs. *"It is the voice of my beloved that calls me, saying, 'Open to me, my love, my dove, my spouse.' "*

His kiss was yearning, both demanding and giving, as if he could never have enough of her, and Meriel wondered how much it had cost him to bank his desire for her sake. His hands caressed every part of her that he could reach, and wherever he touched, her body came to tingling new awareness.

Only a few layers of fabric separated them, but even that was too much. When his drifting hand found the edge of her shift, he tugged it up to her waist so that his warm palms could knead her round backside. As Meriel wriggled closer against him, he gave a soft groan of pleasure, then slid her shift up her torso. Their lips separated when he pulled the garment over her head. *"Behold, you are fair, my love,"* he whispered, *"behold, you are fair."*

"As are you." Meriel gave him a melting smile, half-innocent and half-temptress, then tugged at his tunic. *"His mouth is most sweet, and he is altogether lovely."*

Adrian sat up so she could remove his clothing, a task she performed with great pleasure, her hands lingering wherever they touched. Even the lightest brush of her fingers left trails of fire.

Then they were once more flesh to flesh, as they had been that day in the stream. Though the love Adrian felt for Meriel went far beyond desire, passion was the most powerful way of expressing how she held his heart in her hands; the sight of Meriel's slim body made him ache not only physically but also in his soul. Brushing back her ebony mantle of hair so that none of her loveliness was obscured, Adrian said quietly, "I have wanted you so long and so intensely that it is hard to believe that you are really here, not just a dream more vivid than most."

"I am very real," Meriel said, her deep blue eyes glowing with tender amusement and her smooth flesh warm with passion. Her smile deepened and she quoted, *"His left hand should be under my head, and his right hand should embrace me."*

He laughed and obliged, his lips and hands worshiping his wife. *"How fair and pleasant thou art, O love, for delights,"* he whispered just before his mouth found her breast.

Adrian was glad that this was not the first time they had explored each other's bodies, for now he could savor the pleasures of recognition. It was pure delight to once again spread his hand across the gentle curve of her belly, to once more caress the tender flesh of her inner thighs, to gently probe the moist waiting depths of her.

Her breathing rough, Meriel did not lie passive but thrummed with response like a taut lute string. Her restless hands stroked his neck and shoulders and twined in his hair, arousing him to a point just short of madness.

Using every shred of will at his command, Adrian pulled back, slowing his breathing and laying his head against her soft breasts until the fire in his blood had cooled to a manageable heat. Then he lifted himself and said, "Meriel, look at me."

When her dazed eyes had opened and focused on him, he continued, "The first time for a woman can be uncomfortable. There may be some pain. I'm sorry, I would take it on myself if I could."

A shadow crossed her face. "What if it is not my first time? Since I don't remember, I cannot promise that it is. Will it matter to you?"

Adrian knew that she might not be virgin. In fact, her utter lack of shyness and passionate response argued that she was a woman of experience, and the thought of another man possessing her was agony. But whatever Meriel had done, it was in the past, a past she did not even remember.

Obliquely he said, "A wise woman once told me that one is always a virgin the first time one makes love with one's beloved. In the most important way, this is the first time for both of us. What your body might have done before means nothing—what matters is what is in your heart now."

"What is in my heart is love." She caught his hand and kissed his fingertips. *"I am my beloved's, and my beloved is mine."*

"Then let us make love together." With one arm he held her against him and with his other hand he caressed her intimately until her whole body pulsed with readiness and soft urgent sounds formed deep in her throat. Then he shifted into position between her legs. Finding the entrance, he pressed gently against her and waited just within, so that she would have time to accustom herself to the feel of him.

Adrian had thought that surely now she would feel diffidence, but when she opened her eyes he saw absolute trust. With a slight mischievous smile, she moved her hips against his. He gasped under a surge of passion so intense that his vision dimmed. Then he forced himself to breathe slowly again, knowing how easy it would be to lose himself in his own needs.

In spite of his primitive male possessiveness about his wife, Adrian found himself hoping that this was not her first time, because he could not bear the thought of causing her pain. With infinite gentleness he moved forward until his progress was halted by the barrier that proved her innocence.

For an instant fierce exultation flooded him, but that was immediately damped down by concern. "Steady, love, it will only hurt for a moment," he whispered, hoping that was the truth, for in the ways of virgins he was as innocent as she.

He leaned into her with slow, even pressure as her wide eyes held his, utterly without fear. Then the fragile membrane suddenly gave way and he was inside her. Meriel gave a quick gasp of shock, reaction rippling through her entire frame.

Reining in every natural instinct, Adrian held quite still. "I'm sorry, love," he whispered, clasping her face between his hands.

"I'm not. That did not hurt so very much." She smiled up at him, and in the candlelight he saw the glint of tears in her eyes. "And pain means that you are the first, does it not? I'm glad, my first and only love."

There were no words to speak the depth of emotion he felt, so he kissed her, exchanging the breath of life. Slowly he began to move, slightly at first, then gradually taking longer strokes.

Meriel responded with her whole body, pulsing, learning what it meant to be one with her beloved. The pain had gone within moments, and the sense of strangeness at the invasion lasted scarcely longer. Now each discovery was one of pleasure, a whole world of new awareness and rich sensation.

As they moved together there was heat, there was depth, there was exquisite friction. Deep within her was an indescribable sensation, melting, welcoming, demanding as her body found an involuntary rhythm.

Her arms tightened around him as she trembled on the edge of a delirious new discovery.

Then Adrian slid his hand between them and touched her where he had found fire the first time they had explored each other's bodies. Under the pressure of his expert hand, Meriel once more dissolved in liquid flame. As she cried out, her body wholly out of control, she felt him surrender to his own passion, groaning as he crushed her to him. And the world shattered and reformed in a new configuration that made them forever a part of each other.

In the aftermath of rapture, Meriel found herself so weak that she doubted that she could have walked across the room to save her life. She lay hazy with happiness as Adrian moved his weight from her, retrieved a couple of thin linen cloths from the table by the bed, carefully cleaned away the small amount of blood. Already that brief, insignificant pain seemed aeons ago.

Then Adrian tucked her under the covers and settled down beside her, his arm under her head. "So this is why people get married," Meriel murmured.

He chuckled. "One of the reasons."

"I have a confession to make." Adrian made an encouraging sound, so Meriel continued, "I took some liberties with the translation of the *Song of Solomon.*"

"I know. So did I."

Meriel smiled. "An education is a wonderful thing." Dreamily she ran her hands along his ribs, loving his solid warmth. "Perhaps we made a baby tonight."

She sensed a slight withdrawal on her husband's part.

"Perhaps." There was a long silence, then Adrian continued, "I should have told you before. I have not lived a celibate life, but I have never fathered a child. Perhaps I cannot."

Meriel's sense of well-being was too deep to be disturbed. "Somehow, I doubt that you were one of those men who coupled with a different female every night. Maybe you just didn't try often enough.''

Adrian laughed. "What a wonderfully common-sensical point of view. It's true that I had one mistress for a long time rather than lying with many different women. That makes a difference.''

She was almost asleep by now, but she was awake enough to whisper, "Everything will be all right. You'll see.''

Meriel awoke the next morning with the sense that something was wrong, and after a moment she identified what: Adrian was not in bed beside her. Puzzled, she sat up and looked around. She did not see him, but surely she would have heard if he had unlocked the heavy door and left. A thought struck and she slid out of bed and pulled on her rumpled shift, which had ended up on the floor.

Softly she padded across the room to the narrow door leading into the small private chapel. Inside Adrian knelt before the altar, barefoot and wearing a plain tunic that he had casually pulled on. By the soft dawn light she saw that his posture was relaxed and peaceful.

Understanding why, she went and knelt beside him. Without looking up, Adrian reached out and clasped her hand, and together they gave thanks for the blessing of love which they shared. When prompted, Meriel could recite the Church's formal prayers, as well as hymns and parts of the Bible, but she preferred simply opening her mind to the light and peace all around her, and she did that now.

At length the bells of the village church rang, calling people to early-morning worship. Adrian gently disengaged her fingers and rose. Meriel did the same, then examined her surroundings. While the walls were plainly whitewashed, the furnishings were beautifully made, from the richly carved wood to the jewel-bright colors of the stained-glass window. "This is lovely, and there is such a sense of peace."

Adrian glanced at her thoughtfully. "If so, that is because there is now peace in me. That has not always been so. When my spirit was troubled, even the most beautiful of sacred objects could not enable me to pray."

Meriel's brows knit with immediate concern. "Why were you troubled?"

"Because I was wrestling my own private demons, and losing. In the years after I left Fontevaile Abbey, I prospered in a worldly sense, winning land and wealth and royal favor. Perhaps as a result, the dark side of my nature grew ever stronger." His mouth twisted wryly. *"What is a man profited if he shall gain the whole world and lose his own soul?"*

Meriel shook her head firmly. "I cannot believe that you have such a dark side."

"Everyone does, and it is very black in my case." Adrian put his arm around her shoulders and pulled her close, needing her serenity. "My mother's father, the Sire of Courcy, was one of the wickedest men in France, guilty of the most despicable crimes against God and man. He robbed the Church, broke faith with his liege lord, tortured anyone so unfortunate as to incur his displeasure, and died excommunicate. In Courcy the peasants still make the sign against the evil eye when his name is mentioned. Or when they see me, as I discovered when I visited my cousin who is the present lord."

"Why would they do that?" she asked. "Do you resemble him?"

"Very much so, and not just physically." He winced inwardly as he remembered the terrified faces of the Courcy peasants. They had been vivid proof of his grandfather's evil. "My mother was a pious and loving woman and she feared what she saw of her father in me. From the earliest age, she raised me to be aware of my own capacity for evil, and to fight against it.

She suggested that I enter the Church, and she was wise, for at Fontevaile it was possible to master my weaknesses. But after I left to take up my patrimony, the dark side began to gain the ascendant.''

Meriel shook her head again. ''I still cannot believe that you are so black as you paint yourself.''

Adrian sighed, feeling deeply sad. ''You should, beloved, because I behaved very badly to you. And you have never seen me in battle, where a kind of madness takes over and I am capable of anything. That is one reason I prefer to fight only when necessary—to lessen the likelihood of doing something unforgivable.''

She slipped her arm around his waist and leaned her head against his shoulder. ''Is there not more virtue in struggling against evil and overcoming it than in never being tempted to do wrong?''

''Yes,'' he admitted, ''but that supposes that one overcomes the evil, which I have not always successfully done.''

''Well, if you were already perfect, you wouldn't need to come to earth to grow in grace and humility, would you?'' she pointed out. ''Even the Lord Jesus himself made a mistake or two when he was here. Surely you are not so much superior to him that you can never be forgiven your errors.''

He considered, and found himself smiling. ''I never thought of it quite that way. You'd make a good logician, *ma petite*. But more than that, you yourself are a superb antidote to darkness. Since you began to love me, I have found peace and balance for the first time in my life. I am still a long way from perfect, but I no longer feel that I am poised on the edge of the abyss, a hair's breadth away from doing evil.''

Meriel bit her lip. ''I'm not sure whether I should be pleased that I can help, or concerned at carrying such heavy responsibility for your soul. What if something happens to me?''

''I would rather not think about that.'' His arm tightened around her shoulders. ''But in spite of what

I said, I know that I am responsible for my own soul, not you. It is just that I find it easier to keep it untarnished when you are with me."

Adrian's gaze rested pensively on the altar, and when he spoke next, the subject was only obliquely related to what he had been saying. "The Church is the great force for civilization. Without it men would be little better than the beasts, and probably a good deal worse. One of the best things about Christianity is that it gives us different aspects of the divine to fit our different needs. There is God-the-Father, the all-knowing, all-powerful judge. It is God-the-Father whom I fear when I know I have done wrong."

Then Adrian gestured to the exquisitely modeled crucifix, whose face conveyed suffering, faith, and transcendent joy. "There is God-the-Son, who lived on earth and knows the weaknesses and temptations of mankind, the fears and doubts that trouble us in the night."

Finally he pointed at the circular stained-glass window with its image of a soaring white dove. "And there is God-the-Holy-Ghost, the pure ideals of wisdom and goodness, the abstractions of the spirit."

Meriel smiled and nodded at the lovely statuette of the Virgin in all her sorrowing grace. "Don't forget God-the-Mother."

Adrian looked startled. "I think that might be heresy." Then he chuckled. "Perhaps you are right. Certainly we need her, for she is all-forgiving love. As are you." He led his wife from the chapel to the main bedchamber. "I think the Church has one failing. Theologians are always male, monks and priests who lived removed from real life. As a result, the Church too often condemns passion, denying the body and blaming women for tempting men from higher things, when in truth human love is the closest that mortal man can come to the divine."

"What about mortal woman?" Meriel asked teasingly, sliding her arms around Adrian's waist and pressing against him.

He caught his breath, then enfolded her in a comprehensive embrace. "Perhaps you can work on developing a new theology for mortal woman," he murmured, then scooped Meriel up in his arms and carried her back to the bed.

"I'll start later," she promised as she pulled at his tunic. "Much, much later."

15

BENJAMIN L'EVESKE closed the book and leaned back in his chair, rubbing at his tired eyes. He was getting old. He hoped that he died before it became altogether impossib'e to read the Law. Having someone else read aloud would not be the same, even if his own son were the reader.

The door opened, and without looking he knew that it was his wife, Sarah, bearing two cups of mulled wine. Silently she handed one to him and sat down, sipping the other herself. It was another sign of age that hot wine tasted good even on a summer night. They sat in companionable silence, not needing to speak. When his wine was gone, Benjamin said, "I have come to the conclusion that we should go to Shrewsbury. Of the available choices, I think it is the best."

Sarah glanced up. The topic was one they had discussed frequently in the last weeks. "Very well," she said. "I do not care greatly where we go, as long as it is away from London. The city disturbs me. I will feel safer elsewhere."

"The world is not a safe place, especially not for Jews, but Shrewsbury should be better than here," Benjamin agreed. "Stephen has been a good friend to us, if not a strong king, but I distrust his son Eustace. Stephen is not a young man. He could die at any time, and then what would become of us? All kings squeeze their Jews for gold, but Eustace might take more than money. Living in a town controlled by one of the empress's supporters may be better. It is said Matilda's son is a very pragmatic young man, unlikely to kill those who might help him. If we are lucky, he may be our next king.'' The merchant looked at his lined hands and sighed. ''If it were just us, I would not worry so, but Aaron is young.''

''Aye, and too quick-tempered to know when to submit.'' Sarah wore the faint, doting smile that mention of their son always produced. He had been a late babe, born when they had despaired of ever having children, and was more precious than a storehouse of gold. Turning to the practical, she said briskly, ''When shall we leave?''

''Can you organize the household servants and pack what is necessary in three weeks?'' When she nodded, Benjamin continued, ''Sir Vincent recommended that we follow the old Roman road, since it is the most direct route. He also offered to supply an escort of the earl's soldiers.''

Knowing her husband's ways, his wife cocked a knowing brow. ''But you would prefer otherwise?''

''The more people who know when and how we are going, the more chance of robbers lying in wait. And I would rather be guarded by men who are paid by me.''

''Elementary wisdom,'' Sarah agreed.

''If we go through Oxford and Worcester, we can stay at the homes of friends whom we have not seen in too long.'' Benjamin stroked his gray-streaked beard. ''The southern route would also take us by Warfield Castle. I was disappointed that I could not meet Earl Adrian in person when I was in Shrewsbury, and this would be a good time to remedy that. He has a fine reputation, but there is no substitute for looking a man in the eye.''

Once more Sarah nodded her head placidly. Her husband had not built his fortune by being a fool. ''And if you don't like what you see of him, we can always return here and find another destination.'' But

she sincerely hoped it would not come to that. She
would not mind if she never saw London again.

Married life suited Meriel gloriously. Her house-
keeping tasks were not onerous, for Adrian's household was well trained, and she had the dimly
remembered experience that she must have acquired
at her brother's manor. Unfortunately their respective
duties separated her and Adrian for part of each day,
but the rest of the time they spent together, sharing
the same trencher and goblet at meals, the same
thoughts when they talked, the same pillow when they
slept.

There was no great drama in their everyday lives,
nor did they need any. They talked, walked, hawked,
and laughed, as when Meriel found that Adrian had
had a hole cut in the corner of the bedchamber door
so that Kestrel could come and go at will. A leather
flap covered the hole, and occasionally in the middle
of the night Meriel heard it slap softly as the cat wandered off in search of amusement. More often, Kestrel
stayed on the bed and learned quickly when her affec-
tions would not be welcomed.

Through sunny days and fiery nights, Meriel carried
the blissful secret conviction that she had conceived
on their wedding night. She would wait to tell Adrian
because he would be deeply disappointed if she were
wrong, but she prayed that she was right. A child
would be the best possible gift to return for all he had
given her.

Twice Adrian led his men out, armed for battle, and
was gone once for nearly a week. Meriel hated remin-
ders that outside the enchanted circle of Warfield was
violence. While her husband was matter-of-fact, she
could not help but worry about his safety, particularly
since there was a blood debt between him and Guy of
Burgoigne.

In spite of Meriel's fears, both times Adrian returned unscathed and she gave him the most heartfelt

welcome she could imagine. Every day she gave prayers of thanks for the wonder of her life. More than once it occurred to her that such happiness could not last forever, and she instantly suppressed the thought for fear that it was unlucky.

But suppressing thoughts cannot hold back fate.

It was late afternoon when Adrian was informed that Benjamin l'Eveske wished to see the Earl of Shropshire. He and Meriel were in the garden, where she was enthusiastically describing the plans she had developed, hands flying as she sketched her ideas in the air.

While there was an obligation of hospitality to guests, it was not necessary that the lord of the castle greet visitors personally and Adrian did not welcome the intrusion. Impatiently he asked the servant, "The name is vaguely familiar, but I cannot place it. Who is Benjamin l'Eveske?"

"A Jew, my lord. He said you would know him."

Curious, Adrian said, "Very well, bring him here."

When the servant left, Meriel asked, "Is he a moneylender you have dealt with?"

Adrian shook his head. "I did borrow from a moneylender, Gervase of Cornhill, when I was building the castle, but the debt has been paid and I have contracted no others. I cannot imagine why this Benjamin would think I know him."

A few minutes later the servant returned, followed by a dark, elderly man and a youth who was clearly his son. Both bowed respectfully before the old man spoke. "I was disappointed that I was unable to meet you in Shrewsbury, Lord Adrian. It is most gracious of you to admit me today so that I might thank you for your generous invitation."

Puzzled, Adrian tried to make sense of the older man's words. "Forgive me, Master Benjamin, but I have no recollection of having extended any invitations. Have you had business dealings with my steward?''

"I did not think Sir Vincent was your steward."

Adrian's brows came together sharply. "Do you speak of Sir Vincent de Laon?"

"Of course," Benjamin said, surprised.

"He is not of my household, but of Guy of Burgoigne's. Burgoigne is the king's Earl of Shropshire," Adrian said with a frown. "Tell me what has passed between you."

The older man gave a succinct summary of Sir Vincent's offer of welcome and protection, including a description of the house in Shrewsbury and the fact that much of Benjamin's household and worldly goods were now in wagons in the outer bailey.

Adrian swore savagely under his breath. Seeing that not just his visitors but Meriel looked alarmed, he made an effort to moderate his tone before speaking. "Master Benjamin, I fear that you have been a victim of a hoax. The house you described is owned by Guy of Burgoigne, and the invitation came from him. Knowing Guy, I imagine that there is no good purpose behind it." He thought a moment. "Did you inform Sir Vincent of when and where you were traveling?"

Benjamin shook his head. "It seemed better in these troubled times to let no one know."

"Be grateful for your caution, for it may have saved your lives." Seeing that the older man looked shaken, Adrian waved him to a nearby bench. "You had best sit down. I have heard that Guy is hard-pressed for gold—he might have decided that it was easier to steal it than to borrow it. You would be wise to leave Shropshire quickly, and by a different route."

The youth was leaning with concern over his father, whose face was ashen at the thought of the near-disaster. Two goblets stood on the next bench, and Meriel took the one that had been intended for her and pressed it into Benjamin's hand, saying softly, "Drink some wine, you will feel better."

The wine restored the old man's color, and after a few minutes he said hesitantly, "Lord Adrian, would you allow us to settle in Shrewsbury? Though Guy of Burgoigne may have been ill-intentioned, Sir Vincent's arguments were good ones. Shrewsbury is well-located and would profit by my trading business."

The request took Adrian by surprise. His brows furrowed, he turned away and paced across the grassy turf, hands clasped behind him as he considered the request. It was true that Shrewsbury would benefit by increased trade, and he now recalled hearing that his visitor was a well-respected merchant with interests in England, Normandy, and France.

But he was also a Jew. Adrian was not of the school that held all Jews personally responsible for the murder of Christ; as Abbot William had once said, someone had to be the instrument of the Lord's death or there could have been no glorious resurrection. But Jews were unbelievers, the only sizable community of unbelievers in Christendom. Though the truth was available to them, they rejected it, to the peril of their souls. By their example, other souls might be imperiled. No economic advantage to Shrewsbury was worth such a risk. He turned to face his visitors. "You can settle in Shrewsbury only if you and your household will accept religious instruction from the true Church."

Benjamin sighed, seeming to age right before their eyes. "Do you honestly think that I will consent to such a condition?"

Adrian shook his head. "No, but I would be remiss if I did not at least try. Yours is a stubborn people, Master Benjamin."

"If we were not stubborn, we would no longer be a people." With the aid of his son's arm, the old merchant rose from the bench.

The young man looked challengingly at the earl. "Is Christianity so feeble a faith that Shrewsbury will be threatened by a single household of Jews?"

''Aaron!'' the old man exclaimed, gripping his son's arm. His dark eyes fearful, he said, ''Forgive him, my lord, he is young and imprudent.''

Adrian's face hardened but his reply was level. ''Christianity is not feeble, but among the serfs there is much pagan superstition. I wish no more sources of impiety.''

The old man's head bowed. ''We will leave Shropshire immediately.''

Meriel stood on her toes and whispered into her husband's ear. Adrian nodded, then turned to the visitors. ''My wife has reminded me that I am neglectful of the laws of hospitality. You and your household are welcome to stay tonight, or several days if you need time to rethink your plans. And when you leave, let me send some of my soldiers to escort you out of Shropshire.''

Young Aaron looked on the verge of another remark, doubtless a caustic one, but his father's quelling glance silenced him. Benjamin replied, ''It is late and we will be grateful to accept your hospitality tonight. But I have guards of my own and will not need your escort from the shire.''

''Are you sure? If Guy of Burgoigne has gotten word of your presence, it is possible that he might pursue you.''

''Make no mistake, we shall not be in the area for long.'' There was a bitter edge in Benjamin's voice. Then he rose and left the garden, leaning heavily on his son for support.

When the visitors had disappeared into the keep, Adrian turned to see his wife regarding him with wide, grave eyes.

''Do you really think their presence would be disruptive?'' she asked.

''I don't know,'' he admitted, ''but I prefer not to take the chance.''

Meriel turned away and picked a rose, her eyes cast

down as she sniffed the blossom. "Jesus was Jewish. Should we not welcome his own people?"

"Meriel," he said, his voice hard, "I do not wish to discuss this."

Her gaze flew up to his. "I'm sorry, my lord," she said quietly. "I did not mean to question your judgment. It is just that I could not understand why you would not allow them to stay in Shrewsbury."

"Where souls are concerned, there is little room for compromise." Intensely uncomfortable with this first tension between him and his wife, Adrian said defensively, "It isn't as if I threw them out to starve in a blizzard. There are Jewish communities in a dozen other towns, and Benjamin and his wealth will doubtless be welcome in any of them if he does not want to return to London."

"Of course." Meriel gave him her shining smile. "I know that you would never do anything unkind."

Her absolute belief in him revived the dormant guilt that still lay deep in Adrian's gut. Jesu, if she ever came to understand just what he was capable of, she would never forgive him. Quickly, before the anxiety could take hold, he asked, "What kind of fountain would you like? It would take time, but we could order one to be made in Italy." But he knew that it would take far more than a marble fountain to expiate his guilt.

That night Meriel woke screaming. She flailed and fought, trying desperately to free herself of the relentless dark angel who had captured her. She was near hysteria when the cries of "Meriel, Meriel, *wake up!*" finally penetrated her panic.

"Adrian?" she asked, her voice shaking. By the light of the night candle, she saw that her husband was propped up on his elbow next to her, his gilt hair tumbled, the clean planes of his face drawn with anxiety.

Meriel felt a moment of mind-splitting disorientation, for the dangerous implacable face that tormented

her dreams was identical to Adrian's. She squeezed her
eyes shut, feeling that she was perilously close to
opening a door into disaster. And once it was open, it
could never be closed again.

"Jesu, Meriel, are you all right?"

Adrian wrapped his arms around her and she clung
to him, still trembling with the fear engendered by the
dream.

"You were having a nightmare," he said softly.
"Tell me about it."

"I can't remember it all, but I . . . I think I was a
songbird in a cage. A . . . a demon wanted me to sing
for him, but I wouldn't. I couldn't." Nor could Meriel
bring herself to tell her husband that the demon wore
his face. "I finally managed to break out of the cage,
but I had no wings. When I tried to fly, I could not.
Instead I fell, tumbling and helpless, endlessly. I knew
that I would never stop falling."

He held her tight against his chest, his hand stroking
the back of her neck. "It's all right, beloved," he
murmured. "You're safe. It was just a bad dream. I
won't let anyone harm you ever again."

As her head pressed against his chest, she heard the
drumming of his heart. "I'm so cold," she whispered,
despairing, wondering how she could be cold in Adrian's arms.

"Let me warm you." He lifted her chin and his
mouth found hers. At first his kiss was gentle, but it
rapidly became fierce and demanding.

For an instant panic returned and she wanted to fling
herself away. Then desire flared. Meriel accepted the
kiss and returned it, as fierce as he, her hands and
mouth urgent, for she wanted him so deeply inside her
that there would be no more room for fear.

Adrian was like a raging torrent, and with his intimate knowledge of her body, he knew exactly how to
carry her with him. Reality was touch and taste, demand and plea, giving and taking, so intense that past
and future ceased to exist. And in the inferno of pas-

sion, Meriel was able to forget the terror that had woken her.

When their mutual madness was done, she lay warm and sated in Adrian's arms, her nightmare no more than a distant, fragmentary memory. Enfolded in her husband's love, Meriel slept.

Sir Vincent de Laon was justly proud of the network of informants he had developed throughout the Marches. It rankled to know that Adrian of Warfield had an equally good network, so there was a certain pleasure in gathering information from right under the rival earl's nose. Unfortunately the news itself was not good. The Frenchman swore under his breath and spent time thinking through what must be done to salvage the situation. Then he went to Guy of Burgoigne.

The earl was sharpening the blade of his heavy sword. Usually it was a task for a smith, but Guy enjoyed the work and swore that he could produce the most dangerous blade in Christendom. Perhaps he could. Sir Vincent kept his distance just in case Guy's uncertain temper erupted at the bad news.

"Our Jewish pigeon is a canny bird," Sir Vincent drawled. "He almost escaped our net."

Guy finished drawing the whetstone along his blade, then looked up, his expression ugly. "What do you mean?"

"Benjamin l'Eveske has come to Shropshire at a different time and by a different route than we had discussed." Keeping a wary eye on his lord, Vincent added, "And he is now at Warfield Castle."

"What!" The tip of Guy's upright blade quivered dangerously in the air. "So he knows that you tricked him, and so does Warfield."

"Aye," Sir Vincent admitted, "but no matter. When Benjamin discovered that he had been misled, he asked if he might still settle in Shrewsbury. Warfield, pious fellow that he is, refused permission. So Benjamin, his household, and his three wagonloads of goods, will head east again tomorrow.''

''You're sure?'' the earl asked sarcastically. ''Your certainty before was misplaced.''

''This time I'm sure. Rather than take the southwestern road which brought him to Warfield, he will head northeast to Lincoln. He must pass through the royal forest, so there is only one road he can take.''

Guy considered, stroking the whetstone down the blade with a high-pitched screech that set Sir Vincent's nerves on edge. ''We will have to cross into Warfield's territory to take them, but it should not be difficult. How many guards does he have?''

''Fifteen. Well armed and sufficient to drive off bandits, but hardly capable of stopping an attack by armed knights, and I doubt they will want to die to protect a merchant's ill-gotten gold.'' Sir Vincent's lip curled with disgust. ''Warfield offered an additional escort, but the Jew refused it.''

''The more fool he,'' Guy said dispassionately. ''You know when and where we can strike?''

''Benjamin will leave Warfield Castle tomorrow morning at dawn. The wagons move slowly. We can take them anywhere along the forest road. Presumably we will wish to do that toward the eastern edge, as far as possible from Warfield.''

''Quite right.'' Lightly Guy drew his thumb along the blade. A thin line, beaded with blood, appeared on the pad of callused skin. ''Everyone makes a mistake now and then, Vincent. Just remember that two in a row are *not* permitted.''

''I shall remember.'' Sir Vincent bowed nervously and withdrew. He was used to his lord's bluster, but when Burgoigne became cool and reasonable, real danger was imminent.

From high above on a tower, Meriel watched Benjamin and his household rumble out of the outer bailey and across the drawbridge. The previous day she had sent a servant to ask if they had needed anything, but a polite refusal had been returned. While their men-at-arms had eaten in the castle hall, the merchant and his private household had chosen to prepare and eat their own food. Was that a subtle way of rejecting those who had rejected them, or did they eat differently from Christians?

As the last riders clattered over the drawbridge, Meriel wondered where they would find their new home. Adrian was right, people with wealth had many choices, but she still felt badly that he had sent Benjamin and his family away. No doubt it was her head injury that was the problem, for try as she might, she could not understand why it made a difference that they worshiped God in the same way Jesus had, rather than in the way Jesus's followers had developed. Her husband was right, her thoughts were heretical. Or possibly blasphemous; she had trouble remembering the difference between the two things.

Before going downstairs, Meriel examined the sky. There was a chancy feel in the air and the clouds suggested that a major storm was on the way. Not just yet, perhaps later in the day. She thought of Benjamin and his heavy wagons and hoped she was wrong.

Meriel spent the morning in the kitchen, helping to prepare conserves. After dinner Adrian suggested that they go for a ride and she was happy to agree, knowing that the cook would be not only willing, but probably grateful, to finish the conserves without her.

They rode out at a gallop, which released some of Meriel's tension. Eventually she pulled in her mount to a trot. Looking at the roiling dark clouds above, she said, "I wonder when the storm will break."

"Soon, I think." Adrian reined his mount in and matched her pace. "Perhaps I should not have coaxed you out of the castle."

She laughed. "I am not a sugar comfit that will melt in the rain." Her expression sobered. "I was feeling restless and prefer to be outside."

"Something ominous is in the air," he said slowly.

Meriel glanced at him with surprise. "That is exactly how I feel, but I thought it was just the coming storm."

Adrian's eyes darkened, but his tone was even and good-humored. "This morning a different kind of storm was averted. You remember that Richard learned that Guy of Burgoigne had hired a troop of mercenaries?"

Meriel nodded.

"I asked one of my French cousins to see if he could discover who had been hired, and to buy them off if possible." He chuckled. "My cousin was successful. It is the nature of mercenaries to work for the highest bidder, and I offered them more to stay away than Guy was willing to pay them to come."

"That's wonderful!" Meriel said. "So there is unlikely to be heavy fighting this season?"

"Certainly not on the scale that Guy hoped for." The earl grimaced. "Unfortunately, soon he will learn what I have done, and when that happens, he will turn into a maddened boar. For the last few months he has bided his time, waiting for his mercenaries. When he learns that none are coming, he will turn his rage on my tenants. He might even attack Shrewsbury, though the city wall should hold him until I can send reinforcements."

"Will you be able to stop him?" she asked with quick concern.

"I think so. Around the edges of my lands I have people watching for signs of trouble. When they see something, they signal the nearest castle or keep to bring aid."

Intrigued, Meriel asked, "What kind of signals?"

"Several kinds, depending on the situation and the time of day," he explained. "Colored banners and smoke signals usually. At night, they use something that I read about in an old Greek text. With lamps set in front of polished reflective metal, the Greeks could flash signals for miles to warn ships from rocky coasts. A version of that has proved useful here.''

''So that is how you keep your people so safe and prosperous,'' she said, impressed.

''It usually works.'' He sighed. ''Not always. If the attack is unobserved or moves in too quickly, it is not always possible to get knights there in time.''

''Perhaps Guy will not attack as you think.''

''I hope he does,'' Adrian said with sudden violence. ''I want him to come out in the open and fight, so I can put an end to him once and for all.''

Frightened by what she saw in his face, Meriel asked quietly, ''But there is a risk that he might kill you, beloved, and I could not bear that.''

''He won't.'' Adrian intended his smile to be reassuring, but from Meriel's doubtful expression he must not have succeeded. Changing the subject, he said, ''Do you remember that we rode this way once before?''

She shook her head. They were traveling upland through dense woods, and a few minutes later they entered the clearing of the standing stone circle. On their other visit, Meriel had tried to escape. Now Adrian watched her from the corner of his eye, wondering if she would remember that day.

Meriel did not remember, but she was as fascinated as on their previous visit. ''So this was a pagan place of worship.''

She reined in her mare and surveyed the circle of stones. Sheep had been grazing in the clearing and the grass around the standing stones was cropped like lush green velvet.

They both dismounted and tethered their horses to a low tree branch. Rising wind rustled the leaves with a dry sibilant hiss, and high above, streamers of black cloud whipped across a dark and turbulent sky.

''It's a proper pagan day too, isn't it?'' Laughing, Meriel walked into the center of the circle and raised her arms to the wind. "Perhaps the old gods object to our presence."

With her arms uplifted and her cloud of hair forming a dark nimbus about her face, Meriel looked wild and elemental, a creature not of the earth but of the stormy sky. Adrian was reminded of her falcon, Chanson, of how Meriel had thrown herself from the window to escape him, and the memories were ice in his veins.

Controlling his expression, he joined her in the circle. "Just a blustery English day," he said lightly, wanting to dissipate his deep unease. "I have been here many times and never heard pagan spirits complain of my presence."

"Perhaps they whisper down the wind." Meriel turned her face to the sky and closed her eyes, her mantle billowing like the wings of a soaring falcon. "All we need do is listen . . ." A smattering of raindrops fell, resting on her white skin like dewdrops.

Then the storm hit. Meriel opened her eyes and blinked as her lashes were plastered down by a sudden drenching flood of rain. Her next words were drowned by a flash of lightning and a rapid, staccato crack of thunder. Laughing again, she said, "This is not one of the old British gods, but Zeus the Thunderer himself!"

"Or Thor," Adrian agreed. He put his arm around Meriel's shoulders and hustled her across the clearing. "We had best get out of the open."

Another flash of lightning almost blinded them and the shapes of the standing stones burned eerie blue-white impressions on the inside of their lids. Quickly they ducked under the sheltering branches of the nearest tree, which stood next to the one where the horses were tethered.

Shivering, Meriel pulled her mantle close against the chilly air. Adrian tucked her back against his chest, wrapping his own mantle around them both and resting his chin on her head. Under the cloak his arms linked around her waist so that she was triply warmed.

With a chuckle and a mischievous wiggle of her nicely rounded backside, his wife relaxed against him, saying happily, "What a wonderful way to enjoy a storm."

The wind had risen to a vicious howl, tearing leaves and small branches from the trees and flinging them horizontally through the air. From deep in the woods came a rending crash as a tree went over and took others with it. At the edge of the clearing a sapling bent over parallel to the earth, and above them the leaves saturated until almost as much water was coming through the tree as fell in the open circle. Adrian kept an eye on the horses tethered beneath the tree to the right, but they were surprisingly steady, doing no more than toss their heads and whicker nervously.

A lightning bolt struck nearby, immediately followed by an ear-splitting crack of thunder, and he involuntarily tightened his embrace, as if his arms could protect Meriel from the storm's fury. She was right—this was pagan weather, and it was easy to imagine ancient priests and priestesses invoking storm gods in the heart of the ancient stone circle.

Multiple bolts of lightning slashed the air again and again, and thunder rumbled with such power that the very earth beneath their feet trembled. Pitching his voice over the wind, Adrian said, "If I had known there would be such a tempest, I would never have brought you out."

"I'm not sorry. This is magnificent! It would not be the same if we watched from inside the castle." She smiled and tilted her head back to look up at him, completely unafraid. Then her smile faded. "I don't fear the storm, not when I'm with you. My only concern is a superstitious one, that I am so happy. Perhaps too much happiness tempts fate."

Adrian wondered if that concern was the root of his own dark forebodings. Wanting to forget his disquiet, he bent his head and kissed her. Meriel's lips tasted

of fresh rain and her mouth was a hot, sweet contrast
to the cold air.

When the lingering kiss ended, she wrapped her
arms around his neck and said huskily, "Make love to
me, O my spouse."

He hesitated. Years of ingrained caution warned not
to lose himself in desire when in the midst of danger.
But stronger than caution was Adrian's urgent need to
counteract his deep fear that his wife was bound by
only the frailest of tethers, and that someday she would
fly away from him.

Surrendering to his passionate need to prove to both
of them that she was his, he kissed her again with deep
hunger. The rich wet scents of leaf, rain, and bark
were sharply erotic, as was the wild wind, and within
moments he had forgotten caution, forgotten fear, forgotten everything except the woman in his arms, and
how much he loved and needed her.

His hand slid through the folds of her mantle to her
breast, and under the layers of fabric her nipple hardened instantly. After he had roused both her breasts,
his hand moved lower, across her slim waist, down
the slight curve of her abdomen to the sensitive junc-
ture of her thighs. She moaned and pressed against
him, then fumbled under his tunic so that she might
return the pleasure he was giving her.

Adrian gasped when her deft, knowing hand found
him. Retaining just enough sense to reject the soaked
earth, he turned Meriel so that her back was against
the tree. His mantle protected them both from the wind
as he lifted her heavy skirts, and her waiting flesh was
hot, moist, and eager. She gave a soft cry when he
touched her, then murmured, *"I am my beloved's, and
his desire is toward me."*

There is no aphrodisiac greater than the desire of
one's beloved, and her words dissolved past and future, leaving only the fiery present. Adrian raised
Meriel off the ground and braced her against the tree
trunk as she wrapped her arms and legs tightly around

him. He thrust into her, then caught himself, trembling with the effort of remaining still so that he would not culminate immediately from the exquisite welcome her body offered him.

He would have moved slowly, but Meriel would not let him. She surged with passion, her teeth and nails sinking into him with delirium. Adrian lost the last vestiges of control and they made love with a fury that matched the storm's. And at the end, their cries mingled with the wail of the wind.

Passion spent, breathing ragged, and bodies shaking with reaction, they stayed locked in each other's arms, supported by the tree. In the aftermath of madness was overwhelming tenderness. When he had regained a little breath, Adrian whispered softly in Meriel's ear, "I love you, *ma petite*. Promise that you'll never leave me."

Her eyes opened, the intense blue hazy with emotion. "Why should I ever wish to leave you, beloved?"

Fear had been banished by passion, love, and tenderness, and Adrian wished the moment might last forever. Then the world exploded.

The waning storm had one last bolt in its quiver, and with a flash so bright it etched the bones, lightning struck the tree to the left. Thunder was simultaneous, crashing with a shattering power so far beyond sound as to be a paralyzing physical blow.

The violence of the shock wave hurled them to the ground. Meriel gasped, and in the instant of falling Adrian tightened his arms around her in an instinctive protective gesture. He had a fleeting awareness of the sounds of devastation, and of an acrid, biting smell. Then he knew no more.

16

MERIEL FELT that she had been wandering a long while in darkness, and awareness came in a piecemeal fashion. In time she realized that she was out-of-doors, lying on her back on soft moist earth. A steady rain fell and she could feel it on some parts of her body, but most of her was protected by a warm, heavy weight. The sensation matched nothing in her experience, and questions wound dizzily through her mind. Where was she? And how had she come to be here? When she could find no answers, she made the immense effort of opening her eyes.

The warm weight that pinned her to the earth was Lord Adrian of Warfield. Meriel went rigid with shock at the discovery. The earl lay sprawled on top of her, breast to breast, one of his thighs thrust between hers and their faces nearly touching. His gilt hair was dark with water, and raindrops ran over his closed lids to trickle down the planes of his immobile face.

He was so still that for an anguished moment she was sure he must be dead. No, he was breathing, she could feel the rise and fall of his chest against hers. He was merely unconscious, as she had been.

How odd that the thought of his death was so upsetting after all he had done to her. Her dazed mind solemnly pondered the question of why. Perhaps it was because she wished death to no one, or perhaps it was because his demise would take something wild and beautiful from the world.

Her left leg was cold and wet, bared to the weather.

With a sick twist of horror, Meriel realized that her skirts were rucked up about her waist and that her body was pressed against Lord Adrian's with an intimacy just short of actual coupling. Sweet Mother of God, had he raped her?

She slid her hand down and touched between her legs. Her private parts were tinglingly sensitive and she felt a sense of repletion deep inside her. But there was no pain, and when she withdrew her hand, the sticky moisture on her fingertips was not blood.

Slowly she pushed at the earl's shoulders, tipping him onto his side, then pulling her right leg from between his thighs. She shuddered as his sheathed sword dragged over her ankle. In spite of her panicky desire to flee, she moved with great care, terrified that he might wake and try to stop her.

Meriel pushed herself to a sitting position and looked around. She recognized the stone circle immediately and remembered what had happened here before. It must have been a week or so ago, and had been a sunny day. But she could not remember how they had come here today, in a storm that should have kept decent Christians in their homes.

Had the earl brought her here and raped her? Why could she not remember? She would have fought him with all her strength, but he could easily have subdued her without knocking her unconscious. And she had no pain or bruising, nor any other physical evidence that he had assaulted her.

She shook her head dizzily, knowing that she was a fool to waste time worrying about what had happened. What mattered was seizing this chance to escape. Her limbs trembling and her muddy mantle weighting her down like lead, Meriel stood, almost swooning as she did. She bit her lower lip savagely and the pain helped clear her mind.

To the left lay a shattered tree, yellow flames licking the trunk in defiance of the falling rain. Charred fragments of wood had been thrown in all directions.

Lightning, it must have been lightning, which explained the lingering pungency in the burnt air. No wonder she and the earl had been knocked unconscious and why she felt so badly shaken. Jesu, they were lucky not to have been killed. She remembered the time lightning had struck a tree at Beaulaine when a flock of sheep were huddled beneath. Most of the beasts had been stunned and several were killed outright.

To the right, two horses were tied under a tree. They were wild-eyed and nervous from the storm, but apparently had had time to settle down since the lightning struck. One was the sorrel mare the earl had given her to ride, the other a young bay gelding. She was glad that he had not ridden his great black stallion, Gideon. With a head start the mare could outrun the gelding, so it would be unnecessary to take Lord Adrian's mount with her.

Meriel glanced down at the earl again, wondering if she should do something for him. Lying on his side as if sleeping, he seemed harmless and vulnerable, not the wicked tormentor but the handsome young man who had sometimes made her laugh. She checked his throat and felt a steady pulse. His color was also good and she guessed that he was not seriously injured, merely stunned as she had been. He should waken soon.

In the distance she heard a faint rumble of thunder. At least the tempest had passed, though a steady rain still fell. A man as strong as Lord Adrian was not likely to be harmed by lying on the wet earth a little longer, but she found that she could not turn away without first tucking his mantle around him. She also pulled the hood up to protect his face from the rain.

Moving quickly to the horses, Meriel went to work on untying the sorrel's reins, her fingers clumsy on the rain-swollen leather. Finally she managed to undo them, but before she could mount, she heard movement behind her.

Whirling, she saw Lord Adrian push himself to a sitting position. His head was bowed and his face hidden by the hood, and from the unsteadiness of his movements he was as disoriented as she had been when she first awoke. Hoarsely he called out, "Meriel, where are you? Are you all right?"

She inhaled sharply. With the earl awake, she could not leave his horse, so with frantic fingers she started unfastening the gelding's reins.

"Thank God you were not injured!"

Meriel looked up and saw that Lord Adrian's gaze had found her and his face was vivid with relief. There was something rather touching in his concern for her welfare, though she was not moved enough to want to remain his captive.

Shakily he regained his feet and started to walk toward her.

"Keep away from me!" Her exclamation was reflexive, and she was surprised when he stopped walking.

"Meriel, what's wrong?" he asked, his expression puzzled.

"You have been holding me prisoner for weeks and you have the effrontery to ask me what is wrong?" she said bitterly. The gelding's reins finally yielded. Holding them secure in one hand, she swung onto the sorrel's back. "But that is about to be corrected, my lord."

Even across the distance that separated them, she could see the horrified shock in Lord Adrian's gray eyes. Urgently he asked, "Meriel, what is the last thing you remember?"

"It was . . . it was . . ." What was the most recent event before waking up here? Everything was confused. Uncertainly she replied, "You took me for a walk on the castle walls. Then we went back to my chamber and you almost raped me."

"Meriel, that happened almost two months ago,"

the earl said unsteadily. "Can you recall nothing—*nothing*—more recent?"

She was a fool to bandy words with him rather than fleeing, but she wanted desperately to understand. Squeezing her eyes shut, she tried to remember. "You called me to your chamber. I . . . I think it was the day after we had gone up on the wall."

Her eyes flew open, suddenly fearful that he was going to come over and grab her, but he had not moved. "No, it was the same day, I remember that I was still distraught when I went to your chamber. I . . . I can't remember what happened after I got there." Her voice faltered. "But that wasn't two months ago! It must have been yesterday?"

"Look around you, *ma petite*," he said softly. "That was in the spring. It is summer now. Look at the trees and flowers."

Terrified, Meriel scanned the woods and clearing. He was right, for the leaves were the dense green of high summer, and foxglove was in bloom. Weeks or months had passed, and she had absolutely no recollection of them. On the verge of hysteria, she cried, "What did you do to me that I don't remember?"

The earl took a step closer, then stopped when she jerked her reins. "There was an accident, Meriel," he said, his voice as quiet as if he were calming a bating hawk. "You almost died. When you recovered, you remembered nothing of your earlier life."

When she just stared at him, wild-eyed, Adrian continued, "You agreed to marry me. Do you remember our wedding? The vows we exchanged? Ringing the bells?"

"No!" she exclaimed, appalled. "I would never have married you. Never!"

"Don't you even remember when your brother Alan arrived on our wedding day?"

Startled, she started to speak, then stopped and desperately repeated her earlier story. "My brother's name is Daffyd, not Alan. He lives in Gwynedd."

"No, *ma petite,* you have two brothers. I met the younger, Alan, when he came to Warfield from Avonleigh to find you. He spoke of your family and Lambourn Priory, but you had no memory of anything he told you." A thought occurred to him. "Notice that we are speaking Norman now. Earlier you had pretended ignorance, but after your accident you began using it."

Acute distress rippled across Meriel's face. Then she shook her head. "I could not have forgotten so much. You must have found out about my family some other way."

Adrian's fragile control disintegrated. "Meriel, you are my *wife!*" he said hoarsely. "You said that you loved me and you married me willingly. In fact, you were eager to wed even though I questioned the wisdom of doing it so soon after your accident. Look, you are wearing my ring!"

She raised her shaking left hand and stared at the gold band. "No," she said in a horrified whisper. "I would never have gone to you of my own will. Did you finally tire of waiting and rape me, and I lost my wits after that?"

"Even at my worst, I could not hurt you, *ma petite.* Do you not remember that even when I was half-mad with desire, I always stopped?" Adrian raised a trembling hand to his head, wondering if he was the one who had lost his wits. "For nearly two months we have been together almost constantly. You were so happy, so full of love. Can you remember none of that?"

"You are lying," she cried. *"You are lying!"*

He stepped toward her. Surely Meriel could not have entirely forgotten the passion and tenderness that were between them. If she would only let him touch her . . .

"Keep away from me!" Her face a mask of revulsion, she collected the sorrel's reins.

Before the horse could set off, Adrian dived across the remaining distance and grabbed its bridle. "Meriel, don't run away like this, when you're upset and confused,'' he pleaded. ''If you want to go back to Avonleigh, so be it, but at least let me send an escort to protect you.''

''It is you I need protection from!'' she said furiously. ''You will not stop me from escaping this time, my lord.'' She jerked on her reins and the sorrel reared into the air, breaking Adrian's grip on the bridle. As he leapt away from the mare's flailing hooves, Meriel kicked her mount forward into a full gallop. Leading the gelding, she plunged down the trail away from the stone circle.

''Meriel, stop!'' In spite of his shaky weakness, Adrian hurled himself down the track after her. Jesu, if only he had ridden Gideon today! He could have whistled the stallion back to him, but the gelding had not had the same training.

Within seconds Meriel was out of sight, but he continued running down the muddy track. Though pain stabbed at his side and his lungs screamed for air, he did not stop until one foot slipped in the mud and he fell, crashing down on his side and rolling across the trail.

Too exhausted to continue his hopeless pursuit, he doubled over and buried his head in his hands, his whole body shaking with anguish. Jesu, what right did he have to stop her, even if he could? He had sworn to do anything she wanted, and what she wanted was never to see him again.

Adrian had worried that Meriel might remember her past and despise him for what he had done at the beginning, but he had never dreamed that she might also forget everything else that had happened since. All the love, all the passion and tenderness and vows of fidelity—it was as if they had never existed. For Meriel, they did not. She looked at her husband and saw only her tormentor. *There has never been a woman more blessed than I, for you have chosen me for your wife.*

Her remembered words mocked him viciously. *Why should I ever wish to leave you, beloved?*

Perhaps God himself had sent that lightning bolt from heaven. Adrian tried to dismiss the bizarre thought. It was merely an accident, a result of being in the wrong place—but in his heart he did not believe it. This, finally, was his punishment. He had known that repentance and a vow to atone were not enough to redeem his crimes against Meriel, and the hard self-mastery needed to resist her innocent sensuality after the accident had seemed like God's justice. Living with the guilty knowledge of what he had done to her and the fear that she would remember the past were also punishments.

But this was infinitely worse: to have known Meriel's love for a few brief weeks, then to lose it and have only her hatred. A white-hot dagger in his heart would have been less cruel.

Racked with devastation, Adrian wondered if it was possible to survive such pain without going mad.

Meriel had been riding for hours, and through her haze of confusion and fatigue the thought that sustained her was that she must get back to Avonleigh. From what she remembered of her initial journey to Warfield and her first trip to the stone circle, east was to her right, and she turned that way when she found a well-traveled track. A mile or two along, she released Lord Adrian's horse.

Apart from a brief thinning of the clouds that showed the sun's position and confirmed her judgment of direction, the rain continued cold and steady. Occasionally she saw a serf in the distance and twice she rode through small villages, but few people were abroad and no one threatened her.

Her clothing had long since soaked through and she shivered uncontrollably as the tired mare picked its way through the heavy mud. Because of the weather, the light began to fail early, and it was dusk when she

finally entered the dark expanse of royal forest that
separated Lord Adrian's land from the country she
knew. In spite of her exhaustion, Meriel did not consider stopping. She would not feel safe until she had
reached the other side of the forest.

The violent storm and heavy rain had slowed Benjamin l'Eveske and his party to a crawl as the oxen
struggled to pull the heavy wagons through the
mud, and a broken axle finally stopped them altogether. Since it was nearly dusk, Benjamin signaled
Edwin, the captain of his hired guard, and told him
they would camp here. Benjamin would have preferred
not to spend a night in the dark, ominous royal forest,
but there was no help for it, so he set his servants to
repairing the axle so they could resume their journey
first thing in the morning.

By nightfall they were as comfortable as could be
expected, with the men-at-arms eating around one fire
and the fifteen members of Benjamin's household
around another. The air was chilly and the fires welcome, but the rain finally stopped and the sky cleared
to show a pale crescent moon and stars.

Though most of the travelers retired early, Benjamin
felt a desire to stretch his legs after the fatigue of traveling and Sarah chose to go with him on a short walk
back along the track. They walked side by side, their
index fingers linking them together in a youthful sign
of affection that they were far too dignified to indulge
in before others.

"Do you think you shall like Lincoln?" Benjamin
asked when they were out of earshot of the camp.

"I imagine so," his wife replied cheerfully. "Perhaps better than Shrewsbury. It may lack the trading
advantages, and I suppose there is danger that the city
may be sacked again if the civil war flares up, but as
compensation, there are others of our people there."

"My plan for Shrewsbury did not work out well,"
he sighed.

"No matter. At least we found out about Sir Vincent's deception before it was too late."

They were about to turn back when they heard the muffled sound of hoofbeats on the muddy track. It was a single horse, moving very slowly. Curious, Benjamin drew Sarah back into the shadows so they could watch unobserved.

The rider that came into view was bowed over the saddle as if injured. As they watched, the small figure wavered and almost fell but managed to stay on the horse.

Benjamin called out, "Are you in trouble?"

The rider jerked upright, the slight figure taut with fear. In the dim moonlight they saw that it was a young woman. A face that would usually have been pretty was drawn with exhaustion, and she was muddy and bedraggled.

"Goodness, child, what has happened?" Sarah exclaimed, stepping forward into the moonlight.

Reassured, the girl said, "Nothing has happened. I am just on my way to my brother's manor." Her voice was thin, with a suggestion of chattering teeth.

Taking charge, Sarah moved closer. "You need some hot soup before you freeze, young lady. We are camped just ahead. Spend the night with us."

"I should not stop," the girl said uncertainly.

"If you don't, you might get lost or fall off your horse from fatigue," Benjamin said. "And I understand there are wolves in the forest. Come, let us help you."

The girl looked from one of them to the other, then nodded, too tired to resist. "Thank you."

Benjamin took hold of the horse's reins and led the way along the track to their camp while Sarah kept a wary eye on the girl to see that she did not tumble from the saddle. In fact, when they got back to their campfire and Benjamin helped her dismount, her knees crumpled and she would have fallen if he had not caught her. "I'm sorry," she said unsteadily. "I'll be all right in a moment."

"Of course you will be," Sarah said soothingly. Her voice low to avoid disturbing those who slept, she ordered her husband to take the girl into the wagon, her maid Rachel to heat some soup over the fire, and her son Aaron to see that the horse was unsaddled and rubbed down.

After Benjamin had laid the girl on a pallet in the wagon, he came back to the campfire to find Aaron staring at the wagon. "Father," he hissed, "did you see who that was? The Countess of Shropshire—Warfield's wife!"

"Indeed!" Startled, the merchant compared the strained face of this girl with the sweetly pretty young countess, then scanned the horse whose reins Aaron held. Under its mud and fatigue, it was a very valuable beast. "Perhaps you are right."

"I know I am right!" his son said, fury burning through his low voice. "Warfield would not let us stay in Shrewsbury. Why should we help his wife?"

"It was his right to refuse," Benjamin said mildly. "He could have done a good deal worse to us."

"What if Warfield finds her here and accuses us of abducting her?" Aaron demanded. "He might kill us all out of hand. I say we should put her back on her horse and send her off."

Benjamin shook his head. "You see the Countess of Shropshire. I see an exhausted girl who might not survive the night on her own. A girl, I might add, who was most considerate of us when we were at Warfield."

"You would help her even if it means risking the lives of everyone in your household?"

"If a Jew will not show compassion, then who will?" Benjamin laid a calming hand on his son's arm. "Some things must be done because they are right, Aaron."

The young man's anger deflated and his eyes fell. "I'm sorry, Father. I should not have spoken as I did."

"It is right to be cautious, but not to take out one's anger on someone who is helpless. Now, get you off and see to her horse."

Meriel had only the dimmest recollection of being stripped, put into a warm, dry gown, and wrapped in a blanket. Then the handsome middle-aged woman fed her hot pea soup. Meriel was reminded of her own mother.

At first her teeth chattered against the cup, but eventually warmth began to return and she gained the strength to study the crowded wagon. Her rescuers appeared to be prosperous folk. Canvas walls and roof protected the load, which was mostly household furnishings. A space had been left at the back end of the wagon so several pallets could be laid side by side. A single flickering lamp illuminated the scene as the two women sat cross-legged on the pallets.

After finishing the soup, she said, "Thank you, mistress. I do not know how I would have managed without your kindness." After a moment she remembered to add, "My name is Meriel."

"I am Sarah." The woman cocked her head, her dark eyes bright with curiosity. "Do you mind if I ask what you were doing alone in the forest at such a late hour?"

Meriel swallowed hard. "It is very complicated. I . . . I was in an accident and I don't remember exactly what has happened lately." Thoughts of Lord Adrian and his impossible, confusing claims suddenly overwhelmed her. Linking her arms around her raised knees, she bent her head to conceal her tears.

"Surely you remember that you are the Countess of Shropshire," Sarah said, a faint, questioning lift to her voice.

Aghast, Meriel raised her head. "You mean it's true? I really am Lord Adrian's wife?"

"Well, we saw you at the earl's side at Warfield Castle. The wedding was recent enough that people still talked of it."

Meriel linked her trembling hands together. "What is the date today?"

The older woman calculated. "It was Midsummer's Day a fortnight ago, so today must be the seventh of July."

"Then it must be true," Meriel whispered, her voice almost inaudible. "I have forgotten almost two months."

"Do you want to tell me your story, my lady?" Sarah said gently. "Sometimes it helps to talk to another woman."

Her kindness was a desperately needed balm to Meriel's lacerated emotions. In halting words, her voice sometimes breaking, she recounted all of what she remembered, from the time she met the earl in the forest to her awakening by the stone circle earlier in the afternoon.

Sarah listened intently, sometimes asking for clarification or prompting her with a question. When her visitor was done, the older woman shook her head in amazement. "It's a strange tale. To have lost two whole months, and such significant months!"

Her expression troubled, Sarah continued slowly, "Not remembering all that had happened, it is understandable that you were frightened when you woke up earlier today. But he is your husband. You seemed happy together, from what we saw and heard at Warfield. In fact, the folk at the castle spoke of how you and Earl Adrian doted on each other. Isn't your place with him?"

"Never!" Meriel said vehemently. "The Church says that a marriage is not valid without mutual consent, and I would never have agreed if I were not having a spell of madness." Her hands clenched and she felt the hard shape of her wedding ring. Angrily she tried to remove it, but after hours of holding wet reins her fingers were swollen, and to her intense frustration the ring would not come off.

"You may not be the only one concerned in this, Lady Meriel," Sarah said. "You have been married several months, and might already be with child. Perhaps not—but if you *are* carrying the earl's heir, surely he will fight to keep the marriage."

With child! Meriel's hand went to her abdomen in shock. With startling vividness she recalled how she had woken earlier today, the earl's body intertwined with her own. She had exact memories of the weight and taste and feel of him. Perhaps she had not been just his victim; in her madness, she might have even cooperated in her own ruin. The thought was so sickening that she doubled over, on the verge of nausea.

Sarah's soft arms came around her. "I'm sorry, child, you have already too much to think of. It is best that you go to your brother until you come to terms with all that has happened to you. Perhaps you will remember some of the missing months, which could make the fact of your marriage more acceptable. Your husband is a handsome man. He is also said to have both integrity and compassion." She chuckled wryly. "He would not have us in Shrewsbury, so I suppose that is proof that he is a good son of the Church."

"He is not my husband!" Meriel clung to Sarah until her spinning head steadied. As she straightened up, she wondered about the older woman's last remark. "What do you mean that he would not have you in Shrewsbury?"

"Aye, you would not remember," Sarah murmured. "We are Jews, Lady Meriel. We were looking to settle away from London." Succinctly she explained Guy of Burgoigne's deceitful offer, and how they had learned the truth at Warfield.

Meriel studied her hostess curiously. "I see that my life is not the only one that is complicated."

Sarah raised her dark brows. "You needn't look at me like that. Jews are not so different from Christians, you know, we may prepare our food differently but we don't have horns.''

Meriel blushed. "I'm sorry, I didn't mean to be rude. I have never met any Jews before. I don't know what I expected." After a moment's pause, she added, "You have been very kind. If there is ever anything I can do for you . . .''

"Just lend a hand to the next poor soul in trouble," Sarah said with a yawn. "It is very late, time we were both in bed. I expect my husband is ready as well.''

Stifling her guest's apologies about keeping them up late, Sarah tucked the younger woman into one of the pallets. Meriel was asleep even before Benjamin climbed into the wagon.

The party rose early the next morning, breaking their fast with bread and cheese and ale no different from what Meriel might have had at Avonleigh. All of Benjamin's household seemed to be Jewish as well; so much for the myth that all Jews were rich moneylenders. The household seemed almost like a large family, with Benjamin the patriarch of them all. It was not unlike a Christian manor with a good lord and lady.

All of the servants were kind to Meriel, though Aaron, the son of the house, watched her with wary curiosity. Was he contrasting her present state to when he had seen her as Countess of Shropshire? Meriel's mind veered away from the thought. She was not yet ready to think of what must have passed between her and Adrian of Warfield.

It had been agreed that Meriel would ride with the party at least to the other side of the forest, and she was about to go for her horse when a warning shout came from the lookout set by the hired guards. Benjamin's men-at-arms immediately mobilized to fight, but the attackers had chosen their moment well, when the travelers were ill organized and unprepared for trouble.

Troops of armed men swept into the camp from both

directions and the air was split by shattering war cries. The group coming from the west was led by a huge, burly knight whose surcoat bore the emblem of a blue boar. For a moment Meriel froze, knowing that she had seen that device before. Then she remembered the skirmish she had seen near Lambourn Priory the day she had briefly met Adrian of Warfield. It was also the day she had first seen the blue boar.

The air was cacophonous with swords and shouting men, plus the higher screams of women. Benjamin stood by the wagons, trying to calm his terrified household. Pushing her way through the milling servants, Meriel yelled, "Master Benjamin, it is Guy of Burgoigne!"

"May God help us," he breathed. The old man scanned the fighting around him. His guards were fighting valiantly, but they were outnumbered and none of them had had a chance to mount their horses. Several of them were down, and it was just a matter of time until all were defeated. "There is no point in more men dying in vain," he said grimly. "Which is Guy of Burgoigne?"

Meriel pointed out the leader, whose smashing, bloody sword was the most devastating of all.

Benjamin said, "Give me your veil."

Meriel quickly pulled off the short white veil Sarah had lent her. Waving it over his head, Benjamin plunged into the melee with suicidal courage. "Lord Guy, we surrender," he shouted. "Stop the killing." Catching sight of his own captain, Benjamin yelled, "Give over, Edwin, there are too many of them."

As the message spread through the ranks, the shouting and clashing weapons diminished, then stopped. Benjamin's men were disarmed and herded into a sullen circle, where they began examining and bandaging their wounded fellows.

Guy waited until all was secured, then dismounted and swaggered over to Benjamin, who stood slightly in front of his household, Aaron at his side. Meriel stood beside Sarah, whose grim calm helped steady her servants.

"So you are Benjamin l'Eveske," the earl said, removing his helm. As Meriel saw the broad, coarse face, she knew that this was the Earl of Shropshire that Alan had said was capable of anything. Even at his worst, Adrian of Warfield had never looked so brutal.

Guy stopped directly in front of Benjamin and jeered, "Why were you scurrying away like a rat when I had so kindly invited you to Shropshire?"

His voice calm, Benjamin said, "There was some confusion about the invitation." He nodded at the lean, dark-haired knight who had come to stand behind Guy. "Your man there must have forgotten who his lord was. He led me to believe that he served Adrian of Warfield."

"Vincent is a clever devil, isn't he? He brought you here, which is all that matters." The earl gestured at some of his men. "Search the wagons and bring all gold and jewels to me. And for Christ's sake, be careful with the household furnishings, they are valuable."

For the next half-hour, men-at-arms pawed through the wagons. While respecting the furnishings, they had no compunctions about humbler things like flour and other foodstuffs, which were thrown about with wanton delight in destruction.

One man found a group of books and pulled one out. From where she stood, Meriel saw that it was written in a strange script. With a crow of delight, the man sneered. "Heathens." He threw the book on the ground, fumbled with his chausses, then urinated on it.

There was a gasp of collective shock and revulsion from Benjamin's household. Even Meriel felt the sense of desecration, and Aaron took a step toward the offender before his father grabbed his upper arm with an iron grip. "It is just parchment, Aaron, the true word

of God cannot be tarnished by such as he,'' Benjamin
said softly. In spite of his calming words, the old man's
face was like a mask of granite.

Guy of Burgoigne had been prowling avidly about
the wagons, eager for loot, and now he arrived on the
scene. Before any of the other books could receive
similar treatment, he scowled and struck the man-at-
arms on the side of the head. ''You fool, don't you
know what a book is worth, even a filthy Jewish one?''

The man-at-arms, a large man himself, staggered
back from the blow, then wisely took himself off.

At the end of the search, the clearing was strewn
with lesser belongings, and a small pile of valuables
had been set aside for the earl. Disbelieving, he poked
through the loot, then strode over to Benjamin, bran-
dishing a leather pouch. ''Where is the rest of your
treasure, you heathen bastard?'' he roared. ''Usurers
are always wealthy, but there can't be more than five
hundred silver marks here.''

Quietly ironic, Benjamin replied, ''My deepest regrets, my lord earl. I had not planned on being
robbed.''

Furious, the earl struck the old man with the full
strength of his mailed fist. As Benjamin slumped to
the ground, Aaron shouted with rage and launched
himself at his father's attacker.

There was a blur of movement. A slim sixteen-year-
old boy had no chance against a fully armed knight,
and the earl effortlessly knocked Aaron from his feet.

As Sarah screamed in anguish, Guy set his sword at
the boy's throat. The clearing throbbed with unbearable tension. ''How dare you, you little heathen,'' he
snarled. ''You've won the privilege of being the first
to die.''

Before he could drive the blade home, Meriel darted
out of the group of servants and grabbed the earl's
arm. ''Don't, Lord Guy! Kill Benjamin's son and you
will lose the ransom you might earn for him.''

Startled, the earl looked up at her. ''Ransoms are

paid for battle captives, you witless wench, not for worthless Jews.''

Her heart pounding with fear, Meriel struggled to find arguments that might save Sarah's son, as well as the rest of them. ''Come, my lord, surely you know that merchants do not carry all their gold around with them. Most of their fortunes are in goods and monies of account. If you spare Benjamin and his household, doubtless he can arrange to pay a ransom for their lives and freedom.'' She glanced up and caught Sarah's eye. The older woman was ash-pale at the prospect of what might happen to her husband and son, but she nodded, confirming Meriel's guess.

Meriel turned back to the earl, having thought of another argument. ''And remember, all Jews are under the king's protection, for they benefit the kingdom greatly. Stephen will not be pleased at another massacre of the Jews, even if it is by a man who has served him long and well.''

Burgoigne pulled his sword back from Aaron's throat. He knew about monies of account as well as Meriel did, but he had been so sure of finding instant treasure that his failure had put him into a mindless rage. ''This is the merchant's son? Aye, you're right, he's too valuable to spit like a roasting chicken.''

Aaron scrambled to his feet, then helped his father rise. There was blood on the old man's face, but he did not seem seriously injured.

Guy looked at him coldly. ''How much will you pay for your life, old man? Thirty thousand marks, perhaps?''

''For the lives of myself and all of my people—*all* of them—I would give my entire fortune, but it is not thirty thousand marks.'' Benjamin hesitated, calculating. ''I could raise ten thousand quickly, perhaps another ten when my agents have had a chance to sell my property.''

''Very well,'' Guy said brusquely. ''When I receive ten thousand marks, I will release all your servants.

After receiving the second ten thousand, you, your wife, and your son will also be set free.''

While the bargain was being struck, Meriel saw that the lean dark-haired knight behind the earl was watching her avidly. Uncomfortable under his gaze, she faded back into the crowd of servants. With luck, she would be considered just another maid.

When she reached Sarah's side, the older woman took her hand and squeezed it. "God bless you, child," she whispered. "If you had not thought quickly, Aaron would be dead now, and perhaps the rest of us as well."

"But your freedom will cost you and your family a lifetime's toil," Meriel said soberly.

Sarah shrugged. "What good is gold when one is dead? Our friends will see that we don't starve." Releasing Meriel's hand, she went to her husband and began wiping the blood from his cheek with the end of her long veil.

Guy was about to turn away from his prisoners when the dark-haired knight spoke up. "You've taken a prize richer than Benjamin l'Eveske, my lord."

The knight pushed his way into the group of servants and grabbed Meriel's arm, then dragged her out to stand in front of the earl. His eyes glinting with triumph, he said, "This scrawny wench is Adrian of Warfield's wife."

17

"WARFIELD'S WIFE?" Guy said incredulously. He grabbed Meriel's chin and forced it up so he could look at her. "What would his countess be doing with a pack of Jews? The wench is just one of Benjamin's maids."

"Nay," Sir Vincent said, shaking his head. "I saw her and Warfield together in Shrewsbury shortly before the wedding, and I marked her well because I had trouble believing that he couldn't do better." He gestured toward the back of the wagons. "When we were searching, I noticed a pretty little sorrel mare and thought that it was exactly like the one Warfield's betrothed rode that day. Then I saw her, and knew. This is the Lady Meriel, all right. Ask her."

Guy's fingers tightened cruelly on Meriel's chin. "Speak up, woman. Are you really Warfield's bride?"

Meriel considered denial, but decided not to try. She was a terrible liar at best and would never be able to prevail in the face of Sir Vincent's conviction. And if she did try to lie, they might torture Sarah or her family just to check whether she was telling the truth. "Yes," she said, her gaze steady. "I am Warfield's wife."

"So you are the one he married with no dowry and no family. Truly lust is a marvelous thing. Maybe your pious, thin-blooded husband likes the fact that you look more like a boy than a woman," Guy mused. Then he smiled nastily. "I wonder what he will pay to get you back."

"Very little," Meriel said, instinctively wanting to diminish her value in Burgoigne's eyes. "Warfield was not pleased with his bargain. He was sending me back to my family and considering an annulment. I became lost in the forest and Benjamin and his family took me in last night. They did not know who I was."

Her feeble ploy failed. Releasing her chin, the earl said, "Even if Warfield despises you, he'll want you back if only because I have you." His narrowed eyes were full of vicious calculation. "This will make Benjamin's ransom look like beggar's alms."

With a spurt of fury, Meriel said, "Tell me, Lord Guy, did you choose a boar for your emblem because you resembled one, or did you come to resemble it after you chose it?"

He swung his fist and clouted her on the side of her head, knocking her to the ground. As she lay stunned, he prodded her in the ribs with his booted toe. "If Warfield is willing to pay the price, he can have you back, but I'll make no guarantees as to what condition you'll be in. Any more talk like that and you'll be sorry that I don't kill you."

He raised his head and turned away. "Get these people moving. We're going back to Chastain."

In the dim, confused aftermath of Meriel's departure, the only ray of light was when Adrian found his horse wandering loose on the trail to the castle. As he captured the gelding and remounted, he thought with weary irony that he might return home covered with mud and minus his wife, but at least he was riding as a proper knight should.

Back at Warfield, his expression was so fierce that no one made any attempt to speak to him, not even to ask where the countess was. Adrian withdrew into his room, blindly pacing like a caged wolf as he attempted to organize his shattered emotions. More vividly than the stone walls, he saw the revulsion on Meriel's face when he told her of their marriage. Her appalled denials rang in his ears, yet a few minutes earlier she had been pure loving passion. It was as if there were two different Meriels, one giving herself with absolute love, the other free and unconquerable. Yet her spirit was always the same, and he loved her as helplessly when she hated him as when she had loved him.

He made no attempt to pray for surcease, knowing it would be hopeless. And what could he pray for? Divine justice had already been visited on him, and he doubted that divine mercy would be forthcoming.

Darkness fell, but brought no peace. Adrian lit a candle and continued to prowl restlessly, unable to sit as furious self-condemnations filled his mind. The sounds of the castle had long stilled when he heard a soft sound near to hand. Looking up incuriously, he saw Kestrel emerge from under the leather flap that covered the cat-hole in the door. The comical-looking beast jumped on the bed and sniffed around hopefully, then sat on her haunches and gave the earl a questioning look.

"She's not coming back." Adrian's throat closed on the words. He could not have said more to save his life.

The cat regarded him with grave golden eyes, then stuck one hind foot in the air and began, rather noisily, to wash herself.

For whatever odd reason, the cat's arrival served to bring some focus to his disordered mind. Most likely Meriel had gone to her brother's manor, Avonleigh. Pray God she made it safely; in her state of fear and confusion, she might have gotten lost, perhaps run into trouble. Adrian should have sent men after her to ensure her arrival, but he had been too numb to think of such an elementary precaution earlier.

She would want her cat and her falcon. And what else? He slumped in a chair and kneaded his aching head as he tried to decide what must be done. A man did not die of grief or guilt no matter how much he might want to; daily life churned on, duty must be fulfilled as long as one lived in the world.

That thought produced another, the seductive realization that he might have to live, but he need not live in the world. He set it aside as premature, but a wisp of comfort stayed with him, like a child who had been promised a future treat.

Eventually his sluggish mind ceased to move at all and he slept.

Adrian awoke the next morning cramped and unrefreshed. As chairs went, this one was quite comfortable but it made a poor bed. At least his thoughts were somewhat clearer for the rest.

He was splashing cold water in his face when the door opened. Toweling himself dry, he turned to find Margery, his wife's chief serving woman.

She regarded him doubtfully. "Does Lady Meriel need me this morning?"

He could not deny the truth forever, or even any longer. "I haven't murdered her, if that is what you are wondering," he said harshly. "The countess decided to visit her brother."

The maid's eyes widened, but she wisely asked no more. After bobbing a curtsy, she hastily left.

After dispatching searchers to comb his lands, Adrian himself set off to Avonleigh with half a dozen men. Fortunately his steward knew the manor's location and was able to give accurate directions. Pushing hard, the earl reached Avonleigh by midafternoon.

Alan de Vere was in his stables, and he received his brother-in-law with open hostility. "What do you want?" he snapped, turning from the horse he had been grooming, his feet braced as if for battle.

Responding to the anger in the air, both the Avonleigh and Warfield retainers faded away, leaving the earl and knight alone.

Wasting no time, Adrian asked, "Is Meriel here?"

There was a flash of surprise in the blue eyes that

were so like Meriel's. Then de Vere masked his thoughts. "Don't you know where your own wife is, Warfield?"

"No," Adrian said wearily. "In a moment I will tell you the whole story and you can vilify me to your heart's delight, but for God's sake, first tell me if she is here and safe. I swear that I won't try to force her to come away against her will."

"No, she is not here. I have seen or heard nothing from her since I was at Warfield." De Vere's hostility was now tempered with concern. "What has happened?"

"You were shocked to arrive at your sister's wedding and find that she had no memory of her past, so doubtless you will now be pleased to learn that yesterday she abruptly remembered her entire past up to the time of her accident, and forgot everything that had happened since. Including our marriage." Adrian swallowed hard, determined to spare himself nothing. "We were riding when she recovered her memory. Since Meriel found the prospect of being my wife appalling in the extreme, she promptly stole my horse and rode away. My guess was that she would return to Avonleigh, but perhaps not. Do you know of another place she might go?"

"Sweet Jesu!" Alan said blankly, temporarily bereft of speech. He eyes narrowed. "When I was at Warfield, you never did answer my question about her mysterious 'accident.' What caused her to lose her memory in the first place?"

"I asked her to marry me and she replied by jumping out a window into the Severn," Adrian said flatly.

Having seen how Warfield Castle was sited above the river, de Vere was so stunned that he could not even think of a suitable oath. Finally he asked, "How did she survive? I would have thought that if the fall didn't kill her, drowning would."

"I dived in after her. Fortunately I am a strong swimmer."

De Vere's eyes opened at that, but he was not about to admit respect. "So she lived, but without her memory, and you then coerced her into marriage?"

"Coercion was not necessary, de Vere," Adrian said softly. "You saw her on her wedding day. Did she look unwilling?"

The two men glared at each other, the earl ice cold, the knight molten-iron hot. Adrian gave a wintry smile. Though they loved Meriel in different ways, they were still rivals. "May I leave one of my men here so that if Meriel returns, he can bring word back to Warfield?"

"What do you intend to do now?" de Vere demanded.

"Search until I find Meriel. Once I know she is safe . . ." He shrugged. "As I said, I will not compel her in any way. If she wishes to return here, I will send her with an escort."

"That won't be necessary," Alan said grimly. "I'm going with you, and I intend to stay closer than your own shadow until she is found. You will have no more opportunities to force her."

"As you wish," Adrian said, unsurprised by his brother-in-law's stubbornness. Alan and his sister resembled each other more than just physically. "Come along, then. By the time we are back on Warfield land, the other searchers I sent out may have found her."

But when they arrived back at Warfield Castle late that night, there was still no word of the missing countess.

Benjamin's hired guards had been disarmed and left in the forest. Since none of them were men of means, there had been no profit in holding them for ransom. Guy was in such a good mood over his more valuable captives that he didn't even bother to kill the guards.

Darkness was falling when the prisoners arrived at Chastain after a fast-paced journey that exhausted the frailer members of the party. Guy's castle, like Adrian's, was situated on a crag above a river. Smaller and less impressive than Warfield, it had been built erratically over a long period of time. Nonetheless it was still formidable, and Meriel rode through the gates with a chill of fear that reminded her of her first entry into Warfield. Forcibly she told herself that she had escaped Warfield, and she would also escape Chastain.

The weary group of captives was taken into the keep, then herded down a twisting stone staircase. On the lower level, one of the guards produced a massive key and opened an iron-bound door. "In here."

The flaring torches showed a chamber perhaps twelve by twenty feet in size, apparently built as a storeroom, but now empty. Meriel started to file in with the others, then stopped when a hard hand caught her arm.

"Oh, no, my lady," Sir Vincent said with mocking politeness. "Lord Guy has other quarters for you."

As he marched her away from the group, Sarah gave Meriel a stricken look. Meriel tried to smile reassuringly, but she would have much preferred to stay with the others.

Sir Vincent led her to another stairwell, and as his torch cast wild, distorted shadows on the curving walls, they spiraled into the lowest depths of the castle. At the bottom of the stair was a small chamber with a trapdoor in the center of the floor and a crude ladder leaning against the wall.

"Here you are, countess, a private chamber," Sir Vincent said, lifting the trap. Below was total blackness and a rank, unpleasant smell. Taking the ladder, he lowered it into the dungeon.

Sir Vincent's hostility puzzled Meriel. He had a sly, unreliable face, but he was not the coarse brute that his lord was. Before descending the ladder, she turned and asked him, "Why do you hate me so?"

Sir Vincent was taken aback, so much so that he gave her an answer. "I don't hate you. It is just that you are such an exquisite weapon to wield against your arrogant husband.''

"What did he do to you?" she persisted.

"I asked to take service with him once, and he refused to have me," Sir Vincent replied, his expression ugly. Obviously the Frenchman was not a man to forget a slight.

"So you were forced to serve Guy of Burgoigne instead. I can see how that would be a cruel fate," Meriel said dryly.

None too gently he shoved her toward the ladder. "You've a nasty little tongue, countess. I begin to understand why Warfield might want to set you aside once his lust was satified. At this very moment he is probably looking for evidence of consanguinity so that the marriage can be annulled."

"Very likely," Meriel said with maximum sweetness. "As I said earlier, you will find me a poor weapon for wounding Lord Adrian."

He scowled at her. "Even if he despises you, Warfield has too much pride to allow Guy the victory of holding his wife. You'll see, Guy will make him squirm. Aye, he'll get your worth in gold and a great deal more." He surveyed her. "Even if I hadn't had a woman in a twelvemonth, I wouldn't pay more than a silver penny myself."

Having virtually no personal vanity, Meriel was not easily insulted. Instead, she glanced down into the dungeon and shivered. "If you want me to survive long enough to be useful in your little game, you had best bring me a blanket. And perhaps some straw."

"Very well," he said curtly, unable to deny that a frail female might not last long in these conditions.

The ladder sagged under her weight as she made her careful way down. It was perhaps a dozen feet to the bottom—the dungeon would be impossible to exit without a rope or ladder. As soon as she stepped off the ladder, Sir Vincent pulled it up and slammed the trapdoor, leaving Meriel alone in total blackness.

She stood without moving as she fought her fear. Sweet Mary, she thought in a desperate quest for levity, what was it that made her such an interesting object for imprisonment? Much more of this and she would be eligible for sainthood.

Using extreme caution, she began to explore her surroundings. Sometimes dungeons had deeper pits where prisoners might fall and break their bones for the amusement of their captors. However, that particular feature was not present here.

Arms outstretched, she advanced over the uneven dirt floor until her hands struck the wall. The surface was the roughest kind of masonry, the stones damp beneath her fingers as she worked her way around the irregular perimeter. In the absolute blackness it was hard to decide just where she had begun, but eventually she concluded that her prison was about eight feet square.

In one corner was a drain to channel wastes outside, more luxury than she would have expected. The air was also less foul than it might have been; soon she would not notice the smell at all. In the opposite corner from the drain was a pallet of old straw, noisome but still more comfortable than the dirt floor. She sat down on it, drew her knees up, and wrapped her arms around them in a futile attempt to warm herself up.

Now there was nothing to do but wait. Wait, and try to fend off panic. To think that she had felt trapped by the idea of a lifetime as a nun within Lambourn's welcoming walls! Even her imprisonment by Lord Adrian seemed easy by comparison. There at least she had been in comfortable surroundings, she had been able to see the sky and breathe sweet air. And no matter how unacceptable she had found the earl's passion, she believed that in his strange way he cared for her.

But here she was no more than a pawn, to be kept alive for her value as captive and weapon. How long would it be before Guy decided that it might be amusing to torture his enemy's wife? Even if Adrian would pay a ransom for her—and she agreed with Guy and Vincent, he would do it for honor's sake if not for love—would Burgoigne actually release her? Or would the man who had murdered Adrian's family also murder Meriel after he had received his ransom? If he tried any such trick, she did not doubt that Adrian would make him regret it bitterly, but that would not do her much good.

Her heart was beating frantically and her breath came in desperate gasps. Burying her face in her hands, she prayed: *Holy Mother, help me find the strength to endure what must be endured!*

In the midst of stifling darkness she sought the light, and in time she found it. Her breathing eased, her heart slowed to its normal rate as once more the Blessed Virgin enfolded her with loving arms. Even in the dungeon of a vicious monster, Meriel knew she was not alone.

An unmeasurable amount of time passed. An hour? A night? A day and a night? Then the trapdoor above her head was lifted and someone said in English, "Look out below." The voice was bored but not malicious.

Several armloads of straw were unceremoniously dumped through the trap, followed by a coarse but heavy wool blanket. As Meriel started to shift the straw to the corner, a basket was lowered on a rope. "Here's your supper, countess."

Meriel had no appetite, but she must eat to survive, particularly if she was with child. The basket contained a small loaf of dry bread, a lump of cheese, and a crude earthenware tankard filled with ale. "How long have I been down here?" she called, taking the food from the basket.

"Couple of hours." Feeling the basket lighten, the guard pulled it up and the trap crashed down again.

Only two hours. The first of how many more? Before fear could rise again, Meriel saw a vivid inner picture of Mother Rohese saying: *Sufficient unto the day is the evil thereof.* And good advice it was. Meriel ate her supper, grimacing over the thin, sour taste of the ale, but otherwise the food wasn't bad. Then she wrapped herself in the blanket and sat with her back against the wall. With fresh straw under her, she was really not at all uncomfortable.

There was also comfort in the knowledge that whatever conflict there was between the two earls of Shropshire, it was apt to be settled relatively quickly, in days or weeks. Months at the longest. At least she wouldn't be like those poor devils who spent years in dungeons. Some even died in places such as these, shut away from the sunshine and open sky. Under such circumstances, death would be a blessed relief.

Her mind began to drift, in a not unpleasant way. She should remember that the worst Guy could do was to kill her, and she did not fear death, though she was not much looking forward to purgatory. But when all was said and done, she had not lived such a wicked life. She smiled a little; she had had precious few opportunities for wickedness, and even less aptitude!

Meriel began to doze off, floating between waking and sleeping. Yes, death would be preferable to endless imprisonment. . . .

With heart-pounding suddenness, she jerked awake. Once before she had thought exactly that: that death would be better than endless imprisonment. A scene began unscrolling in her mind like a vivid dream. Lord Adrian had called her into his chamber. It was the day he had nearly raped her, and she had been distraught, not merely philosophical about possible death, but desperately eager to embrace it. She had grabbed his dagger . . . Shuddering, she remembered the flash of light on the blade as she plunged it toward her own throat.

Lord Adrian had stopped her, prevented her from committing a crime that would condemn her to eternal hell. Was that the accident that had caused her to lose two months?

In spite of the cold air, she was sweating under the heavy wool blanket as she furiously commanded her mind to remember. Adrian had taken the dagger from her, then told her he wished to marry her. Sweet Mary, first he had promised to let her go no matter what, then he had asked her to marry him!

But she had not believed him. She had been so sure that he was just trying to torment her, even though his face had been raw with guilt and honesty. What happened next? *Jesu, what had happened next?*

Her hands clenched, the nails biting like claws as she remembered. Disbelieving, strung to the point of madness, she had whirled away from him, across the room, onto the window seat. She remembered raising her arm as she hurled herself forward—and then she knew no more.

Had she been aware during that endless plunge to the water at the time? Or had she already been blessedly unconscious? Pray God she had been unconscious—even at this distance, the thought was horrifying. Falling . . . spinning helplessly through the air like a broken-winged bird—perhaps smashing into the cliff—and then sinking under the flowing dark waters.

Thoughts of the fall made her stomach twist with nausea, and she forced herself to think of other things. How had she survived? Possibly one of the little fishing boats had been near and the occupants had rescued her. Perhaps she had floated downriver and washed to the bank before she drowned.

There was another possibility, perhaps a more likely one. Dispassionately she visualized the height of the chamber above the river and decided that it was possible to dive safely into the water if one hadn't first crashed through the heavy leaded glass, and if one dived far enough out to avoid the cliff.

Was that what Lord Adrian had done? It was more likely that he had gone in after her than that a boat had been in exactly the right spot or that she had washed ashore still living. If it was indeed the earl who had saved her, she had to give him reluctant credit: he had done his best to atone for what he had forced her to.

Meriel thought about that, and another unwelcome thought intruded. Yes, he had captured her, tried to break her will, but he had not forced her to attempt suicide: she had done that on her own. If she had been stronger, more accepting of God's inscrutable will, she would not have been desperate to the point of madness. The earl had said he would release her, and she had responded by trying to kill herself, not once but twice.

Looking back, there was no reason to have disbelieved the earl's word. He had behaved wickedly, but he had never lied to her. Therefore, when he said he would free her, very likely he had meant it.

Which meant that if Lord Adrian pulled her from the water, saved her from suicide, he had saved far more than her life. He had saved her soul, and at the risk of his own life.

A strange thought, that she had reason to be grateful to her captor. Meriel lay back on the straw, her body curling in an instinctive search for comfort. If there was a lesson to be drawn from her newly discovered memories, it was to try to endure this captivity with more strength and grace than her previous one.

18

GUY HAD COME BACK from his mysterious journey in such good spirits that Cecily was immediately mistrustful; her husband's good nature was invariably founded on some other poor soul's pain. He said nothing directly to her, of course, he never did. Silently she helped him remove his armor and ordered food and wine for him and Sir Vincent.

Then Cecily sat down at her embroidery frame and went to work, though by candlelight it was hard to set the stitches accurately. No matter, they would be pulled out tomorrow. It was more important that she discover what was going on. She had learned early that being well informed was essential to survival.

As Cecily listened, her lips went tight with distaste. So Guy had used false pretenses to capture and imprison a Jewish merchant, his family, and his entire household, innocent people whose only crime was that they had wealth. Thank God Cecily's father was not alive to see such shame, that Chastain had become a den of thieves. Of course, if her father were still alive, life would be unimaginably different: Guy would never have been allowed to defile Chastain with his presence, and Cecily would have been given a decent husband, a man of honor.

There was worse to come. Guy and Vincent began laughing uproariously as they worked out the wording of a message that was to be sent out immediately. At first Cecily was puzzled, but when she realized what they meant, she was so shocked that she accidentally stabbed herself with her needle, staining the embroidery with her blood. Merciful Mother, they had captured Adrian of Warfield's wife and thrown her into the dungeon like a common felon! A Norman woman of gentle birth, and she was now imprisoned under Cecily's own roof.

Not for the first time, Cecily lamented that she was neither brave enough nor ruthless enough to have murdered Guy in their bed years ago. The world would be a better place without his wickedness, as would Chastain. These lands had been in Cecily's family for so long that the first owners were lost in the mists of time. There had been British farmers, then Saxon, a Dane or two. After William had conquered England, one of his knights had married a daughter of Chastain and the blood of Norman and Saxon had mingled. And now the line had dwindled to her, a woman unworthy of her ancestors.

A tear fell on the linen stretched across the embroidery frame, then another. Cecily closed her eyes against her tears and prayed that if an opportunity ever came to retrieve her honor, she would have the courage to take it.

Her angel was holding her in his arms, his voice gentle and poignant with longing as he said, "I loved you from the moment I saw you, ma petite." Then he held her differently, not with tenderness but desire, whispering, "Behold, you are fair, my love, behold, you are fair."

Slow waves of rapture swept through her as he did miraculous, exquisite things to her ardent body. And she responded in kind, discovering the wonders of his beauty, and of pleasuring him.

They joined and were one, body and spirit, and in the joining there was shattering joy, the closest mortals could come to the divine. She cried out, "I love you!" and her body echoed her words with uncontrollable abandon.

Meriel was woken from her sleep by the cry of her own voice and the shuddering convulsions of her lower body. Gasping and dazed, at first she could not remember where she was or what was happening to her. Doggedly she started with the evidence of her senses. Straw, stench, absolute darkness: of course, this was Guy of Burgoigne's dungeon.

And what she had just experienced was a dream, the most vivid dream of her life, for her loins still shuddered, replete with pleasurable warmth. Uncertainly she moved her hand beneath the heavy blanket and touched one of her tingling breasts, and was shocked when sensual delight shafted through her. Blessed Mother, what did it mean? What kind of shameless creature had she become?

Her fingers clenched the edge of her blanket and straw rustled beneath her as she shifted, trying to hide from the knowledge that she had dreamed of Lord Adrian. She had always thought him as handsome as an angel, the proud fallen Lucifer, who had chosen to rule in hell rather than serve in heaven.

But in her dream Adrian was not the dangerous, unpredictable man who had terrorized her; he had been all tenderness and gentle love. And much as she loathed admitting such a bitter truth, Meriel could not deny that she had loved him back—totally, without reservation, she had loved him back. She had welcomed him inside her, not merely willing but eager. Between them there had been such perfect love and harmony that on waking Meriel felt as cold and bereft as a babe torn away from its mother's arms. For what she felt now was not love, but the memory of love.

Was that perfect love the true tale of their marriage? Or was the dream her mind's attempt to flee dreadful reality by creating a happiness she had never known?

Meriel bit her lower lip until it hurt. That passionate dream was only that, a dream; she could never have loved Lord Adrian. He was as much a monster as Guy of Burgoigne, and infinitely more dangerous because he was so fair. She could never have loved him, never. . . .

Denying, she squeezed her eyes tight against the dark. But as Meriel slid once more into sleep, the edge of her blanket soaked in tears as she wept for losing what she had never had.

Alan restlessly paced across the dais at the end of Warfield's great hall. "We should be doing more."

The earl leaned back in his high chair of state. "I think it is more useful to talk to the searchers as they come back, but I understand your impatience to be more active. Perhaps you should take several men and ride out yourself."

"I prefer to stay where I can watch you," Alan said coldly.

Warfield accepted this churlishness as dispassionately as he had accepted all of his brother-in-law's other edged comments. At first Alan had thought Lord Adrian cold, but he had come to recognize that tension had stretched the other man taut as a bow. Whatever his crimes toward Meriel might be, the earl did care for her, and even his rigid control could not disguise his fierce anxiety.

Sitting idle allowed Alan far too much time to recall his own despairing search for Meriel several weeks before, but privately he admitted that the earl was probably accomplishing more here with his probing questions and quick decisions. The night before, they had stayed in the great hall until past midnight, Lord Adrian interviewing his men as they straggled in and checking their information against a large map of the area.

But there had been little news, and this morning had been no better. Because of the weather the previous day, visibility had been poor and few people abroad, so Meriel's passing had left only the faintest of traces. A lady on a sorrel mare had been sighted several times between the point where she left her husband and the royal forest. Then, somewhere on her eastward trek, she had vanished.

Having faith in his sister's ingenuity and good sense, Alan himself was less concerned for her safety than Warfield. Possibly her horse had gone lame and she had taken refuge with a forester in some remote cottage. Or perhaps she had thought it unsafe to go to Avonleigh and chose another destination, though Alan was uneasy at the thought of her riding any great distance alone.

The only report of any interest was that a large body of armed men had been seen crossing the northern edge of Warfield territory the morning before, then returning later the same day. The earl had frowned when he heard that, but it did not seem likely that Meriel would have been so far north, so the news was set aside as not relevant.

When they found his sister again, Alan might exercise his brotherly prerogative and tan her little backside for running off alone again. Even as the thought crossed his mind, he knew that he would do no such thing, for he had never struck his sister in his life. But for a sweet, mild-tempered girl, Meriel had certainly been causing more than her share of trouble lately!

The bad news came in late afternoon. Alan had been roaming the hall, talking to those Warfield retainers who were about. He had learned that Meriel was universally popular, which did not surprise him, and that the earl was also, which did.

Then a messenger arrived, a travel-stained man wearing a blue-boar badge. He bowed, then handed his parchment to the earl. Alan was vaguely aware of the sound of a seal being broken. Then a well-developed instinct for danger jabbed Alan. His head shot up and with narrowed eyes he watched his brother-in-law.

As he read the message, Lord Adrian's face turned cold and hard as a carved marble statue. Savagely he crumpled the parchment, saying in a low, deadly voice, "Tell your master that I shall bring my army to Chastain to discuss this with him. Now, get out if you value your life!''

No fool, the messenger left faster than he had come.

The earl turned to one of his retainers. ''Send a message to Montford. Richard must come immediately with his full complement of knights and men-at-arms.''

As the servant hastened away, Alan said sharply, ''What has happened? Does it concern Meriel?''

White-faced and wordless, the earl handed over the parchment that had just been delivered. It took a moment for Alan to decipher the script. Then furious, annihilating rage swept over him. The message said that Guy of Burgoigne, who styled himself the true Earl of Shropshire, had captured Meriel of Warfield. And if her husband did not meet the ransom demand, Lady Meriel would be returned to her home in pieces.

Guy was dining in his hall when the message arrived from France, and the earl immediately handed it to Sir Vincent to read aloud. ''It must be from Ulric. When will he be arriving with his troop?''

Sir Vincent hastily wiped his greasy fingers on a piece of bread and took the parchment. After scanning it, he pursed his lips in a soft, not unadmiring whistle. ''He isn't coming. Lord Adrian found out that he had been hired and paid him more to stay away. Ulric said that he is sure you will understand that this is strictly a matter of business and no personal insult is meant. The money you offered him on account will be returned to the London goldsmith whom you used for your initial payment. By the time you receive this, he and his men will be on their way to Italy on a new commission.''

''What!'' Guy roared. ''How dare that bastard interfere with me!'' He leapt up and swept his arm furiously across the table, scattering meat, trenchers, and tankards to the floor. Half a dozen dogs converged on the unexpected bounty. Swearing, the earl kicked out viciously, catching one of the hounds in the ribs. The dog yelped, then snatched the joint of beef in its jaws and raced away, pursued by its fellows.

Ignoring the canine byplay, Sir Vincent said, "But you don't need Ulric now that you have Warfield's wife. You'll be able to get whatever you want from him, and will be saved the cost of paying mercenaries as well."

"That isn't the point!" Guy said savagely. "That effete bastard thinks he's so clever. He thinks he's stolen a march on me. Well, by all the saints of hell, he'll be sorry for this." The earl whirled away from the table. "Get his wife and bring her up to my chamber. *Now!*"

When Meriel woke in the morning, she discovered an unexpected blessing: the dungeon was no longer completely dark. High on the wall, an air shaft led to the outside. Because of its height and the thickness of the massive walls, she could not see out, but fresh air and a little light managed to find their way in. There was a world of difference between absolute blackness and even the dimmest of illumination, and she was passionately grateful for that narrow slit above her head.

The trap was lifted and she was required to send up the previous night's empty tankard before receiving more bread and ale to break her fast. After she had eaten, Meriel sat cross-legged on her pallet and relaxed. It wasn't easy, but eventually she was able to attain a state of meditation where her circumstances no longer mattered greatly. She was aware of her body, and of the danger that surrounded her, but her spirit was serene, and in such a state time flowed by easily.

In her detachment, at first she did not notice that the trapdoor had opened again. Only when the ladder was dropped into the cell did her awareness return to her circumstances, and at first she was a little disoriented.

Someone was calling her name, and when she didn't respond, Sir Vincent himself came down the ladder.

"Come with me, countess," he said gruffly, grabbing her wrist and pulling her to her feet. "The longer you keep the earl waiting, the angrier he'll be, and believe me, you won't want him any angrier than he is now."

Obediently she climbed the ladder, Sir Vincent right behind. A man-at-arms waited above. Did they really think that it would take two armed men to keep her from fighting her way to freedom? Her calm mood still on her, she decided with amusement that she must be more dangerous-looking than she realized.

The two men led her up an endless series of stairways and passages until they were a floor above the hall. Then Sir Vincent grasped her upper arm and escorted her into the lord's bedchamber. "Here she is, Lord Guy."

When the earl saw Meriel, a look of dangerous gratification crossed his face. "You may go now, Vincent. Unless you would like to stay and watch, and maybe have her yourself when I am done?"

Sir Vincent's hand tightened on Meriel's arm, then fell away. "She holds no charm for me, my lord," he murmured, then bowed and left the room.

Outside in the corridor he hesitated, uncharacteristically perturbed. It was one thing to rape a peasant girl. Serfs were scarcely more than animals and didn't matter, for chivalry was a code of behavior among nobles and had nothing to do with the lowborn. But Warfield's wife was a lady, and ravishing her was outrageous even by Vincent's flexible standards. Worse, in his present mood the earl might get carried away and kill her, like that wench last year in Nottingham. It would be a great waste, since alive Warfield's wife was valuable, and dead worth nothing at all.

Sir Vincent had too much respect for his own neck to suggest that when Guy was in such a rage, but there was one person who might be able to do something.

If Sir Vincent could find her in time, and *if* the stupid cow had the courage to interfere. It was a long chance, he decided, but worth trying.

Inside the bedchamber, Burgoigne very deliberately unfastened the brooch that held his mantle in place, then tossed the garment over a stool. "Your husband has interfered with me, and you are going to pay the price for it. Come here!"

Meriel's calm fractured at his unmistakable meaning. Her eyes fixed on him, slowly she began backing the length of the room. No matter how hopeless her case, there was no way she could make herself approach him voluntarily.

Swearing impatiently, he closed the distance between them in a few quick strides and grabbed her by the wrist. "Come here, you whey-faced bitch. And don't flatter yourself that I am doing this from desire."

Rationally Meriel knew that fighting him would be useless and would increase the likelihood that he would seriously injure her, but her revulsion was far stronger than reason. As he started to pull her toward the bed, she furiously raked his face with the nails of her free hand.

At first Burgoigne just stared at her, so startled by her opposition that he was not yet angry. Then his complexion turned wine-red with rage and he struck the side of her head with his open hand. He was enormously tall and broad, easily double her weight, and the force of his blow caused her vision to dim and her knees to buckle. Still she continued to struggle feebly. Infuriated by her resistance, Guy shoved Meriel down. She struck the floor so hard that all her breath was knocked out, leaving her temporarily helpless.

His face savage, he stripped off his belt and outer tunic. "Perhaps I shall let you live to go back to your husband. If you do, he'll never be able to take you again without remembering that I have had you too, that my shaft has reached depths his puny rod never will," he jeered. "If you bear a child soon, he can wonder whose it is. He will never be free of the knowledge that his meek, virginal little wife has been my whore.''

Frantically Meriel tried to scrabble sideways away from him, but Guy dropped to his knees and grabbed her tunic so that the fabric tightened around her throat with choking force. He shoved her flat on her back again, pulled her skirts up and straddled her thighs so that she was immobilized, then ripped her bliaut and shift to her waist.

Guy smiled evilly at the sight of what lay beneath the loose, oversize clothing that Sarah had lent Meriel. ''You are less boyish than I thought,'' he panted as he opened his chausses. ''There may be some enjoyment here after all.''

He stopped her thrashing by pinning her wrists to the floor with one of his massive hands, then pinched her left nipple until she gasped with pain.

Merciful Mother, help me endure! Meriel prayed. Tears streamed down her face as he separated her legs, and she knew that only a miracle could save her now.

Then, just before he could force his way into her, the door was thrown open with such force that it slammed into the wall with a hollow boom. Meriel looked up, desperate for any interruption, and saw a tall, heavy woman whose green robes were so rich that she must be the lady of the castle.

Though her face was white with fear, she strode across the room toward her husband. ''Let her go! I will not have this!''

Guy could not have looked more startled if one of the chairs had stood up and begun talking. Releasing his grip on Meriel's wrists, he sat back on his heels, an ugly expression on his face. ''What do you think you are doing, you stupid bitch? Have you suddenly become so jealous of my favors that you would dispute my right to plow another woman? Does that mean you will no longer be an icicle in my bed?''

The countess came to a stop just out of his reach. "It means that this time you go too far," she said, her voice shaking. "You have dishonored the name of Chastain for years, but I will not permit you to ravish a gently born woman under my roof."

"You will not *permit* me?" Guy stood, his beefy face incredulous at her effrontery, then struck his wife across the side of the head. "Just how do you propose to stop me?"

The countess staggered back from her husband's blow, but she was much larger than Meriel, and she managed to stay on her feet. "I cannot stop you myself," she agreed unsteadily, the mark of his palm blazing red across her white face. "But remember, this castle was mine before it ever was yours! To most of the servants and men-at-arms, *I* am Chastain, not you. You can abuse me as all men abuse women, but you cannot murder me with impunity, not without risking revolt."

Maddened, he shouted, "Do you truly believe that you have any power here? *I* am the one who gives the orders, and I am always obeyed. I could flay you alive in the great hall and there is not a man at Chastain who would try to stop me!"

The countess stood her ground, though Meriel saw that her hands were clenched knuckle-white. "Are you sure enough of that to test it?" she asked softly. "Do you think you are so well loved that men will follow you no matter what atrocities you commit? Your power is built on fear, my lord husband, a foundation no stronger than sand. Perhaps no one would oppose you publicly, but are you proof against a knife in the back? Or poison in your wine? Are you fool enough to want to find out the hard way? Kill me and you will never sleep peacefully at Chastain again."

With a howl of frustrated rage, Guy hit his wife again, this time in the chest, using such force that she went reeling back against the bed. But to Meriel's amazement, the other woman's arguments had prevailed. The earl strode to the door and bellowed for a guard. When one appeared, he snarled, "Take this skinny bitch back to the dungeon."

During the confrontation Meriel had scrambled to her feet and stayed away from the combatants, praying that the gallant countess would not be murdered right in front of her eyes. Now she darted out the door with the guard before Guy could change his mind. As she escaped, she heard him say with cruel deliberation, "And now, my lady wife, I will give you what you were reluctant to see go to another."

Meriel cringed as the countess uttered a dark, anguished cry. Then the door slammed shut and Meriel heard no more.

After the scene with Guy, the dungeon seemed like a welcome refuge. Meriel wrapped herself in the blanket for warmth and modesty, then prayed to the Blessed Mother to preserve the countess. It took hours for her shaking to subside.

Under her fear was the strange thought that even at his worst, Lord Adrian had never inspired the revulsion she felt for Guy of Burgoigne. Adrian had been a man obsessed, dangerous and capable of ruthlessness. But she doubted that he was ever wantonly cruel, like Guy. Lord Adrian knew the difference between right and wrong and was capable of feeling remorse at his own lapses from grace. Indeed, his real struggle had been not with her but with his better self. Guy was merely vicious, with none of the qualities that made men more than beasts.

The dim light was beginning to fade when the trapdoor opened. Meriel expected that it was her next meal and was surprised when the ladder was dropped. Looking up, she saw the countess descending the ladder, a bundle awkwardly tucked under one arm.

"Merciful Christus, my lady!" Meriel exclaimed, horrified. "Is Lord Guy imprisoning you too?"

"No," the other woman said. "I just came to assure myself that your condition is not unbearable."

Reaching the bottom of the ladder, she turned to face the prisoner. Meriel gasped at the sight of the savage bruising on the larger woman's cheek. "Sweet Mary," she breathed, tears forming in her eyes as she gently touched the marks. "I'm so sorry. He beat you because of what you did for me, didn't he?"

The countess's lips twisted in a bitter line. "He did nothing that he hasn't done to me a thousand times before. At least this time I was beaten for doing something worthwhile."

Meriel said quietly, "I thought your action was the bravest thing I have ever seen."

Their gazes held, and Meriel saw an easing in the other woman's eyes at the tribute. "Thank you," the countess said, her voice equally low. "I have not always been brave." Then, more briskly, she handed over the bundle she carried. "My name is Cecily. Here are some garments to replace those that he tore. They are nothing very fine, but should fit you reasonably well. I have given orders that you receive some of the same food that is served in the hall. Is there anything else you need?"

Meriel thought wistfully of a hot bath, but did not think it a practical request. "Might I have a bucket of water a day to wash myself, and a comb?" After a moment's hesitation, she added, "Also, do you know if the people who were captured with me are all right?"

Cecily nodded. "I have already visited them. They are a little crowded, but otherwise well enough. The master and mistress have done a good job of maintaining the spirits of their people. I shall do my best to see that they are not abused."

Her voice dropped so that no one in the chamber above could hear. "I'm sorry I can do no more. My husband ordered two of his personal guards to follow me everywhere. If it weren't for them . . ." She shrugged expressively.

"You have already done a great deal, particularly for someone who is a stranger to you." Meriel shifted the bundle of clothing, and was surprised to feel something hard in the middle. Unfolding the top garment, she looked down to see the wicked glitter of a small, narrow-bladed dagger.

Meriel lifted her head, and her gaze met that of the countess for a long, wordless glance of acknowledgment and thanks. Swiftly concealing the weapon again, Meriel said, "May God bless and keep you, Lady Cecily."

"May he keep both of us," the countess murmured. She touched the smaller woman lightly on the shoulder, then climbed the ladder.

Meriel wondered how old Lady Cecily was. Though she was much too heavy, her complexion and features were good, but years of hopeless misery had drained away whatever youthful prettiness she had once possessed. It was something of a miracle that she had survived years of marriage to Lord Guy; perhaps it was her sense of responsibility for Chastain that had enabled her to endure.

As Meriel changed into her new clothing, it was impossible not to hope that soon Guy would be facing heaven's judgment for his crimes.

19

It took two days of furious activity for Adrian to assemble his army and take it to Chastain. Alan de Vere had chafed with impatience, but privately admitted that the task could not have been done any more quickly. Richard FitzHugh had brought his men from Montford in little over a day. The morning after FitzHugh's arrival, the combined troops made a fast march to Burgoigne's castle, the mounted men arriving late one afternoon with the foot soldiers half a day behind.

Before leaving Warfield, Alan had asked the earl what he intended to do in response to Burgoigne's demands and was told that it depended on how events unfolded. It was a cool answer, but the expression in his brother-in-law's eyes reassured Alan that Meriel's safety was not going to be forgotten in the excitement of going to war.

In point of fact there was not yet war between the two earls, but both sides undertook the preliminary steps with the ordered rhythms of dancers. It was child's play to force the gate in the village wall, and the Warfield forces arrived at the foot of Chastain to find the drawbridge raised and the castle ready to defend itself against possible siege.

In his turn, Lord Adrian drove everyone from the village, giving them an hour to collect their essential possessions and leave. Since it was summer the villagers' lives were not threatened by eviction, but they left with the grim expressions of people who did not expect ever to see their homes again.

Alan thought Lord Adrian would fire the village immediately as a message to Burgoigne, but instead he quartered his troops in the newly empty cottages. If there was going to be a long siege, his men would have the advantage of being well-housed.

Richard FitzHugh, as second in command to his brother, took an escort of knights and rode to the main gate. In a shouted exchange with Burgoigne's lieutenant, Sir Vincent de Laon, time and conditions were set for the two earls to meet. The time would be mid-morning the next day, the place the Chastain drawbridge, which would be let down only after the Warfield troops had visibly withdrawn half a mile from the castle.

Alan watched the negotiations, approving how Warfield's brother handled the details. Richard FitzHugh had played the role of peacemaker when Alan had showed up at Meriel's wedding, and further acquaintance had proved that he had a naturally equable disposition, though negotiating with Sir Vincent had visibly strained his temper. Occasionally something in FitzHugh's eyes made Alan suspect that darker currents flowed under Richard's golden surface, but he was a far easier person to be around than the earl, who radiated cold, lethal fury.

Until the meeting actually took place, there was little to be done, so Alan occupied himself by exploring the village and environs, for the knowledge might prove useful later. He stopped at the parish church, which was set on a hill at the farthest end of the village from the castle. In the nave he found the priest tending several sick parishioners who had been given special dispensation to stay rather than being forced into the fields.

After stopping at the Lady Chapel to pray for success, Alan climbed to the top of the bell tower. Because of the church's elevation he was almost on the same level as the curtain wall of the castle. Under the slanting golden rays of the setting sun, the scene was a deceptively peaceful one. The wind rippled both Guy's blue-boar banner above the castle and the silver hawk planted before Warfield's headquarters in the village.

Perhaps it was just Alan's imagination that an air of tense expectancy lay over castle and town. It was like a chessboard, with white and black kings opposing each other. And somewhere in the castle was the captured queen, Meriel. Alan did not doubt that his sister was alive; she was too valuable a prisoner to kill. Did she know that her husband and brother were here, drawn up in full feudal array to fight for her to the death if necessary? Or was she locked away in ignorance?

During his years of service with Lord Theobald, Alan had fought his share of skirmishes and sieges, and had even been in one full-scale battle, but never before had a prospective encounter been so important to him personally. He would have offered to fight Burgoigne in single combat with Meriel's life the stake if the other man would have accepted, but well he knew that Warfield was Burgoigne's true target. Neither Alan and Meriel were of any real importance to that old enmity, though both of their lives might be forfeit in the coming struggle.

Alan did not much care if the two earls killed each other. But as the sun disappeared below the horizon, he vowed that he would do all in his power to save Meriel not only from Burgoigne but also from the man who had coerced her into becoming his wife.

"Let us lie down and just relax in each other's arms," Adrian suggested. *And she did, finding infinite peace and comfort.*

Then she awoke, and peace became passion. "What is in my heart is love," she had whispered. "I am my beloved's, and my beloved is mine." They made love

*with sweetness and wonder, and in the morning they
had prayed together, holding each other's hands, as
innocent as children.*

Meriel gradually emerged from sleep. She was no
longer shocked by such dreams, for she had had them
every night since she had been brought to Chastain.
And now the dreams were invading her days as well
as her nights.

Critically she judged the light in the cell and decided that it was very early. Her morning meal would
not be served for some time, so she began on the routine she had developed. First she softly sang one of
the Benedictine offices. After that she performed a series of exercises to prevent her muscles from stiffening
with inactivity. Not a great deal could be done in a
room that was eight feet in its longest dimension, but
she felt better if she stretched and trotted in place twice
a day.

Exercising done, she washed herself as well as she
could in the bucket of water that was now provided
daily. During her first bath two days before, she had
discovered barely healed scars on her arm and leg,
apparently a legacy of her attempt at self-destruction.
Her lips had thinned as she realized that not only her
mind but also her body had become strange to her.

Still more difficult to accept was the message im-
plicit in the sensitivity of her breasts and her occasional bouts of nausea. She did not doubt that she
carried the child of her captor; what she did not know
was how she felt about that shattering fact. Meriel
loved children, and her chief regret when she had
thought she would never marry was that she would
never have a babe of her own. But she had never
dreamed of having a child in circumstances such as
these.

After her sparse bath, Meriel unbraided her hair,
combed it out, then braided it again. When her hair
was nearly finished, the trapdoor lifted and her first
meal of the day appeared.

The guards must have been ordered to silence, for they no longer made even the simplest of comments. Meriel had spoken with no one since Lady Cecily had come to the dungeon three days before. Meriel suspected that when Guy had learned of that visit, he had ordered his wife's guards to keep her away from the captives. Lady Cecily might have some power, but it was not of a kind that could be exercised freely.

After Meriel had eaten, she sat cross-legged on her pallet and cleared her mind. She had chosen to spend as much time as possible in prayer and meditation, since floating in the hazy worlds of the spirit was the best way of dealing with the fear, loneliness, and lethal tedium of her prison.

Ever since the second day of her captivity, strange new images had begun drifting up from the lower levels of her mind. The scenes showed an Adrian who was tender and loving, a Meriel who adored him in return. As though she were a spectator, Meriel had seen herself marry; she had laughed with her new husband, exchanged secret thoughts with him in the intimacy of the night, made love with him speaking the words of Solomon's Song.

Piece by piece, the lost weeks were being restored to her mind. Meriel was no longer horrified but grimly accepting. She comforted herself that it was better to know the truth, no matter how dreadful, than to be at the mercy of ignorance. She no longer doubted the dreams and images, they were too detailed, too full of the texture of life, to be false.

Meriel forced herself to accept the devastating knowledge that when injury had returned her to a state of primal innocence, she had fallen in love with Lord Adrian and it had been the most richly rewarding experience of her life. Just as Adrian was two different men, she had been two different women, and it was impossible to reconcile the differences.

In the face of such unpalatable truths, Guy's dungeon was almost appealing. She was reasonably well-fed and comfortable, and she knew what to expect each day. Far more alarming was the prospect of being freed and brought face-to-face with Lord Adrian again. In the name of all the saints, what would she do then?

Captor and enemy; husband, lover, and father of the child she carried: Lord Adrian was all of those things. Meriel had both hated and loved him. And after all that had happened, she had not the remotest idea of how she truly felt about him.

In the full armor and panoply of an earl, with Richard at his right hand, Alan de Vere on his left, and his hawk standard carried before him by a squire, Adrian rode the short distance from the village center to the gates of Chastain. He was not surprised to find that the drawbridge had not yet been lowered; he fully expected Guy to try to provoke him with every kind of minor humiliation possible.

When they reached the edge of the moat, he and the others dismounted, leaving their horses in the charge of squires. Then they went through an elaborate show of casualness, as if they had nothing better to do than chat idly of the state of Chastain's defenses. Fortunate that Richard was present to carry the burden of the charade, for Adrian was strung tight as a crossbow and Alan was little better. It was Richard's particular job to keep an eye out for bowmen who might have been charged to shoot the rival earl, since neither brother had any faith in Burgoigne's honor.

Finally, after an hour or so, Guy and several of his men appeared on the wall walk above the gates, their mailed figures silhouetted against the sky. Adrian guessed that Guy would stay up there rather than lower the drawbridge, since it gave him the pleasure of looking down on his enemy.

As Adrian walked unhurriedly to the closest approach, one of the men said in a voice intended to be overheard, "Warfield is the short one, Lord Guy."

Adrian almost smiled. Burgoigne's taste in insults

was crude; he must think that all other men envied his burly height and breadth. Adrian was not in the least upset by the fact that Richard and Alan both had several inches on him, so he called out pleasantly, "Is your eyesight failing with your advancing years, Guy?" His early training in monastic chanting had left him with a voice that carried easily without shouting. "Or is it your memory that fails you?"

Guy scowled; age was a far more sensitive issue than height, and Adrian was a dozen years younger. He shouted, "I have had second thoughts about trusting your honor, so I've decided to carry on our discussion from up here."

Another insult. Once more Adrian turned it with the comment, "Far be it from me to force a man beyond the limits of his courage."

Even at this distance, Guy's flush of anger was clearly visible. He was many things, but never a coward.

Seeing Burgoigne's expression, Adrian reminded himself sharply that he was not here to bandy insults. Guy's mind might not be the quickest, but he had the power to hurt Meriel, and the angrier he was, the greater the risk to her. "Let us waste no more time, Burgoigne. You say you have my wife. Prove it! Show me that she is alive and well, or we have nothing to talk about."

Guy's expression eased with the knowledge that he was in control. "I had thought you would ask that," he replied, then gestured to someone below him.

Within a minute, two more people came up onto the wall walk. One was a man-at-arms, his hand clasping the upper arm of a slim, blindfolded woman whose hands were tied behind her back. It was indeed Meriel, her black braids falling over her shoulders, an oversize gown billowing around her. Beside him Alan drew a shaky breath, his relief as palpable as Adrian's own.

Shading his eyes with one hand, Adrian stared, hungry for the sight of her. Meriel did not move like someone who had been injured or tortured, but his lips tightened when he saw that the blindfold had been arranged to cover her ears as well as her eyes so she could neither hear nor see. It was a pointless cruelty on Guy's part, and Adrian put it to the other man's account as another crime that must be answered for in the final reckoning.

Guy said something inaudible. Then, to Adrian's horror, the guard put his hands around Meriel's waist and lifted her from the wall walk into one of the battlement embrasures. Her balance distorted by blindfold and bound hands, she swayed forward between the merlons and almost pitched off the wall.

Adrian's vision dimmed around the edges, and he took an involuntary step forward, only to be jerked to a halt when Richard grabbed his elbow. "Restrain yourself," his brother snapped under his breath. "You can do nothing, and it will merely confirm for Guy what she means to you."

As the man-at-arms caught and steadied Meriel, Adrian reestablished a fragile control over himself. His heart ached as he wondered if she thought she had been brought to the wall to be hurled down to her death. But if she felt fear, she showed no sign of it. Her slight figure stood erect against the wind, her chin held high as the fabric of her gown snapped around her.

He saw that Richard had also gripped Alan, whose reaction had been much like Adrian's. Thank God one of them could keep a cool head. Raising his voice, Adrian said, "Very well, you have captured my wife. What is the ransom you are asking?"

Guy gave an unpleasant smile, exulting in the power that was in his hands. "Are you so besotted a new husband that you will pay any price I ask?"

"I won't know until you ask it, Burgoigne," Adrian said, feigning indifference. Alan shifted restively, but he was intelligent enough to recognize the principles of bargaining in spite of his anger.

Meriel's guard lifted her from the wall, then escorted her from sight. His voice full of malice, Guy said, "I wondered at first why you married her, but I've learned the reason in the last few days. My God, she's a hot little minx, Warfield, she kept begging me for more and more. If I don't send her home soon, she may wear me out." He laughed nastily. "Of course, she may not be like that with you. She told me her marriage bed has been a grave disappointment."

Richard made a warning sound, but his concern was unnecessary. Though it took every shred of willpower he possessed, Adrian showed no reaction to the other man's taunts. In truth, the insult to his masculinity bothered him not at all; what was unbearable was the likelihood that Burgoigne had raped Meriel, perhaps repeatedly. May God forgive me, *ma petite,* for what has befallen you, Adrian thought with anguish.

What he said aloud was, "By your actions you are diminishing her value, Burgoigne," a note of boredom in his voice. "Now, will you stop wasting time and tell me what ransom you have in mind?"

This was the moment Guy had been waiting for, and he drew it out before answering. "I want Shrewsbury."

Adrian sucked his breath in with surprise, but Burgoigne was not finished.

"I also want Warfield Castle." He drew another breath, then ended, "And Montford Castle, and all the lands belonging to each."

Adrian could feel Richard's flinch at the last. Ignoring everything but the mocking figure of Burgoigne, Adrian replied, "Wives are easily come by. Did you seriously think I would hand over everything I possess in return for a woman?"

"Oh, I'm not asking for everything," Guy said jovially. "That would be an unchivalrous thing to do to a fellow nobleman. You may retain the keep and demesne of Cheston, plus those manors you hold in other shires. That is more than you started with a dozen years ago. Perhaps in time you will parley it into another fortune.''

Adrian shrugged. ''I am willing to pay a substantial ransom in gold, the same as if the woman was a captured baron, but you're mad if you think I will hand my half of Shropshire over to you. Send a message when you are ready to talk seriously.'' He turned and began walking to his horse.

Furiously Guy shouted, ''I am talking seriously, Warfield. You have twenty-four hours to think about what I have said. Then I will return part of your wife to you as earnest of how serious I am. One of her fingers, perhaps.'' He stopped, then continued with glee, ''No, one of her pretty little breasts would be better. Will that convince you?''

Adrian had the same sensation of blurring that he had felt when Meriel had teetered on the wall. It was the feeling that heralded one of his berserker rages, and if Guy had been down at this level he would be a dead man.

Instead, Adrian said with as much unconcern as he could muster, ''I will be back here tomorrow at the same time, to see if you are ready to ask a reasonable price. I can offer you quite a lot of gold, but if my wife is dead—or even disfigured—she is worth nothing. Remember that between now and the time we talk again.''

Then he swung up on his horse, his hands trembling with the force of his suppressed emotions. If he allowed Guy to know just how much Meriel meant to him, the situation was doomed.

Grim-faced, Richard and Alan also mounted, and they rode away together, the squires behind them. Except for Alan's low, steady stream of oaths, they traveled in absolute silence.

* * *

It took only a few minutes to reach the house that had been made headquarters because it was the largest in the village. Leaving the horses to the squires, the three knights went inside. Richard immediately crossed to a table in the corner where a flagon and several goblets stood. Splashing some of the contents in two of the goblets, he handed one each to Adrian and Alan. "I thought we might need something like this after talking with Burgoigne," he said dryly. "Drink up. You both look like death."

Alan obeyed automatically, then almost choked on the unexpected fierceness of distilled spirits. "God's blood," he muttered, staring at the cup. Then he took another gulp. The drink helped his blood start moving again but did nothing for his temper.

The earl had sipped a little, then slumped in the room's only chair. One elbow was propped on the wooden arm and his raised hand obscured his face. Perhaps he was thinking, perhaps merely succumbing to the same black rage that threatened Alan.

Turning his ire to Richard, who was drinking more slowly, Alan snapped, "Easy for you not to care what happens to Meriel. In fact, I should think you will be delighted if your brother's wife is murdered or, better yet, imprisoned for the rest of her life so he can't marry again."

Richard slammed his goblet down on the table, a dangerous flash in his eyes, but before he could speak, Adrian's voice cut across the room. "Don't be a damned fool, Alan. You should be grateful that someone has his wits about him, because neither you nor I do."

Suddenly realizing the magnitude of the insult he had offered, Alan muttered, "I'm sorry. I should not have said that." After Richard had relaxed and given a forgiving nod, Alan took another gulp of the spirits, welcoming the way the drink burned his throat. "Is Burgoigne as wicked as he seems?"

"Worse," Adrian said without looking up.

"How much of a ransom are you willing to pay,

Warfield?'' Alan asked. No matter how mad with lust or guilt he might be, it was hard to imagine that his brother-in-law would give up his entire earldom for his wife.

Adrian didn't reply, just shook his head, his face still and withdrawn.

Richard sighed and sat down on a stool. "To deal with Burgoigne is to walk the edge of a sword, with the fires of hell below if you fall to either side. If Adrian had agreed to his demands today, Guy might well have decided that since Meriel meant that much to him, it would be more enjoyable to kill her as a way of spiting Adrian.'' He emptied his goblet and set it back on the table. "I seriously doubt that Guy expects to get what he asked for today. The critical question is, what will satisfy him instead? And what will he do to Meriel if Adrian doesn't judge his state of mind perfectly and make all the right responses?''

"Merciful saints,'' Alan whispered. Remembering Burgoigne's threat of mutilation brought a cold sweat out on his palms. "Might he accept me as a hostage in her place?''

Adrian spoke up. "No. He might possibly exchange her for me. It would give him the chance he has wanted for years. And it might be the best solution.''

"No!'' Richard exclaimed. "You'll not put yourself in his power.''

Adrian dropped his hand and looked at his brother. "Do you think you could stop me?''

Richard glared back, his usually pleasant expression furious. While he doubtless did care for Meriel, clearly he cared a good deal more for his own brother.

Alan would unhesitatingly pick Meriel's life over the earl's if forced to choose, but after today he was loath to see any man fall into Burgoigne's vindictive hands. Given what he was willing to do to an innocent, God alone knew what he might do to the man he hated. "Surely there must be another way,'' Alan suggested.

"Perhaps the king can bring Guy to heel and persuade him to release Meriel."

Richard looked derisive. "Stephen has had precious little success bringing his barons to heel—that is why England has known a decade of war. And do you think he would use what influence he has on behalf of the wife of one of Matilda's supporters?"

Alan had temporarily forgotten their political differences, which seemed unimportant just now. "That might not matter. Stephen is an honorable man, as even his worst enemy admits. He would never condone the abuse of an innocent woman. And while you are for Matilda, my Lord Theobald is not. He and his lady are very fond of Meriel, and they have considerable influence."

Adrian spoke again. "Even if influence could be brought to bear, there isn't enough time for that. Burgoigne wants some kind of satisfactory response tomorrow. So I must either guess what is in his mind correctly or try something else." He glanced at his brother. "Do you think that you could locate one of the Chastain villagers who is knowledgeable about the inside layout of the castle?"

"I've been inside Chastain," Alan said. Both heads swiveled toward him, surprised. Answering the implied question, he said, "You never asked me. Several years ago, Lord Theobald spent a night with Burgoigne and I was with him." He grimaced. "I saw nothing of Lord Guy, or I would have known better what kind of man he is. But I did have time to explore the inner ward. One can never tell when it will be useful to know a castle's defenses."

A faint smile, the first in days, touched Adrian's lips. "What a very astute brother-in-law you are. Did you happen to discover where the dungeon is?"

Alan started to say that surely Burgoigne would not put a lady in a dungeon like a common thief, then thought better of it. That might be exactly the kind of thing Burgoigne would do. "I'm not sure," he admitted reluctantly. ''My guess would be that the dungeon is beneath the northeast tower, but I did not actually see it.''

The earl nodded, regretful but unsurprised. Even the most curious guest was likely to be wary of probing the darkest corners of another man's castle. ''In that case, Richard, you had best discover whatever retreat the villagers have withdrawn to. Sorry to send you to face their ire, but I am off to do a little exploring.''

Apparently knowing what his brother had in mind, Richard gave him a look of disgust. ''You're mad.''

''Perhaps,'' Adrian said equably. ''Perhaps not. Have you a better idea?''

''I'm going with you,'' Alan announced.

Adrian gave him another faint, rather charming smile. ''Somehow I did not think I would escape you. Very well, get your cloak and come along.''

An hour later, Alan echoed Richard's statement, saying flatly, ''You're mad.''

The earlier sunshine was now obscured by drizzling rain, and he and the earl had used the poor visibility and their dark cloaks to make their way unseen to a spot which gave them a clear view of the back of the castle. The massive stone keep loomed high above the river. A steeply angled bluff rose from the water to the base of the castle, and the curtain wall itself rose sheer for another two dozen feet.

Ignoring his brother-in-law's comment, the earl narrowed his eyes as he studied the cliff and wall. ''When you visited, did you notice what kind of night guard Guy kept on the river side?''

Alan thought back. ''I have the impression that there were only a few watchmen, and all were posted on the land side.''

''He always was a careless devil,'' Adrian murmured. ''He may be a bit more cautious with us on his doorstep, but I'd be surprised if the river side will be watched very thoroughly tonight.''

"The reason it won't be watched is that no one can attack that way," Alan said with exasperation.

"The cliff and wall at Warfield are steeper, and I've climbed them," the earl said mildly.

That momentarily silenced Alan. He had the irreverent thought that Lord Adrian would be a great asset in capturing eyases. "Did you scale Warfield at night, in the rain, when the cliff and wall were wet and the wind tearing at you?"

"Not in the rain," the earl admitted, "but this is an easier climb. Not so steep, and with more handholds."

Alan cast another disbelieving glance at the precipice. If that was Lord Adrian's idea of an easy climb, he really was mad. "What good will it do Meriel if you get yourself killed?"

The earl's humor vanished. "Do you think I can possibly go on living if Burgoigne murders Meriel?"

The dangerous light in those burning gray eyes silenced any retort Alan could think of. For the first time, he believed that his brother-in-law might actually be willing to give his entire earldom in return for his wife's life. The hell of the present situation was that even that might not be enough to save her.

Alan's gaze traveled back to the castle. It was not as formidable as Warfield, but it was quite ominous enough. Ignoring the chill that prickled his neck, he said gruffly, "If you go in there tonight, I'm going with you."

Lord Adrian arched his blond brows. "You are mad enough to climb a wet precipice in the dark and the rain? I hadn't realized that you would carry this shadow business quite so far."

"I'm not sure I could manage the climb in the light, much less the dark, but if you reach the top, you can drop a rope," Alan said, ignoring the other man's levity. "There is a much better chance of getting Meriel out safely if you have someone to guard your back."

A wicked gleam showed in the earl's eyes. "You won't succumb to the temptation to put a dagger in it yourself?"

Alan felt himself color. At some point his hostility to the earl had dissolved, probably because of Lord Adrian's unmistakable devotion to Meriel. Not yet ready to admit that, he said shortly, "I will forgo that pleasure until my sister is free."

A hint of smile playing around his lips, Lord Adrian wisely refrained from answering. Instead, he went back to studying the dangerous heights he planned to scale that night.

20

A PITY THE NIGHTS were so short this time of year,
Adrian thought. They were starting late so that the
castle would be sleeping, and there would be only a
few hours of full darkness before the sky began to
lighten. It would take time to scale that cliff, more
time to find where Meriel was imprisoned. If she were
on the upper level of the main keep, it might be impossible to reach her.

He pulled a dark cap over his head, covering the
bright hair which might attract unwanted attention. For
similar reasons he had rubbed earth on his face, aim-
ing for a neutral tone, neither too dark nor too light.
Climbing the bluff would be impossible in a hauberk
so he wore a padded leather gambeson, which would
provide a little protection in the event of trouble. He
carried a long hemp rope, looped diagonally around
his body. It would be a hindrance to climbing, but
there was no help for it.

Richard had used his gilded tongue to convince the
wary villagers that Lord Adrian had no intention of
using them as ill as Lord Guy did. Hoping that cooperation might save their homes, two people had offered
their help. One was a young laundress who usually
worked in the castle. She had been visiting her family
when the drawbridge was raised, marooning her outside.

The girl and Alan had worked for hours with pieces
of charcoal to draw a plan of the castle. She had shown
the precise location of the dungeon, with suggestions

of other places Meriel might be held captive and warnings of where guards would be found. She was particularly knowledgeable about the castle's nooks and crannies. Adrian suspected that the girl had discovered them while pursuing private pleasures with various men-at-arms. Thank God for native English lustiness.

The other helper was a fisherman who would take them to the base of the bluff in his boat, then wait to take them away again. Adrian had had some doubts about trusting him, until Richard took him aside to say that the man's daughter had been raped by Burgoigne. After that, Adrian had accepted the offer with no further demurrals.

Richard watched the preparations, tight-lipped but silent.

As Adrian buckled his swordbelt, he said to his brother, "If anything should happen, both Matilda and her son have agreed to accept you as heir to my title and holdings. You'll probably have to fight some of Stephen's people for the right to keep them, but you can manage that handily."

"Come back and do your own fighting," Richard snapped.

Adrian understood his feelings; with so little of their family left, neither of them could easily spare a brother.

In spite of his concern, Richard made no attempt to talk his brother out of going, for it wasn't as if Adrian was attempting this mad plan from sheer high spirits. A clandestine rescue represented the best chance of getting Meriel away from Guy before she was further injured or killed, and Adrian could no more have held back from going than he could have voluntarily chosen to stop breathing. But one did not speak of such things. Keeping his voice light, Adrian said, "Alan, do you have any last requests for Richard to execute?"

Alan de Vere, attired much the same as Adrian, shrugged his broad shoulders. "Avonleigh will revert to Lord Theobald. Anything personal can be sent to my brother William at Beaulaine in Wiltshire. Just do what you can for Meriel.''

Adrian knew that last comment was unnecessary; Richard would do whatever was possible to free Meriel. If Adrian were dead, Guy would likely lose interest in her and she could be freed by payment of a moderate ransom. At least, Adrian devoutly hoped that would be the outcome.

As Adrian and Alan left the house, Richard gave his brother a quick, rough hug. ''For God's sake, be careful, you foolish bastard.''

Adrian punched him lightly on the shoulder. ''I'm foolish, you're the bastard, remember?''

Alan tactfully pretended not to notice the byplay; other families' rituals were often obscure.

The weather was wet, somewhere between drizzle and mist: poor for climbing but excellent for concealment. Leaving the village, Adrian and Alan made their way around the castle to the upriver site where Turbet the fisherman waited.

It was a short journey, and the current was strong enough to carry the small boat to the foot of Chastain Castle without paddling sounds, which might carry across the water. Turbet left his passengers on a small thumbnail of rocky beach at the base of the bluff, then let his boat drift a bit further, concealing it under a nearby willow that grew horizontally above the river.

Having worked out their plans earlier, there was no need to say anything now. Adrian stripped off his cloak, then his boots, for bare toes gripped better than leather. He also left his sword with Alan, but retained his dagger in case a welcoming party greeted him above.

Then there was nothing left but to begin. The first part of the climb was relatively easy, up a bluff of earth and stone with numerous holds. Then the angle increased sharply, as did the number of smooth stone expanses that offered no handholds at all.

Adrian's world narrowed to the fierce and unremit-

ting concentration required to climb. Even the fact that
Meriel was somewhere inside was only a distant
thought, of no current significance. Reality was
stretching one's hand up a rough surface until questing
fingers found a narrow crack; the trembling strain of
shoulder muscles forced to support the whole weight
of a body. It was the coarse brush of wet stone against
one's cheek, the slow shift of weight onto an uncertain
foothold, the necessity of instant retreat if it broke
away.

Three-quarters of the way up the cliff, a fragile ledge
crumbled away in a flurry of gravel after Adrian had
already committed his weight to it. Unable to maintain
a grip on the wet stone, his fingers broke loose and he
began sliding across the rock face. Only an instant
from disaster, he twisted his body like an acrobat, using what little leverage he had to hurl himself sideways
toward a scraggly bush that had found a precarious
home in a crack. He managed, barely, to catch the thin
branches. The bush started to tear loose, but held long
enough for him to find better support.

As a scattering of pebbles rattled down the rock,
Adrian clung to the cliff face for a long minute, shaking with reaction from the near fall, thinking that anyone above must surely hear his heart pounding. In spite
of the cold, he was sweating as hard as if he had just
spent an hour in sword practice.

Then he resumed his laborious progress. Twice he
retreated when he ran out of holds and needed to try
a new angle of attack. But eventually—how long had
it taken? how much precious time had been consumed?—he reached the narrow ledge of cliff at the
base of the castle wall.

After Adrian hauled himself onto the grassy turf, he
allowed his shuddering muscles a few minutes to re-
cuperate from the strain, knowing all the while that
the worst of the climb still lay ahead. The sense of
time wasting away finally got him to his feet. Silently
he explored the length of ledge. It did not run all

around the castle, just along a stretch of the river side. Doubtless the folk in the castle considered it inaccessible, which was why the rugged little tree he had noticed earlier in the afternoon had not been cut away. Careless of Burgoigne.

He unslung the rope, tied one end around the trunk, then tested it. It bent a little, but held, and he decided it was strong enough to bear Alan's weight. Softly he mimicked the cry of a bittern, a water bird more nocturnal than most. Adrian doubted that he would fool a real bittern, but a moment later he heard his brother-in-law echo the call from below, so he tossed the rope out, wincing at the noisy rasp of hemp against stone.

The rope quivered as Alan tied on a bundle containing swords, cloaks, and Adrian's boots. Alan tugged twice when it was secure and Adrian pulled the line up slowly, hand over hand, grateful that it didn't catch on the way. After detaching the bundle, he tossed the rope back down. It took about ten minutes for Alan to walk his way up the cliff, the line looped around his waist for safety, his arms and shoulders straining with effort.

When his companion reached the top, Adrian untied the rope, then rewound it and pulled the coils over his head again. Wasting no words, Alan braced his arms against the wall and Adrian used his brother-in-law as a ladder to give himself a six-foot head start. Then he began the painstaking process of working his way up the wall. Whichever lord of Chastain had built this section of the castle must have stinted on paying his masons, for the stonework was very coarse. In some places the mortar had crumbled away—poor maintenance as well as poor masonry.

Nonetheless, as Adrian's fingers and toes slipped, broke, and bled on the wet sandstone, he knew this was the most difficult climb of his life. He was never afterward quite sure how he had managed it, but divine intervention seemed likely.

When he finally got his fingers over the edge of an

embrasure, he gave a sigh of what turned out to be premature relief. Before he could pull himself onto the battlements, he heard the sound of footsteps sauntering along the wall walk. Apparently divine intervention had been withdrawn, leaving him to his own devices again.

For an infinity of time Adrian hung against the sandstone face of the wall, all his weight supported by his hands. He occupied his time praying that the watchman would not notice his clutching fingers, or choose this spot to look down at the river. His luck was in, for the leisurely guard noticed nothing and continued his progress, doubtless thinking his duty unnecessary, for no one would be fool enough to attempt the castle on this side.

Adrian would have preferred to wait until the watchman was farther away, but since his numb fingers were on the verge of failing, he pulled himself up into the embrasure. He crouched there for a moment, listening and watching, but heard no signs of alarm. According to the laundress's map, he should be above the piggery, and judging by the smell, she was right.

He stepped down onto the wall walk. Keeping low so his figure would not be silhouetted against the night sky, he dropped the rope to Alan and they repeated their earlier actions, this time with the rope anchored around a merlon rather than a tree as Alan came up.

While waiting, Adrian had donned boots, sword, and cloak, and wiped the earth from his face, since inside the keep it would look suspicious. When Alan had reached the top and put on his own cloak, they made their way to the nearest stair, still keeping low. The rope, invisible in the shadows, was left tied to the merlon. While there was a chance that it would be discovered, that faint risk was offset by the much greater likelihood that they might need to use it to escape in a hurry.

Once they reached ground level they raised their hoods against the drizzle and walked upright, as if they had every right to be in the inner ward. Since he had some familiarity with the castle, Alan took the lead.

As they passed the stables, a door screeched and a man ambled out in front of them. Alan raised his hand in a vague greeting. The man responded with the same gesture, then turned and relieved himself against the wall, completely incurious.

Adrian's senses tingled with the heightened awareness that danger always brought, but there was no alarm, no sign that their intrusion had been noticed. With rising excitement, he began to wonder if they might actually succeed.

He forced himself to stay calm. Climbing the wall was the hardest part physically, but locating Meriel held the greatest risk of disaster. And to the east, the dark was less dense than it had been.

The watchman looked longingly at the sky. The drizzle had ended and the sky was noticeably lighter. Soon his watch would be over, saints be praised, and he could have some food and sleep. A waste of time having him patrol the back half of the castle wall; if he were posted at the main gate or even above the postern, he would have felt that he was doing something worthwhile, but this night would have been better spent cuddled up with the new kitchen maid.

Doubtless Lord Guy was nervous about the other earl being camped in the village, but so far there had been no fighting, not so much as an exchange of arrows. Still, if the other earl, Warfield, didn't get his wife back soon, there might be hell to pay. The girl was a sweet, pretty little thing. A pity she was caught like a bone between two dogs. One dog was more than enough—look at how Guy had chewed up their good Lady Cecily.

The watchman leaned against a merlon and looked down. The mist had lifted enough so that he could see the river, which was as quiet as one would expect at

340 • MARY JO PUTNEY

an hour when good Christians were abed. Still, the
kitchen would be at work soon, and by the time he
went off watch, there would be hot fresh bread.

Already anticipating, he straightened up. As he did,
his knee brushed against a ridge more yielding than
the sandstone merlon. Curiously he touched it. Then
his blood chilled as he identified the unmistakable
prickle of hemp.

Peering over the battlements, he saw that a rope
dropped to the narrow ledge below. By Christ's
blocked bowels, someone had either gotten out of or
into the castle. Escape was not quite so bad, but if one
of Earl Adrian's men had gotten inside, at this very
moment he might be opening one of the gates to let
his fellows in. Even if such a plan failed, there would
be a very slow, very unpleasant death in store for a
watchman who had been insufficiently observant, and
arguing that there had been too much wall for one man
would be futile when Lord Guy was in one of his rages.

Running as fast as his middle-aged legs could manage, the watchman warned the guards at both gates to
beware of possible attack from inside. Then he went
to wake the captain of the guard with the unwelcome
information that there might be an enemy within the
keep.

The door at the foot of the northeast tower opened
with an excruciating squeal. Worse, when they entered, Alan tripped over a man sleeping in the small
vestibule. The sleeper came half-awake with an oath
but subsided when Alan muttered a gruff apology. The
laundress had not warned them of possible occupancy,
but the castle had lifted the drawbridge when day
workers from the village were inside, and such workers were probably bedded down in any corners they
could find.

Feeling their way along in the thick, choking darkness, they found the staircase that led to the lower
level. Once they had gone down several turns of the

spiral, they stopped and Alan struck his flint and steel to light the candle he carried. With light, they were able to move much more quickly, and in another minute they were outside the storeroom that the laundress had said was sometimes used for prisoners.

The storeroom was locked. The two men looked at each other, wondering if Meriel might be inside. Then a deep cough, unmistakably masculine, was heard on the other side of the door. Meriel might also be inside, but by unspoken consent they began looking for the smaller stairwell that led to the dungeon.

The captain of the Chastain guard always slept with his hauberk arranged so it could be donned instantly, and he did that as soon as the watchman woke him. As he belted on his sword, he ordered the watchman to alert the other men-at-arms to turn out and begin searching the keep. Then the captain went himself to wake Lord Guy, who would forgive a false alarm more readily than he would forgive not being notified of possible intruders.

The night candle showed that the countess slept as far from her husband as was possible. The captain, a long-time Chastain retainer, preferred not to think about that. He shook Lord Guy's shoulder and the earl woke quickly.

"A rope has been discovered tied around a merlon above the river," the captain said succinctly. "One or more men might be in the castle. The gate guards have been alerted and the men-at-arms turned out to search."

Guy swung his legs over the side of the bed. "It's Lord Adrian," he exclaimed, his face exultant. "Make sure Sir Vincent has been roused, he will want to be in at the death."

"Aye, it must be one of Warfield's men," the captain agreed.

"No, it's Warfield himself. He came to get his wife, the lackwit, I can feel it in my bones." The earl struck his own wife in the shoulder to ensure that she was awake. "Help me with my hauberk. This time I will put an end to him, as I have been longing to these dozen years."

Her eyes wide with alarm, Lady Cecily helped her husband into his armor. Then Lord Guy and the captain of the guard left to find and destroy the interlopers.

"I want the whole of Shropshire to know we have wed," he cried, pulling the bell rope. As Great Tom boomed, she had laughed and pulled the rope of Little Nell, whose soprano chime added a high clear sweetness to the glorious sounds of celebration. She had felt pure joy, pure love, absolute certainty.

Meriel awakened abruptly from her sleep, the sound of bells still ringing in her head. No, not bells, a voice, a familiar beloved voice, calling her name. "Meriel," came the cautious whisper, "are you down there?"

"Alan?" she gasped in disbelief, sure she must be dreaming. She looked up and saw a square of flickering light where the trapdoor had been lifted.

"God be thanked," he said, exuberant but still muting his voice. "Move back while I lower the ladder."

She stepped aside and a moment later the ladder dropped to the dungeon floor.

"Do you need help climbing up?"

Even before Alan had finished speaking, Meriel was halfway up the ladder with no backward glances. Alan half-lifted her the last several rungs, pulling her into a crushing hug.

Half-laughing, half-crying, Meriel hugged him back, her eyes hazy with tears. "How did you find me? And how in heaven's name did you manage to get in here?"

"It's a long story," Alan replied, "and it must wait until we are outside."

He released her and Meriel turned toward the door, then halted in her tracks with a horrified intake of breath. At first she thought the dark figure behind the candle was a Chastain man-at-arms who would try to stop them.

Then she recognized him. Even with his gilt head covered, Adrian of Warfield was unmistakable. The flickering candlelight played over the elegant bones and planes of his face, and twin flames reflected deep in ice-gray eyes. The Earl of Shropshire had come to reclaim his property.

Her husband watched her, utterly expressionless. "I will not harm you, *ma petite,*" he said, his words so low that she could scarcely hear them.

The cold face was that of her tormentor, the soft voice that of her lover, and Meriel stood paralyzed, torn between fear, longing, and confusion. At her reaction, Adrian's expression became even colder.

Breaking the charged silence, Alan laid an encouraging arm around his sister's shoulders. "Lord Adrian scaled the cliff behind the castle. Now we must be off the same way before it gets any lighter. Here, put this on." He handed her a boy's hooded mantle of coarsely woven wool.

Alan was right, there was no time to waste on confusion. Meriel donned the cloak, then followed the earl up the winding steps, her brother right behind her. As they climbed, her eyes were fixed on the back of her husband's mantle as it swung from his shoulders and swirled in the draft that blew down the stairwell. It was eerie knowing that she could have described in intimate detail the lithe body beneath the dark fabric, yet could say nothing at all about his soul.

At the next level, Meriel shot an agonized glance toward the storeroom as they hurried past. Forcing the lock, rousing fifteen people, then escaping down a rope would be time-consuming and dangerous. Probably the older people would be physically incapable of leaving by such a route, and to even try would risk the lives of her brother, her husband, and herself. Nonetheless, she felt like a traitor for leaving Benjamin, Sarah, and their household behind.

They made their way up the second stairwell. Just below the top, Adrian reached back and whispered, "Take my hand."

After she hesitantly did so, he doused the light. In the thick darkness his hand was the most potent reality, warm and strong as he guided her up the last few steps. She forbade herself to think beyond that. Better to pretend that it was Alan leading the way. This was not the time to worry about what Lord Adrian would expect of his wife in the future.

At the top of the stairs they made their way slowly across an entryway. Meriel sensed that at least one person slept there, but no one woke or challenged them. Adrian released her hand and opened the door, which swung in with a threatening creak.

Outside it was on the verge of dawn, light enough to see a hand held before the face. Already there would be people working in the kitchens, and very soon the whole castle would be awake. Adrian turned to the left, and they hastened single file along the wall of the keep. Then they rounded a corner, and Meriel saw the fires of hell come racing down at them.

21

AFTER HER HUSBAND LEFT, Cecily dressed herself, convinced to her very marrow that the old enmity between Warfield and Burgoigne was about to be resolved. It was incredible to think that Warfield would have climbed into the castle in a mad, doomed attempt to save his wife, yet she believed that Guy's guess was correct. Warfield was said to be fearless, and likely he believed none of his men would care as much for his wife's life as he himself did. With a stab of pain, Cecily wondered what it would be like to have a husband so loving.

Ruthlessly she dismissed the thought. For his devotion, Warfield was about to die a bloody death and there was nothing she could do to prevent it. But she might be able to accomplish something else.

Summoning two menservants with torches, Cecily went outside and climbed a stair to the wall walk, where she would be able to see everything that happened in the inner ward. The nearest stair was the one by the gatehouse, and at the top she stopped for a moment, her attention caught by the sounds of impatient horses beyond the wall.

Peering into the gloom, she made out a darker mass on the other side of the moat. It was a body of waiting troops, likely with Warfield's brother, Richard FitzHugh, at their head. Was he waiting for Warfield to open the gate so that Chastain might be attacked and captured?

Cecily considered the question, then shook her head.

A battle inside the castle would endanger everyone inside, including Lady Meriel, which was why Warfield had tried to quietly spirit her away. Most likely FitzHugh was there in the wishful hope that he might be able to do something.

Well, there was nothing he could do to save his brother. Perhaps, if he were heir, he would not be entirely sorry about Warfield's demise. Dismissing him from her mind, she swiftly started around the wall walk, seeking a position where she would have a clear view of the river side of the inner ward.

When Warfield was caught, perhaps Cecily's intervention might save Warfield's wife. Though she scarcely knew Lady Meriel, the fragile young woman had become a vital symbol. If Meriel could be saved, perhaps somewhere, somehow, there might be salvation for Cecily as well.

Adrian stopped dead at the sight of the torchbearing men-at-arms who came swooping down the stairs from the wall walk. Somehow the intruders' presence had been discovered and they were trapped like rats in a barrel. It was light enough now to distinguish individual figures, and the soldiers shouted triumphantly as they sighted their prey.

They might be trapped, but they were not yet caught. "Back this way!" he commanded.

They had just passed a place where keep, curtain wall, and another stone building met to form a kind of blind alley. When they reached it, Adrian and Alan drew their swords and daggers and took positions side by side, blades at the ready. Adrian ordered, "Meriel, get behind us and stay there."

Wordlessly she did as she was bidden. The area was wide enough to give both men space to fight, but narrow enough that it might be held against a much greater number, at least for a while, until exhaustion, error, or archers claimed them.

Feet pounding, hauberks jangling, and torches

streaming out behind them, a half-dozen men came charging up to the mouth of the alley. Even more noisily, they skidded to a halt just short of impaling themselves on the waiting steel. There was a temporary standoff as the men-at-arms considered odds and strategy.

Before anyone could make a move, another group of soldiers swept up, this one led by Guy of Burgoigne himself. Fully armed, his blue boar rampant on shield and surcoat, he was a huge, intimidating figure, even his shadow grotesquely multiplied by the half-dozen torches.

Burgoigne stopped and stared at Adrian. "So . . ." he breathed, his voice an ominous hiss of satisfaction. "At last we meet. It is just like you to be soft for a woman, Warfield. Your weakness has cost you your life."

"It will cost a few other lives if you have to take us by force," Adrian replied, his mind racing. Though a quick fighting death would be infinitely preferable to putting himself at Guy's mercy, either way he was a dead man. Deciding that it would be worth surrendering if his death would buy freedom for Meriel and Alan, he offered, "If you swear to release my wife and her brother, I will yield to you now."

"Nay, Warfield, I do not want you to surrender," Guy said softly as he drew his sword. "I will not deprive myself of the pleasure of killing you." His expression was invisible behind the nasal bar of his helmet, but his voice was unmistakably gloating. "Single combat, to the death. Perhaps after I have carved your bones for the ravens, I will be in such a good mood that I will set your companions free."

"This should be a splendidly equal fight, since you are fully armed and I am not," Adrian said ironically. His own life was forfeit no matter what, for even if he killed Guy, the Chastain men-at-arms would surely take instant revenge. But Burgoigne had half-promised freedom to Meriel and Alan, so there was a reasonable chance that they might survive. Especially since it would be easier—and much safer—to release Alan than to try to kill him. "So be it—single combat to the death. My brother-in-law will not interfere if your men do not."

Sir Vincent de Laon, who was behind Burgoigne, gestured at the surrounding men to fall back. Quickly a semicircular line formed around the end of the alley. The torchbearers spaced themselves around the edge to give the best illumination, for the ward was still too dark for clear seeing.

Adrian looked over to Alan, who lifted his sword in a wry salute. "In an odd sort of way, it has been a pleasure knowing you, Warfield. Good luck."

A faint smile on his face, Adrian nodded in acknowledgment, then glanced back at Meriel, feeling an ache deep inside that he might never look on her again. She was a slim, erect shape, a shadow among darker shadows, her face invisible. Quietly he said, "I'm sorry, *ma petite,* for bringing you to this. Can you forgive me?"

Her shoulders lifted in a shrug. "You would not be here facing death if it were not for me, so perhaps the scales are balanced and there is no need for forgiving." There was gentle sorrow in her voice, but no bitterness. "We are all in God's hands. May he protect you now."

It was more absolution than Adrian had expected. He turned back toward the arena, temporarily sheathing his weapons so that he could remove his cloak. But as he reached for the ring brooch that secured the garment, Alan gave a shout of warning.

Adrian looked up to see Guy charging across the arena, sword upraised, blatantly ignoring the rule that combat would not begin until both parties were ready. But of course this bout was hardly a normal judicial combat. Adrian leapt to one side barely in time, Guy's sword stabbing through his cloak and gambeson and grazing his side without drawing blood.

Burgoigne reeled as his blade caught in the entangling folds of cloak. After spinning out of the garment, Adrian yanked on it with enough force that he pulled his opponent off-balance. The ground beneath was damp from the night's drizzle and Guy went down clumsily on one knee. By the time he had regained his feet, Adrian had drawn both sword and dagger and was fully prepared. "Send for your priest, Guy," he said in a low, deadly voice, "for now is the hour of your death, and even treachery will not save you."

With a bellow, Guy struck out with his great sword. Adrian knew how disastrous his own position was, for he began with the lethal disadvantages of being unarmored and already tired by his climb up the cliff. Any of Guy's blows that connected would be serious and possibly mortal, while Adrian would need both luck and skill to deal a killing stroke around his opponent's armor.

Yet at the first clash of steel, fierce joy flooded through Adrian. It was a dozen years since he had sworn his solemn oath of vengeance. He had bided his time, honing his skills, rebuilding his patrimony, staying his hand when revenge would have taken innocent lives. But now the hour had finally come. Though in the end Adrian would die himself, first he would settle his score with the man who had destroyed his home and family.

For the next few minutes the deafening clang of swordplay echoed from the stone walls as they took each other's measure. Adrian found that his opponent was a ferocious and deadly fighter, possibly the most dangerous he had ever met. If Adrian made even the smallest error, he would be a dead man. But because his sheer brute power ended most fights quickly, Burgoigne's technique was surprisingly crude, and therein lay the seeds of his doom. The longer he fought, the greater the chance that he could be lured into making a lethal mistake.

As he considered possible stratagems, Adrian con-

centrated on defense and kept his own swordplay as
conventional as Guy's. He was younger and quicker to
begin with, and unweighted by armor, he was enormously faster. Guy would tire first. Until then, Adrian
would bank his battle fury and concentrate on staying
alive.

For most of the onlookers, the bout was a dazzling
lesson in the art of swordfighting. Appreciative men-
at-arms began laying bets on the outcome. Most
backed their own lord's strength and superior equipment, but some of the more reckless put money on
Warfield. Though he was continually on the defensive,
he moved with swift, sure skill, always keeping a hairbreadth ahead of disaster.

Suffocated with tension, Meriel understood none of
the fine points as the sights and sounds of battle beat
on her raw senses with painful clarity. At first she feared
that each of Guy's mighty blows would be the last,
cleaving Adrian in half. Next to Burgoigne he seemed
small and vulnerable, at a deadly disadvantage. Yet soon
she realized that the two men resembled their emblems.
Guy had the crude, vicious strength of an angry boar,
while Adrian soared like his own silver hawk, swooping
in for a quick slash, then darting away from the boar's
tusks.

Meriel might be hopelessly confused about her feelings for her husband, but she had no doubts about
Guy. He was a monster of wickedness, a man whom
even God must have trouble loving, and she prayed
desperately for Adrian's victory.

Years ago at Lambourn she had seen his fighting
skill from a great distance. Now that she had an intimate view of his fierce concentration, she saw once
more the unholy beauty of his dance with death.
Adrian moved with sinuous power, his trained muscles
taut and swift as he parried and evaded, his beautiful
face remote and uncompromising under its sheen of
sweat.

She also learned that a fight to the death was a noisy

business. Blades not only clanged like broken bells but also slithered along each other with ear-torturing squeals. Blow and counterblow were accompanied by ragged breathing, wordless exclamations, and harsh oaths from the combatants. From the watchers came a constant murmuring, like the curling sea, punctuated by gasps of excitement at a particularly deadly move.

It was a bystander's action that led to the first spilling of blood. As Adrian backtracked yet again, one of the men-at-arms, bored that no one had yet been wounded, took a step into the ring and thrust the handle of his lance between Adrian's ankles. His attention focused on his opponent, Adrian was caught completely off guard and crashed heavily to the ground, falling on his right side so that his sword arm was pinned beneath him.

A chivalrous knight would have stepped back when his opponent was unfairly tripped, but there was no chivalry in Burgoigne. Raucous with delight, he smashed his sword down in a killing stroke. Involuntarily Meriel cried out, one hand to her mouth as panic burned her veins, certain that the end had come.

Her anguish was premature, for Adrian responded to disaster with stunning swiftness. As Guy's sword slashed down at his throat, he whipped up the dagger in his left hand and used it to divert the sword. The dagger's blade shattered under the impact. As Guy's sword slanted by into the ground, Adrian hurled the dagger's hilt into his opponent's face, the jagged edge of broken steel slicing along Guy's jaw before bouncing off his nasal bar.

As Guy recoiled, Adrian rolled onto his back, drew his legs in, then kicked up, both booted feet landing in Guy's belly and groin with the force of a bucking mule. The other man howled with pain and staggered back. Still on the ground, Adrian chopped upward with his sword. He was not in a position to strike a mortal blow, but he managed to slash his enemy's leg from calf to knee.

"First blood to Warfield!" His chest heaving with exertion, Adrian sprang to his feet. His dark cap had fallen off and his gilt hair shone like a beacon fire. "That blow was for my father, Lord Hugh of Warfield, murdered defending his home on Christmas Day. It is God's justice that today you shall die by his own sword."

In the same handful of seconds that Adrian was wounding Burgoigne, Alan crossed the arena and attacked the treacherous soldier whose lance had tripped Adrian. His blade cut deep into the man's forearm, and as his victim's scream reverberated from the walls of Chastain, Alan shouted, "I'll kill anyone else who interferes!" He retreated to his former position but kept a threatening eye on the circle of soldiers to ensure that there would be no more foul blows.

It was now light enough to see clearly without torches, and the men-at-arms began quenching the flames. Guy's legs wound was bloody but not critical, and now he returned to the fray, his heavy blows raining down on Adrian. Loss of the dagger had seriously affected Adrian's ability to defend himself, and he was driven into hard retreat with no chance to strike offensively.

Abruptly Meriel remembered the slim dagger that Lady Cecily had given her, and which she carried hidden beneath her tunic. It was not as heavy as the broken dagger, but the blade was narrow enough to penetrate chain mail. Perhaps it would help balance the odds again.

She pulled the knife out and unwrapped the rag that muffled the blade, then waited for the right moment. It came when Adrian dodged one of Burgoigne's charges, dancing back into the alley. Meriel called, "Adrian, take this!"

She tossed the knife hilt-first so that it landed on the ground near his left hand. Deftly he scooped it up, then glanced at his wife. For a fraction of a second his gaze met hers, and Meriel flinched under the impact of Adrian's savage eyes, even though she knew his violence was not for her. His lips tightened. Then he turned away to meet Guy's next assault.

There was a collective gasp of shock when the onlookers saw that Adrian's guard had dropped when he picked up the dagger and his right side was unprotected. Meriel's nails bit into her palms, knowing that if he was killed because she had distracted him, she would never forgive herself. Indeed, within the hour she would likely be as dead as he, for she did not believe that Guy would release her or her brother.

Seizing the opening, Guy swung his sword with enough force to cut Adrian to the backbone, bellowing with triumph that turned to fury as once more Adrian slid aside. Guy lurched forward with sword arm extended and discovered too late that his opponent's apparent error had been a deliberate feint, designed to lure Guy into exposing himself.

Moving with lightning speed, Adrian slashed the tip of his blade across the inside wrist of his enemy's sword arm. As blood spurted from severed veins, he panted, "That was for my brother Hugh, and his murdered wife and son."

The combatants exchanged another series of strokes and counterstrokes, but the balance had shifted. Guy had lost much of the strength in his sword arm and now he was the one falling back before the smaller man's lethal whirlwind of steel.

A strange, uneasy hush fell over the watchers. Burgoigne was perhaps the only man present who did not realize that his doom was sealed. Now Warfield was in control and he played with his opponent as a cat torments a mouse, his blade making teasing stabs at unarmored parts of Guy's body.

Guy's parries slowed as his strength trickled away. When an attempt to protect his legs caused him to lower his sword and shield too far, Adrian thrust in with a high stroke and sliced the left side of his enemy's face, destroying one eye and cutting through his

cheek to the bone. "That one is for my brothers
Amaury and Baldwin, may they rest in peace!"

Except for one hoarse, animal cry of agony, Guy
was silent. He did not ask for quarter, for he knew it
would never be granted. Instead he fought on, and
even half-blinded and bleeding from three wounds, he
was formidable. Since he lacked power in his sword
arm, he unexpectedly tried the desperate expedient of
lunging at his enemy's mocking voice, his arms
stretched out for an ironbound embrace.

The wrestler's attack took Adrian by surprise and he
made the dangerous mistake of countering with his
sword rather than leaping away. His blade skidded
harmlessly off Burgoigne's mail but did nothing to stop
the larger man's bull-like momentum.

Before Adrian could dodge to safety, Guy's hurtling
body knocked him to the ground and pinned him there
with crushing weight. The two men lay face-to-face,
years of hatred compressed into a few taut inches of
distance.

The links of Guy's mail ground into the smaller man,
and his hot breath and vicious eyes were those of the
wild boar. Moved by sheer angry will, his blade inched
toward Adrian's throat. "I may go to hell, you pious
bastard," Burgoigne snarled, "but you'll be there before me."

"Don't be too sure," Adrian gasped. He had been
stunned by his fall, and shattering pain knifed through
his side, but he had not come this far to die at Guy's
hand like a butchered lamb. Concentrating all of his
remaining strength and tenacity, he began working his
left arm free of the other man's armored bulk.

Guy's sword was a hairbreadth from his neck when
he succeeded. Adrian raised Meriel's dagger, then
plunged it into the other man's back, the narrow blade
slipping between the links of chain mail to sheath itself in solid flesh and bone.

As he wrenched the dagger free in a gout of blood,
Adrian's hoarse voice rasped across the courtyard.

"This is for all the innocent people of Warfield who died by your command!"

Mortally wounded, Guy choked and spewed blood as his sword dropped from swiftly numbing fingers. Adrian heaved the other man's body away and staggered to his feet. Guy lay sprawled on his back, undiminished hatred burning in his eyes even as his lungs coughed up his life's blood. He groped feebly for the hilt of the sword, but he was no longer able to lift it.

Meriel thought the fight was over, but Adrian was not yet done. His fallen-angel face blazed with a merciless rage unlike anything she had ever seen. As she watched in sickened disbelief, he leaned over to yank Guy's hauberk upward, then straightened and thrust his sword into the other man's belly.

Guy gave a raw, choked scream of agony, but it was Adrian's harsh voice that filled the yard. "That is on behalf of all the others you have killed and maimed in your misbegotten life."

Even now, vengeance was not yet satisfied. Adrian jerked his blade loose from Burgoigne's gut. Then, with cold, deliberate brutality, he emasculated his enemy. Softly, so that only those who were closest heard, he finished, "For Meriel. And for your crimes, may you burn in hell for eternity."

Guy's lips twitched and he gave one last hate-filled gurgle as the turf around him saturated with his blood. Then his throat and eyes closed forever.

Drenched with sweat, blood dripping from his blade, his own blood pounding in his ears so loudly that he could hear nothing else, Adrian stared down at his enemy. Now that justice was done, his madness began to subside, leaving him weak with reaction. Instinctively he looked toward Meriel, craving her loving sweetness to soothe his shattered spirit.

Instead he found revulsion. His wife had retreated to the farthest corner of the alley, one of her slim hands clenched against her midriff as if she fought physical illness. In her white face was not love but horror, as if he were the loathsome spawn of the rankest pit of hell.

Soul-deep despair swept through him as he realized that in the process of defeating Burgoigne, he had lost Meriel. In that moment Adrian wished that Guy had dealt him a mortal blow, for he would have welcomed death as a cherished friend.

Then a hoarse muttering from the men-at-arms drew his attention. Adrian turned to find that there was no time for despair, for danger still surrounded them and he was not, after all, quite ready to welcome death. Warily he scanned the circle of soldiers before him. Even though Guy's men were hardened fighters, their expressions registered shock and revulsion at their lord's mutilation.

Slowly Adrian stepped back from Guy's body, his gaze flickering around the frozen faces. He was so drained physically and emotionally that the tip of his sword wavered, and every breath was stabbing pain. Probably some ribs had cracked when Guy fell on him, but there was no time to notice pain, not if there was to be any hope of getting Meriel safely away.

''He has murdered your lord,'' Sir Vincent snarled. Furious at the loss of a master who had favored him, he raised his sword in the air, then slashed it down. ''Kill them—kill them all!''

Some soldiers hesitated, but others drew their weapons and moved forward, their expressions fierce as a pack of hungry wolves.

Aching with grief that Meriel and her brother were to die for his sins, Adrian summoned the last of his strength for a final desperate effort. He and Alan could never defeat a whole crowd of determined men, but they would sell their lives dearly.

Grim-faced with the same knowledge, Alan came to his side, his own blade ready.

Then a woman's voice cut through the tense deadly silence. ''No, damn you!'' Lady Cecily shouted, running down the stairs from the wall walk, her veil

gave Adrian such an enthusiastic embrace that the earl nearly fainted from pain.

There followed a confusing period of introductions and explanations. Though Adrian's attention faded out whenever he moved too suddenly and his ribs stabbed, he managed to keep track of events. He welcomed the pain, welcomed the confusion—anything that would keep him from thinking about the shuddering revulsion he had seen on Meriel's face.

Just as he had had a tingling awareness that she was behind him when he fought, he knew now that she was gone, though he had not seen her and Alan depart. He was too much a coward to seek her out, but even cowardice was no protection, for a few minutes later Meriel came to him. She rode the sorrel mare, Alan mounted beside her on his own horse.

Meriel's night-sky blue eyes were the only color in her stark face as she reined the mare in. "My lord, imprisoned in the castle are the Jewish merchant Benjamin l'Eveske and his household. Guy was holding them to ransom. They helped me when I was lost and ill in the royal forest. I beg that you will see that they are released."

"It will be done." Adrian would have given all he possessed to take her hand and not have her pull away, but he dared not touch her. Meriel's expression was bitter proof of how much she feared and loathed him.

"Thank you, Lord Adrian," she said with formality. Meriel hesitated a moment longer, as if considering further speech, then turned to Lady Cecily. "My lady, from the bottom of my heart I thank you for what you have done for me. You are a brave and honorable woman, and I shall pray that your future brings all the happiness you deserve." Then Meriel collected her reins and rode toward the main gate.

Alan nodded at Adrian. "I have never seen a warrior to match you." Rather to Adrian's surprise, Alan offered his hand. After a firm shake, he wheeled his mount and rode after his sister.

As Meriel disappeared from view, Adrian felt his heart tugging after her as tangibly as if a rope connected them. Strange to think that a heart could be pulled from one's breast, yet leave one living, an empty shell.

Puzzled, Lady Cecily glanced from Meriel to Adrian. Then she looked away, embarrassed at what she had seen on his face.

Richard was less tactful. "For God's sake, Adrian, don't let her ride away," he said roughly. "Meriel is your *wife!* In the last twelve hours you risked your life a dozen times over to save hers. Let me bring her back so that you can talk to her."

Adrian shook his head. On his face was an expression of such raw, primitive pain that it hurt Richard to see it.

Before he turned away to take up the duties that awaited him, Adrian said so softly that the words were almost inaudible, "If she were truly mine, she would come back of her own free will."

22

THE MOST IMPORTANT of Adrian's tasks was Benjamin l'Eveske. It was several hours later that they met in the solar, which Lady Cecily had put at the earl's disposal. Adrian stood when the old man entered. "Good day, Master Benjamin. I hope that no one in your household was seriously injured?"

"No, we were very fortunate." Benjamin's clothing was torn and soiled, but he was admirably calm for a man just released from captivity. "Lady Cecily has directed that all of our possessions be returned, including the captured arms of our guards, and my wife is now supervising the repacking of our wagons."

Wincing, the earl sat down again and gestured to the merchant to do the same. "Please, help yourself to the wine."

Benjamin poured himself a goblet full. "Did you take some injury in the combat with Lord Guy? I had heard that you escaped unscathed."

"A few cracked ribs, and not the first time that has happened." Adrian shrugged dismissively. "After you and I have finished our discussion, I will find someone to bind them up."

"If you wish, I can send my household physician." Benjamin stopped, then gave a dry little smile. "I'm sorry, I forgot that for a Christian to seek medical aid of a Jew is to endanger his soul."

One corner of the earl's mouth quirked up. "At the moment, I would welcome the devil himself if he were an experienced bonesetter." He took a sip of his wine, then leaned back in his chair, his face gray and exhausted under his pale hair. "Lady Cecily and I have conferred. As compensation for her husband's transgressions, she wishes to give you the house in Shrewsbury that Sir Vincent had offered to lend you."

Benjamin's bushy brows rose. "That is very generous of her. I will be able to rent it for a sizable sum."

"If you still wish to—and I will certainly understand if you do not—you may settle in Shrewsbury with your household. You may also tell others of your people that they will be welcome," Adrian said with some diffidence. "I offer my personal support and protection. After I have spoken with the mayor and my sheriff, I do not think you will have any problems."

The old merchant was too startled to be tactful. Acidly he asked, "Are you no longer concerned that we will threaten the souls of the good Christians of Shropshire?"

The earl's gaze shifted away. Obliquely he replied, "One of Jesus's parables tells of a man who fell among robbers, who stripped and beat him and left him for dead. A priest came by and passed on the other side of the road, pretending not to see. Another holy man, a Levite, did the same. Then came a Samaritan, a member of a despised race, who bound the man's wounds, took him to an inn and tended him, then left money to pay the innkeeper until the man was well."

After a long pause, Adrian said, "You helped Meriel." His gaze returned to Benjamin. "The people of Shrewsbury will not be threatened by the actions of a good man. I was a fool to forget that what matters most is what is in a man's heart."

"No man of woman born is not occasionally a fool." The old merchant smiled reflectively. "You are an admirable man, Lord Adrian. It takes courage and humility to admit fault, and to change one's mind." It was perhaps too honest a statement for a man of a subject race to make to another who held great power, so Benjamin moved briskly to the next point. "I shall confer with my wife, but I think she will agree that it would be be an honor and a pleasure to accept your invitation.''

''I hope so.'' The earl raised his cup in a salute. ''I should like to engage in theological disputation with you sometime. That would doubtless be excellent for my humility.''

Benjamin laughed and lifted his own goblet, then drank deeply. At times like this, it was possible to believe that someday men might live together in peace.

After Benjamin's physician had bound his ribs, Adrian lay down and slept like the dead, not wakening until the next morning. The castle had an almost festive air, for Lord Guy's demise had been greeted with near-universal relief. Lady Cecily and Richard had the situation well in hand, so there was no reason for Adrian to stay at Chastain.

Nonetheless, he found that he could not yet face returning to Warfield, where every chamber was haunted by images of Meriel. When she had first recovered her memory and run away from him, he had clung to the faint hope that when she had had time to reflect, she might accept the marriage. Now that hope was gone, as was the marriage itself.

Taking only two of his men, Adrian rode to Fontevaile Abbey. For years he had been a regular visitor, but never had he so much craved the abbey's peace. He stayed three days, immersing himself in silence and worship, and at the end he knew that he had survived the crisis. Proof was in the fact that once more he was able to pray as simply and directly as when he had been a boy. During one of his meditations he had a brief vision of the silver chalice that was his symbol for his soul. There were a few dents in the metal that would never come out, but the surface shone bright and untarnished again. While he would never cease to mourn losing Meriel, he had no doubt that letting her go had been the right thing to do.

The evening before returning to Warfield, he went to the abbot's study after vespers and asked William to hear his confession. Adrian had not confessed since Meriel had entered his life, because he could not be shriven of sins which he had been unwilling to stop committing. But now Meriel was gone, and it was time for penance and absolution.

Making formal confession eased some of his tension, though it could not touch his deepest grief. Then, because William was friend as well as priest and abbot, Adrian went on to explain the full story of what had happened over the last months: not just what had happened, but why.

When his tale was done, the earl rose to his feet and drifted across the study, not looking at the older man as he spoke of something that had been much on his mind. "I would never have left Fontevaile had it not been for the massacre of Warfield. You know that I swore then to rebuild my patrimony and to revenge my family."

Adrian stopped in front of the finely carved crucifix that hung on the wall. The Man of Sorrows looked back at him with a face that knew all there was to know of pain. "Those vows have been fulfilled. Now it is time to return to Fontevaile and swear a vow of service to God."

There was a rustle of coarse woolen fabric behind him as the surprised abbot shifted position. "You will abandon your patrimony? There is more than one way to serve God, and you have served him well as lord of Warfield."

Adrian turned to face William. "Richard can have Warfield, and welcome. He will rule it better than I, and his position will be so strong that no one will dare challenge him on the grounds of his illegitimacy."

The abbot knew Adrian well, perhaps better than any other man alive. "And what of your wife? If Lady Meriel had come back to you, would you still wish to become a monk?"

William's words triggered an instant image of Meriel as she had been in the handful of days when they had been truly wed. Adrian could hear her gay laughter, feel her silken skin under his fingertips. As his body tightened in response, he said harshly, "But she did not come back, so I have no wife."

"When you were a novice here, I thought that you had a true vocation for the religious life. Perhaps you did." Slowly the abbot shook his head. "But you are no longer that lad. You may rest at Fontevaile for as long as you wish, but I will not permit you to take binding vows."

"Why not?" Adrian demanded, feeling his fragile peace dissolve beneath his feet. To become a monk had seemed the perfect—the only—solution. "Is it because you prefer me as a wealthy patron rather than an impoverished monk?"

Abbot William's mouth curved with amusement. "Not a very Christian remark, Adrian."

The earl flushed. "I beg your pardon, Father, I know that is not so. But I feel compelled to enter the religious life, and if you will not have me at Fontevaile, I will find another house that will accept me."

"I'm sure that you would have no trouble finding an order that would be delighted to have you. But, Adrian, by the affection we have for each other, I beg that you consider long and hard before you take such a step." The abbot sighed. "Too often monastaries are used as refuges from the world. That is not always a bad thing, but I would grieve to see you take vows for the wrong reasons. Can you truly say that you would be entering Fontevaile with a full and joyous heart, because you can imagine no better life? Or would it be because you wish to flee a life that at the moment is intolerably painful?" William smiled. "My guess is that if you had a choice between living with God or with your wife, you would choose your wife. A man who feels that way should not become a monk, for it is not right that God be second choice."

After a long silence, Adrian gave a twisted smile. "I had not thought of it in those terms, but you are right. In truth, even as a lad, part of the reason I came to Fontevaile was to flee from myself and my own potential for evil. God deserves better than servants who come to him from fear rather than faith."

"It is not a question of faith, but of works. You have done much good as an earl, and can do much more, for there are few lords who have your faith and justice." The abbot stood and offered his hand. As Adrian kissed it, William said, "If the day ever comes when you can say from the bottom of your heart that God is your first and only choice, I will welcome you here as a brother. Until then, I shall pray that you find peace."

The Avonleigh garden had been neglected in Meriel's absence, and she had worked in it every day in the fortnight since she had returned home. Nonetheless, she admitted ruefully as she cut dead blossoms from a rosebush, she needed the flowers more than they needed her, for it was very healing to be in a garden.

Meriel had received a loving welcome at Avonleigh, and it had been balm to her bruised and aching spirit. Sometimes she felt as if she had never been away, but those moments were few and far between. Avonleigh had not changed, but Meriel had. In the past months she had learned much about fear and courage, about passion and anger, about the dark and mysterious depths of the human soul. She had lost more than one kind of innocence, and come to realize how sheltered her previous life had been.

Day and night she was haunted by images: Guy of Burgoigne lying butchered in his own blood, her husband standing over him as wild and savage as a bird of prey. Adrian of Warfield as her implacable and frightening captor. And infinitely worse, images of Adrian as her tender lover. No matter how hard she tried, Meriel was unable to reconcile the different aspects of her husband.

She guessed that his obsession with her had waned, for he had made no attempt to stop her when she left Chastain, just watched wearily, as if she were an unwanted guest departing. At the time Meriel had been intensely grateful for his disinterest, for she had been desperate to escape the terror and slaughter of Chastain. Indeed, she had been near hysteria when she had begged Alan to take her away immediately. If Adrian had refused to let her leave, she might have broken down entirely.

But after she had recovered from shock, she knew that her flight had been a mistake. For better and worse, Lord Adrian was her husband and that was a fact that she could not ignore. Another fact that could certainly not be ignored was the child growing inside her. Soon she must inform the earl that he would have an heir. And after that, what would happen? She had no idea, did not even know what she wished for.

Meriel realized that she had been staring at one rosebush for quite some time, doing nothing. Resolutely suppressing the queasiness that had been with her since waking, she moved to the next bush and set to work. She had almost finished her pruning when Alan came from the house, a frown on his face. Concerned, she asked, "Is there trouble?"

"Not precisely trouble," her brother said slowly. "A message just arrived from Warfield. I suppose he sent it to me, since I am in effect your protector."

Very carefully Meriel sat down her shears. She had a feeling that whatever the message's contents, they would not make her happy. "What does Lord Adrian say?"

"The gist is that since you wed him without true consent, the marriage can be annulled. Warfield will pay for all the legal costs and petitions. I suppose that includes any bribes that might be necessary," Alan added as a cynical aside.

"Also, for your future maintenance and as a dower should you choose to marry again, he will settle on you several manors worth a total of six knight's fees. He will return all of your personal possessions, including clothing, jewels, Chanson, and"—he glanced at the parchment—"a kestrel that he says misses you."

Alan offered her the letter so that she could read it for herself, adding, "Warfield is amazingly generous."

Lord Adrian had even thought of Kestrel. Yes, his obsession had ended. Meriel stared at the parchment, not reading it. Of course he would be generous, it was one of the traits that defined a nobleman.

The faint queasiness she had been feeling abruptly became full-fledged nausea. Meriel swayed dizzily, then turned, dropped to her knees, and began retching under one of the rosebushes. Even her body was betraying her. She felt Alan kneel beside her, and when there was nothing left in her stomach, he lifted her in his arms, deposited her on a nearby bench, and wiped her mouth with the corner of her apron. "Would you like something to drink?" he asked.

"Water, please," she said thickly.

He left and returned a few minutes later with a goblet of water, which she drank greedily. When she had emptied it, Meriel leaned against her brother, her mind a gray blank.

"I think we had better talk," Alan said, putting his arm around her. "Are you with child?"

"I'm certain of it."

"Warfield will have to know."

"Of course," she agreed, her voice leaden.

"I don't suppose he will want to go through with the annulment under the circumstances." Alan paused, then asked quietly, "Will you?"

Therein lay the problem. Meriel leaned forward and buried her face in her hands. "I just don't know," she said wretchedly. "I had not told you this, but gradually I have come to remember what happened in the weeks between the accident and the return of my memory. And, Alan, I loved Adrian then. I thought the sun rose and set on him, and he was so kind, so gentle.''

''Do you love him still?''

''Again, I don't know. I remember how he imprisoned me, and how vicious he was when he fought Burgoigne.'' She shuddered. ''That was not honest combat, but butchery, and Burgoigne's blood flows between me and the happy memories. How can I live with a man capable of such cruelty?''

''Yes, I suppose he was cruel,'' Alan said slowly, ''though as a knight myself I can understand why. There is a wildness that comes over a man who is fighting for his life. In that state men are capable of great bravery, and great wickedness.'' He shrugged. ''Warfield took a little longer to kill Burgoigne than he might have, but the provocation was great. If someone had murdered my family and abducted my wife, I would have behaved no better, and possibly a great deal worse.''

''You admire him, don't you?'' Meriel lifted her face from her hands but continued to stare into her lap, where her frantic fingers intertwined. On her left hand was the gold wedding band. She had started to remove it a dozen times, but something had always stopped her.

''I do,'' he admitted, ''for sharing danger forges a bond. But more than that, I like him. He is honorable, he behaved with great restraint when I was doing my best to provoke him, and he is possibly the bravest man I have ever known.'' Alan's voice softened. ''Warfield also loves you as I have never seen a man love a woman. While his original behavior was unconscionable, he has done everything possible to atone. If you have any fondness for him, you could not ask for a better husband.''

''He does not love me,'' Meriel said, wondering if her words were true, or if she even wanted them to be. "When we first met he swore that he would never let me go, but he has. I was a brief madness to him. Now he has recovered and wishes to be free of me. The marriage is over."

"It is over if you want it to be," her brother agreed.

Meriel bent over and picked a daisy that grew below the bench and absently began plucking the petals one by one. *I love him, I love him not.* "I think," she said as white petals drifted soundlessly to the grass, "that I should go to Warfield and talk to Lord Adrian." *He loves me, he loves not.* She crumpled the ruined flower in her palm.

"I agree," Alan said. "When do you want to go?"

Having made the decision, Meriel knew instantly that it was the right one. Meeting Adrian again was the only way to free herself of her tormenting confusion. "Now?" she said hopefully, slanting a glance up at her brother. "This morning?"

"Very well, I'll order the horses." Alan stood and went to the stables, his heart considerably lighter. Meriel might not know what she wanted, but he thought that he did.

During their journey, Meriel varied between terror and anticipation, and it was a distinct anticlimax to arrive at Warfield to find that Lord Adrian had gone out riding alone. No one knew just where he had gone, or when he would be back, but likely it would be very late.

Meriel gnawed her lower lip at the news. The idea of waiting for hours more was intolerable. Her morning fatigue had vanished and now she brimmed with energy in spite of the long ride. But how to find Adrian on the vast Warfield lands?

An absurd idea struck her. Alan trailing behind, she went to the mews and swept inside.

"Lady Meriel!" the falconer said with delight when she greeted him. "It's good you're back, my lady, Chanson has been missing you, and so has the earl.

Some folk have been saying that you left him and that his lordship is going to become a monk, but I never believed that for a minute. My lady has just gone to visit her brother, I said.''

A monk! Shocked, Meriel stared at the falconer, knowing that it was quite possible that Adrian might do such a thing. Is that why he wished to dissolve the marriage? Masking her reaction, she pulled on a leather gauntlet. "I wish to take Chanson out now, I've been neglecting her.''

It was a delight to have the falcon on her wrist again, and she and Chanson spent several minutes exchanging nonsense greetings. When they were outside again, Alan asked, "Care to explain what you are up to, little sister?''

She grinned. "Perhaps Chanson can find Lord Adrian for me.''

"For heaven's sake, Meriel,'' her brother expostulated, a smile tugging at his lips, "he's not a hare or a partridge.''

"It can't hurt to try. I'll go mad if I must wait here for hours.'' Meriel swung onto a fresh horse, Rosalia the First having earned a rest. "You don't have to come if you are tired.''

Alan snorted and remounted his own horse. "Haven't you been cured of riding alone yet? Look at what happened the last two times you did it.''

Meriel decided not to dignify his remark with an answer. They rode out of the castle until they were in the middle of the broad water meadow. Then she took off the falcon's hood and stroked the bird's throat. "Find him for me, Chanson.''

As she spoke, she concentrated on a mental image of Adrian as she preferred to think of him: his beautifully molded face, the warmth that came into his eyes when he looked at her, the way light played on his gilt hair. For a moment the picture came so alive that she forgot why she had created it. Then she gave herself a mental shake and tossed Chanson into the wind. On powerful beating wings, the falcon arrowed into the sky. Holding to the thought of Adrian, Meriel tilted her head back and watched Chanson ascend. *Find him.*

Soon the bird was no more than a black speck high in the sky. Meriel told herself that this was a foolish idea that would never succeed; even if Chanson understood, the falcon could only see Adrian if he was in the open. But the activity was harmless, exercised the bird, and distracted Meriel from her fretting.

Nonetheless, Meriel prayed for a small miracle. When the falcon began to fly south, she followed.

After they had ridden two or three miles, Chanson stooped, knifing from the sky toward the top of a hill, then winging upward to wait on again. When they came to the foot of the hill, Meriel looked around in sudden recognition. Of course. Perhaps fate bound them to this place; at any rate, she offered inner thanks for having received her miracle. She dismounted and took out the lure, then called the falcon down from the sky.

After Chanson had returned, eaten, and been made much of for her cleverness, Meriel hooded the bird and gave it to her brother. "There is an ancient stone circle at the top of the hill and Adrian is there. You can return to Warfield now. I will see you there later."

"Meriel," Alan said warningly, "will you never learn?"

"I won't come back alone," she promised. "I have done with running away. Even if Adrian wants to wring my neck like a barnyard fowl, he will chivalrously insist on escorting me back to where he can do it in safety."

"You're in love with him, aren't you?"

She thought of her husband's complex nature, the bright strands woven with the dark, and shivered. "Perhaps I love one aspect of him, Alan. I don't know if that is enough."

"I'll ride up behind you. When and if you see Warfield, signal and I will leave, but not before then."

Meriel nodded agreement, then started up the path. The last time she had traversed this trail, she had been leading Adrian's horse through a violent storm, terrified out of her wits at having woken up in her enemy's embrace. Now the summer sun beat hot on her shoulders, and she was going voluntarily to the man who had been both enemy and lover.

Wryly she thought that over the last several months she had been trapped in the midst of a jongleur's tale, her emotions pushed to exhausting highs and lows as she suffered from other people's whims. It was time and past time to take control over her own life. Surely when she saw Adrian, her doubts and confusion would resolve and she would know what was right.

Her horse's hooves were muffled by thick leaf mold and Adrian did not hear her approach. He sat on one of several stool-sized rocks on the far side of the stone circle, his gaze focused on nothing, his fingers absently plaiting strands of grass.

Meriel turned and waved to Alan, who nodded and turned back down the track. Now her fate was in her hands alone.

She took a moment to study her husband without being observed herself. It was hard to believe that this quiet man was the same one whom she had last seen mercilessly butchering his enemy. Now he was once again the ascetic, the man who might have been a scholar or monk, his expression remote and otherworldly beneath his bright hair. Yet his dark, restrained dress only emphasized the lithe fitness of his body; if he were a monk, it would be of a warrior order.

She swallowed hard, then signaled her horse forward into the clearing. It was time to determine her fate.

To Adrian, the stone circle had become a symbol for all that had happened between him and the woman who had been his wife—coercion and companionship, passion and estrangement—and he had come here to try to make his peace with the past. Everything he saw reminded him of Meriel—the rough stones that had fascinated her, the tree under which they had made love, even the falcon that had briefly swooped from the sky.

Then he heard the sound of hooves. He turned his head, and with a twist of his heart he knew that he would find no peace today. Meriel was riding directly toward him, slim and lovely and grave, and the sight of her was more frightening than any sword Adrian had ever seen.

God only knew what showed in his face in the first unguarded moments. Why did Meriel have to come to him when it meant that once again he would have to watch her leave? It was too much to ask of any man. But he had released her once, and somewhere he would—*must*—find the strength to release her again.

Clamping rigidly down on his emotions, Adrian stood and walked toward her. "Good day, Meriel."

"Good day," she replied. Such flat, meaningless words. Her deep blue eyes met his, and in their depths Adrian saw nothing. Not joy, not fear, not grief. Nothing.

A little helplessly, Adrian wondered what came next. If they were strangers, it would have been easy to speak of casual things, but there was so much between them that it might be impossible to speak at all.

From the speed with which Meriel slid from her horse, it was obvious that she did not want her husband to touch her. She was wise, but it was a hurtful wisdom, one more pain he must conceal.

She tethered her mount under the tree by Adrian's horse, then turned to face him. "Your message arrived at Avonleigh this morning. It seemed time for us to talk face-to-face."

"What I suggested was not satisfactory?" Though he would have given everything he possessed to take her in his arms, he forced himself to stop six feet away from her. "I cannot relinquish any of my inheritance from my father, but I can assign you more of the lands that I have acquired myself."

"That isn't necessary, my lord. Your offer was very generous." Meriel's restless gaze shifted away from him and fixed on her gold wedding band. Strange that she still wore his ring; perhaps she had come to return it. She asked, "You really think it will be possible to have the marriage annulled?"

Adrian nodded. "The Church maintains that there is no marriage without the full consent of both parties. Therefore, since you wed while in a condition where you could not give true consent, you are not bound by the vows. An annulment will take some time, perhaps a year or two if it must go all the way to Rome, but I do not doubt that it will be granted."

After a long pause, he added in a voice of absolute neutrality, "Then you will be free to marry again. Or as the Church will consider it, for the first time."

He could not have been less expressive if he had been a stone wall. It was hard to believe that this was the man with whom Meriel had lived such high drama. Did he really not care what happened to their marriage? Or did he care too much? Uncertainly she said, "You will also be free to marry elsewhere."

Her husband shook his head. "You did not give true consent when we married, but I did. I made my vows with full knowledge, and in my heart they will always bind me. I will never take another wife."

His quiet, passionless sincerity was devastating. Meriel swallowed hard, wondering what lay beneath his words. "Will you become a monk?"

"I have considered the idea," he admitted, "but Abbot William convinced me that I have insufficient vocation. I shall merely . . . go on living."

Somewhere beneath his surface calm was the inner fire of the real man, and Meriel must touch that fire if she was to truly understand her husband. Needing to establish some kind of connection between them, she stepped forward and laid a tentative hand on his forearm.

Hawk-swift, Adrian jerked his arm from her clasp and spun away, not halting until he was a dozen steps away. "It is not wise to do that, *ma petite,*" he said, his steady voice belied by his desperate eyes. "I am trying my best to control myself, but I cannot vouch for the consequences if you touch me."

Now Adrian blazed with the fire Meriel had sought, and Meriel knew that he still cared for her, perhaps too much. With dismay she wondered if she possessed the courage to really know him, the strength to endure his intense, demanding love.

Unable to answer her own questions, Meriel turned to another subject that must be spoken of, a subject that should please her husband and take the desolation from his eyes. Baldly she announced, "I am with child."

Adrian became absolutely still. Then, to her shock, he asked, "Is it mine?"

Meriel stared at him, aghast. "What kind of woman do you think me?" she exclaimed. "Whose child would it be but my husband's?"

"I'm sorry, I did not mean that as you think." He made a spasmodic movement toward her, then halted. "It is just that . . . when I first spoke with Burgoigne about ransoming you, he boasted what a passionate mistress you were."

Seeing the revulsion on her face, Adrian lifted one hand. Composure was a thing of the past; now pain was written vividly across his face. "I know that you would never have lain with him voluntarily, but a child can be born of rape as well as love."

"He did not rape me, not quite." It had been a long and wearying day, and suddenly Meriel felt that her legs would no longer support her. She sank down on a rock, her voice uneven. "He decided that assaulting me would be a satisfying way of striking at you, but

Lady Cecily stopped him before he could accomplish his aim.''

"God be thanked.'' Adrian's eyes squeezed shut, as if he could not bear to expose the intensity of his relief. After a moment he opened them again. "That is another debt I owe the lady of Chastain. I am so very glad. You have already borne too much because of me.''

Meriel realized that it said a great deal about Adrian that even at his most obsessed he had never physically harmed her. It was Burgoigne who had taught her what real fear was. "Do not blame yourself for everything, my lord,'' she said. "The responsibility for violence lies with the man who commits it.''

"True. But you would not have been at Chastain if not for me.'' He sighed. "It was foolish of me to ask what I did. Even if Guy had . . . fathered a child on you, you would not know when only a fortnight had passed.

"I shall acknowledge your babe as my heir so that its rights will not be affected by the annulment. Will you let me take the child for fostering when it is old enough?''

"Of course,'' she answered, her throat tight. In his humility, the earl was yet again a stranger, neither the dominating lord nor the tender lover.

Adrian turned away from Meriel, his blind gaze resting on the tallest stone. His voice raw, he said, "When you were dying, I swore to obey your will in all things. Tell me what you want of me, Meriel, so that we can be done with each other.''

Watching his still profile, Meriel said softly, "I want to know who you truly are, Adrian. When I was at Chastain, I began to remember what had happened between the time of my injury and when I recovered my memory here.''

His whole body went rigid, but still he would not look at her. "What did you remember?''

She flushed deeply as memories of passion darted

through her mind. Of how she had cried out his name with love and desire . . . "I remember recovering from my injury. Our courtship and marriage. Almost everything, I think. But though the events are very clear, it is as if they happened to someone else, not me."

Meriel paused, struggling to define what she meant. "It is as if the woman who married you is separated from the real me by a wall of clear glass, like the window in your chamber. I know that I loved you then, but those feelings are not quite real to me. Just as I was another woman, you were another man. Not the one who imprisoned me in his castle, nor the one who terrified me by butchering Guy of Burgoigne. You were so kind, so gentle." Her voice broke. "I had never dreamed that such love and gentleness could exist."

Suddenly too distressed to sit still, Meriel stood and paced away until she reached one of the standing stones. Halting, she leaned her forehead against the coarse gray surface and drew a deep breath. These stones would still be here, a mute testimony to mankind's need for faith, when she and Adrian were gone and forgotten.

Calmer, she turned back to her husband. "Who are you, Adrian? A butcher? A devil from hell, sent to torment me? Or the angel of kindness who loved me, and whom I loved in turn?"

"I am neither, *ma petite*," he said, his bleak gaze finally meeting hers. "I am just a man. Though of the two, I have more of the devil than the angel."

His mouth twisted with self-mocking bitterness. "I have never felt free. I suppose it is my own fault. All of my life I have felt driven—compelled to master my own lower nature, to discharge my responsibilities to Warfield, to fulfill oaths I swore as a boy. Then I met you."

He moved away from her with the dangerous grace of a predator. "I loved you from the moment I saw you, Meriel, not just because in my eyes you are beautiful, but because you spoke to some deep, aching need in my soul. I think it was because you were so wholly yourself. And so free, as free as your own falcon."

Adrian stopped facing away from her, the lines of his body taut. "Abbot William said that too often we kill what we love most, and he is right. Being a man and a fool, I tried to cage you, to bind you to me, to destroy what I most loved about you. I did not see that I was trying to kill your spirit until I came so very close to killing your body as well."

Finally he turned, his expression as bleak as death. "But you won, *ma petite.* Your will to be free is stronger than my ability to break it. So go in peace, beloved. I will not use the law to hold you against your will."

Meriel stared at her husband, tears forming in her eyes at his anguished honesty. She thought of a verse from the Bible, not from the Song of Solomon, but from Luke, the healer: *His sins, which are many, are forgiven, for he has loved much.*

Only God could know all the dimensions of a man's soul, but finally Meriel felt that she understood what the essence of Adrian was. Loving her, he had sinned against her, imprisoning a woman whose soul could not survive without freedom.

And now, loving her, he had set her free to make her own choice. As if she were a falcon to be whistled down the wind, he had cut the jesses of law and custom and obligation. There was nothing to bind her to him now.

Nothing but love, the strongest bond of all.

Finally she had her answer, and it was a very simple one. Though there were fearsome qualities in her husband, she had no reason to fear him. Yes, he had harmed her in the past, but he had learned a bitter lesson and she knew that he would never harm her again. When injury obliterated her anger and stubbornness, when she had seen Adrian with fresh eyes and discovered the good in him, she had fallen in love. Together they had found passion, trust, and joy, and now that she was finally free to choose, Meriel discovered that there was only one possible choice.

Though she had sworn a vow never to submit to him, some vows should not be made. Or if they were made, they should be broken.

Trembling a little, Meriel walked to her husband, stopping an arm's length away. He tensed at her approach, his expression a blend of undisguised longing and despair.

"When I came here I did not know what I wanted of you, Adrian, but now I do." Meriel gazed into his eyes, wondering how best to speak her heart. Then the Song of Solomon came to her tongue once more. Softly she said, *"By night on my bed I sought him whom my soul loveth. I sought him, but I found him not."*

Adrian's face flared with unbearable hope, but he did not touch her. Instead he answered, *"Rise up, my love, my fair one, and come away . . ."*

"For lo, the winter is past, the rain is over and gone." Meriel completed the quotation, then put her hands on both sides of his face and pulled his head down so she could kiss him. Even now she felt a shiver of fear, until her lips touched his.

Then the wall of doubts that had separated her from the woman who was Adrian's wife shattered like glass and she felt the full force of her love in every fiber of her being. "As God is my witness, I love you, Adrian," she whispered, weeping and laughing together. "I don't know how I could have forgotten, even for a moment. Perhaps deep down I knew that if I admitted how much I love you, I could never be wholly free again."

Adrian's arms came around her with the force of a dying man seeking salvation. "It doesn't matter that you forgot," he said, his voice shaking. "All that matters is that now you remember."

The hungry intensity of his emotions ignited Meriel's own yearning. Words were not enough—only passion had the power to express such joy and need. They had married and separated, and now they would renew their vows forever.

Meriel's memories of lovemaking were dreamlike,

but now desire was achingly real. Every sense in her body responded to the pressure of Adrian's mouth and seeking hands, every nerve tingled as taste, touch, scent, and sound intoxicated her. And she knew that she was beautiful because she saw her beauty reflected in his eyes.

Such was their urgency that Meriel never after remembered mundane details such as disrobing and spreading a mantle to make a bed of the grassy turf. Passion was the only reality, for her desire was as feverish as Adrian's. She wanted—*needed*—to join her flesh to his, as their hearts and spirits were already joined.

And at the height of their divine madness, their spirits soared to the gates of heaven, together, yet free.

Afterward they lay twined together on the mantle, utterly content. Adrian drew a caressing hand down Meriel's sun-warmed body. "I thought I had lost you forever, *ma petite,*" he said quietly. "I did not think I would ever be happy again this side of the grave."

Meriel's lashes swept up to reveal the full force of her sky-deep eyes. "God works in mysterious ways," she said with a smile that very nearly melted his bones. "When I was sore of heart about whether I should take the veil, I prayed for guidance and had a vision.

"I saw that two possible roads lay before me. One led to the religious life and was straight and clear and narrow, while the other was dark, mysterious, and rather frightening. Yet there was no true choice, for the religious road was barred by an angel with flaming sword. He had silver-gilt hair and was the most beautiful and dangerous being I had ever seen." She smiled and slid her fingers through Adrian's hair. "He was, in fact, the very image of you, beloved. I think we were destined to be together. Yet I did not realize that until you set me free to choose."

Idly Adrian untied and loosened Meriel's braids, then proceeded to spread the silken veil of hair across her body. "Why did you lie about your background when I first found you in the forest?"

"It seems foolish now," she said ruefully, "but I was afraid that you might endanger Avonleigh. You looked so fearsome, and I had heard evil things about the Earl of Shropshire."

"Richard guessed that might have been the reason. I shall have to cultivate a milder demeanor." His expression turned serious. "Though I was joyful when we first wed, there was always fear of what would happen if you remembered the past. Only now do I feel that we are truly married."

"I'm sorry, beloved," she whispered, "for the wasted time, and for the grief I caused you."

Adrian stretched out beside her and propped his head on his hand. "You needn't apologize. The last few weeks have been so wretched that even I think I have suffered enough for my sins." He lifted her hand and kissed the palm, then brushed a soft trail of kisses along the fragile skin inside her wrist.

Meriel's fingers tingled with pleasure at his caress. "I think it would have been a very great waste if you had become a monk."

"Abbot William was right," Adrian agreed. "I lacked a true vocation, for I can think of no higher earthly calling than loving you." He leaned over and kissed the gentle curve of her abdomen. "You are so slim. It seems hard to believe that you carry our child here."

Meriel smiled with wry amusement. "You will believe it in the morning when I turn a delicate shade of green."

Laughter was the final gift, and laughing, Adrian drew his wife into his arms again. They had made love once with wild abandon. This time passion would be slow and thorough and infinitely tender.

I am my beloved's, and my beloved is mine.

Historical Note

IN 1153 Stephen's older son and chief heir, Eustace, died unexpectedly. Stephen's younger son, William, had neither the training nor the inclination to be king, and Stephen was persuaded to adopt Matilda's son Henry as his heir. Stephen himself died in 1154. He is generally regarded as a good man but a disastrous ruler. His successor, Matilda's son, has gone down in history as Henry II, one of England's finest kings.

Between them, Stephen and Matilda created twenty-seven earldoms as bribes for support, and the situation of two earls competing for the control of one county was repeated several times. At this period Shropshire did not have an earl; probably Henry I had assigned the revenues to his young widow, Adeliza, and neither her stepdaughter Matilda nor Stephen would have disputed the grant.

Names and titles were much more fluid then, and a nobleman might be styled in several ways simultaneously: Adrian de Lancey, Adrian of Warfield, Adrian of Shropshire, or Adrian of Shrewsbury (the principal town of Shropshire). Surnames were only just beginning to come into use (in Wales they did not become common until the eighteenth century), but for the sake of simplicity I have given family names to the protagonists.

The years from William the Conqueror to the end of Henry II's reign were generally a good time for the English Jews, who were protected by the kings and valued for their economic contributions. The Jews were considered fairer and more consistent in their money-lending practices than most Christian moneylenders. (And there were a number of Christian moneylenders in spite of the Church's prohibition against usury.)

The Jews were taxed heavily and unpredictably, but everyone was then. (One of the accomplishments of modern society is that taxes are now somewhat more polite and predictable, though there are those who will disagree with that statement.)

After Henry II died, the position of the Jews deteriorated as Henry's sons Richard and John treated their Jewish subjects as resources to be wrung dry. Also, the rise of crusading fervor sometimes led to anti-Semitic persecution and violence.

In 1290 Edward I expelled the Jews from England, and they did not return in any numbers until the seventeenth century. Interestingly, it was the Puritans, who were great believers in reading the Bible for themselves, who developed respect for their Old Testament brethren and allowed the Jews to come back.